De'Ath in Corsica

By Paul Humber

Acid Crime

First Edition

All characters are fictional.

All locations have been altered and some have been re-named.

ISBN 9798647400642

You can follow Paul Vincent Humber on Facebook

Other books in the De'Ath Series

De'Ath in Sicily

De'Ath in Venice

Part One

THE WORLD ACCORDING TO PETE

ONE

It was Friday evening and there was a knock on the door and there was Little Sarah from the office. I didn't realise she even knew where I lived.

'Okay now don't freak out,' she asked.

'Why would I freak out?'

'Promise me you won't freak out?' It was the sort of thing a young person says to their parents. Just how old did she think I was? How depressing.

'Okay.' She took a deep breath.

I looked forward over her, to see if the explanation for her arrival somehow lay in the street beyond. It didn't.

'Okay well the thing is, it looks like I've done a murder. But I haven't done a murder.'

And with that handful of words my entire weekend was comprehensively buggered up.

Normally I have near-perfect Friday evenings. I live on my own. If I want to watch a film or a box set – Game of Thrones, Mad Men, Love Island, Casablanca, Earth Girls Are Easy – I have a wide and varied taste - I can just choose it and watch it and drink a glass of wine, and what the hell a second glass of wine, and I can pause it whenever I like and make a bacon sandwich or get, what the hell, a third and fourth glass of wine; one in each hand.

The point is I don't have to think about whether someone else is enjoying themselves, or indeed what someone else makes of my alcohol consumption or the fact that I am only wearing my underpants. I don't have to worry that someone else is sitting alone in a room gazing at a paused film while I fry the bacon and get distracted by the internet. Also, to be clear, I wouldn't just wear underpants - I was being figurative - even in a hot country I find my feet get cold easily, so I would also at the very least wear socks as well. The point is, because I live on my own, I can just be myself.

And it is bliss.

Let me just take a moment to stress this.

It is bliss.

I live somewhere amazing – Corsica - one of the most beautiful islands in the world. If I want something, I can have it. If I want to walk from my sun-scorched house down the coastal path to the sea; if I want to sit at a café table on the old quayside and watch the boats come and go; if I want to go sailing or walk in the mountains or visit Paris or Nice or Tuscany for the weekend, I can do it.

Some people's lives are a desperate flight from loneliness. Mine is a desperate flight from getting involved. I love my own company and I love the company of others. And that makes me the luckiest man alive.

Little Sarah's real name is Sarah-Jayne, but largely goes by the name of Sarah which - to confuse matters further - she pronounces as Sara. If someone calls her Sarah she gets really shirty which is totally unreasonable – how are people supposed to know Sarah is not pronounced Sarah? Broadly speaking, she is likeable though; she's a young Tigger of a thing who joined our office about six months ago, increasing the English contingent in the building by exactly 50%. My initial reaction when I saw her, therefore, was that her problem was somehow related to work.

Our business is insurance, and our office is a tiny backwater branch of a huge multinational insurance empire. Our area shows a slightly high level of claims for boating accidents and life assurance generally, but the latter is due to the fact that Corsica routinely has the highest murder rate per capita of any French territory – you've got to be good at something, it might as well be murder - so there has been repeated interest in the high pay out level for deaths from head office, which is irritating. On the other hand, we have below average statistics for burglary, fire, and car theft and so the figures balance out. It is the way of management, however, that you never get praise for the figures that look good, you just get earache about the figures that look bad.

I am digressing as usual.

Sarah was wearing a flimsy summer dress and some plastic sandals.

In fact, coming to think of it, this is probably the first important fact about the murder: the clothes Sarah was wearing. If you were going to plan a murder, you would wear something practical like leggings or a pair of jeans. Sarah was wearing a mid-length spotty cotton dress that was white and blue. It had a slight puff at the skirt and it would have left her upper back and shoulders completely bare, were it not for what she was wearing underneath which was – as far as I could see - a black nylon halter neck body stocking with a lacy pattern to it. It was meant to look racy as in, 'Look I am wearing sexy underwear under my dress,' but the effect didn't work. Apart from the fact that the underwear looked cheap and didn't match the dress, it showed off too much of her back and shoulders which were doughy pale and dotted with a distracting number of black moles. The point is – and I am repeating myself on purpose – these were not the clothes of a murderer. These were not even the clothes of a skilled seductress. You could see she was going for a 'game girlfriend' look, but instead of looking flirty, it just looked forlorn.

I appreciate this is not amazing evidence either way, but consider the opposite: when the case got to court, if she had been wearing black leggings and a mask and somehow it was caught on camera, then the prosecutors would have had no trouble saying 'Does this look like the sort of clothes you wear on a date?' If you allow one line of logic, then you have to allow the other.

So anyway.

Sarah stood there and she said, 'I don't know where to begin.'

Oh and she was a dreadful colour. She wasn't just pale; she was Uma Thurman Pulp Fiction pale.

'I suppose,' she began. 'I suppose that you're the only English person I know here. Well there's your sister Emily, but you know what I mean. You know, here in Corsica, I've only been here a few months and I don't really know anyone. I certainly really don't know what to do in a situation like this. I mean what do you do? Well what could you do? The answer is I don't know what to do.'

I tried to look patient - it is the social protocol in such situations to look patient - but I was well within my rights to just look irritated: it was the weekend, and she owed me an explanation.

'It looks like you've killed someone?' I repeated. 'And you don't think you did it. But you're not sure.'

'I didn't kill him, but it looks like I did,' she repeated.

Well I knew she didn't kill this 'him', or certainly didn't kill him on purpose, because - bottom line - she's Little Sarah from the office. How do we know anything? The answer is we don't; I just knew in my heart that Little Sarah from the office was not a crazed professional killer.

Sarah then breathed in sharply which I took to mean she had made a decision of some sort. 'Come on. I'll show you,' she said. She made to walk across the street.

'Hang on Sarah!' I said. 'Hold on. I will need some trousers.'

As well as my trousers and a shirt, I needed my keys, because I didn't want to lock myself out. My keys were in my bedroom along with my trousers – and this is an important detail for later - the keys were exactly where I thought they would be; on my bedside table. I am willing to state irrefutably and categorically therefore that the only item I remember being on my bedside table in the early evening were my keys. There was nothing else on the bedside table.

Sarah's car was parked across the road from my house. Much was made of the car as the evidence was gathered for the trial, so it is worth stating as a minimum that it was a neat little red Renault Clio. There was the finest film of sand over it, as there is over almost everything you touch on the island at certain times in the summer when a southerly wind catches sand from North Africa. But other than that, nothing special: it was just a normal cheerful second-hand car that a woman might buy cheap and then not put any oil in and wonder why it seizes up. It was a celebration of summer island life and the supposed carelessness of being young. There was conjecture that Sarah must have had help with the dead body because of the nature of the car. I am not sure about that. When you are desperate, you can manage the most Herculean of tasks; you're pumped up, you're adrenalized, if that is a word.

Sarah looked up and down the street and checked sight lines as to who might be able to see what we were doing.

She took another deep breath and said, ‘Here goes.’

She opened the back of her car, and in the back there was a dead man.

TWO

How old am I?

I am at an age where I am constantly surprised at having middle-aged thoughts.

When you are a teen and you see a house, you just see a house. Last week, a friend pointed out a pretty house that an acquaintance had bought and my next words were, and I quote myself exactly, 'I bet that's a bugger to heat.' No teenager in the history of humanity has ever uttered the words, 'I bet that's a bugger to heat.' Similarly, I was at the theatre recently and our seats were high up. I looked down on top of a male actor and my exact words were 'That's a fine head of hair.' Again, no teenager has ever said those words.

How old am I?

I am at an age where 'pulling an all-nighter' means going the entire night without once getting out of bed for a pee. I have recently become so obsessed by my bladder - largely for no reason - that it is pathological. Again, youngsters are not like this.

How old am I?

I am old enough not to panic when I see a dead body.

In fact, I am happy to say that broadly speaking whatever was thrown at me in the subsequent months I kept pleasingly calm. Okay, so when I was kidnapped I might not have been *totally* calm, and when I was surrounded by forty Corsicans with guns on the steps of a church during a wedding, I might not have been too calm either. But for the rest of it: the wrestling with corpses, meeting witches, the police interviews, the dashing about in boats in the Mediterranean: for all the rest of it, I was pretty darned calm.

Anyway, back to the body...

The body in the back of the car was that of a man. He was young, he looked Corsican as far as I could tell. He was of medium build, or coming to think of it a Clio isn't very big and the body probably appeared bigger than it actually was by comparison, so he was perhaps small to medium build; he was pretty squashed in.

One fact was for sure: he was definitely dead.

I knew he was dead, not through some superior medical knowledge, but because in any meaningful sense he didn't have a head. He had a fair amount of neck, but after that, there was tissue and some skin and some hair from the back of the head. It was like the face had exploded outwards. There was a fair amount of brow but the face was a pulpy mass of red flesh. There was a profusion of red shredded cheek muscle and a tongue that was part severed and hanging forward beyond what remained of the mouth. It was beyond disgusting. Because I am a normal person, I felt queasy and had to look away.

So the salient points to my mind so far were: the clothes Sarah was wearing, the look of shock on her face, the items on the bedside table, and the fact the body was definitely dead.

I closed the boot of the car in case someone else saw the body. Of course, looking back, that put my fingerprints on the door, but that was to prove the least of my problems. I nodded my head towards the house, and we moved back inside.

'What did you do to him?' I asked.

'I did nothing,' she said. She let out an involuntary exhalation of incredulity; incredulity that this was happening to her, that this was real.

'Why hasn't he got a face?' I asked.

'He's got a lot of face. I mean that's his face,' she replied. 'There was a gun. Like a shotgun.'

'Like a shotgun, or indeed a shotgun?'

'A shotgun,' she clarified.

'You had an accident with a shotgun?' I asked.

'No!' she replied.

I seemed to be upsetting her, so I brought my voice down a bit.

'Okay,' I said. 'And who is he?'

'He's called Jacob.'

'Is he a boyfriend?' I asked.

'Yes.' She said this with certainty, but then she corrected herself. 'No, well sort of. It was like our first weekend away together. Our first night away. And we...' It was as if she was struggling to recall, but in fact I think she was struggling to understand what had happened. 'We... had been lent a cottage in the mountains and we thought we would go there for the weekend and it was our first weekend away and we would go for a walk in the mountains and, I don't know, watch a film, have a drink. I was going to cook.'

'Okay,' I said. 'So you were in a lodge, in the mountains, and you were playing with a gun?' We were whispering all of this even though no one could hear us.

'No,' she replied. 'There was no gun. Jacob was, I don't know, testing out the bed. You know how you find the place you've rented, and you go through the house and look in all the doors and open some windows to let some air in because a holiday let is often a bit musty. So we found the bedroom which was at the back on the ground floor. There was only one floor. So we had found the bed and Jacob was like bouncing on it to kind of test it. You know, like a fun thing. I can picture him: he was kind of sitting up on it, and I left the room to get some stuff sorted out, like food unpacked getting the wine in the fridge, and I had to go out to the car because I had left some stuff in the car, and I had just stepped back into the house and then there was a huge bang.'

'There was a bang?'

'I mean huge. A huge bang. Could I have mistaken it? No I couldn't have mistaken it. My ears were ringing, and it was ringing around the mountains. I dashed straight back to the bedroom and then there was a shotgun. For the first time. There was no shotgun before and now there was a shotgun, and there was Jacob and his face was blown off lying back on the bed.'

'There was no shotgun?' I asked.

'No. I mean, you would remember if you brought a shotgun on a date,' she said. 'In fact, now I think about it I have never ever seen a gun in real life before.'

'So he shot himself?'

'No. Or I don't think so.'

'Was anyone else there? Was anyone else in the house?' I asked.

'No. We were alone together.'

'You and this Jacob were totally alone together in an isolated summer house, a hut or something in the mountains?'

'Yes,' replied Sarah.

'Are there other houses nearby?'

'No not at all. It is in the middle of nowhere. In the mountains. There is space all around the house. You can see if anyone is there. And how would they get there without a car?'

'So he must have shot himself?'

'No,' said Sarah.

'Why not?'

'Because the gun was nowhere near the body when I found it. It was like, two metres away leaning upright against the wall.'

'So he shot himself and the gun bounced off and by chance ended up leaning against the wall. Things like that happen.'

'Not to me they don't.'

I laughed.

'And there's another thing,' she continued. 'I have reason to believe there were two shots. Could he survive the first shot and then pull the trigger a second time? He couldn't. And anyway, as I said, the gun was standing bolt upright leaning against the wall. It just wouldn't land that way. It would have fallen over. I've had some time to think about this in the car, and that is what I think.'

'How long were you gone from the room?' I asked.

Sarah stopped to think a long time about this.

'Well I wandered off to the car, and I was cleaning the kitchen area. The kitchen is at the front of the house. The bedroom is at the back. The front door leads straight into the kitchen which is also the sitting around place. Everything takes time. I was looking for a bread knife. I thought we would cut up some bread, so I was looking for a knife. I don't know. Certainly five minutes, but perhaps ten minutes.'

I said, 'The most obvious option is to take the body off to the authorities.'

'Why?'

'Why? By driving around with a body in the back of your car you look guilty Sarah. It is better to take it to a hospital or the police.'

'The trouble is,' said Sarah. 'I was alone with him in that house and the police will feel that I murdered him. Who can blame them?'

No, the real trouble was that I now seemed to be involved.

Sarah was staring at my face waiting for some reassurance.

I smiled. 'Everything has to have an explanation,' I said. 'We just need to get to the bottom of what happened. The more we cover up what has happened, the more we *seem* to cover it up, the worse it will look.'

'The gun is still there,' she said, apparently remembering this for the first time.

'Did you touch the gun at any stage?'

'No,' she said.

'Okay. That's good.'

There was a knock on my front door.

I jumped at the noise and that was when I realised proper nerves had crept in. I could feel myself going white. We both went quiet.

'We could choose to not answer the door,' I said. 'People are out all the time. We could simply not answer it.'

'Do you think it's the police?'

'Well I do think that *now*,' I said.

Sarah sat rigid and silent. This was not her house, so she didn't know what to say or do.

'People sometimes leave lights on when they are out,' I reasoned, largely to myself.

We sat not speaking for a few seconds.

'What were you thinking, putting the body in your car?' I whispered. We looked like two naughty children trying to get our story straight before the adults returned.

'I panicked! I didn't know what to do,' she replied. 'There is no phone reception at the lodge, and I didn't want to leave the body, but I did want to talk to someone.'

'To me?'

Sarah considered this.

'I did think of you quite quickly,' she conceded.

Cheers for that.

The door was knocked again.

'I can see you're there,' said the voice. It was a woman. 'Open the door!'

It sounded like family, but my heart still sank to my boots.

THREE

'Who died?'

'What?'

It was my sister Emily; she had let herself in through the front door. Gorgeous, random, over-confident – disastrously over-confident – always relaxed Emily now stood looking over us.

'Who died?' she repeated.

'What do you mean?' I asked.

'The atmosphere in here is awful.' Emily then mouthed to me in plain view of Sarah, 'What is she doing here?' My family are not renowned for their manners.

'Man trouble,' I mouthed back. It was an understatement.

My elderly mum was the next to speak; it turned out it had been her at the window. She was now somewhere near the front door, shuffling down the corridor. 'What's wrong?' she asked.

'What do you mean what's wrong?' I asked.

'There's something wrong,' she said.

Just how awful was this alleged atmosphere? Just how much do we give ourselves away without realising it? And how come Emily had brought mum along to my house on a Friday night?

Mum, when she arrived, pressed her face unspeakably close to mine and scrutinised me. She swears she has good eyesight 'Because I never wore it out by reading,' but I have my doubts.

'You look like you're ill. You're pale.'

As a rule, no one is pale on Corsica. In fact, we have a special word that we reserve for pale people: 'tourists.'

I recovered myself a little. 'You're standing between me and my Friday night drink. Literally, you are standing between me and my Friday evening drink; of course, I'm pale,' I said. 'Oh and no one's died,' I added unnecessarily. 'So what can we do for you?'

'Ludic! He won't return my texts,' said my mum.

'Your octogenarian married lover, who does not reciprocate your love for him, won't return your texts?' I turned to Emily, 'And what are you doing here?'

'Our mother's romance is beginning to lose its considerable power to fascinate me. I thought I'd enhance the experience by letting you listen to her for a change, while I cadge a drink.'

'Or my calls,' said mum. 'Ludic won't return my calls. You try. Anyway, he's not in his eighties and neither am I.'

My mother is in her eighties.

Mum rooted about in her handbag and produced a crumpled piece of paper with pencil writing all over it.

'Look. Look. That's his number,' said my mother. 'I want you to text him.'

'Why don't you do it yourself?' I asked.

'I haven't got my reading glasses.'

Ever. What happened to 'I didn't wear my eyes out with reading?'

I looked at the number on the piece of paper.

'You do know you are trying to text a landline?' I asked. 'The best that could happen is nothing, and the worst that could happen is that his wife answers the phone and they have that system where a text gets read out by a computer.'

My mother considered this. 'Piss!' was her considered reply. My family are not renowned for their manners.

I scrutinised Emily. 'What's wrong with your hand?' I asked.

'What?' she replied.

'You're holding your hand strangely, like you're cupping it.'

She said it was nothing, but I felt she was being a bit mysterious about it.

My sister has had a lifetime of getting away with being mysterious until it all goes wrong, and then we all have to get involved.

To explain: our mother is currently stalking a man called Ludic. Ludic is substantially younger than my mother and apparently has a fine pair of legs. We know this because my mother drops it into conversation whenever she's not getting enough attention. 'Oh Ludic, he is so dishy, ooh you should see his legs.' Dishy is her 'go to' word for good looking men. Ludic is married - inevitably - and his wife plays the church organ during the services they all attend. My mother, who in my lifetime never showed any interest in religion, attends church twice a week, and when Ludic's wife is playing the organ my mother sidles up to Ludic to simper at his jokes.

'Isn't Ludic married?' I asked my mum.

'So?'

'So you're carrying on with a married man,' I said.

My mother shrugged. 'When you're married you'll have an affair, you'll see.'

Thanks for that mum.

'Not that you're likely to get married,' she muttered. 'You'd have to attract a woman first.'

I was having trouble believing my evening.

Then I had a thought.

A terrible thought.

In the heat of the moment - and the surprise at opening the boot of Sarah's car and seeing a dead body - I hadn't checked something. To get the body into her car, Sarah must have put the back seats down to make space. This meant the body must be clearly visible through the side windows. The body wasn't covered in any way. Anyone walking past the car could look in and see a corpse with most of a head missing.

The road outside my house is narrow and a dead end to cars but not to walkers. Plenty of people come up from the main town via a set of stone steps and use our road to walk dogs. It is also a popular tourist route for holiday makers to get to an ornate chapel called Scala Santa where disabled people over the centuries crawl up the red and gold carpeted staircase on their knees to seek a cure from the Almighty Himself. It's well worth a visit – and you don't need a disability to have a look - but you probably have to go past my house to get to it.

I hurried to the window to glimpse at Sarah's car. In my mind there would already be crowds of onlookers peering through the passenger window and phoning the police on their mobiles. There would be the leader of a tourist group holding a pink umbrella aloft guiding forty Japanese tourists each armed with overactive cameras. These are people pleased enough with photographing street signs and the breakfast buffet at their hotel; imagine how thrilled they were going to be when they had a decapitated body to film. Instagram was made for this moment.

There was nothing in the street.

I looked left and right.

Then there was a slight movement at the edge of my vision. It was a dog.

Then there was a youngish couple sauntering. They were chatting and taking their time. The dog was sniffing lampposts and clumps of grass and probably belonged to the couple.

I would need to go out and put a blanket over the body to hide it from view. Should I do it straight away, though? By the time I found a blanket, and Sarah sourced her car keys and opened the car, would the couple be alongside and witnessing me tucking the legs of the corpse under a travel rug?

'Nice day for a murder!' I could hail to them. They would nod and smile, and I would compliment them on their dog. Dog owners like that.

'Sarah, you're going to need your car keys,' I said.

'Why?' she asked.

I leant into her to whisper as best I could.

'The body can be seen through the side windows of your car,' I said.

Sarah shrugged. 'Yeah I suppose.'

'Yeah, you suppose?' I said. 'We need to cover it up.'

'Okay.'

Sarah didn't move. We had lost countless valuable seconds already.

'We need to put a blanket over it or something.'

'Okay,' she said, still not moving.

'You need to put a blanket on him.'

'You do it. You're the man.'

Presumably my face was the picture of incredulity because she then added, 'Look. I don't know where the blankets are. You do it.'

Rather than waste time arguing with a woman who was making no sense, I went off to find a blanket. I looked in the airing cupboard for something not too decent. I wouldn't be able to use the blanket ever again, so I didn't want it to be my best blanket. Did I have a best blanket? It was a thought for another time.

I chose a blanket I usually use for picnics and returned to the sitting room.

'Sarah! Car keys! Please!' I tried not to bark.

'What are you up to?' asked Emily.

'Sarah wanted to borrow a blanket,' I said.

Emily just looked me and stared me out. She seemed to be trying to determine something from my face. She shook her head at me, I think in incomprehension. Sarah handed over her keys and I ran out to the car.

Sure enough there was the dead body, clearly visible through the side windows. And sure enough, there was the young couple and their dog ten metres away. They were laughing at something. How dare they laugh at something. They were holding hands; they were in love. How dare they be in love. Smug marrieds. In fact, they're probably not even married. So what are they so smug about?

I fumbled with Sarah's keys and got the back of the car open.

I daren't look back but I felt in my head that the couple were now five metres away and approaching. Approaching unduly fast for a couple in love, if you ask me.

I could clearly see the body laid out in front of me and so it was only a matter of moments before it would be also clear to the couple should they look my way. The dog was now in the periphery of my vision. It was just a matter of time before it lifted a leg against the wheel arch of the car. I shook the blanket to get it unfolded and inevitably – inevitably – the blanket had no inclination to unfold.

I imagined the couple would now be a few feet behind me, their mouths aghast, their eyes wide in horror.

The blanket was now more loose but still had a stubborn folded section near the bottom. It would have to do. I threw it forwards into the car. It covered the legs and torso but stopped short of covering the head.

I tried to not run to the side of the car; it would draw attention. I affected a casual but firm saunter to open the passenger door and leant in and pulled the blanket over the head area of the body. The boot was still open. Why hadn't I thought to shut the boot? Why hadn't Sarah done all this already? If I pulled the blanket up over the head area it may inadvertently pull the other end to reveal the feet of the dead man. The boot would have obscured the view at that end. I pulled the blanket towards me.

So far so good.

I slightly tucked the edges of the blanket over Jacob's shoulders – it's what he would have wanted – and I tried not to panic when I saw the other end of the blanket shift a bit to reveal a shoe.

My only option was to stay calm. I retrieved myself from the car and shut the passenger door. I sauntered to the back and closed the boot. Then, and only then, did I allow myself a look down the street.

The man of the couple locked eyes with mine.

He was about three metres away.

The girl of the couple was observing the dog who was sniffing its way almost through my gateway and onto my property.

Was that my leverage? Could I affect an air of indignation and get angry with them to get their dog off my land? How dare your dog sniff the edge of my gate!

The man looked away.

There was no reason to believe he had seen anything.

I locked the car, and walked towards my house. There at the window was Emily's face. Surely she couldn't see anything from there? I was pretty sure she couldn't.

I got back in the house.

'Have you got anything to eat?' asked Emily turning from the window to me.

'Have you not both eaten?' I asked Emily and mum. I wanted to appear normal but sounded breathy.

'I never eat after six,' said my mother. She said it as a reprimand that we never listen to her and never take to heart her manifold unproven medical conditions; if we had listened over the years then we would know that she doesn't eat after six.

She does eat after six

'It plays havoc with my indigestion and then I can't sleep,' she said. Then she added, 'Why what have you got I can eat?'

'Yeah can we eat?' asked Emily.

I had some risotto on the stove left from earlier. I went off and placed some in two bowls for her and Emily, and gave them both a fork. The risotto had gone a bit sticky in the centre and a bit dry round the edges but it smelt good. Nonetheless my mum sniffed it with aloof disdain - she wanted us to know she wasn't impressed - then inevitably tucked into it with gusto.

'Have you got cheese or something to go with this?' asked my mother. No wonder she gets indigestion and then tells anyone who will listen about her bowels.

'Can you not talk with your mouth full?' I asked her. 'And can you not put more food in your mouth before you have swallowed the last lot?'

I turned to Emily who was finishing a phone call I didn't realise she was even making.

'Why does it fall to me to do the parenting with her?' I asked.

'Because I'm her favourite. And I plan to remain her favourite,' said Emily.

Funny. Emily is making a joke while we have a dead body in a car outside.

FOUR

My uninvited family did finally get round to leaving and as Emily left she raised an eyebrow at me and pointed to Sarah. I think she might have come to the conclusion that Emily and I were having a relationship, possibly based on Sarah's 'come hither' apparel. When I later read the police files there were a couple of allusions to such a thing, although in fairness these didn't originate from my sister. Unbelievably, when this was finally clarified, there was then a stray inference that I was gay. My irritation about all this is the repeated inability throughout the saga for anyone to get basic facts right. The police, the prosecutors, the media, the internet - well, of course the internet - consistently got more details wrong than right. What hope for justice? It became quite an obsession for me: how different people go about getting to the truth, or not, and their relationship with it when they find it.

Gay?

My house is a veritable mausoleum to dead relationships with women.

The kitchen. In the kitchen there is a whiteboard for writing on. It was placed there by Amy an ex-girlfriend. Her constant stream of conversation was on the ageing process - she was against it - or her thickening waistline; she was against that too. Somehow it was all my fault. 'I've aged since I've been dating you,' she'd say. 'I've put on weight since I've been dating you.' Thus the whiteboard. 'Must eat less' 'Buy more vegetables' 'Buy less wine' - that kind of thing. Who would buy less wine? It was very irritating. But I liked that it was there. She was fun when she was drunk, and she was fun when she was eating. Which was all the time incidentally. And none of it was my fault.

The bedroom. In my bedroom there is a huge china vase that Colette bought me. Ah Colette. She was kind, and attentive and good-looking and fun and gave me lots of space and organised great trips for us and she bought me great presents. But she had a very slight nasal whine when she breathed. It was almost inaudible, but I knew it was there.

All I could hear was the whine. My sister claims that no one else could hear it. Ultimately the nasal whine got the better of us and she had to go.

In the sitting room is the battered couch where Bridget used to lie and flick chewed up bits of paper at the ceiling. They're still up there: a tribute to both Bridget's desire to irritate me, and my laziness at cleaning. I would sit on the floor on a cushion next to her and when she wasn't getting sufficient attention, she would flick me with her finger. Hard. Some days she'd say she'd turn up to see me and she didn't. Some days she'd turn up when she said she definitely wasn't going to, and when I'd made other plans she sulked. Some days she wouldn't return my calls. Some days she'd ring me every ten minutes. She was the only woman I ever dated who never wore a bra. Heaven knows she wasn't flat chested. I loved that woman.

But, as usual, I digress.

'Why did your mum come, exactly?' asked Sarah. It was a reasonable question. 'They often visit you on a Friday night perhaps? Does Emily always visit?'

'Emily is hopeless with money,' I replied. 'Any money she gets she spends on travel. I think she hangs around with Mum just to get fed.'

'I can see that,' said Sarah.

'Anyway!' I said purposefully.

'Yes?'

'Let's get the body to the police station or a hospital.'

'Why?'

Why? Seriously? What kind of a question was why?

'We don't have any other option,' I said.

I couldn't believe the look on her face; it was like I was talking alien.

I came to the conclusion that Sarah was in some kind of shock so I explained slowly and carefully that our only real option was to report everything to the authorities, but Sarah refused to agree or indeed even stand up to go.

It took me over half an hour of reasoning with her. What on earth did she imagine we were going to do for a plan? Bury the body in the woods? And more pertinently, are all the women in my life insane?

Eventually she said, 'Okay but we'll go to the hospital not the police. The police will just try and arrest me.'

'The hospital is fine by me,' I said.

'But we've got to go via the lodge first,' she said.

'What?'

'I've left my handbag there.'

'You've left your handbag there?'

'Yeah,' she said, 'I had my car keys out because I was unloading the car and then everything, you know, kicked off, so I forgot my bag. If the police get involved, they will cordon off the lodge and then I won't be allowed my handbag. It's got all my stuff in it.'

I reflected that it was perhaps like when a plane has a crash landing; the passengers still go back for their hand luggage regardless of how many cabin crew are screaming at them not to, and that the fuel tank could explode at any minute. I sort of related to it, and certainly wasn't going to argue; her just agreeing to go to the hospital was progress of sorts.

'We will go back for your bag,' I said. 'Then on to the hospital here in Bastia.'

She nodded and blinked a bit. She was still a terrible colour.

I stood on the threshold of my house to go, and as I looked back into the house to check I'd shut the windows, I had one of those quasi-paranormal feelings you sometimes get where everything seems hyper-real. The corridor, the sitting room beyond, the light making beams through the skylights, it all seemed to telescope and feel overly 3D. It was like that feeling you have when you have a bath by candlelight and you have a glass of wine on the go and somehow the rings of light and the reflections on the ceiling feel profound and spiritual. I am the least spiritual person on the planet, so it was all very odd. I suppressed all impulses to take it as an omen - as I always do, and I always will - and locked the door behind me.

We crossed the road to the car.

'Can you drive?' Sarah asked me.

'I'd rather not,' I said. 'I hate driving other people's cars. Also I am not insured. It would look terrible if someone who worked so prominently in insurance was found driving without insurance.' Like that was our biggest problem.

'Please drive,' she said.

'I am not going to drive,' I said.

‘Well I’m not going to drive,’ she said. ‘I’m all shaken up.’

‘Sarah, if we are going to go anywhere. You are going to drive.’

She really wanted me to drive. She really, really, wanted me to drive.

I conjured my face into the grumpiest sternest middle-aged expression I could summon. I kept my face that way until she drove, and then continued like that because by then I was indeed feeling grumpy.

I sat beside her in the passenger seat. We both avoided looking in the back of the car.

‘So what’s the plan?’ she asked. I can only assume she was in shock.

‘We are going back to get your handbag and then we are going off to the hospital.’

Sarah didn’t make eye contact; she just kind of stared into space; sometimes even in the direction of the road.

‘Okay but you’re making me do this,’ she said.

‘What?’

We drove for a mile or so.

I reflected that I was already thinking like a guilty person because I had deliberately left my phone at home. In my line of work, I get to investigate a lot of crimes, and one of the first things the police do is contact the phone service providers and find out the location of their suspects at different times. They then let the suspects talk themselves in circles before revealing that they already know where they were and how much they are lying.

The island of Corsica is not called the Granite Isle as an act of whimsy. It is basically a mountain range that emerges from the Mediterranean, with port towns dotted around its edge where the mountains drop into the sea. As a result, to get around Corsica at the best of times you need patience and the locals routinely describe journeys in terms of time not distance: ‘That’s an hour into the mountains’, ‘That’s two hours down the coast’; even the train takes three hours to go what is less than thirty miles as the crow flies. We knew we were in for a bit of a ride, therefore.

‘So tell me about how you met this man, Jacob,’ I asked.

‘How do you mean?’ replied Sarah after a pause.

‘When was the very first time you met him. How many weeks or months ago?’

'About four weeks ago. A little under four weeks.'

'And where did you meet him? Where exactly?'

A long pause from Sarah. I didn't prompt her further; I was just grateful that she was scrutinising the unlit road.

'I was leaving work one day,' she said at last. 'He bumped into me. He was on his phone and he wasn't looking where he was going and his shoulder caught me. He apologised. He like, held my two shoulders and looked at me and said, "Are you okay? Are you sure you are okay?" and I said I was fine. Why wouldn't I be fine? I was fine. Was he making a bit much of it? I thought he was. Then I was due to meet Benedettu from the office for a drink at the bar we all go to.'

'You are friends with Benedettu?' I asked. Benedettu is a feral looking lad who has a mixed role at work including office manager, clerical work and responding to general queries from the public. It is the sort of job where you don't realise how much the person does until they leave, and then it's too late 'cos they've already left.

'Later on we were chatting in the bar, Benedettu and I; and Jacob came over. "You were the lady I bumped into," he said.'

'What bar?' I asked.

'What does it matter?' she asked.

'I'm just trying to picture it.'

'Les Palmiers,' she said. 'You know. The sort of stately one on the main drag.'

'So then you dated,' I said.

'Yeah,' she replied.

'Every night? Or was it off and on for a few weeks?' I was trying to ascertain how much she knew about the man.

'Yeah, so, it was off and on for a few weeks. We got on well. We didn't, like, stay over at each other's place or anything if you know what I mean. Why, what are you implying?'

'I'm not implying anything.'

'So, we just had some drinks and swapped numbers,' she continued. 'You know we didn't really do much. There were often other people there, so we took an interest in each other, but nothing special happened. But then one day you realise you have seen the same person six times or whatever and so it obviously does mean something, doesn't it?'

'Who suggested you go away for the weekend?' I asked.

'Yeah, so, he rang me,' said Sarah. 'He suggested it. He said he had a friend who had a holiday place in the mountains and would I like to spend the weekend there. I said, "Is anyone else coming?" and he said "No." But I didn't want to seem uncool, and I was interested in him. I just wanted to understand what the deal was. There is a world of difference between going away in a big group and two people just going away on their own to a place in the countryside.'

'Indeed.'

'I could hardly say no because it was clear even to me that I was interested in him.' She then turned to me and was very earnest when she said, 'He's very good looking.' Like that explained everything.

'Perfect!' I said. 'So tell me about him. Tell me what sort of person he was.'

'Well he's like most men. He's all well-groomed and polite at first and then it all gets a bit grunty and sticky, and you have to sort of cling on and hope for the best.' Sarah laughed. She had a lovely round laugh full of warmth; it filled the car like a hug. It surprised us both, and then Sarah chuckled to herself like she was relieved to discover she could laugh at all.

Sarah got back to driving for a while. We were now already deep in an area of the mountains I didn't really know.

'You know,' she said. 'With some relationships, you wonder whether the boy is just behaving himself because he is only after one thing. You try to think about the conversations you had, what did we actually talk about? Was there something more there than two people who are trying to say the right thing and show themselves off best. I think there was. I found that something would happen in the day and I would turn round as if I could talk to Jacob about it, but he wasn't there and I would think, "Oh I'll tell him later" and I remember so many conversations we had about films or books, and I remember us chatting about some other people in the bar and, oh I don't know..'

'What kind of books and films do you enjoy?' I asked.

'Is that relevant?'

'No,' I replied, but perhaps it was – who knows what information is useful in a situation like this?

She looked as if I was bothering her.

'So you said yes to a weekend away,' I said, trying to get us back on track.

'And could he have killed himself?'

'No,' she said firmly. 'He just wasn't that sort. He wasn't brooding, he wasn't dark. He radiated life.'

He radiated life.

Less so now.

'But young men do famously try to kill themselves,' I said. 'You've seen the statistics: it's our line of work. Suicide is the biggest cause of death amongst young men, if there isn't a war on.'

'Not him,' she said.

'How do you know?'

'I know,' she said. 'Some things you know, even if you can't prove it.'

I let the subject drop.

I became obsessed by Sarah's key fob. I had used it before to open the car, but I hadn't really focussed on it. The key to her car was of course in the ignition, but dangling from it was a plastic unicorn that was covered in pastel coloured rainbows. It had a tuft of pink hair and big over-accentuated white eyes and black eyelashes. How old did Sarah think she was, eight? We knew for a fact she was old enough to have a dead boyfriend. I tried to look away from the swinging key fob, but its ghastliness was hypnotic. That unicorn was so profoundly irritating; how had I not noticed it earlier?

I tried to picture what I would see when we got to the lodge.

'What did the room look like?' I asked. 'Was there blood everywhere?'

Sarah paused to try and remember.

'It was such a shock,' she said. 'I didn't really take in the scene. There must have been a mess. I remember his face. There was a smell. A sort of gun powdery, fireworky smell. The window was open, pushed open, and there was like a smoke swirling around. I don't remember a huge mess. It's hard to recall.'

We came off the main road and onto an upward path that was mostly earth and rock. Previous vehicles had churned up the mud to form scars and furrows that were now dried solid, so the car bounced and creaked and strained alarmingly as the path got steeper.

Jacob shifted uneasily in the back. He'd evidently sensed something.

At the top of the road the vegetation gave way left and right to a granite belligerence, with a path somehow carved into the rock that was just about wide enough to allow for a car. The view was now of a phalanx of mountains standing shoulder to shoulder in a clear act of intimidation, each peak grander than the one before, all the better to dwarf and magnify what was in their middle - the hunting lodge - dwarfed by being so small by comparison to the landscape, and magnified by being the only evidence of man in a terrain unchanged in a hundred thousand years.

The lodge was a simple but effective construction of darkened wood formed by a heavy triangle of roof held up by short thickset vertical beams that were darker still. Set in the side facing us there were two small square windows and a solid door. The land was clear and flat to each side. Sarah had been right; you would definitely know if anyone else was in or near the house.

The headlamps of our car lit up the lodge in a beam and showed us something we didn't expect.

There was a car parked outside the front of the building.

Sarah stopped and turned off her lights.

'Was that car there before?' I asked.

'No. Jacob's car should be here, but it's parked further along round the side. That's not Jacob's car.'

'I didn't see anyone in the car. Can you see anyone in the car?'

'No.' She looked rigid and slight and afraid.

'If there's someone in the house we would expect to see a light on in the house. Can you see a light?' I asked.

This went unanswered.

'Perhaps there is someone in a back room,' I said

'What is someone doing here?' said Sarah at last.

'Perhaps it's the police,' I said. 'Perhaps someon

to investigate.'

'They must often hear a gunshot in the countrysi

police,' she replied. 'And how would the police know

Sarah put the car into reverse and craned her neck to direct the car back down the road. We retreated into the darkness. Just before we lost the view of the villa, a light did indeed flicker inside the house, and then the front door was opened but I couldn't be sure because our car was soon back down the hill.

At the bottom of the drive, Sarah chose not to get back on the main road.

'What shall we do?' she asked. 'There is someone in the house. Why is there someone in the house? Who could possibly be in the house?'

'We can't just leave the body in the car. And if that is the police up there, we can hardly drive forward and present them with the corpse. We need to drive to the hospital.'

'Yes,' she replied. 'But who is in the house?'

We sat in silence for what felt like forever, but was probably seconds rather than minutes.

'This is like the most weird nightmare ever. The whole thing. A weird nightmare,' said Sarah.

'You got that right.'

It wasn't plain what to do; we were gloomy or shocked or just plain shattered.

'What sort of car was it? The car up by the villa, I mean,' I asked.

'I don't know.'

'I mean it could be a police car. Were you expecting a visit, from one of Jacob's friends or something?'

'I don't think so,' said Sarah. She sounded so wretched. 'I met a few of his friends. But we were in a bar and it was just, you know, Corsican lads. They were nice. There were quite boisterous. There was a curly haired friend who was very chatty, there was... well they all look the same. Sort of.'

We were disturbed by a bird or a bat flitting across in front of the car. It somehow [illegible]ad the effect of changing our conversation.

[illegible]t's keep the car lights off, and then creep up to have a look,' I suggested.

[illegible]t of the car and have a look? Or stay in the car and have a look?' she asked.

[illegible] the car and have a look, and that way if we need to speed away we can,'

Sarah drove slowly back up the hill. Every creak of our car over the hard mud sounded a hundred times louder than a minute earlier.

It was getting darker now, but we could clearly see the lodge. The front door was open and the light was on inside. I saw one figure move from the door to the car and then possibly a second person – the movement was so fast it was hard to be sure. Then the light in the lodge went out and it was difficult to adjust my eyes straight away but I felt there was a second person shutting the door and then all bets were off because the car put its headlights on and we were caught in the beam.

Sarah jolted into action. She reversed the car like a good'n and got us back onto the main road in seconds. Then she just drove and drove and drove with her head set forward and without a word spoken.

'Lights,' I said.

'What?'

'You need to turn your lights on,' I said.

FIVE

The principle roads in Corsica are very safe and well designed. However, there was a time not long ago when many country villages were only accessible by donkey track through a forest, and there are still a number of coves around the island best visited by boat. In the last few decades a number of great roads have been laid down, built largely with money from the EU and mainland France. The locals' inevitable response to this is to vote for separatist parties in ever increasing numbers, presumably safe in the knowledge that the EU won't dig up the roads and re-possess them once they have been spurned. So to recap: I would recommend the principle roads in Corsica to anyone.

And then there are the minor roads.

Sarah's bright idea - assuming she was thinking at all and not just panicking - was to get off the main road as soon as possible and get lost in the darkness of an unlit mountain track so that we could have a hide and a think. And this is exactly what happened.

The route we found ourselves on was one of those mountain roads whose sole apparent function was to be the perfect location for a car chase in a Bond film. Actually, it was worse than that; car chases in Bond films usually take place during daytime so that we can appreciate with our eyes the many ways in which the car could crash, fall off a cliff, or hit an oncoming farm vehicle. On the road we were on that night, there was no light whatever so I had to rely solely on my overactive imagination to guess how exactly I was going to die. There were the hairpin bends where the only clue to their border was a wilting bunch of flowers to signify the death of previous motorists. There were the roots of trees extending from the cliff that rucked the tarmac and made the car lurch to the right where a hundred foot drop beckoned. There were the rock falls half blocking the road, there were fallen trees; there were the abandoned cars on the verge with one corner jutting out to make oncoming cars swerve into your two yards of space.

Sarah didn't seem to care about any of this. She just careened on.

'Why was there someone at the lodge?' she asked.

'I don't know. Did anyone else know you were there? Were you expecting anyone?'

'No! No one,' she replied. 'At least, I didn't tell anyone I was there.'

'When you say Jacob's car was there just now. So you travelled separately to the lodge?'

'Yes.'

'Who got there first?' I asked.

'He did,' she answered.

Sarah took one side turning too many; the road we were now on was darker, more vertiginous and more random than I could stand.

'Can we stop?' I asked.

Sarah didn't stop.

The road was no wider than one single car. It hugged the contours of the mountain but with no sign whatever that it was an official route. If an oncoming vehicle came we would have died there and then.

And then there was a section of the road missing.

Simply missing.

A massive bite had been taken out of the road by a land slip. There was perhaps one metre missing on the right and a metre and a half remaining on the left. Even the section that remained had a curious tear in it; a tear that had been there so long a plant was growing up through it. The plant was caught in our headlights and the fact that it looked so healthy implied that no one, not even a crazy local drunken youth of a driver – categorically no driver at all - was silly enough to use this road.

Except Sarah.

Obviously.

Sarah hunched herself into a tense knot of elbows and bony shoulders, and edged us forward into the gloom. Her tactic appeared to be to push the wheels up onto the edge of mountain and away from the precipice. This ruse definitely succeeded for a few metres - if success can be measured by narrowing our options still further - but our progress was soon impeded by a sign post. The post was a metal sign warning us to beware of rock boulders that could fall on top of us from above. The sign was suitably battered and bent where it had itself been hit by the falling boulders it alluded to. This is true irony, not Alanis Morrisette irony. At least I think so.

Finally, mercifully, Sarah stopped the car and applied the handbrake.

'We're going to have to reverse,' I said over the sound of my heartbeat.

'I don't like reversing,' she said.

'Well you are going to have to reverse,' I said.

'Reversing scares me,' said the woman who had reversed the car with no fuss whatever only ten minutes previously back at the lodge.

'Sarah, please.'

'I don't want to discuss it.'

'You don't want to discuss it?'

She went on not discussing it.

We sat in silence for a very long time.

'And now you're crying,' I said.

Sarah cried more, and in a manner that implied her extra crying was all my fault.

'I'm having a terrible day,' she said.

'So... am... I...' I said calmly.

I couldn't get out my side of the car because there was a sheer drop to the valley below. So I decided my best bet was to climb out the back of the car and either guide Sarah back, or swap with her and drive myself.

'Open the back of the car and I will climb out,' I said and set about trying to manoeuvre my bulk between the two front seats. Inevitably, I was soon wedged and then when I did finally lurch free I fell face first into the dead man's groin. I could feel his cock against my upper lip. Like the rest of the body, it was stiff. It was the most macabre 69 in the history of all things vile. You wouldn't even find something as sick as this on the dark net.

I... will... never... have... sex... again.

Then without any notice, Sarah reversed us off the edge of the cliff.

SIX

The car fell about ten metres then came to rest upright, wedged against something unseen; probably a tree.

Jacob and I were silent and still.

Sarah, for her part, threw herself into an energetic regime of whimpering and shuddering, accompanied by a mantra of 'I can't believe this is happening to me.'

To *us* Sarah. It's happening to *us*.

'You told me to reverse, so I reversed,' she muttered. So it was my fault.

It turns out that a dead body makes for a reasonable ladder, if you aren't too fussy about placing your foot into their pelvic bone. Who knew? I stood on Jacob and tried to break the windscreen above us with my fist. It refused to crack. Sarah, meanwhile simply wound down the window and climbed out. After much more cursing and swearing – all from me – I somehow joined her standing upright on the grill and the edge of the bonnet, but this proved the last straw for the car itself; it gave way from under us.

Now we were scurrying with our hands and legs - and in my case also my stomach - against the side of the mountain trying to secure a purchase and get ourselves to the safety of the road. The tiny surface of topsoil was turning to dust against my clawing fingers, and the edges of the granite were scraping our knees and shins.

Sarah took the view that momentum trumped meticulous planning. Her feet were soon well above my head, so out of pride I also scrambled up as fast as possible. It wasn't self-preservation that got me up that mountain that night, but the desire to not be shown up by a woman half my age. Happily – or rather unhappily – at one stage when Sarah was above me she slipped. I put my hand up to stop her fall and ended up with her bare arse against my palm. Her arse, for the record, was quite firm with one central bony bit pressing against my palm. There was nothing flabby going on.

Don't judge me. I am a bloke.

Other crimes of mine that I'd like to be taken into consideration, include once admiring the bottom of a cyclist in front of me in traffic only to discover the bum belonged to a man, and having unclean thoughts about the woman who delivers the post at work.

Once Sarah had her foothold again, I went into over-drive. I was determined to beat her up.

I managed to overtake her and there was a moment when the obvious option was to place my foot on Sarah's shoulder to get a better purchase, but even I refrained from doing that. Before I knew it, I was up on the road and able to offer a hand to help Sarah as she had floundered - yes floundered - a few feet below. As a result, I had the satisfaction of being able to say down to her 'If you take my route it should be easier,' so it was worth it. Or rather, I would have said that sentence if I hadn't been so profoundly unfit. I was so out of puff that suddenly I was aware of opening my eyes and seeing Sarah's face peering down at me concerned. I think I may have passed out for a second or so. Or taken a judiciously timed micro-nap.

'Are you alright?' she asked.

'Yeah,' I wheezed. Eventually I added, 'That was something wasn't it?'

A little while later I had a thought.

'I've left my blanket in the car,' I said. 'I should have rescued the blanket. I left my blanket with a dead body.' And my fingerprints and, no doubt, a profusion of DNA.

SEVEN

It was going to be a long, horrible walk back to Bastia from the mountains, and it transpired that Sarah's sandals were largely decorative.

Somehow in the excitement of scrambling up the mountainside I had twisted my ankle and Sarah had ripped her dress up the front. From what I could see and feel we were both also covered in mud. I also discovered I had hit my head at some stage; I felt round in my hair and found blood. Just great. I had no idea how that happened.

We hobbled along the pitch black road with my foot swelling in my shoe and Sarah periodically moaning. 'My feet really hurt.' or 'How much further is it?' In other words, she had reverted to being a drip and – worse – was stealing my thunder about feet that hurt; I was the one with the ankle injury, not her.

At one stage I said to Sarah, 'I suppose that the act of an innocent person would be to ring the police now.'

'I did think that,' she replied. 'But in all the panic I left my phone at the cabin. I think it's in my bag.'

Somehow we got down to the next, slightly larger, road and I realised Sarah was no longer with me; she was some way behind.

'What are you up to?' I asked.

'I've ripped my dress so I've got to turn it round. I've torn the front of it.'

A car came from nowhere. The headlights caught Sarah in the middle of the road with her clothes half turned on her body. She had threaded her arms inside her dress and they were now stuck in the main body of the fabric. Presumably she was trying to turn the dress back to front, without taking it off.

At the precise moment that the headlamps caught her in the middle of the road, she was an abstract pole of summer fabric hopping up and down with a mop of struggling hair on top: a sort of mardi gras pogo stick with anger issues.

Happily, it proved plenty enough to stop a car.

Sarah hopped up and down more vociferously in an effort to both communicate with the driver and to set herself free. She added a yelp which was along the lines of 'Hel-ep hel-ep.' Then she added in French, 'Sauvez-moi, sauvez-moi.'

I myself then half hopped, half lurched, out of the darkness towards the driver. It looked to any reasonable onlooker that Sarah was asking to be 'sauvezed' from 'moi.'

We were destined to be very memorable to the driver should the police ask later.

The car was large and old, but I couldn't say what make it was. The window came down to reveal an elderly male driver. He certainly wasn't one of the wealthy yachting community we encounter on Corsica; he had the dark features, hooked nose and lit cigarette of a traditional Corsican; if he had a washing label it would read '70% Italian 30% granite.' Although it was not in fact clear that he had ever washed.

'Bonsoir,' I said in French. Good evening.

'Bona sera,' he replied.

'Vous pouvez nous aider?' Can you help us?

'Un capiscu mica,' he replied. He was clearly a Corsican who spoke Corsican. I think he'd said something like 'I don't understand.'

I smelled a rat.

It is vanishingly rare to meet a Corsican who doesn't speak any French at all, so when I come across the Corsican language I either assume that they will switch to French in due course, or that they are making some sort of point at the expense of foreigners - a entirely hostile point. There is a well-worn aphorism that the older generation speak Corsican but want to speak better French, while the younger generation speak French but want to speak better Corsican, so at least I was getting a clue as to this man's age.

My Corsican is not up to much but I take an interest in languages, so I tried what I could.

I wanted to say, 'We need the police' which would be something like 'Avemu bisognu di la polizia.' But I think I actually said something like, 'Ci tocca à esse pulizzìa.' This means 'We need to be police.' The situation wasn't helped by the fact that there is more than one traditional Corsican language. Northern Corsican is different from Southern Corsican which is also spoken in northern Sardinia.

Naturally the Corsican was confused and I think he replied with, 'I have done nothing wrong.'

In return I replied with what I hoped was, 'We need a lift in your car,' but in fact was probably more like, 'We need your car.'

'You can't have my car,' he replied. I bet he spoke French really. I scrutinised his eyes. I tried to work him out. He was unblinking, but I could see some French in there somewhere.

Given the ongoing communication problem, I resorted to the fall back strategy of all Brits abroad. I became slow, demonstrative... and *very* loud.

'We,' I said tapping my chest earnestly. 'Go to house.' I mimed a house. My fingers drew a roof, some upright walls, a door, some French windows. I threw in a conservatory for good measure, a patio for barbecues...

'We go to house,' I said again.

'I not go to Police station,' he said. In English. In English. He... said... it... in... English.

He reluctantly beckoned us into his car, drove us in silence for about ten minutes, then turfed us out the car.

Without any explanation at all, he simply turfed us out the car and drove off.

Sarah and I peered gloomily into the gloom.

'The odd thing is,' I said. 'I think we're back at the lodge where you and Jacob were going to spend the weekend. The man might have done us a favour,' I said.

'I doubt it,' she replied.

'Look it's over there!'

And there it was. We were back at the lodge. The other odd thing was that when approaching the lodge from this angle it didn't appear as isolated as I previously thought; judging by a few lights we could see, there was a dusting of houses about a hundred yards away down the valley.

We hobbled and moaned our way up the path to the hunting lodge, and paused to look for any sign of life. There was no light at all, no sound, and no car parked out the front.

'Jacob's car is still round the side,' I noted. 'Where are the keys for it do you reckon?'

'I don't know,' she replied.

'Do you reckon they were in his pocket?'

'Maybe,' she replied. 'I doubt it though. He was, like, bouncing on the bed, lying on the bed. I think you would kind of empty your pockets of keys before you settle on a bed.'

'Well you yourself probably would, but yeah, I agree,' I said. 'So we might be able to use his car.'

We were still wary as we approached the house, but somehow we all have a sixth sense about whether a building is empty or not, and I felt in my heart it was empty.

Sarah nipped round the corner and came back with the key to the front door.

'The key is kept on the top of the guttering on the side,' she explained.

'Did you lock the house after you left with the body?' I asked.

'Yes.'

'And yet when we were here earlier, there was a light on in the house and people,' I said. 'That means whoever was in the house knew how to get in.'

'Yes,' said Sarah.

'Who would have a key or who would know where the key was kept?' I asked. 'Did you put the key in that hiding place for the first time yourself, or were you told that was the hiding place to leave the key?'

'We were told that was where to leave the key?' she somehow asked it as a question, as young people often do. I hate Australian inflection - it drives me insane out of all proportion - but tonight this particular grievance would have to take its place in the long long queue of my other grievances.

'By whom?' I asked. 'Who told you where to leave the key?'

'The owner,' replied Sarah.

'Have you met the owner?'

'No, Jacob organised everything,' said Sarah. 'Presumably a lot of people knew where the key was. I think the lodge was hired out a lot; it was maybe a family lodge? So everyone who ever hired the lodge would know where the key was kept.'

'Yeah,' I said. 'Good point.'

We were inside the hut now. We instinctively felt guilty for being there, even though presumably Sarah and Jacob were officially entitled to be there that weekend because they had rented it; either way we didn't put the lights on at first.

'Found my bag!' trilled Sarah.

'Well that's a relief,' I replied.

I wanted to see the famous bedroom – the room where it had all happened.

'So this place is basically a front room with a kitchen area,' I said. 'The bedrooms are where?'

'The bedrooms are down the corridor?' she said. 'There's the main bedroom and there's another little bedroom to the left,' said Sarah. 'Like a children's room.'

'Look we should turn the lights on,' I said. 'We have to start thinking like innocent people. Because we are innocent people.' The kind of innocent people who cart a dead body around in a car and don't report it to the police, and then lose it off the side of a mountain. It's a special kind of innocence; one for the connoisseurs.

Sarah turned on the kitchen lights. The hut was very wooden and rustic, but otherwise quite modern in its fixtures and fittings. It smelt of pine needles and wood smoke. There was a comfortable looking corner sofa, and a convoluted lamp hanging over it that was styled in the self-consciously trendy style that the French often fall prey to; it was sort of three big orange flying saucers suspended by some polished steel.

We made our way down the little corridor to the bedroom where the murder or suicide had occurred.

Before turning on the light I breathed deeply and measured my breath out through my mouth. I turned the light on and it revealed...

Nothing.

'Is this the bedroom you mean?' I called.

Sarah arrived at my shoulder.

'Yes.'

'This is the bed where Jacob had his head blown off with a shotgun?'

'Yes.'

'I can't see anything,' I said.

Sarah stood silent. Her tongue was poking out slightly against her upper lip. Her eyes were moving left and right.

An eternity later she spoke.

'There was a gun by the window there,' she said pointing to the right.

'There is no gun there now,' I said.

'I can see that,' she replied. 'It was there.' She pointed again to just below the window.

She dramatically opened a wardrobe as if the contents would explain all. There was nothing.

'Where was the body?' I asked.

'On the bed. It was there.'

'There is nothing there now,' I said. 'No blood, no mess, nothing.'

'No,' she said. 'The sheets are clean and everything. Someone's changed the sheets.'

'You are sure this is where Jacob died? He was lying on this bed?' I asked.

'He was lying on this bed. There was blood everywhere,' she said. 'There was a body. There was, you know, flesh. There was flesh all over the bed sheets'

She was absolutely floored by what she saw.

Which was nothing.

This was just a perfectly normal clean room with no sign of a murder or suicide. Just a nice pleasant holiday let kind of bedroom. It even smelled nice; not murder-sceney at all.

'What about the walls?' I asked. 'Was there blood on the walls?'

'I think so,' she said. 'I mean. I didn't really stop to think or look. I was, well, I wasn't panicking, well I was panicking, but it was more like shock? I was in shock? I mean, wow, it's all such a thing.'

'Well there's nothing here,' I said. 'There was blood?'

'Yes! There was plenty of blood. Or I think there was. There was flesh. I remember flesh. Flesh and I don't know. You believe me, don't you?' asked Sarah.

'Of course I believe you. I have spent the evening driving around with a dead body in the back of a car. I believe you.'

'But you believe I have been telling the truth?' she asked.

'I believe you,' I said. 'I know you. If you say something happened. It happened.'

'Thank you,' she said.

'And this is the right house?'

'Of course, it's the right house,' she wailed.

I followed Sarah's lead and walked/limped warily back through the house with her.

She stopped in the kitchen.

'Well, I left stuff out in the kitchen; wine and food and they are now in the cupboards, except for the wine: that was tidied to the back of the counter next to another bottle. Also, the window in the bedroom was open when I left the place.'

'You left the window open?'

She shrugged a yes.

'So it's like a maid came and tidied and cleaned,' I said. 'I mean, we did see someone here.'

'Sort of, but if a maid came then they would alert the police about the blood and bits of body, and also who does cleaning at this time of night? Overnight is not when you visit a house to clean. Particularly if you think the place is rented out that evening to a couple.'

'Indeed,' I said. 'Do you reckon the gun is anywhere?'

We looked in cupboards, and we also looked inside the other little bedroom. It had a simple bunk bed in it, but no gun.

I walked around outside a little. The light was coming up now, sending tendrils and horizontal shadows across the downs. You could tell it was going to be great day; it was one of those mornings where you could smell it was going to be sunny later. It is said that Corsica is so fragrant that sailors can smell it when they are out at sea. Eucalyptus, sage, juniper, rosemary, heather, myrtle, thyme, lavender and mint form a murmuration in the air that soars and swirls and dives and beguiles. They say Napoleon longed for the smell of this place; I could see why. I love this island. I wouldn't be anywhere else in the world.

I looked around a bit. Sarah had been right about one thing. The house was in a clearing such that you would see anyone coming and going: you would have to approach by the same drive we had used. If Sarah said they were alone, they were probably alone.

Sarah called from inside, 'I've found Jacobs keys! They were in a drawer. And I've found my phone.'

I walked back to the front door and Sarah emerged looking happy, dangling a car key on a small chain.

'Well we could drive back to Bastia in Jacob's car,' I said. 'We could get some sleep. In fact, I need some sleep.'

This was the first time I realised I hadn't been to bed. I love sleep. If only it was an Olympic event then it would be 'gold for Britain' every time. I can sleep every night without fail, I can catnap at any time of day with no notice whatever, I can sleep on all known modes of transport and on all known furniture and flat surfaces. Sleep: it's a glorious indulgence, it's plentifully available, and it's free. Who doesn't love it? Between the pain and the exertions and the terror I would need to go to bed before I could possibly face the police and get all this on the record.

Sarah drove us home in Jacob's car. It was an old Peugeot whose paint was bleached and blistered from a life spent on an island and left repeatedly on the edge of beach. It was even more tatty than Sarah's. My plastic seat made a springing noise when we went over bumps. But other than those things, there was nothing of interest about the car apart from the fact that I can report that driving a dead man's car is pretty unsettling. Not so unsettling, however, that I didn't instantly fall sleep.

I woke outside my own house having had a pleasant little dream about having afternoon tea with Leonardo DiCaprio. It was sunny and we had a strawberry coloured cake with plenty of cream in the middle. Leo - we were on first name terms - was in fine form: gentle and funny, erudite but down to earth.

'What are you going to do with the car?' I asked Sarah.

'Just park it outside my flat and have a think,' she replied.

I had been dwelling on the fact that Sarah had been funny about going to the police and had only reluctantly agreed for us to go to the hospital with the body. Now, clearly, we would have to go to the police and report events exactly as they occurred as a matter of urgency. The trouble was, I didn't fancy a lengthy haggle with Sarah about doing all this and I did need some sleep.

I settled on a coward's strategy: as I left the car I shot over my shoulder, 'We'll need to go to the police in the morning!' and dashed off.

I had no idea whether Sarah heard me.

It was a problem for the next day.

EIGHT

The Saturday after the night before was, if anything, even more unsettling.

I woke up fully clothed on top of my bed and with my head pointing sideways to the bedside table. When I focused on it, I realised there was a piece of paper lying on it that hadn't been there before.

There was no other item on the table; just the piece of paper.

I reached out, picked it up and read it.

It said, 'Don't get involved with Sarah. Get her to deal with the body.'

I froze.

The paper was slightly yellowed and a coarser quality than used for writing paper. It was a little frayed on the left hand edge, so it was most probable that it had been torn from a paperback book. The writing was in blue biro.

It was terrifying.

Someone had stolen into my house at night and left a note by my bed.

Had they been looking over me as I slept? The note was about a foot from my face.

I read it over and over again, even though there was nothing more to read and no more that could be understood.

Another odd aspect was the quality of the handwriting. It was atrocious. There was no rhyme or reason to the size and shape of the letters, and it was barely legible. It was like the scrawl you'd see if a ghost from the spirit world tried to write a note during a séance. Who writes like that? A ghost. I might have answered my own question there. Except I don't believe in ghosts, obviously.

I picked up the corner with the tips of my fingernails and placed it sideways on some books on a bookshelf, in case it turned out to be evidence. I don't know why I used my fingertips, given that when I first picked up the piece of paper to read it, I had got my fingerprints all over it.

I then realised the room light was on. I hadn't noticed it at first because the sun was up and so the bulb was not the brightest source of light in the room. Whoever had stood over me and left that note had turned the light on. And failed to draw the curtains shut the night before. Okay, so one or both of those actions might have been down to me collapsing exhausted in bed after a long evening, but it was still unsettling.

'Don't get involved with Sarah. Get her to deal with the body.' I ran the words over and over again in my head.

Then I was distracted by my bladder. I was going to need to go to the toilet.

A word about my prostate gland.

I am pretty sure there is nothing wrong with my prostate gland. However, at some stage or other I have become obsessed about it.

I have heard, and then endlessly read on the internet, that all men over seventy when they die and have a post mortem will show they have a degree of benign prostate cancer and a degree of prostatitis. This will place pressure on your bladder and make you think you need to go for a pee when in fact you don't, or it will squash off my 'tubes' so that I will half go, stop again, and then be convinced there is more in my bladder that hasn't come out yet.

My basic thesis, therefore, is that if what I euphemistically call my 'flow' is always good then I haven't got to worry about cancer. I have been totally overthinking the whole issue.

As a result, I endlessly contrive to have a lengthy and, dare I say it, satisfying pee whenever I can. Just to reassure myself of my general health. To make this possible, if I think I need to go off to the bathroom, I first ask myself a whole series of questions. When did I last go? How much have I drunk? Is it just that I might not have the chance to go to the toilet later – because I am going to the cinema or on a long trip perhaps – and I am just having a panic about when I will next be able to go?

The trouble is, the more I think about going to the toilet the more I want to do it, regardless of how full my bladder is. As usual, over-thinking is my enemy.

I am happy to report that that morning I had a long and satisfying pee, so all was right with the world - apart from the note on my bedside table, obviously.

And the dead body we had left in the mountains the night before.

Have you ever stood in front of a bathroom mirror and looked at the blood on your face and wondered which bits were your blood and which bits were the blood of a dead man? No of course not. These things don't happen in normal life.

I scrubbed.

I scrubbed again.

I got a nail brush to my brow and then my cheeks and then when I still didn't feel clean, I took the brush to my lips and my nose and then showered and scrubbed some more. I was totally obsessed that I had a dead man's human flesh stuck in me and on me; in my creases, under my nails, and in my pores. No matter how much I showered, I would never feel clean.

Until I remembered how hungry I was, and got over it in a trice.

Breakfast over, and I rang round to get Sarah's number. We were going to need to go to the police station.

'But I don't want to go to the police station,' she protested. 'They will only arrest me.'

'They are not going to arrest you,' I replied.

'Why not? And why not arrest you too? You've got your DNA all over my car, all over Jacob... how do they know you didn't kidnap me and murder Jacob and...'

What? Seriously?

'Sarah, enough. The longer we leave it, the worse it will look when they find your car.'

'And you are saying they are not going to arrest us?' she asked.

'They are not going to arrest us,' I said.

'Promise?'

'I'll see you outside the police station in forty minutes.'

I trudged down into town with a very bad feeling in my heart. What if Sarah was not as innocent as she seemed? What had she meant earlier when she talked about how it could look as if I had kidnapped her? Where did that train of thought even come from?

I tried to think things through afresh. Why had Sarah singled me out to visit the previous night? What if she was trying to frame me? I dismissed the idea before I had barely thought it. But now my head was spinning with all these ideas. Sarah had established evidence that I was having a relationship with her – we had been witnessed together by my sister no less, with Sarah wearing her supposedly sexy clothes - and she had my DNA all over the murder victim. Meanwhile some unknown accomplice had cleared the true murder scene so that I had nothing to offer as proof for any scenario other than that I was responsible. Was Sarah trying to establish some sort of love triangle and I, the wronged lover, had done away with Jacob and kidnapped Sarah? It made no sense.

Then there was the man who gave us a lift in his car - the old Corsican farmer - what might he say about the strange couple he met? We looked like a couple arguing. When we first got in Sarah's car the night before, she had wanted me to drive it. Was she hoping to get my DNA and fingerprints on the steering wheel? Sarah could be so wet so often but on a number of occasions she had been surprisingly resolute; on the occasions, I now reflected, when she needed to frame me.

But the fact remained I had seen the look on her face when she saw that the murder scene had been cleaned up – my paranoia hinged on Sarah being quite the actress - and why would she take me back there at all? It made no sense. But then nothing made any sense. I reasoned with myself that ultimately, surely, she was Little Sarah from the office. My instincts couldn't have been that far wrong all along? Little Sarah from the office couldn't possibly be a calculated killer. But on the other hand someone had gone to a lot of trouble to leave a note to warn me off her. I suppose the trouble was I didn't really know her. I knew Emily, I knew mum, but I didn't really know Little Sarah.

I felt instinctively that Sarah was innocent, but it was a credo based entirely on a woman's stature.

NINE

The police station in Bastia is a fine modern building at the north end of the harbour. It is made of flat slabs of white stone and shaped - improbably but with some style - like a container ship. It has the words 'Hotel De Police' carved deep into its sides and running the whole length of its hull. Above the sides of the 'boat' is a ship's bridge that is five stories of offices. I have never heard the locals pass comment on it, but to my mind it is a good example of how the French are willing to take chances at architecture that might be too quirky for British blood. The building, to my mind, is a success. It mirrors the ferries and cargo ships in the harbour it faces, but also has the general air that it would be the last building standing in a nuclear attack. The clear assumption is that sooner or later the locals will get restless, and the building needs to be able to withstand a siege that, given the determination of the average Corsican, could last upwards of forty years. As a result of all this, you can't just walk in. You need an appointment to get yourself arrested these days.

Outside the police station there is a little green hut where a sentry could stand guard. There was no one in the hut, and worse, there was no sign of Sarah.

I figured I would give it ten minutes before I allowed myself to succumb to a full panic.

Ten minutes passed. Still no sign of Sarah.

I checked myself in the reflection of a window. My face looked pale, my hair looked out of control where I hadn't dried it properly, and somehow my eyes looked deep set and desperate from tiredness.

In short I looked like a murderer.

Sarah was now walking along the road towards me. Well that was something at least. She looked fresh and neat; her clothes looked ironed and she had a spring in her step.

'You're making me do this you know,' she said.

What, on earth were the other options?

After much pressing of buzzers and talking through intercoms we finally found ourselves sitting in front of a rather taciturn detective. He squinted at us both in silence for what felt like an eternity.

'I recognise you,' he said to me finally. 'You're often in here. You sometimes work with my colleague Luc Cadin on insurance matters.' He went silent again.

'This is Sarah-Jayne Hoskins,' I said. 'She's a colleague from the same company, Society Metropolitan. She and I work together on insurance cases.'

We exchanged pleasantries and then Sarah was suddenly assertive.

'I need to tell you what happened,' she said. 'Not him.'

'Okay,' said the inspector.

'First of all, I want to say that I am here under duress.'

Seriously?

Sarah smiled, breathed, smiled again. She was composed.

'It started early yesterday evening. I have a boyfriend called Jacob and he has been murdered.'

'Okay,' said the inspector.

'We had organised a lodge in the mountains to stay in. Him and I...'

With each word that Sarah spoke I was getting more and more tense. I was convinced she was going to somehow land me in trouble. I dared not breathe in case the sound of me breathing prevented me from hearing even one word that she said. But she started the story exactly the way she had started it when she had first seen me the day before, and bit by bit, word by word she explained about the shotgun and the room where Jacob was bouncing on the bed. She kept exactly to the story she had told me originally.

I almost fainted with relief.

The inspector was happy to let Sarah talk at length. In fact, Sarah talked for so long that it made me jump when the inspector finally interjected.

'How did you get the body into the car?' he asked.

'I am wondering that myself,' replied Sarah. Her demeanour had become quite jolly - perhaps from relief at getting the whole story off her chest. 'I think when it is a big astonishing thing like that, you kind of have the strength to do it.'

'Who owns this lodge where you stayed?' asked the inspector.

'I don't know,' replied Sarah.

Sarah got on with the story. When she came to the part where the murder scene had been cleared up she re-iterated again and again her amazement. 'I just don't know what to make of it,' she said. 'I know what I saw. Someone had shot his head off with a shot gun, and then when we went back there was nothing. Nothing!'

The inspector had other concerns. 'This Jacob. What is his second name?' he asked.

'Lluberas.'

'What town did he come from?' he asked.

Sarah perked up. 'Corte, I think,' said Sarah. This turned out to be wide of the mark, but we didn't know this at the time.

The inspector pulled a slight face at this news, but I might have imagined it. Corte is one of the more nationalist strongholds on the island. They weren't necessarily the most helpful to the police.

'Why didn't you report all this last night?' asked the inspector.

'We were trying to report the crime on the Friday,' I said. 'But as Sarah said, we crashed the car. The car fell off the side of the road. We were pretty traumatised. When we got home we were shattered.'

Sarah spoke. 'It was awful. It was a terrible, terrible, night. I ripped my dress.'

The inspector had heard enough.

'Take me there,' he said.

TEN

The police car we drove in was a straightforward little Renault. The child in me was eyeing up the various buttons and dials that presumably turned on sirens and flashing lights, and operated the radio links. Sarah and I had to sit in the back seats like naughty children or - to be more precise – suspected criminals.

The inspector was his taciturn self.

Just before our car had left Bastia, the inspector unexpectedly stopped at the side of the road and wound down his window. He addressed a teenager who was walking along eating an ice cream from a large tub with a purple plastic spoon. He was just a normal looking lad wearing trainers and a t shirt that said 'Don't forget to breathe' in graffiti style writing. It wasn't clear what this lad could have done wrong.

The inspector shouted at him, 'I'll tell your mother what you're doing!'

The lad looked startled and then pulled a face in a mock laugh.

The inspector wound up his window and drove on.

Even Inspector Fortini realised we were owed an explanation. 'He's a diabetic,' he said.

What I took from this was that Inspector Fortini knew his patch and cared about who everyone was, and for him it wasn't all about crime; it was about community. These were all good signs. Again, I was extrapolating this from very little, because Inspector Fortini gave us very little.

Sarah chirped, 'It could have been, like, frozen sugar-free, yoghurt he was eating.'

'Yeah, right,' I said.

The inspector added, 'He's not a girl!'

I felt the inspector and I bonded over the frozen yoghurt thing.

As a footnote, the ice cream in Bastia is amazing.

It wasn't too long before we were high up in the countryside at the road where our car came off the side of the mountain, and Sarah and I had scrambled to safety.

Inspector Fortini parked in a meticulously safe place and placed a hazard sign five metres before his car. The three of us walked the last section of road. It was the first time that I was struck by how small Inspector Fortini was and how lumbering I was by comparison. By lumbering, I mean fat.

'It should be here,' I said.

Sarah nodded in agreement.

But then her mouth stuck open and was clearly never going to close again in our lifetime.

The police inspector, Sarah and I were staring at the broken edge of mountain road where Sarah's car had slid down the mountainside.

There was no car there now.

There was a lot of broken tree damage. This was clearly the correct place.

There were a few torn branches where you could see the white wood of various trees at the point of break, showing it was fresh damage, but there was no car, and no sign of where it had been.

I tried peering down from different vantage points. There was definitely no sign whatever of Sarah's car.

'There's a tyre mark on the soil there,' I said, pointing it out to the policeman.

'Sort of,' he said. 'Are you 100% sure this is where your car came off the road?'

'Yes,' I replied. 'We stopped near the sign that says "Beware falling rocks" and we reversed back.

The three of us leant forward as a group in case we were all somehow missing something. Sarah and I had previously been there in the dark and so it had been difficult to be sure of the exact distance the car could have dropped; five metres and fifty metres look pretty much the same when there is no light to go on. With the benefit of daylight, we could see that perhaps the car could have fallen a total of about twenty metres – perhaps a little more – before it would have been stuck again on rocks and trees. A little forward from the rocks and trees there was a small farm track that ran parallel to the road we were standing on.

I squinted at the area for a long time. Cars are not huge but they are quite heavy. A space made by the car might not be wide but it should leave a mark in the soil. There was more than enough space down there to imagine where a car could have landed, but no clear marks in the earth.

'I think I can see some broken fragments,' I said to the inspector.

I pointed down below and Inspector Fortini was attentive enough in looking.

'I think I can see a few fragments where the car first settled, and then again some glass down below at the bottom.'

'Perhaps,' he said, but he was being polite.

'Perhaps someone has winched the car up?' I suggested.

'I can't see any tyre marks up here on the road from a tow truck,' said Sarah. 'I think there would be something. Perhaps it was moved from the track below?'

I literally scratched my head, and then regretted it; I had disturbed the skin where I had cut it the night before and blood had matted my hair. My problem was clear; I had pursued a strategy of laying out all the facts to the police, but the facts were refusing to be consistent with the evidence of our own eyes; and consistency is how we judge the truth.

'It is possible the car was removed from below. From that lower track. Perhaps we should go down there,' I said.

'If someone found a car with a body in it, then they would ring us,' said the inspector. 'They would ring the police.'

'Well perhaps they have,' I said. 'Where would they ring? Perhaps they have just recently rung, while we have been in your car,' I suggested. 'Perhaps they rang the wrong police station.'

The inspector accepted this; he looked at his phone.

'There's no signal here,' he said.

He turned to me and looked at me for an eternity.

'And you are 100% sure this is where the car came off the road?' he asked looking at me: evidently this was a question for a man to answer.

'100% sure,' I replied.

'Well who's taken my car?' asked Sarah. 'It's my car! Someone's stolen my car!'

I shrugged.

The Inspector walked up the road a little way and sniffed around, then walked back. He had the demeanour of a man who had seen a lot of things in his life and this was not the most bizarre by a long stretch. However, we had dragged him away from a quiet afternoon at the police station to look at a road in the mountains where clearly nothing had happened, on account of what appeared to be the fantasy of two British people with a convoluted and far-fetched tale of body snatching. Looked at in that light, it was a tribute to Inspector Fortini that he was simply impassive.

'Okay then, let's go to the lodge you mentioned,' said the inspector. 'At the lodge I will ring around to check if there has been anything reported. You are quite right. Sometimes something is reported and gets lost in the system for a little while. It is Saturday, after all.' These were his longest sentences so far. So long in fact that I think he must have shocked himself; he then didn't speak for another ten minutes.

We drove to the lodge. As it came into view, I was relieved to see that there was no one apparently there and no cars were present. I was fed up with unexpected events that had no rational explanation.

The inspector walked away with his phone to find reception. He had to walk quite a long distance and then we could see him walking in little circles as he talked. Once or twice he stopped to punch in a few different numbers into the screen and make different phone calls.

Sarah and I waited outside the lodge. We felt we weren't supposed to go in without him.

At length the inspector walked back towards us looking sunny enough.

'Did you have anything called in?' I asked.

He looked at me steadily. 'Something was phoned in last night around this area, but it wasn't much.'

'It wasn't much?' I asked.

'Someone telephoned the local police that they heard something happen here last night. The local police briefly visited here. It is my understanding that they found nothing here that was unusual and left again.' He nodded that he felt he had told us enough.

We unlocked the house.

'The police?' I mouthed to Sarah behind the inspector's back. 'Were here?' I added.

'Did the police let themselves in?' I asked the inspector.

He seemed to not hear me.

I pointed out the various rooms to the detective – the kitchen, the seating area – as if I were somehow an estate agent, then we made our way through the house and into the bedroom at the back. The three of us stood in the doorway.

I thought Sarah was going to cry. It has to be the first time in history that someone has been upset because there was no murder, no dead body, no gun, and no problem at all. We already knew that this was how the lodge would look, so I think it was the realisation that we had such a big tale we wanted the inspector to understand but absolutely nothing to show him. We had acted correctly by going to police – in fact we had been picked up on not going to the police earlier – but now it looked like we should have not gone to the police at all. We should have been happy - after all, we were now totally in the clear – if there's no body there's no crime. The worst that could be levelled at us was that we had wasted police time - I'll take that - I'll take that, and I'll offer a hearty handshake to the person who gives it to me.

'Which way was the man lying?' he asked.

Sarah showed him miserably.

'What is the last thing he said?' he asked.

Sarah thought about that for a long while. Her eyes had a habit of darting left and right when thinking, in the pace and style of someone watching a tennis match.

'Are you still there?' said Sarah. 'He said "Are you still there?" and I replied "I'm just popping out to the car."'

'So he checked where you were?' said the Inspector.

'Yes,' crumpled Sarah. 'Look! I promise there was a dead body here.' She sounded angry with the detective.

'Don't worry! The inspector is looking into it!' I said. But was he? I felt we were losing his interest.

Sarah was looking more miserable by the minute.

'I saw the body with my own eyes,' I helped.

The inspector said, 'If he shot himself with a gun. Was he lying back with the gun over him, or was he sitting up and the debris went over the wall behind?'

This was a great question. This is why he is the inspector and we are the little people.

'He was lying back,' said Sarah carefully. 'I don't remember any blood on the wall.'

'And you feel the sheets have been changed?' he asked.

'Yes,' she replied. 'The sheets have been changed.'

'Okay,' said the inspector. 'So I can see there was time for the sheets to be changed, but there wouldn't be time to change a whole mattress. Where could someone get a mattress at short notice on a Friday night and have it delivered?'

This was a good point.

We stared at the bed for an eternity.

Sarah started crying; her crying was at least silent, which was something.

'I am going to pull back the bed covers,' announced the inspector. 'Don't touch the bed. I will get some gloves and then we will pull back the covers. If there had been a shotgun shot from above the bed down, then there would be a hole in the mattress.'

Indeed.

We waited in the room.

At least the inspector trusted us to stay at the murder scene without contaminating the evidence; that had to be a good sign - or a sign that he didn't think this was a murder scene at all and he was humouring us.

The inspector returned with some blue non-latex gloves on his hands. He went to the bottom of the bed and unpicked the sheet at each corner. He pulled up the sheet and the duvet in one careful but firm manoeuvre to reveal the bare mattress surface.

The mattress was intact. There was no way at all that a shotgun had been discharged into it. Shotguns make a big wide hole in things - they are not sniper's rifles. If there had been blood then it would have made a mess, if only from the cleaning fluid and water that had been used to clean the area.

'Perhaps the mattress has been turned over,' I said.

The inspector lifted the mattress a little way to reveal a large label that denoted the underside. The mattress had not been turned. He put it down again.

'Everything in life has an explanation,' I said.

Sarah shoulders were shaking rhythmically up and down.

'And the window was open and then it shut again,' she blubbed, pointing to the window.

'When you first ever arrived at this house,' I said. 'Did you walk through the length of it?'

Sarah nodded.

'And you didn't see a gun?'

She shook her head.

'It could have been under the bed?' I asked.

The inspector and I leant sideways to peer under the bed. It was dark down there, but there was nothing apparently there.

'Or he could have opened the window and hopped out and got the gun while you were in the kitchen and hopped back in again.' It sounded ludicrous the moment I said it. I was going to add, 'He could have opened the window to a murderer who then hopped back out again.' But it sounded so stupid I let the words stay in my throat.

Eventually I said, 'Look, I'm sorry we have wasted your time inspector.'

'But we haven't wasted his time!' cried Sarah. 'Jacob died in this room! We need. We need. We need to find his body! We had his body, and we need to find it again.' Now her head was swaying and she was swaying as a whole. I didn't think she was actually going to faint, but I wasn't a 100% sure.

'You believe me, don't you?' she said to no one in particular.

'Of course, I believe you,' I said. 'I drove around Corsica with the body in the back of the car. I got his blood on my face.' I had a thought. 'Yes inspector!'

Inspector Fortini raised his eyebrows inviting me to speak.

'I had his blood on my face. I had his blood on my clothes.'

I was waking up now. I had been asleep, but now I was awake.

'There'll be something. I have washed, I have scrubbed, believe me I have scrubbed because it is horrible having someone else's flesh and blood on you, but there is still a chance there will be something under my fingernails, or on my clothes, or on my bed where I slept. Sarah will have information thanks to her phone.'

'What?' asked Sarah.

'How did he contact you when he was dating?' I asked. 'If you spoke on the phone then the phone company will have some locations for where he was when he made phone calls, and where his phone is now.'

'Yes! Yes!' she said. 'And we could ring him now. His phone would ring. Wherever he is, and we should do it before his battery runs out.'

'We are going to ring Jacob Lluberas, whom you say is dead?' I asked.

Without thinking, Sarah got her phone out of her handbag and set about ringing Jacob. We had no better ideas, and psychologically we were going to call it a day, so we let her.

'The trouble is that there is no reception here,' said Sarah.

'You'll need to walk over there, outside, for reception; it's not too far,' said the Inspector who seemed oblivious to the madness of ringing a dead person.

We all went outside. The inspector and I stood in the shadow of the house and admired the mountains while Sarah wandered forward looking at the bars of her phone. She'd gone about twenty or thirty metres when she called out 'Lucky strike!' She had found a little hotspot of reception.

We waited by the house.

Sarah rang Jacob's number and waited.

'It's getting through!' she called.

'Look,' said the inspector. 'Without...'

'Ssssssh!' I said.

'What?' asked the inspector.

'It's gone to voicemail,' said Sarah.

'Do it again,' I shouted to Sarah.

'What?'

'I thought I heard the phone ringing somewhere. You know, like when you've lost a phone and so you ring it? I thought I heard it ringing somewhere near here.'

'Where?' asked the inspector. This was the very first time he had looked truly interested.

Sarah rang the phone again and we all listened.

Somewhere, somewhere not close, but definitely somewhere, there was a phone ringing.

'It's up near that hill or on that hill,' said the inspector.

Perhaps our hearing was a bit different because the inspector and I moved forward at slightly different angles – him to the left and me to the right.

'Can you still hear it?' I asked: I was furthest up the slope.

'No,' called the inspector.

'It's gone to answerphone,' called Sarah.

'Ring again!' I called.

A slight breeze picked up; just enough to make you feel you might not be able to hear quite so well.

The phone rang by my feet.

'It's here. It's right here!' I shouted. This was our first bit of success in terms of showing there was some substance to our story.

'Don't touch it,' said the inspector, closer now. 'I will get an evidence bag.'

He went to his car and opened the back. He returned with a metal case and opened it on the ground. It was terribly impressive; it contained evidence bags, tubes with swabs, sachets of blue rubber gloves, marker pens, some test tubes with mystery white crystals, and all sorts of fun. Either he was a meticulous man who kept his evidence case in order, or it was a new case.

'Why would his phone be out here?' asked the inspector.

'I don't know,' replied Sarah. 'But it is something isn't it? This is Jacob's phone. It proves he was here.'

'If this is Jacob's phone,' said the inspector. 'Then it shows that Jacob's phone is here. It doesn't show he was here. Did he move from the house? I thought you said he was in the bedroom bouncing on the bed.'

'He was,' said Sarah. She had visibly cheered up.

'So how is it that his phone is out here?'

'I don't know.'

'Did he go for a little walk to find reception, but if so why did he drop his phone and not pick it up again?' asked the inspector.

'Sarah said that Jacob came out to the lodge first, a while before Sarah arrived. Perhaps he made a phone call from here. Perhaps he was sitting on the grass. Did he smoke?' I asked.

'Sometimes,' said Sarah.

'Perhaps he walked out here to where he could get reception and made a phone call and sat on the grass, and after the phone call he had a cigarette and forgot that he had left his phone on the ground where he was sitting,'

We all nodded at that idea. I felt it was a great bit of deduction. There was no sign of a cigarette butt, but I was loathed to give up my new idea too quickly.

'We will see from his phone records what calls he made and when,' said the inspector.

He crouched down, presumably to look for cigarette ends, but found nothing. From where he was crouching, he looked up at me.

'Stand upright,' he requested.

He stood in front of me holding an oversized cotton bud. He was scrutinising my face for blood.

'Let's look at your fingernails,' he said at last.

All three of us looked at my fingernails.

'I can't see anything,' he said. 'As you say, you washed last night.'

He placed Jacob's phone in a plastic evidence bag and wrote on its docket with the marker pen.

At least the phone showed that Jacob was not a figment of our imagination and the inscrutable Inspector Fortini had something tangible he could analyse.

'Perhaps we could pick up your clothes that you wore last night,' he said.

'Sure,' I said. 'But' – I started to mumble now – 'They have been through the washing machine.' I had a thought. 'You might have some luck with my bedding though.'

'Yes?' asked the inspector.

'I fell asleep on my bed last night with my clothes on and I hadn't washed. I haven't washed the pillows or the duvet cover. And there is Jacob's car,' I remembered.

'What?'

'Sarah drove Jacob's car back to Bastia last night. It must have evidence in it,' I said.

The inspector looked doubtful.

'All we are really going to learn is that it's his car,' he said. 'Confirm his DNA perhaps.'

'I am just trying help,' I sighed.

'Absolument,' he said.

Sarah re-iterated to the inspector that she had parked Jacob's car outside her house, so we set about driving there.

It transpired that Sarah lived in the hills a little inland from the centre of Bastia. It's a nice patch – both scenic and convenient. For once, it didn't seem too long before we had reached her neighbourhood.

'How do you get to work?' I asked.

‘Why are you asking?’ said Sarah, suspicious for no reason.

‘I’m just interested.’

‘Car? Could I cycle? Yeah, I probably could,’ she said.

I had already noted that Sarah is prone to Australian inflection – making a statement as if it was a question. Or I should say, making a statement as a question? But to this she added the further crime of asking an actual question of herself and then answering it as she went along.

‘Would I be fitter if I cycle? Yes, I probably would,’ she said, right on cue.

‘Which apartment block is yours?’ asked the inspector.

‘I live at the end of this street?’ she said.

Could I live at the beginning of the street? Yes, I probably could. Was that the thought I was having in my head? Yes, it was.

‘And where is the man’s car? Jacob’s car?’ asked the inspector.

‘Right in front. I live on the first floor,’ she said.

‘The car is where?’ I asked.

‘I live here?’ she said, pointing out the window to a three storey house. ‘And Jacob’s car is, er...’

It was clear from Sarah’s expression that the car was missing.

Jacob’s car was missing.

It had been parked outside Sarah’s flat and now it was gone.

Of course it was.

We dutifully looked at the empty parking space where a car could well have been.

‘What sort of car was it?’ asked the inspector.

Sarah shrugged miserably.

‘A Peugeot 206,’ I said. ‘Quite old. A reddy, faded red sort of colour.’

‘Anything unusual about it? A Dent? A modification? There’s no chance you remember the registration of the car, I suppose?’ asked the inspector.

I couldn’t remember the registration of the car.

There is only so long the three of us could gaze at an empty bit of street before calling it a day.

‘Do you have the keys?’ asked the inspector.

‘I have the keys,’ said Sarah.

She looked in her handbag. After the day we had had, I half expected them to be missing as well, but no, she handed over the keys to Jacob's car.

'I'd best bag it up,' said the inspector.

We stood in silence for a while.

'It was here first thing this morning,' said Sarah. 'I went off to find Peter and then visit the police station and when I left my apartment, Jacob's car was here.'

'I suppose the car could have been stolen, just like any car can be stolen?' Now it was me doing Australian inflection. Good grief.

We were all so stunned by the whole day, I doubt we knew what normal meant any more.

The inspector made some more notes and got out the evidence case again. He took out a camera and photographed the parking spot where Jacob's car had been. I myself had never seen Sarah park the car there but I could think of no reason why she would lie or get it wrong.

When the inspector was satisfied, he said brightly, 'Let's go to your place and test the sheets!'

He seemed to be enjoying himself for the first time. Possibly because he could see the end was in sight.

'Do you not need a forensic team?' I asked.

'I don't know if we even have a crime yet,' he said. 'And it's Saturday. We need a very good reason to call out resources on a weekend. Everything costs money.'

We said goodbye to Sarah and the inspector drove me to my place.

I was a little abashed at how untidy my house was. You get used to how you live, but then when a guest arrives, you see things through their eyes. There were dirty dishes in the sitting room from when Emily and mum had been over on the Friday night, there were the red stained wine glasses; many, many, red stained wine glasses.

'I haven't had time to clear up,' I said.

He didn't care – or to be more accurate, he was not a man prone to facial expressions, so who knew if he cared?

Inexplicably, when we got to my bedroom, it turned out I had previously taken the time and trouble to make my bed look neat. I suppose you sometimes tidy the room you are in, but don't then have the time or instinct to go through the house cleaning and tidying other rooms.

Inspector Fortini opened his forensic case again.

This time he put on white gloves.

'Why do you have white gloves this time?' I asked.

'What?'

'Well you had blue gloves before.'

'Ah yes,' explained the inspector. 'Those gloves were blue. And these gloves are white. That is the difference.'

I looked blankly at him.

'They just happen to be a different colour!' explained the inspector. 'Where is your sense of humour? I thought you British had a sense of humour?'

'Not after the day I've had!' I replied. I forced out a laugh. To prove I was British. What with my British sense of humour and everything.

It was then that I remembered the note that had been left by my bed. The note saying 'Don't get involved with Sarah. Get her to take the body back.'

Looking back, there was a little part of me, even at that stage, that understood the note and its true significance – either way, my instinct was that I didn't want the inspector to see it.

Inevitably I did all the wrong things.

If I had left the note on the bedside table, then the inspector would have seen it and I wouldn't have had a dilemma. But I had moved it and placed it sideways on some books on a nearby bookshelf. This was at waist height and therefore could be seen quite clearly. On the other hand, the inspector had no interest in snooping around my room.

I was standing about two metres from it.

What I should have done was not move towards the note or in any way look at it.

What I actually did was look at it for about three seconds then look away. Then when the inspector was clearly looking at me, *I looked at it again*.

My instinct was that the note contradicted the line that Sarah and I had been taking; the line that we were both totally innocent. I then shuffled round in front of it, but it was too late.

'What is that?' asked the inspector pointing straight at the note.

'When I woke up it was by the bed.'

The inspector peered at it and read it aloud. '"Don't get involved with Sarah. Get her to deal with the body." Who wrote this?' he asked.

'I don't know. I woke up this morning and it was by my bed. Just there. And the lights were on in my room.'

We both looked at the light bulb as if it would make a difference looking at it.

'Was your house locked last night?'

'Yes.'

'With a lock? With a chain?'

'A lock,' I said. 'I'll show you in a minute.

'Were any windows open this morning?'

I hadn't thought about this at all.

'I keep a window open in the bathroom at night, but I don't think you can climb in there: it is too small. I keep my bedroom window open in the summer. But it is a large climb up.'

The inspector photographed the note where it lay.

'No I found it there,' I said, pointing to the bedside table. He dutifully photographed the bedside table.

The inspector then placed the note in an evidence bag.

We both then looked at the open bedroom window. We leant out to assess how easily someone could climb up the side of the house.

'It's difficult but not impossible,' I said.

We walked to the bathroom and looked at the window in there. It was a much smaller aperture but it was not impossible to get through if you were slim enough.

'I think the climb is a bit easier. It is best viewed from the outside,' I said.

'Who has access to your house?' he asked.

'No one,' I replied.

'No girlfriend or relative or friend has a key? A cleaner?'

I hadn't thought about that either. I tried to think of various girlfriends from the past. One or two had had a key for a while but they handed them back when dumping me – I was led to believe it was part of the ritual. I suppose they could have had a spare key cut and kept one, but why? It didn't seem to fit the picture of the crime as a whole.

'So no one has a key to your house apart from you,' said the inspector. His pen was ready to write on his pad.

'I don't think so. Various ex-girlfriends I suppose,' I said.

'You can perhaps provide their names and addresses?'

'Yes.'

'And you rent this house?' he asked.

'Yes.'

'So the landlord has a key? I will need the name of the landlord.'

'Good point,' I said.

He sighed.

He closed his notebook and set about swabbing the pillow case and bed instead.

'I think I will also seal this room and ask the forensic team to come this week. I will need to talk to a judge first, and I need to think a bit about all these...' He swept his hand around in the air. 'All these events.'

'Okay,' I said. 'Fair enough.'

'So don't go in this room again, until I say so,' he said. 'Have you got somewhere else you can sleep?'

I figured I could sleep on the sofa.

'I am going to need to clean. And tidy,' I said to the inspector.

'Okay, well I will leave you then,' he said.

'So I am free to go?'

'I have your numbers. I have your addresses. I haven't got a body. I haven't got a car.' He paused by way of emphasis that he was letting me in on his thinking. 'I am inclined to believe you. The stranger the tale, the more I am inclined to believe it. I mean no person would make up a story like this. I am inclined to believe something happened, so you aren't wasting police time. And as a professional courtesy after all,' he concluded. 'We are colleagues!' He patted me on the shoulder.

'And tell Miss Hoskins not to worry. She looks like a worrier,' he said. 'You. Not so much.'

I don't look like a worrier apparently.

He turned to go.

‘I will try and get a forensic team here on Monday morning. Then you can use your bedroom again. I will phone you,’ he said.

And with that, the inspector departed. He had been almost chatty by the end.

ELEVEN

How do you spend a Saturday night, after you have totally committed your weekend thus far to losing a dead body in the mountains of Corsica? A bottle of wine and a box set, of course. Largely because it's my emotional go-to response to most events in my life.

I decided to watch 'The Bridge' again.

I selected a bottle of good quality local red – I deserved it – and poured myself a generous glass. I watched the now familiar opening credits. I tilted my head back against the cushions and let the melancholic theme tune drift over my eyes and let the 'bright vivid flavours of flowers, red fruit and stony earth' – I am quoting from the label on the wine bottle – soothe my taste buds.

This is heaven.

This is relaxation.

This is near impossible.

I was supposed to be cleaning and tidying and making the sitting room better for sleeping purposes, not watching TV.

I didn't do any of that. Instead my thoughts kept going back to the murder - or was it suicide? - and the body, and the car falling off the mountain.

Okay.

The necessary prescription – clearly - was more alcohol, and perhaps if I tried watching something I had never seen before? Something new would engross me more and distract my brain.

I tried 'Sneaky Pete' - a TV show from a few years ago recommended by a colleague at the office. 'Colleague': a word used by the inspector earlier.

Sneaky Pete is a comedy drama about a man stuck in prison for a long time with a cell mate who yawns on about his life in the outside world. Upon his release, our hero decides to pass himself off as the cell mate.

I wondered what kind of cell mate I would get when I was – inevitably – arrested and convicted. Would I sink like a stone in prison or would I be able to find a niche for myself as a more educated inmate who can help the others with their court appeals and stuff. Okay, so basically that is the plot of 'Orange is the New Black.' Oh, who am I kidding? I'll just get beaten up and left for dead for the crime of looking someone in the eye, or not looking them in the eye - who knows what the rules are about looking them in the eye? - I might have to Google it - and if by some miracle I do survive the beating, I'll get back to my cell to discover someone had peed on my bed.

Okay, not 'Sneaky Pete' then. And I'd better not watch 'Orange is the New Black.'

I might watch 'Prison Break.'

For some tips.

I decided instead to join my sister down in town.

'We're down at Pinocchio's,' she said on the phone. 'I supposed we have space for a middle-aged grump.'

The bar isn't really called Pinocchio's; it's just that the proprietor has a big nose. And I am not a middle-aged grump. And last, but not least, Emily is only two years younger than me.

Oh, and Emily smells.

But not so much that I'm not grateful to piggyback on her social life when I'm bored.

Emily. What can I say about Emily? She's my sister, she is bonkers popular with the boys, and she always seems to be broke. Actually when I say she's my sister, in fact she's my half-sister even though we are close in age. My mum got pregnant with me by someone I have never met and soon moved on to Emily's father. She has never really talked about it.

'Well who was he?' I would ask as a child. 'What was he like?'

'I don't know,' she'd reply. 'It was so *dark*.' My mother would say this with a twinkle; she knew who he was all right, she just wasn't going to tell. She must have been quite racy in her day. My surname – De'Ath - is unusual but not rare, so if I wanted to track down my biological father it probably wouldn't be too hard, but I have always fought the impulse. I do know it is a name that is common in and around the French Belgium town of Ath, or that if it is in fact English in origin then it denotes that my forebears sold wood or kindling; but beyond those generalities, I know nothing.

It was Emily's father who brought us up. It was Emily's father whom I think of as Dad. So for all intents and purposes Emily is my sibling and that's that. A sibling: the only person in the world you are allowed to hit. At least I am pretty sure that's the rule. In truth, in our childhood Emily would largely do the hitting.

Picture it. A wet Sunday in our childhood and Emily and I at the age of five and seven lying on the floor of the living room of our creaking Victorian house which had floor to ceiling bookshelves that our mum insisted on to insulate the cold external walls and Dad, who was not a practical man, had built with as much good grace as he could muster. The bookshelves were now as dusty as the rest of the house and full of books I don't recall and which certainly no one had read in recent memory.

Emily and I had fallen out earlier that afternoon about what channel to watch on the TV or whose turn it was with a toy, and we had stalled into an uneasy truce where we sat side by side about two feet from the TV, distracted by the adverts for toys on the run up to Christmas. With each new advert I would say 'I want that' or Emily would say 'I want that' in turn.

Then for no reason that I recall except that it is what Emily routinely did, Emily hit me and then I hit her back. We were used to the routine: she would hit me and then when I retaliated she would call out for Mum or Dad and when they came in the room she would say 'Pete hit me!' and she would time her tears to spring from her eyes at the exact same moment that Mum or Dad arrived so that I was the one who got told off. Emily would then finesse her crime by peeping at me from behind Mum's legs and gloat. If she was lucky she would get ice cream to cheer her up.

So Emily did this. She hit me, and then she waited for me to hit back, but before I did so our dad told Emily off because he had been standing against the door frame watching us all along.

Emily was totally rumbled and was duly told off.

This had never happened to Emily before. And as a result of being told off, Emily... was... outraged. Even though she was 100% in the wrong, she was incandescent.

She saw herself as the sibling who never got told off. She expected the natural order to be that I was the one who got reprimanded, and she was a saint. Not that our dad did much in the way of telling off and not that he told us off severely. It was just all about Emily's perception of herself.

Our dad was chewing on the remains of a croissant that looked second hand and chewy, and he came and sat down on the sofa and watched TV with us in a distracted manner. He was only sitting there so that he could feel he spent some time with the kids, or get out of doing something useful elsewhere in the house. He was only in his twenties, and he had been very matter of fact about being a father to Emily and taking me on to boot. He was always calm and a little distracted and he always seemed to have jeans and a t shirt and always the same battered brown sandals – I can remember the look and smell of them like it was yesterday. Or were they moccasins? And he would make us Alphabites and fish fingers and peas for tea for as many times as we would ask, and that is about all I recall about him because he sat on that sofa that day and we thought he had fallen asleep, but in fact he had died.

One of us was climbing on Dad and the other was sitting watching the TV a foot or two from the screen. Oddly, I can't remember which of us did what. Then sooner or later one of us was hungry and we thought Dad was asleep and so we went off to find mum.

'Why can't Dad get your supper?' asked mum.

'He's asleep,' we said.

When the ambulance came, Emily and I watched the paramedics trying to bring our Dad round. We had both gone outside and stood in the front garden and looked in through the window at the heart paddles and the body that arched up and slumped with each electric shock, and my mother standing tall and willowy and lost like a ghost, and the blue piercing lights of the ambulance, and Emily and I held hands as we watched. And somehow we felt guilty. Somehow we felt we were to blame for Dad's death, and of course that was silly, but that was how we felt. But less silly was that from then on, Emily and knew that somehow it would always be me and her against the world. We were in it for the long haul, and we were in it together.

As for our mother, it is fair to say that, broadly speaking, she's always been insane, but these days it's nice insane.

When you are a child, you just accept your parents for who they are; only later do you see that they have personalities and foibles, psychoses and neuroses. I only realised as an adult that my mother had some form of personality disorder of which she was totally unaware.

I once said to her. 'It is not normal to shout and scream for three days and three nights without any sleep. And this is exactly what you used to do in our childhood.'

She reflected on this for as long as it took for a cup of tea to go cold – quite some time - and concluded, 'Well that is just how I express myself.'

Indeed. That was just how she expressed herself.

I wandered down to the bar on foot to meet Emily.

Pinocchio's is a pleasant watering hole; it is modern without being in-your-face trendy, it plays music in the evenings - but not too loud - and it does a good line in big bowls of interesting food and well-chosen local wine. Coming to think of it, I'm surprised I don't go there more often.

Another word about Emily.

Emily is a man magnate. Yes, a man magnet, but also a magnate: she seems to own and control large swathes of willing men. It's a phenomenon. When I watch her in action I feel like applauding her, but I don't, because I can't give my sister praise: she'd only use it against me at some unspecified time in the future.

I have often wondered at Emily's success with men. She is not classically attractive, nor is she particularly charming. She has Medusa hair and an ungainly gait – she has a sort of 'leg on each corner' thing going on. She will unapologetically wear the same flimsy dress all summer and the same leather sandals. But it's her confidence and the way she always has one eye on the door. She doesn't quite care, and it makes men want her to care. Anyway, whatever it is she's got, I have seen - with my own eyes - men come to blows over Emily.

Emily was standing with one foot on a chair and a glass of white wine slung against her palm that was attempting to spill with each gesture. She was entertaining her entourage.

'...so I said to her, if I could do that would I be lesbian too?' she finished.

The table erupted with laughter. Whatever story Emily had just told, it had made these men – and one woman - very happy.

'This is my brother Pete,' announced Emily.

I toured the table, shaking hands with everyone in the French style. One of the men had his big puppy eyes fixed on Emily and when she moved a little, his head moved to match.

On a whim I whispered to him, 'Emily likes you.'

'Do you think so?' he asked hopefully. He raised his jaw a little, encouraged, or perhaps to reduce his double chin. His posture improved as he puffed out his chest. Good grief, men are pathetic - not me, you understand - other men. They are all pathetic.

Emily called to me, 'You look like shit!'

'Thank you Sis!' I replied.

There was a bottle of wine in the middle of the table that seemed to be anyone's. It was now largely mine.

I went to explain my shell-shocked demeanour to Emily, but she had bounded on to another subject.

'So Carlu... .' This was addressed to a relaxed looking man with more than a hint of George Clooney about him. I wondered if she actually fancied any of these men. I wondered what she actually wanted from life. This was probably not a thought that she herself had ever had; so there lay the answer, I guess.

'So Carlu, have you ditched that girlfriend of yours?' asked Emily.

'No!' he replied testily, but he was enjoying the attention.

'She's not here!' said Emily. 'You can say what you like.'

'To be fair to Lucia,' he began. The others groaned, clearly this absent Lucia was not popular with this group. 'She is...'

'Great at sex?' offered Emily.

'Emily!'

'I am just searching for an explanation for events,' she protested. 'Come on team! Can anyone think of any other explanation for why Carlu puts up with Lucia?'

'To be fair to Lucia,' he persevered. 'We had a great time the other day. I drove her to Porto-Vecchio, and the whole time we drove in that car we talked. You know? We talked, and it was good.'

'Carlu has another girlfriend,' Emily explained to me and, indeed, the restaurant as a whole.

'I don't have another girlfriend,' said Carlu loudly to the restaurant.

And it was at this moment that I made my mistake.

Carlu said, 'All I am saying is that I drove all that way with Lucia and we found ourselves chatting effortlessly.'

'Well,' I replied. 'That is more conversation than I got from my passenger the other day. I drove around the island with a dead body in the back of the car and I'll tell you he was not the conversationalist.'

I have no explanation as to why I felt the need to confess this to complete strangers in a restaurant. It could have been tiredness; it could have been that I was weirded out by events; but I fear – and this is a terrible reflection on me - that it was sibling rivalry. My sister is clearly a huge social success, and I am just, well... a bit plodding. I had only been there five minutes and I was trying to upstage my sister in her natural territory. And I had no reason to do it. Emily puts in many hours with my mother and never moans about it, and she certainly never does me any harm and never would do. But whatever the reason was, I would rather increase the chance to going to jail for twenty years for being an accessory to murder, than pass up the opportunity to upstage my own sister.

I despair.

All eyes were turned to me.

There was no turning back.

'On Friday night, there was a knock on my door, and a colleague, a young female colleague, was standing on my doorstep and she explained she had a dead body in the back of her car.'

And I went on to tell the whole tale.

I left out Sarah's name, but let's face it, anyone who knew our office would work that out.

I fleshed out the story with all the details at my disposal. I then started to re-enact several scenes physically.

Me scrambling up the cliff edge.

Sarah pogoing in her dress to turn it round her body.

The look on my face when I saw the note by my bed.

The good news was that I had enrapt the audience. Indeed – not to brag too much - I enrapt most of the restaurant and half the waiting staff.

There was even a supplementary question from a complete stranger who looked in his seventies two tables away.

'The gun was missing?'

'Yes, she said for sure there was a shotgun propped up against the window about a metre, two metres from the bed. When we went back to the lodge, it was gone.'

'She did it, and she's framing you,' said the stranger.

People pulled faces at that; it didn't seem to be the consensus opinion, but a few people nodded.

'How did she get the body in the back of the car? If she had an accomplice to help with the body then what else is she hiding?' asked one of the men at the table – I'm not sure which one - the male Corsican's tend to look similar with their thick dark hair and Italianate complexions.

There was much debate about around the table about how easy it is to move a body.

'I could move a body,' said Mia, the one woman present.

We all looked at Mia, who put her phone down. Ha, Emily! I am more interesting than you; when you were talking Emily, Mia was playing on her phone.

Mia was diminutive.

'I could move a body,' she re-asserted.

Noses were wrinkled in disbelief.

'I am a dentist,' she said. 'I tell you, if you ever need a tooth taken out, get a woman to do it.'

'Er, what, and why?' asked Emily.

'A big man, if he takes out your tooth might use brute force,' said Mia. 'Ouch!'

We acknowledged her logic so far.

'A slight woman,' said Mia. 'If she takes out a tooth, she has to use good technique. You have to push and lever the tooth. You have to get the right pathway, and use the correct angle. You can't use brute force. You have to use intelligence.' The implication was that men might be short on the latter.

'You have to use the man's weight against himself,' I said. 'Like they say in self-defence.'

'Precisely,' said Mia. 'Good technique.'

We all accepted the logic in theory, but no one moved from their original opinions; it still seemed unlikely that Sarah had moved a body by herself and successfully bundled it into a car.

The man with the puppy eyes said, 'I can just about understand the first car going missing. You might come across a car that looks crashed and winch it up to the road, but then surely when they found a body in the car, the police would know. But why would the second car go missing? You say you had the keys?'

This is how evidence gets tainted; people half hear, or half remember, or they paint information into place that wasn't there; suddenly it was me who had had the keys to Jacob's car.

'No I didn't have the keys to the car,' I said. The bar seemed noisier than before, so I was not sure I was heard. I felt some person said to another 'He had the keys to the car?' and I said, 'No!' but it made no difference and probably didn't matter.

'It might be burnt out somewhere,' said someone else. 'A lot of youngsters on the island steal cars for a joy ride. It could just be a coincidence.'

'I will look into this,' said another man. He said it very firmly, which piqued my interest.

'Who's he?' I asked Emily.

'He's Bernard.' She pronounced it the French way with all the stress on the 'ar' and she added, 'He's something to do with the police. A detective?'

What?

Oh just great.

I had been blabbing in front of a detective.

Emily had seen my face fall.

'I'm joking!' she said. 'I'm joking. He's not a detective; he's a journalist.'

'How could that possibly be better than a detective?' I asked. 'Seriously. How could that be better? We will have the whole story on the front page of the local... .'

'Pete,' said Emily. 'Pete! It's fine. It... is... fine. Your story will not be on the front of a paper. For one thing, it's a really weird story that no normal person can understand, and secondly, he's not a newspaper journalist. He's a TV journalist.'

I was distracted by the food that arrived. It was to die for. It was imaginative but not over-fussy. It was good and honest and based on local tradition but still drew on the best of what is modern. Coming to think about it, I might be describing myself. Chestnuts. The food in my line of vision was all about the chestnuts.

In 1584 it was decreed that every landowner and farmer in Corsica had to plant four trees every year; a chestnut tree, an olive tree, a fig and a mulberry. The chestnuts were used to make everything from soup to a very agreeable stew made with venison, and this still goes on today. There is a very likeable chestnut beer available on the island that I would thoroughly recommend, but in the restaurant that night, it was all about the flour. Chestnut flour is a big staple on Corsica and can be made into a kind of cake-like bread. In this instance this was used as a base for an over-flowing bruschetta of tomato, red pepper and basil salsa with rosemary and fried slices of goat's cheese. Suddenly it was all I wanted in the world.

That was the last clear thought that I remember having.

After my long day, I had fallen asleep at the table.

TWELVE

Monday, and I was out at Calvi, the port and tourist town at the top of the island.

I was doing a day's work.

I really enjoy work a lot, and I maintain this happy state of affairs by doing it as little as possible; I try to do an honest day's toil so rarely that doing one comes as a wholly satisfying fillip.

Calvi in the summer gives me flashbacks of childhood summer holidays. Sure, it has a lovely old town with narrow streets and a tiny hidden market; sure it is overlooked by a fine looking citadel with some excellent restaurants and views, and yes it has yachts, a working port, and dramatic snow-capped mountains across the bay; but the most important aspect of Calvi is that all this goes on by a beach. The smell of suntan oil sizzling on the sunbathers, the sight of over-excited toddlers running with buckets of water, a balding man asleep in a deck chair with his head beginning to redden and not one of us civic minded enough to wake him up and tell him, young women in bikinis enjoying turning the heads of young men. The Brit in me will never get bored of the trappings of summer.

I was investigating an insurance claim with a shopkeeper. I like to get truly to the bottom of a case and proceed from there and in this instance it took less than an hour to decide that the man was more or less honest and make a deal with him. I knocked the claim down a bit to save the company some money and the rest of the day was my own.

I decided to favour a restaurant called The Hole in the Wall: they do ample salads with fresh mozzarellas, boiled eggs and - inevitably for Corsica – something boar-based. After lunch I was going to have a chat with an acquaintance of mine called Francois from whom I often rent a boat. I am probably deluding myself but I feel that by popping by and having a chat I will ensure I get a slightly better rate than a 'mere' tourist when renting a boat.

My phone rang. It was Inspector Fortini.

My heart sank to my balls.

'Hello inspector,' I tried brightly. 'To what do I owe the pleasure?'

'Good news.'

'Do speak!'

'The forensic team have finished at your house. Do you want me to keep the key or put the key through your door?'

'Through the door would be great!' I said. 'And dare I ask how we are doing? Should I be a worried man?' I was trying to affect a light tone of insouciance but probably achieved 'irritating' and 'transparently self-interested' instead.

'Everything is fine,' he said. 'We still don't have a body, so it is difficult to know exactly how to file it. But file it we will.'

I think that was an attempt at humour, so I laughed.

'What's so amusing?' he asked.

'Nothing,' I said. 'What about the lodge and Sarah's car?'

'We have sent a forensic team to the lodge and there is no news on Sarah-Jayne's car.' That was all he was willing to say, but I was happy with this. In fact, all in all, I felt better after the phone call.

My phone rang again. It didn't recognise the number.

'Pete?'

'It's Sarah-Jayne!'

Sarah. I must store her number, so I can be better prepared emotionally for any murder-related phone calls.

'My car has come back,' she said.

'What?'

'My car has come back! It is parked outside my place.'

'Was it, like, towed there?' I asked. I wanted to ask if there was a body in the back, but it seemed too big a question.

'I don't know!' she said. 'I popped home for lunch. I mean, I was at work all morning, by the way where are you? I was looking for you at the office?'

'I am in Calvi,' I replied.

She made a disappointed noise.

‘What shall I do?’ she asked.

‘I have no idea,’ I said.

I looked at my gorgeous salad that smelled of olive oil and summer sun. I looked at my beautiful, beautiful half-drunk glass of ice cold white wine which had condensation frosting its side. I sighed the sigh of someone resigned to a lifetime of suffering.

‘I’m coming,’ I said.

By which I meant I was coming after my salad and wine, obviously. And maybe dessert.

THIRTEEN

It takes about two hours to drive back from Calvi. I sat in my car and almost straight away I wondered if I needed to go to the toilet. The truth was, I had definitely visited the facilities in the restaurant and so by rights my bladder was empty. I knew for a fact it was empty. I drove along telling myself it was all my imagination. I can go days on end without being paranoid about my bladder, but when the paranoia strikes, boy does it strike hard. I coasted along the road that runs parallel to the sea trying to distract myself with the view. I played games with myself to have something to think about. The game was I tried to guess how many cars would come from the opposite direction before one of them was a Fiat – eleven, and then nineteen - but all the time I felt a rising pressure in my bladder. I had had one solitary glass of wine. That is less than half a bladder full, surely? Perhaps there was undue pressure on my lower abdomen. I undid my trouser buttons. It made no difference. Perhaps it was the seat belt. I adjusted it looser. It helped a little, but not much.

I won't succumb. I won't stop. I must keep on driving.

Was it orange juice? Sometimes orange juice irritates me and I think I need to go to the toilet but I don't. I did have some orange juice earlier. I find it is quite a good pick me up. Curse the orange juice.

I stopped the car at the side of the road and stood behind it to pee.

Nothing came out.

I jiggled up and down to move any fluid in my bladder around a bit.

Nothing.

I loosened my trousers more.

A car honked on its way past. It could have been a coincidence they honked their horn, but I am sure they were mocking me and my prostate.

At most I got two dribbles out.

Okay, new rule. No more orange juice.

Best just to stick to wine.

One hour, forty-eight minutes later – another of my many obsessions is timing my car journeys - and I found Sarah in her flat. She ushered me inside with a stage whisper, and closed the door behind me.

'Why are we whispering?' I asked.

'I don't know,' she replied, still whispering.

By her front door, and causing an obstacle to the free movement of humans, stood an upright vacuum cleaner.

'Is that the best place for that?' I asked.

'As I leave the flat I can pull it behind me until I'm out of the door. That way everything is clean that's left in the flat,' she said.

'Okay, but we're now inside again.'

Sarah shrugged her incomprehension. Evidently, as usual, I was the one making no sense.

I smiled and nodded as a way of curtailing the topic.

'Oh can I just use your toilet?' I asked.

Marginally placated by events in the toilet, I returned to Sarah.

It was dark in her living room - in fact it was dark in every room - Sarah had drawn all the blinds down.

From what I could see, her apartment was as neat and tidy as you would expect. There were some square pictures on the walls – pictures of flowers - but the pictures were too small for the wall and there were only three of them so Sarah had spaced them too far apart from each other. It wasn't a look that worked.

Sarah beckoned me to the front window. She placed her hands on top of each other, and stretched her fingers forward to part the horizontal slats of the blinds.

'Look!' she said.

I peered forward.

'Can you see it?'

'Can I see what?'

'My car! Look, it's my car!' she said.

We looked down into the street at what certainly looked like Sarah's car.

'How do you know it's yours?' I asked.

She was irked by the question. She said, 'It's the right colour, it's a Clio, and it's in my parking space.'

'Yeah, but,' I said.

'It's the correct registration number!' she said.

'That is indeed a clincher,' I said.

I peered at it. The afternoon sun was low and glinting off the windscreens and bonnets of the cars; it left flashes in my eyes.

'Is there anything in the back of the car?' I asked.

'No!' she replied.

'And why aren't there any dents?'

'I don't know!' She was very distressed. In fairness, she had every right to be distressed.

She didn't look well.

'Are you sleeping alright?' I asked.

'No,' she replied.

'Me neither,' I lied. 'Are you eating, alright?'

'No,' she replied.

'Me neither,' I said. I could feel some olives in my stomach trying to repeat on me. There are just so many olives you should eat in one go, but they were free with lunch and...

'I was doing well at first,' she said. 'On Saturday I hadn't slept, but I gave myself a talking to, and you had been so kind, and I had a shower and I put some clean clothes on, and then there was the police, and I thought that went quite well? I thought it went well.' She looked to me for reassurance.

'I thought it went very well,' I replied. 'Bizarre! But well. And Inspector Fortini rang me today.'

'He did?'

'Yes,' I said. 'He sounded most encouraging.'

'In what way?'

'He just sounded relaxed and that he was filing a report.'

'He said he was going to file a report?' she asked. 'To whom?'

'I think he meant he was going to put it in a filing cabinet, because that is where files go.'

'I don't feel well,' she said. She sat down. 'I seem to have crumpled. I went to work. I thought could I work? Yes, I could work. But everyone asked me if I was alright. I said I was a bit unwell but I didn't get much done. I mean I meet someone I like. I mean I have barely met anyone since I have been here. I meet someone I like, and I was just beginning to think things were happening. I mean you look forward to living in a place like this, like Corsica. When I came here I gave up England, I felt kind of sad to think that I really didn't have much in England keeping me there. I mean that's pitiful isn't it? That's pitiful right there. I had no one special in England and I had lived there all my life. I mean the odd friend, but really not much. Everyone else these days seems to have like a thousand friends from uni and from school and home and work, but I don't know, maybe I am like timid or something; I've got my sisters and that's about it, but you're born with your sisters. Well they're younger than me, but you know what I mean. Maybe people just don't like me. So anyway, I come to Corsica for a new life and I finally find someone and I am thinking yes, yes, this is why I came here. The sun, the beaches, I like my job. I do like my job. And I had met Jacob. Jacob happened and it was fantastic, and then, and then this happens!'

Sarah continued talking in the same vein for quite a while and I listened with man sympathy; I nodded occasionally and said 'Yeah, I agree' a few times. In my experience when women have a moan like this, they don't actually want any advice, they just want to talk a lot.

I couldn't even put my arm around her because, though she was now crying, she's a colleague and she's half my age, and also we were both English, and the English don't hug unless we're at gun point.

I realised she had finally stopped speaking, so I said brightly, 'Shall we look at the car?'

'Sure,' she replied. 'It's not like I've got anything else to do on a Monday night.'

Now the boyfriend's dead.

We both laughed.

We went downstairs and looked at the car from across the road. Sarah was loath to even get close to it. Clearly it was bewitched or it was the harbinger of ill, or to engage with the car at all was to engage further with the worries we thought were behind us.

'If that is your car,' I said. 'Someone's knocked out the dents. And replaced the back windscreen. It's got to be a different car, and that is that,' I said.

We stayed looking at the car from across the road.

'Can I ask a question?'

'Sure she replied.'

'Your flat?' I asked.

'Yes.'

'It's so clean and spotless,' I said.

'Thank you,' she replied.

'But your car when I first saw it, hadn't had a wash for ages.'

'I don't like cleaning my car,' she said. 'I don't like standing outside doing that. I'd be seen.'

I was the first to brave crossing the road.

'When did you say it arrived?' I asked over my shoulder.

'I don't know. I am pretty sure it was not here when I went to work, and to be fair I didn't notice it when I came home for lunch. I was upstairs in the flat and something made me want to look out the window. See that's spooky isn't it? Sometimes you know to look somewhere. It's paranormal.'

Er, no it's not. People look out of windows all the time. It's what they're designed for.

Sarah continued without pause, 'I double-took when I realised I was seeing my own car. I mean I had like a heart attack. But I mean we saw that car. You and I saw the car. My car was smashed up. There is no way it could be repaired and there it is! Well I suppose it's like a dream. Did we dream all of this?'

I had learnt during my crash course of getting to know Sarah that there were various Sarahs: there was Refusenik Sarah, there was Garrulous Sarah, there was Methodical Sarah, there was Game Sarah, there was Irrational Sarah. They all had their cons. At least with Garrulous Sarah I knew what she was thinking. The downside of Garrulous Sarah was that I could no longer hear what I myself was thinking. Oh well.

'Did your car have the same stickers on the screen?' I asked.

'What?' She still wasn't going to cross the road. She had crossed her arms over her chest to give herself extra security.

'This sticker for the garage that sold the car?'

'Yes that's the same,' she said.

I peered inside.

'It looks cleaner inside than before.' What with there being no corpse in there. But the issue of the dead body aside, it was all cleaner.

'What about the key?' I shouted.

'What?'

'You heard me,' I said. I noticed I was getting impatient - not necessarily with Sarah - more with what life was throwing at us.

'Well, have you got the key to your car, and if so, does your key unlock this car?'

Sarah thought about this for a bit.

'I will go and get my key,' she said. But she didn't move.

'When we crashed the car and left it, did you take the key out of the ignition and keep the key?'

'Yes,' she replied. 'I found it in my handbag later.'

'Where is the key now?' I asked.

'The key is upstairs in my handbag.'

'Can you go and get it please?' I asked.

She obediently went upstairs and an eternity later reappeared holding the key.

It had the irritating plastic unicorn as a key fob; there was no mistaking or forgetting her car key, and this was the correct one.

'Now see if you can unlock the car,' I said.

She was reluctant to do this.

'Press the key to unlock the car,' I insisted.

She frowned and braced her shoulders, as if the pressing of the car key involved considerable physical strength.

The car's indicators blinked and it made the standard 'dud-up' noise.

These really were the keys to her car. This was her car.

'This is doing my head in,' she said.

‘Okay now please Sarah, come across the road and look at your own car.’

She reluctantly crossed the road. She hugged herself even tighter against the unknown forces that were bedevilling us.

‘Tell me something about your car that only you could know,’ I said.

‘What do you mean?’

‘Well, what is in your glove compartment?’

‘I don’t know,’ she replied.

‘A map, some insurance documents, a bulb, a biro?’

‘Yeah maybe?’

‘Okay. So for example, where do you put the car de-icer? For when the screen is frosted up.’

‘We live in Corsica. We don’t get frosts.’ Sarah can be very hard work.

‘Okay. In the boot of your car, underneath the floor of the boot where the spare wheel is kept. Did you store anything there?’

‘Car oil. A small, like, bottle of car oil. It is in a plastic bag in case it leaks.

‘What brand of plastic bag? Tesco or something.’

‘Spar. It’s a Spar bag.’ Sarah was cheering up. She could finally see the point of my questions.

‘Okay, let’s open the boot,’ I said.

I breathed out long and hard to steady my nerves.

We opened up the back of the hatchback.

Sarah wrapped her fingernails around the edge of the carpeted flooring and pulled it up. She scrunched her eyes up against what she might see.

‘The oil is there. It’s in the bag like you say,’ I said.

Sarah looked.

She peered deeper into the car.

‘Here’s a receipt,’ she said. ‘Look it’s a crumpled up receipt.’

She pulled it out and we looked at it together.

It was from a supermarket that we all use on the edge of Bastia.

‘How would it get there? How would it get under the bottom mat flooring thing?’ She asked.

'Well I guess you put shopping in the back of your car and the receipt fell out of a bag,' I reasoned.

'But how did it get under the floor?'

'Well, when you last picked up the mat to, say, get the oil it could fall in. When did you last lift up the floor of the boot?'

'I got someone to do my oil. Someone from work. Kind of topped up my oil when there was a light on the dashboard?' she said.

'When?'

'Quite recently.'

I looked at the date on the supermarket receipt.

'Since May 2nd?' I asked.

'Yes.'

We were silent a long time.

'This is my car,' she muttered.

She curled into me and hugged me and she wouldn't let go.

The good news was, her hair smelled good.

FOURTEEN

My first proper day back at the office after 'the event' and everything was ticking on exactly as before. How could everyone possibly look so bored and nonchalant? Didn't they know what had happened at the weekend? No, of course they didn't. It's just that I felt that on some sort of spiritual level a little acknowledgement of my travails was in order.

Our office is in an old building above a bakery in the centre of town. It is a street with an air of crumbling wealth. A top-of-the-range designer shop will be as well appointed as any that you would see in Paris, but when you look above the well-dressed windows you will see a building that is pockmarked and friable with rotting wooden shutters, derelict rooms, brickwork turning to dust, and a faded handwritten sign saying 'beware falling objects.' But look even higher and you will see a new satellite dish and a very classy roof-garden where someone has done up the top floor.

Most people would argue that Bastia is one of the less attractive parts of Corsica but I feel its strength lies in its contrasts: it is elegant but crumbling, business-like but louche, add some top notes of charisma and a dash of serious wealth and... well you get the idea: if it was a person it would be an ageing Peter O'Toole, or Bill Nighy looking awkward at a wedding. But beware falling objects.

Although we do meet the general public in our work, they don't have to visit us in our offices and so we have stuck with our original central site rather than something more sensible at the edge of town. It is well located in that it is near the police, should we wish to liaise with them about a theft, and it is near the ferry terminal should I want to suddenly flee the island to avoid – oh I don't know - a prison sentence for abetting a murder.

I share a large creaking wooden floored office with two large creaking colleagues.

The first is Niculaiu – a good Corsican name which has the hints of Italian that you might expect from an island that is twice as close to Italy than it is to France. Niculaiu is older than the rest of us and has the demeanour of a poorly revived corpse. When he speaks he has a tone that implies that he's on the brink of breaking bad news to you. This is quite useful if you are an insurance claims adjuster - it is a career wholly based on breaking bad news; when we adjust claims, we never adjust *up*. He is my nap time buddy. According to all sources Niculaiu and I are capable of having a 'snore-off' each rumbling louder than the other, and sometimes talking over each other in our sleep. It livens up an otherwise tranquil afternoon at work, and I only have other people's word for it that this all goes on, and clearly they are all lying.

My second colleague is Jean-Marie. Jean-Marie is a sort of human chameleon. He will agree with you to your face about anything you have to say regarding a colleague, and you will assume you are at one with him on a subject; he will laugh at your jokes; he will tell you he 'loves the English sense of humour' and then, and then, you will catch him later – wait for it – being perfectly nice and pleasant to the very person you have just slagged off, and agreeing with that person, and laughing at their German sense of humour or whatever. It is beyond outrageous. The only good thing about Jean-Marie is that he keeps watch while Niculaiu and I have our afternoon naps.

So anyway, I was at work getting through paperwork and wondering quite obsessively about where we stood, given there was no body and Sarah's car was back, when I made the mistake of leaving the office to get coffee and a pastry.

I was only gone five minutes, at most twenty – the pastry was so delicious it would have been a crime to have hurried it – but when I returned the atmosphere of the office had completely changed.

As I entered the room, Niculaiu stiffened at his desk and wouldn't meet my gaze while Jean-Marie had his head buried downwards.

'Peter?' called Daniel from the other room. 'Peter' - not even 'Pete'.

Jean-Marie's head was now buried so deep, he was almost under the desk.

'Daniel wants you,' said Niculaiu clearly knowing that I had heard already.

This allowed me to reply to Niculaiu, 'What's it about?'

Niculaiu tried a shrug that visually meant 'I don't know' but that he could later plausibly deny meant anything at all.

I stopped right in front of Niculaiu and stared him out.

'What is this about?' I persevered.

After an eternity of me staring at him and him keeping his face blank, Niculaiu concluded that I was going nowhere until he talked.

'You might be in the newspaper,' he replied.

'I might be in the newspaper, or I am indeed in the newspaper?' I tried to clarify.

'You are indeed in the newspaper.'

'What about?' I asked.

Judging by the whimpering sounds coming from Jean-Marie, whatever was in the newspaper it was very bad.

Right. We lived on Corsica, the birthplace of Napoleon. What would he do? He would attack. I pulled myself up to my full five foot nine, I plastered a smile on my face, I noticed a flake of pastry on my shirt front from earlier, I wet a finger, retrieved the pastry flake and ate it, and thus fortified I lumbered down the corridor to do battle with Daniel.

'Close the door,' he said.

I chose to close the door.

What can I say about my boss Daniel? I find him irritating beyond belief. There is little he does that isn't irritating.

Breathing is a case in point; he has a sort of 'gasp gasp breath, gasp gasp breath' pattern to how he breathes. What is that? Is it asthma? Is it nerves? Is it that he is deliberately breathing strangely? No to all three; I know this because I have asked him.

'So, um,' began Daniel not making eye contact. He says 'um' far too much and he doesn't make eye contact. Words do not express how irritating I find him.

'So, um,' he said again. He just can't stop himself.

'What can I do for you?' I asked.

'There's um, well there's a newspaper and you are on the front page,' he said. 'It is not the only story on the front page.' And that's another thing. He habitually starts a subject and then immediately backtracks and apologises before he has even bothered to tell us what he is on about. No! Sometimes you just have to spit out what you have to say because - guess what? – sometimes it's actually interesting and important.

'There's, um, a newspaper article about you and I feel it is, well, it doesn't 100% reflect on your work here but it doesn't show you in a good light, um, well, we wouldn't suspend you or anything, but it is important.'

'Daniel!' I barked.

'What?' he jumped.

'Just show me the newspaper.'

And then he didn't hand it over. He didn't hand it over.

It would have been quicker for me to leave the office, go downstairs and just buy a copy of my own. Worse than not handing over the paper, he decided to breathe instead. 'Gasp gasp, breath' 'Gasp gasp breath' 'Gasp gasp breath.' Then, unbelievably, there was a pause. I can only assume he was not breathing at all for four or five seconds, then 'Gasp gasp breath' he was off again. Who does that? And why? Seriously! Why?

I tore the paper from his hand.

'Brit in Dead Body Drama.'

By our crime correspondent.

A Bastia man drove around Corsica with a dead body in the back of his car for a weekend in a story confirmed by police sources. The red Peugeot travelled around the north of the Island to Corte and the Morosaglia region and twice returned to Bastia for reasons that are unclear.

As the flesh of the body began to rot the driver scattered baking soda on the body to help cover the smell and preserve the body. The car was found crashed and abandoned in the mountains near Corte.

A British man, Peter De'Ath from Norwich, England, has been helping Bastia police with their inquiries. Mr De'Ath who works for the insurance company Society Metropolitan in Bastia moved to the island two years ago with his sister.

Where do I begin. No, really, where do I begin?

First of all, there is no mention of Sarah and her involvement. Second of all, every detail was wrong. Seriously! Every single detail was wrong. Third of all, who talked to the press? Fourth of all... well whatever... it was all just so irritating.

Also, have they got a body or haven't they? I mean the whole weirdness from my point of view is largely about the fact we seem to have lost the body. Bodies just don't disappear. It has to be somewhere. Fiftieth of all? I just didn't know what to do.

My first instinct was to have a team talk with my partner in crime Sarah-Jayne.

No, in truth, it turned out that my first instinct was to completely ignore my boss Daniel even though he was in the room looking at me.

I tried to put that right.

'Daniel,' I said. 'Literally every detail about this story is wrong.'

He just looked at me, waiting for an explanation. Oh and he breathed. Of course, he breathed. 'Gasp gasp, breath.' 'Gasp gasp, breath.'

He... is... just... so... irritating.

'I just, um, don't understand what could have happened for this to be on the front page of a paper,' he said.

'Neither do I,' I said. 'We had a weird experience on Friday. It was reported to me that there was a death. I reported it to the police. I think maybe something I said in a bar on Saturday, perhaps that was misinterpreted.'

I tapped the paper firmly and raised a finger for full effect.

'I am going to have to look into this,' I said grandly. 'I'm going to talk to the journalist who wrote this.' This is something I never did.

'We?' asked Daniel.

'We?'

'You said, "We"?' he asked. 'You said, "We had a weird experience... "'

'Yes I did say that,' I said. 'I am not sure why I said that.'

I relied on Daniel being weak and a bit thrown.

'Anything else?' I asked brightly.

'No,' he replied. Prat.

I left his office.

The worst aspect was that it was all probably my fault for shooting my mouth off in the bar.

FIFTEEN

I managed to catch up with Emily the next day.

'What an unexpected surprise!' She looked pleased to see me.

'Did you see the paper?' I asked.

'What paper?' she replied. That explained her unguarded reaction to me.

Emily, as usual, was wearing the same dress as ever. How does she get away with wearing the same dress day in and out and still look glamorous? 'Oh well that's Emily,' people must say. 'What does she do when it's in the wash?' 'She's the sort who would walk around the flat naked,' another might say. They would all nod then and get on with their work.

In the average workplace, a man can get away with having two suits in rotation and people will say he looks well-dressed, but for a woman it's different – it's less fair, of course – but it's different: they have to have quite a few outfits.

Anyhow, we were on the floor above my own floor at the office, which is where Emily and indeed Sarah work, and so I took her to her desk and showed her the article which was now available online.

'Wow!' she said.

'Do you think your friend I met in the bar had anything to do with this?' I asked.

'Bernard? I don't know what you were thinking mouthing off that night,' said Emily.

'No indeed,' I said. 'But anyway, do you think it was him?'

She shrugged.

'I'll ask,' she said. 'I'll ring him, and we can meet up. He's a nice guy. He wouldn't deliberately do us harm.' To my ear she didn't sound sure of this; it was more she was trying out the words to see how they sounded. 'And we need to talk about all this,' she said. 'This is all huge. I mean, I really want to hear every last detail.'

'Hmmm. I told you about it in the bar that night, and as I didn't throw talcum powder or whatever on the body there isn't much to add.'

She changed the subject back to the journalist. 'He might be useful Pete. To have someone on the media who you keep onside. That sort of thing.'

I think she was implying, 'Keep onside when this blows up.' Or perhaps she meant 'When you get to court.' Okay so that's my paranoia speaking again.

And so it was that Emily arranged for me to meet Bernard. I had been told at the time that he was a TV journalist, but when Emily and I trundled off to meet him at the restaurant in the old town square he was quick to put me right.

'I make documentaries,' he said.

He ordered a bottle of red wine and three glasses, so naturally I warmed to him. It was a Clos Reginu from the top of the island; an excellent wine that is complex, full bodied and particularly comes into its own then accompanied by a hearty meal. Again, I'm describing myself.

'Did you tell anyone about the story I told at the bar?' I asked.

He gave it some consideration. 'My girlfriend,' he said at last.

Emily was more direct; it was better that she probed, being an established friend and a female. 'Did you contact any friends in the press?' she asked firmly.

'No,' he replied, equally firmly.

He was a genial and relaxed individual. He said, 'Look, you know how Bastia is; it is a tiny place and everyone knows everyone. The journalist had obviously heard some tittle tattle. They work to deadlines and it is better copy to include the most sensational details they hear. As long as they don't libel you then the story is good to go. I have a question for you though Peter. Don't be offended at this question. Is there any chance you imagined any of the events?'

'No,' I replied.

'You didn't fall asleep at any stage?' he asked. 'Do you have vivid dreams?'

'Quite vivid,' I replied. I didn't know what to make of this line of questioning. 'I didn't imagine the events that took place. I really didn't. You don't make up having a dead body in your face.'

'No of course not,' he said. 'It's just that... well we live on a crazy island.'

'We do,' said Emily with the air of someone who felt she ought to join in with the conversation occasionally, but in fact is easily distracted by food and wine - after all, she is my sister.

'And at no stage did you fall asleep?' asked Bernard.

'I would have fallen asleep at some stage.'

'He's always falling asleep,' confirmed Emily.

'I have someone I think you should meet,' he said. 'Do you know what a mazzere is?' He had clearly thought through this conversation in advance.

'The witches?' I asked.

'They're not witches.'

'How irritating,' I said.

'Pete finds everything irritating,' said Emily. 'This is why he lives alone.' She turned her attention to me and looked serious. 'Bernard wants to show you something, and I think Sarah should come to.'

A few days later a car drew up outside my house and inside was Bernard, Emily and Sarah.

We were off in the direction of Chera, a region of remote mountain villages in the south. It would take a long time to get there and so there was a general sense in the car that it was like a big family outing. Bernard was to be Dad and he took it upon himself to 'big up' the trip to the children in the back, and explain to us what he knew.

'There are thought to be about thirty mazzeri active in Corsica; they are mostly in the south of the Island. They are mostly women and just normal women at that. They aren't feared or maligned, but neither are they, shall we say, central to society.'

Sarah's face was a total delight. She was like a dog scrutinising her owner's face – totally attentive and yet totally uncomprehending.

'Go on,' she said. She clearly loved all known nonsense, without fear or favour.

'The mazzere will dream about a person and the person who has been dreamt about will die,' continued Bernard. 'Perhaps in a few days' time and perhaps in a year, but they will die.'

'How?' asked Sarah.

'They could die by any manner or means,' said Bernard. 'And they die on an uneven day after the dream.'

Sarah gasped on cue.

'And when they die,' I added. 'Their eyes close.'

Sarah gasped again.

'Then their eyes open suddenly.'

Sarah gasped some more.

'And their pupils are now white.'

'Noooooooooo,' said Sarah.

'No indeed,' I said. 'I made that up.'

'Ignore my brother,' said Emily.

'What is important,' persevered Bernard. 'Is that you remember what day you experienced the death of Jacob. Because, as I said, he can only die on an odd day after the hallucination.'

'No. No. No,' I protested. 'Jacob is dead. We hadn't hallucinated anything.'

Bernard looked pityingly at me. At least I think he did; I only had the back of his head to judge by, but I am sure I could feel pity radiating back towards me.

'We cannot warn Jacob of his impending death,' I said. 'Because... he... is... already... dead.'

There was no support from the rest of the car. I was smelling a rat.

Sarah swung her face from me and back towards Bernard. Bernard, evidently, was The Keeper of the Truth.

Despite the nonsense, I liked Bernard. He was laconic and polite and not at all like the love-sick puppies who normally hang out with Emily.

'They can die in any normal manner,' Bernard re-iterated. 'But it is the duty of the mazzere to go the next morning to the person they have dreamt about and tell them about the dream and then they can take precautions.'

'Or make sure their will is up to date,' I added.

'What precautions?' asked Sarah.

'According to ancient traditions that go back 6000 years, there are various ways to cheat death,' said Bernard.

'Such as?'

'Certain incantations. Eating certain foods on certain days. Going to a priest. My favourite is walking up a hill backwards.'

'Does it work?' asked Sarah.

'Of course it doesn't work,' I said.

'Sometimes the remedies work and the person survives,' continued Bernard. 'And timing is important. You can only die on the third day, the fifth day and so on, so you take special precautions on those days.'

'Oooooh yes,' said Sarah. 'I wouldn't even go out on those days if it was me.'

'How would you hold down your job?' I asked.

'I would have to work from home,' she said firmly. 'And my bosses would have to accept that.'

It was going to be a long journey. I tried not to encourage them by interacting, but cracked after less than a mile.

'So if the person dies, it proves the premonition was true, and if the person doesn't die it shows that walking up the hill backwards was a success,' I said.

Silence from the car.

I need some new friends.

The village we were taken to was as remote as it is possible to be, and was a total treat. It was up a steep hill, surrounded by mountains, with some extra mountains thrown in for good measure, all topped with a lavish coating of forest.

When we got there it was still light. Bernard slowed the car to a crawl, all the better to admire the misshapen cobbled streets and the stone slab houses which were excellent examples of the time honoured 'make it up as we go along because no one knows what we get up to in the countryside' school of architecture.

Some of the houses looked as though they were created with waves of volcanic lava. There was one very eye catching – and huge - spew of solid rock that went up in the air like a tidal wave, and where there was a hollow at its base, someone had piled up stones to form a house. Between the lava eruption as the roof and the two square windows placed in the wall below, the resultant edifice looked like the face of a startled woman buried up to her neck and turned to stone on the whim of a passing god.

Another house was formed from a quiff of rock that, again, someone had placed stones under, but this one looked like a Teddy Boy who'd been punched in the face. Another 'house' - they are known as 'Oriu' on the island - was formed from a huge forward jutting piece of rock. Again, someone had placed stones below to fill out the space left underneath and this one looked like a giant turtle that had given birth to a cottage. What fun. Any one of these wonders would have been worth the journey and that made the witch - I mean the mazzere - the bonus on top.

Bernard took us for a walk through the forest. The air was heavy with the smell of eucalyptus and lemon; it was soporific and portentous. Of *course* this is where a witch would live.

Unexpectedly we emerged to a clearing of wet grass that was in the shadow of a mountain. It was the size of a cricket pitch and caught the moonlight like a lake.

We jolted when a voice called us. We turned to find a woman standing at our backs. She was right behind us in the field and yet we hadn't passed her by. Had she been hiding? Had it been a trick of the light and we hadn't noticed her? Had she simply been following behind us? Either way we screamed. Or rather I screamed, and Sarah screamed at my scream, which served to hide my blushes.

'I'm sorry,' said the woman. She clearly wasn't sorry at all. 'I saw you walking through the woods and followed you.' She spoke in French which was to her credit: she could easily have started speaking in Corsican for added effect. Or in tongues.

She was tiny. I mean really tiny. Her face was a perfect circle with two huge eyes. She looked weathered, and handsome rather than pretty. She had long wispy black hair that caught the wind and swirled around her head and face.

'Bernard hello,' she said. 'Peter hello. Sarah hello. Emily hello.'

Okay so Bernard had probably rung her in advance and she'd asked our names, but she didn't look like the sort of person who owned a mobile phone. Or soap.

She could have been forty or seventy – it is easy to age badly when you spend too much time outdoors, or leaning over hot cauldrons.

'Walk with me,' she said. 'It is a lovely night. Why would we spend it in a field?'

For some reason Sarah shivered visibly and uncontrollably; Emily felt the need to hold her hand.

The mazzere led the way across the clearing. She had long looping strides that meant that although she seemed to be half the size of any normal human, we were the ones scurrying to catch up.

Her clothing was loose and vague and seemed to hollow out the darkness as she walked. Inexplicably it flapped out of rhythm to the way she moved.

We were soon at a cliff edge. There was a hundred metre drop to a river.

'Sit, do sit,' said the mazzere.

The other three sat swiftly, which made me feel lumbering and truculent, so I sat also.

Then as if by a split timing that must have been coincidence, the valley lit up. When we were in the field before there was a mountain between us and the setting sun - it was lit by the moon - but here the setting sun was still reaching out and across the land; it had changed its colour and was giving a full final blast that crashed and exploded in front of us. It caught the sides of the ravine with such a wallop that the walls of rock sparked into a fire of reds and pinks. Individual clumps of gorse and broom a quarter of a mile away were picked out like a laser and became so detailed and 3D that by some optical trick they now seemed close up to our faces.

We then watched as the old lady - I had decided by this stage she was old - seemed to rub the ground in front of us. She used both hands in a rapid movement forward and backward to rub the soil in opposite directions. This continued for some time without any of us feeling the need to question or stop her. Then...

Whoomph!

A fire sprang up from below the old woman's hands.

'Oh well done!' said Emily. For her, then, it was all a piece of theatre.

Bernard, meanwhile, had the air of someone who had seen it before and was eager for us to share the experience; he kept grinning and shooting glances at us to see our individual reactions.

The old lady stroked the fledgling flames with her palms so that yellow wisps of fire appeared between her fingers and a white smoke swirled in circles between our bodies. She started to alternate her hand action with a motion that gathered small twigs and bracken from the forest floor. In very little time we had a hardy fire illuminating our faces.

The mazzere cocked her head like a bird to better assess her handiwork, and then breathed deeply through her nose and addressed us at the same time. It gave her voice a rumbling 'fresh from the coffin' timbre.

'So Sarah and Peter,' she inhaled. 'Bernard has told me a little of your story. There was a young man. He was your lover... and you were preparing your lover's food as he prepared your bed. He died.'

This was laying it on a bit thick; Sarah had just been getting a few bottles of wine out the car while Jacob was bouncing on the bed. And as for 'lover' – they hadn't even had sex.

The mazzere reared up and extended her arms in a circular motion that allowed her billowy clothing to catch the wind. She was now a spectre, an eagle, towering and threatening us. Her face came close to mine and the smoke from the fire puffed and swirled in my face; she was blatantly pushing it deliberately at me with her wings. Her face was now right in my face; her eyeballs were black and two inches from mine and swaying forwards and backwards, and what with the asphyxia from the smoke, I was feeling quite queasy. It was all most unnecessary.

'Boo!' I shouted, but I clearly hadn't caught the mood of the party.

To her credit, it didn't put her off her theatricals, but she did give up on me and move on to Sarah. Again there was the flapping arms and the suffocating smoke in Sarah's face, but this time the woman fixed Sarah with her eyes and somehow locked into her. The crone - I am sure she wouldn't mind being called that; it was, after all, the general effect she was going for - started to sway her head in horizontal circles and, because her eyes were locked with Sarah's, Sarah also started to sway. The mazzere increased the size of the circles and kept billowing the smoke into Sarah's face and Sarah in turn was swaying in a more and more alarming fashion. Her whole body was now twisting and cavorting, her eyes were flickering, and her head was floppy on her neck.

Then CRACK!

It was like an explosion or a flame, and it was a loud noise, like a gun going off.

My best guess is that the crone dropped some sort of powder in the fire and it ignited in the heat - health and safety regulations may not have reached all of Corsica - either way, the firecracker trick caused us all to jump.

Sarah then slumped and the mazzere caught her face in her hand.

'Dream...' she said in English. 'Dream.'

I went to catch my sister Emily's eye ready to exchange some sibling cynicism but - oh for the love of all I hold dear - Emily was fascinated. She was restless, moving from one micro vantage point to another to get the best view.

'You are travelling. You are running barefoot through the woods,' chanted the crone to Sarah.

Sarah slumped more; her shoulders were now folded down, her knuckles were lying limp in the dusty soil.

'You are running...' The crone was swaying, and Sarah's head was tilting left and right in her palm. 'The woods are dark and the twigs are snapping under your bare feet. You can smell the leaves, you can smell the damp grass. You are running. There is dew on the grass, round clear spheres of dew. It is dark in the woods but the moon guides the way. You are running.'

The crone's eyes widened and then appeared to retreat into her skull.

'There is movement in the woods. You see eyes behind a tree, a shadow that moves. It is your prey. The eyes blink and catch the moonlight. The prey turns to run away. You run. You run through the woods, you tear through the woods, you are hurtling forwards to catch the prey. But the prey is running fast. It knows the paths and tracks through the trees. But your legs are like springs and your body is a gazelle. You are faster now and certain, and you know you will catch it. The prey knows it has chosen a dead end. Its legs trip on a root. It trips and falls on its stomach. It scrambles to push its body back up, but it is no use. You are towering over its matted body. The prey is beneath you and it knows it will die. It turns and its eyes fix yours. Who do you see? Who are you killing? Who do you see?'

Sarah screamed. It was a long rasping terrified scream. Then she reared up and her eyes were wide with terror.

'It's Jacob!' she gasped.

Sarah was at her full height now. Her face was impassive and unblinking.

Emily stepped forward and took Sarah in her arms and kissed the top of her head.

The mazzere had completely disappeared.

SIXTEEN

When we got back in the car I sat in the front with Bernard, and Emily and Sarah sat in the back. Sarah's head nestled into Emily's armpit to help her rest from her experience, and to better protect her ears from the non-believer in the front.

In the event, I restricted myself to a simple 'What the fuck?' and when I did speak again I said, 'Shall we go to Porto-Vecchio for a late supper? There's an excellent place that has wooden decking that stretches across the edge of the water, the decking is supported by huge boulders – it's very picturesque. I happen to know they do fabulous fresh swordfish with capers.'

'Of course you do,' said Emily.

Bernard drove us to the restaurant without protest, and I was soon lost in the menu. When I came to, I realised Bernard was halfway through explaining something.

'This is exactly what happens,' he said. 'It is not like it's a bloodline. People get called in their dreams to be a mazzere. Most of them are unwilling. Some of them are distressed when they are called and try to get exorcised by a priest.'

'Oh please,' I said.

'You saw things for yourself!' protested Emily.

'I saw an attention seeking crone leading Sarah on and asphyxiating her with wood smoke until she started to hallucinate through lack of oxygen.'

'That too,' said Emily dreamily reading the menu. 'That too.'

Bernard adopted a tone with me as if reasoning with a child. 'The idea with the mazzere is that once in a while they will have a vivid dream that they are outside in the countryside and they are carrying perhaps a stone or a stick. And they may hunt down an animal – it could be sheep, or a wild boar, or a dog; any animal I think. And at the point of kill the face of the animal reveals itself as a person you know. This means the person will die.'

'I'm going to need to tell him,' said Sarah, who had totally recovered from the smoke-and-crone incident; in fact she now seemed energised. 'I am going to need to tell Jacob I dreamt of him,' she murmured.

'He's dead,' I mouthed, entirely to myself.

'If I have one dream, I will have others,' said Sarah. 'Well if I have the gift then I will have more dreams. If I dream of someone then that it will be my duty to report to them that they might die.'

'That'll go down well at the office,' I said.

'But I have to!'. she insisted. 'Because they need to then do the right things to prevent death. I am going to have to get used to this.'

I pretended to consider this.

'Promise me one thing,' I said.

'Uh huh?'

'If you dream of someone from the office and you have to report to them that they are now cursed and they have to walk up a hill backwards wearing garlic in their hair on the second Thursday of the month to prevent their death, then promise me - promise me - I can be there when you explain this to them.'

'Okay,' she replied.

I asked Bernard a simple question. 'Did you know that mazzere? Did you liaise with her before this evening?'

'No,' he replied. 'I didn't meet her or phone her if that's what you're thinking.'

Then how did she know our names?

Bernard smiled. 'Peter. We all have faith, we just don't realise it. We routinely accept whole piles of things we don't understand; Einstein, gravity, crying when we hear an opera... you have taken it on faith that Sarah did not kill Jacob, because you have faith in Sarah...'

I wasn't sure where Bernard was going with that or what it had to do with operas, and I never found out, because Sarah alerted us that she was going to speak. She did this with a long 'Hmm' noise.

'The thing is,' said Sarah. 'That I am beginning think that is not the issue. I am now quite sure that Jacob is not dead at all.'

Oh good grief.

I looked to Emily to share my frustration. She looked sunny and relaxed. When is she ever *not* relaxed? Oh dear Lord, I have been forsaken by all those I walk amongst.

And then Sarah got arrested.

I didn't see Emily, Sarah, or indeed Bernard for several days after that, but one evening I was outside my house admiring the bougainvillea which has taken up most of one wall and that, when it puts its mind to it, flowers as a mass of vibrant purple, and I was wondering if it sometimes blocks my nose and/or is eating away at the mortar of the house, and whether I care about the latter because I rent the house and don't own it, all while fumbling for my keys to get in the door, when my phone rang.

It was Sarah.

'You said they wouldn't arrest me,' she said.

'What?'

'You said they wouldn't arrest me.'

'I did say that,' I conceded.

'They've arrested me.'

I wasn't having a good week.

'I've been arrested for murder,' she said.

'Where are you?'

'In Bastia.'

'Is this your one phone call?' I asked, my heart sinking like a stone.

'Yes.'

'Okay. Right. Don't worry,' I said.

'I'm not worried,' she said.

'You're not worried?'

'No, I'm not worried,' she replied.

'Why aren't you worried?'

'Because as I said he's not dead. Jacob isn't dead.' I could hear her shrugging her indifference down the phone.

'You are adamant Jacob isn't dead?' I said.

'No, he's alive. I'm sure of it.'

'Okay.'

'Oh,' she added. 'Also I think the police are going to arrest you next.'

Part Two

THE WORLD ACCORDING TO EMILY

ONE

So. My brother. My effing brother. My effing ineffectual brother. The entire point of the walking health hazard that is Pete De'Ath is that he is lazy and ineffectual. If he had just stuck to his core strengths of being a) lazy, and b) ineffectual and refused to get involved with Dippy Sarah, we wouldn't have had half our problems.

If he has inexplicably decided he wants to be less lazy after all these years, then why not use this newfound energy to help more with mum? He barely gets involved at all with our mother except for a quick stint on Saturday mornings, which he never stops moaning about; whereas I am endlessly at her house running around doing her jobs, and unlike Pete I do have a life. There is a perpetual assumption that I always mysteriously have the time to help mum and this is because I am a woman. It is somehow a woman's job.

Breathe Emily, breathe.

Don't get me wrong. I do like Pete. He is totally agreeable company. At work, the management absolutely adore him and paradoxically this is because he is lazy. He is supposed to investigate big insurance claims, examine the facts and remove the inflated claims and the criminal activity; but the truth is, he simply half reads the folder and if he doesn't like the 'smell' as he calls it, he doesn't pay the claim. He then looks to see if the claimant gets angry or if they appeal, and takes his cue from their behaviour.

Pete is always looking at the percentage of claims he is rejecting, and he ensures he is paying out less than his similar colleagues around Europe, and that way he has risen to the top of the firm. But the trouble is the colleagues in his own office quietly detest him because they sold the insurance policies to people who have just lost their farm or their boat in a fire and these will be friends or friends of friends because the island is small; they will then find it more difficult to sell an insurance policy to the same people in the future. As a result, Pete never gets any invitations out to drink or eat with the other people at the office, and he ends up sitting at the café table across the street from the office stuffing his face with cream pastries, all on his own.

Oh yes, then there's his 'Let's get ready to ramble' style of conversation. He accuses other people of being taciturn, but it is largely because he is doing all the speaking himself. That man could, oh I don't know, be kidnapped, and rather than working out how to escape he would somehow be talking about his bladder using a sentence that went on for a week. He claims he has had his prostate checked at the doctors, but if that is true, why is he so obsessed about it? And if he isn't talking about his bladder, that's only because he's talking about food and drink. If that man was on board one of the planes in 9/11 hurtling towards the Twin Towers, I swear he would be texting me a commentary on the relative merits of the different white wines available in the little plastic bottles on the drinks trolley; then the end of the text would read 'P.S. we look as if we might hit an office block.' Pete, it's not always about the booze.

Breathe Emily, breathe.

And then there is his dating. Despite his enormous stomach and lazy ways, he somehow thinks he is entitled to have petite attractive girlfriends who are complete raunch buckets. How can he think that? Amazingly enough, he does sometimes attract such women. There was a lovely girl called Colette who was a complete poppet and inexplicably adored Pete. But between the red wine teeth, the endless monotonous TV he watches and, according to Colette, an inability to always finish sex because he gets caught up in a coughing fit. It didn't last.

So. Sooner or later Pete finds faults in these women. A particular pet peeve he has is the way people breathe. Once he notices their breathing patterns he gets obsessed by them. These are breathing patterns that are barely discernible to the rest of us. But people are indeed allowed to breathe, and we could do with an extra female in the family.

I don't really have any girl friends. Men? I am lousy with men. In both senses. I have men all over me like lice, and I treat them in a lousy manner. I have always had boyfriends since I can remember, so I suppose I am a bit careless with them. I am a weapon of mass seduction. It's not my fault; it's just a statement of fact. But at least if I was really keen on a man I would know what to do to keep them. Like Antone. I like Antone. I am putting in some effort and it's going fine. Well we have even organised a crime together. And it was totally ad lib. How many couples can say that, eh?

And then don't get me started on Dippy Sarah, how is it possible that she pulled that body into the back of the car? It was never a reasonable possibility, so why would we ever have factored that in? She is a twig. She is a petite dried twig at that. A dried irritating histrionic twig. I repeat. How is it possible she dragged that body into the car? It defied all logic. It defied all I knew about Sarah. It defied physics.

In fact, the plan was all going fine, and the cousins had put in a call to the police that they had heard shots at the lodge when somehow, just somehow, the little twig dragged the body of a man the length of the house and across the gravel drive and into the back of her sad little car. The point of Dippy Sarah, the entire point of Dippy Sarah, is that she is dippy. Okay, other points include that she was new to the island, she didn't have any friends, and most importantly of all, she works in insurance; but ultimately, she is dippy.

Perhaps we cannot trust stupid people to act consistently. Perhaps that is the one big lesson of the whole venture.

Antone and I had just that moment fired the gun at point blank range at Jacob's head and then because I had slightly failed to get the gun central, I fired a second time which looking back was a big mistake, and we jumped back out the window sharpish because Dippy Sarah was returning faster than we thought. We thought she was near her car, but perhaps she was in the kitchen. While trying to shut the window behind us, I somehow pinched my palm in the hinge. It hurt like hell and I ended up leaving the window ajar, which was not the plan.

So anyway, we were crouched down just below the window on the outside and somehow almost immediately we heard her pulling at the body of Jacob, but at the time we didn't understand what she intended to do. Because Sarah was so quick to return, I left the gun by the window, and yes it would have made far more sense to leave it near the body if it was going to look like suicide.

The noise of the shotgun was ringing in my ears, and I couldn't see into the room from our position outside, so we had to guess what Sarah was doing. I think I heard the door of the bedroom open and I think I heard Sarah gasp or cry, but I wasn't sure, and as I said, we heard a bit of movement. Antone and I just stayed low and moved slowly towards the wood pile area at the back of the lodge. My heart was getting louder and louder and I was trying to breathe in a shallow manner. I hadn't flapped at first but when I shot the gun, it had all got real. Up until that moment I hadn't really broken the law; Antone had broken the law, but not me. But from that moment on I felt I was a proper accessory to the crime. Oh well, it's better to live and let die and all that jazz, and other films from the seventies.

So, we were soon safely hidden behind Jacob's car and then like thirty seconds later we managed to get away to a sort of small hill that lies quite some distance beyond. We assumed we were going to stay there for twenty minutes or perhaps an hour until the police came. When we had planned everything a few days previously, I had known there was no phone reception at the lodge. I once stayed there with Antone and I had got a little obsessive about it at first; probably because I spend too much time on the internet. But when planning everything I decided it was quite useful that the lodge didn't have phone reception: basically, it stopped Sarah ringing people. However, the fact remains, I had been a bit obsessive about it at the time and I had done that thing where you wave your phone in the air and walk around looking at the bars on the screen. I had finally discovered a bit of reception up and near the hill nearby and that was when I decided this was the best place for us to have our temporary refuge, after shooting Jacob.

In the event, we had elected to leave our phones off for the evening in case we were tracked retrospectively by the GPS system or by triangulation with radio masts. The trouble was that we didn't have an accurate estimation for when Sarah would turn up. She had said very vaguely that she would come out after work and pick up some stuff on the way. That could mean anything, especially from Sarah who was so vague by nature. So by the time she had gone home and showered and changed and then packed and then gone off to a shop to get some food for the weekend, and then found her way out into the countryside, it could be any time of night from six-thirty to nine.

It was a flaw in our plans that when we had shot Jacob I needed to text a simple message to one of our partners in crime. It was a nondescript text that meant nothing at face value but when they received it, that was the cue for them to report to their friends in the police from a neutral phone that they had heard the gun shot. The police would then swing by to investigate. This meant we had some of our people in the area as well as Antone and myself, and in fact this proved useful later.

The fact remains that if for some reason my phone was investigated then it was possible I would be placed at the scene of the crime. So as far as I was concerned the trick was for my name to not be in the frame at all. That way they'd never check my phone records

The other trouble we had was finding somewhere to park my car. It had to be, like, near the lodge but not noticeable. There is a small mountain village quite nearby and we didn't want to be witnessed by anyone living there. The car ended up half in a ditch a little way down the road. I just had this residual fear that the car would be remembered by someone if they saw it. I am a great believer that if something can go wrong, it will go wrong, and the phone being on for a few moments and my parked car were the two potential flaws in our plan that I had identified. Apart from that, I felt it was all fine if the correct policeman was called out to the shooting; they knew the stones to leave unturned. It wasn't fine if it fell into the hands of the wrong police.

So, I settled myself on my stomach next to Antone and my only concern was that I was beginning to think that if I needed to go to the toilet I couldn't think of where I could go. No, I do not have an obsession with my bladder like Pete; it is just that I had been at the lodge for a very long time hiding out. Antone couldn't text me when Sarah was arriving at the lodge in the first place because there was no phone reception at the lodge and we didn't want a paper trail of events. The only reason I was needed at all was because we thought it would take two people to drag a body (take note Dippy Sarah) and I was needed to drive Antone back home.

So of course I was as surprised as anyone when Sarah opened the front door of the lodge and kept it open with a rock. I thought to myself 'We know she's found the body, so why is she propping open the front door. To let some air in?'

An eternity later we saw Sarah's little frame appear again in the doorway, her back against the sun, straining at something, and still wearing that sad little summer dress, and she was dragging the body of Jacob by the feet onto the path in front of the house. I couldn't believe my eyes. Antone nudged me with the side of his arm, and I opened my eyes wide by way of reply. There was nothing we could do. I couldn't run down to her and give her advice because she knew me and I would have to explain why I was there. Oh well, they say the best laid plans of mice and men, are... actually, I have no idea how that quote ends.

The act of Dippy Sarah dragging the body along a drive now seemed easy by comparison to what she needed to do after that. It seemed like her next big idea was to pull the body up and into the back of her Peugeot. Yes. It was me who thought it was a Peugeot when in fact Dippy Sarah drives a Renault Clio. And, no, I never understood the thing about the talcum powder mentioned in the newspaper article. Anyway, I don't know why Sarah didn't re-park her car a bit nearer the front door, it would have helped her efforts more than a little, but the next bit was near impossible. She was clearly a very methodical person because she carefully put down the seats of the car and then she pulled Jacob's shoulders up until he was sitting against the back of the bumper of the car. She then got in the passenger door of the car and climbed into the back, leant forward and grabbed the body to try and get it up and into the back of the car.

So you simply had to admire her. She is like one of those little determined dogs you see in the park that doesn't understand how small it is. She was never going to give this up. What I didn't get was what her plan was. Was she going to take the body to a hospital? Did she think that because she didn't have phone reception she shouldn't leave the body and should deliver it to the police in person? She would have to be mad if she thought the hospital could bring the body back to life. His head was missing; no one can come back from that. Actually, I just didn't know what to think, except that Sarah-Jayne had just created a massive problem for us, and our little operation had barely begun.

When she realised that the body wasn't a natural fit for her sad little car and she wasn't a natural fit for the task of lugging the body of a grown man, she walked off in an unhurried fashion to get a thick branch of a tree from a woodpile and then went back for a log the size of a tree stump. She staggered with the log and propped Jacob's shoulders and back onto it, then reversed the car a few inches and then used the branch to lever the body up nearer to the aperture of the open boot. To be fair, it was really heroic. The little dippy terrier was heroic. It was methodical and ingenious.

And then, bless her cotton socks, when she had finally got the body all sorted in her car, she lugged the tree stump back to the woodpile and then came back for the branch. She closed the back of the car, locked it and then went into the house.

And then she tidied. At least I presume she tidied, because she was gone a long time and Antone and I just lay on our stomachs with our eyes trained on the front door waiting for a glimpse of her again. It must have been ten or fifteen minutes later that she emerged and when she re-emerged she was holding a plastic spray gun of kitchen cleaner in one hand and a cloth in the other. She was wiping down the door and door handle. Then we saw her bend down and clean the floor. Then she went off, presumably to rinse her cloth under a tap and repeated the process but without using the kitchen spray.

'She's crazy,' I whispered to Antone. 'You don't clean a murder scene unless you're guilty.'

A long while later Sarah re-appeared with the door key in her hand and she carefully placed it round the side of the house where people who rent the place were supposed to leave the key. Then she adjusted her sad little summer dress and, honestly, she picked a bit of feather off the fabric that caught her eye and then examined that bit of the dress for creases and then, and only then, she got in the car. She adjusted the rear-view mirror, checked all around her that it was safe to drive, and set off. She was a meticulous little thing.

So, we now had to rush off to get to my car and could cut across through some undergrowth. I mean we really had to run. The thing was, Dippy Sarah was driving left and onto the very road we ourselves needed to run along. So we hid behind the tiniest tree; the smallest thinnest twig of a tree you have ever seen. It is fair to assume Dippy Sarah may have had more on her mind than to take in the view and see who was half hiding behind a twig at the roadside. On the other hand, it was impossible to know anything for sure with Sarah.

The problem was we didn't know what Sarah's plan was, and so we couldn't divine where she was going. That meant we needed to follow her car in our car, and that meant we needed to get to our car really quickly. Our plan was for Jacob's death to look like suicide. If Sarah now did the wrong thing, it may look like she had committed a murder, and even I didn't want Sarah done for murder. Either way, we didn't know if we had a problem, and wanted reassurance.

We drove as fast as we could and we could see Sarah's car on the mountain roads in the distance which was something at least. I assumed at that time she was going to drive to a hospital, but when she took the road to the coast, Antone spoke for the first time in a while.

'Do you think she's going to dump the body off a cliff?' he asked.

'I don't know what to think,' I replied. 'Corte hospital is the other way, and Bastia hospital is at the southern end of Bastia. I don't think she's going to either of those. She might be going to the police, I suppose.'

Sarah stopped her car by the side of the road a little before hitting Bastia proper, and we were forced to wait, like, fifty metres further back in our car. I felt she would assume she was not being followed and so she wasn't looking behind her. Just to be safe, it made sense to keep a good distance, though. I don't know what she was doing in the car, but it took more than a little time. Perhaps she was checking something on her phone now she had some reception.

She finally moved on and then I was absolutely gobsmacked to see her drive off to where my brother lives. The last thing I wanted, was him involved.

My brother's place is on a hill above the old harbour; his road is a dead end, so we parked at the top. I followed on foot a little to see what Sarah was up to. At least now if I was spotted I could say I was visiting Pete.

Sarah didn't get out of her car at first. In fairness it must be quite a big thing to knock on a colleague's door and say 'I've got a dead boyfriend in my car, can you help me?' In any event, whatever the reason, Sarah had decided to sit in her car. It gave us some time to think.

'I'll ring up you know who,' said Antone, presumably meaning his cousin. 'But I need to go back to the lodge and clean it and get rid of the gun. I wonder how much Sarah decided to clean up, surely she didn't clean up the bedroom. It would have taken too long.'

'She's a meticulous little flower; perhaps she just wanted to clean up the bit she was responsible for, like the drag marks on the kitchen floor where she moved the body,' I said. 'Why do you want to go back?'

'The plan was for a specific local policeman to come to the lodge and when he filed the report it would say suicide. If Sarah and Pete go to the police in Bastia, it could be anyone who comes out investigate. If you think about exactly what we did, my DNA is everywhere, absolutely everywhere. Probably yours too. We need to clean up the place for if the wrong police go there. We also need to get rid of the gun.'

'I still don't see why,' I said.

'That gun has a bit of history,' he said.

'Oh great. Just great.'

'It's okay. We will get rid of it,' he said. 'Besides, if Sarah's story doesn't square with the facts then the police won't be able to see beyond that. They will assume she is lying. They certainly won't be looking for a third party; they will just keep pressing her for what they feel is the truth. Sarah will just look like a crank.'

'They might convict Sarah,' I said. 'I don't like the sound of that.'

'They won't convict Sarah. Just look at her!' replied Antone. 'We will clean up all the evidence, change the bed covers, and then the police will just be puzzled by why Sarah appears to be lying or a fantasist. They won't suspect us, and we can be sure we left no DNA of our own.'

I obviously looked unsure. He pressed the point. 'Think about it, Emily. Think carefully about everything I did. I definitely left my DNA. That's why we needed our own policeman; one who wouldn't look beyond suicide as an explanation.'

And then there was the issue of Pete. If Sarah roped him in, it was a disaster. Never in a million years did I want Pete involved. I wouldn't want my own brother arrested or in trouble for something. More importantly, I also wouldn't want him to know what I was up to.

I tried to think of things from Pete's point of view. If he rang the police the moment he knew about the body, they would talk to him at length first before heading off to the lodge so we had at least a bit of time to clear up the scene if we started now. But it wasn't much time. If we were going to clean the lodge we should do it as soon as possible.

I kissed Antone farewell and he disappeared off into town. I presumed at the time this was to get his car but in fact it was to get a lift with someone. The kiss was on the lips but quick. I mention it because it never ceases to amaze me that a French man is never too stressed to remember to kiss.

I went to get Mum for some cover. Mum, bless her, was sitting gazing into space. It appears to be her favourite pastime in all the world, second only to praising Pete over me. I can feed her, I can entertain her, help her with her cleaning and take her shopping, and her only comment will be, 'Look at this lovely card Pete got me at Christmas.' A Christmas card. A Christmas card is, literally, the very least Pete could do for his own mother. If he could do less, believe me, he would do it.

In fairness, the sad thing is that Mum probably does this because she does in fact like my efforts and so she wants to make a bit of conversation with me, but she doesn't get out much apart from when she is stalking her boyfriend so she doesn't really have any conversation to offer. She knows she can always talk about Pete, so she does; but it grates.

But say what you like about Mum bless her, she is amenable. I just had to walk into her flat and say brightly 'I'm off to see Pete, do you want to come?' and she replied, 'Do you think he will help me with my texts?'

I said, 'Of course he will!' And we were up and running. Or up and shuffling, in Mum's case.

It took less than ten or twenty minutes and we were back at Pete's.

So, Dippy Sarah was there in Pete's living room, perched rather primly on the edge of Pete's sofa. She looked remarkably composed for a woman with a dead boyfriend. Pete, on the other hand, looked clammy. He was the colour of silver. He looked guilty as hell. That's the funny thing. He was the one who had done nothing wrong, and if he just rang the police he would still be doing nothing wrong. Okay, so if he rang the police that could land me in trouble, but it would help him. When did life get so complicated? Crime, eh? Who'd do it for a living?

I wondered what tale Sarah had told him. I wondered if Pete was going to say anything to us about the body.

I scrutinised Pete and Sarah. I wondered if they had previously had a relationship. It was unlikely. It was more likely that she was simply taking advantage of Pete's good nature, which was outrageous; taking advantage of Pete is my role in life, not hers.

Mum, meanwhile, was angry about her so-called lover Ludic, and Dippy Sarah and Lazy Pete were trying to sort out Mum's phone so she could text him a dirty message or whatever goes on between the elderly and infirm, and I tried to think how I could somehow dictate events. I was desperate for Pete to not be involved at all. If I stayed around the house then at least Pete wouldn't be able to do anything in the short term at least, and it would give Antone some time to clean up the murder scene. But how long could I realistically string out my visit and what would be my next move? I decided to ask after some food and the like. Pete is used to me sponging food off him, and it would take up some time. In fairness, shooting people does make you hungry.

As Pete sorted out some paella I had a little think. I needed to instil a simple message, like in some subliminal way. A message like 'Just don't get involved' or 'What are you thinking? Just get the body back to the mountains!' In desperation I tried saying the words out loud but pretending I was on the phone talking to someone unseen.

I said, 'Don't get involved. Just don't get involved,' as if I was reasoning with them. But I really don't think Pete noticed at all. He was probably too busy thinking about the body in the car.

The other thing I did was to pretend to go off to the toilet, but in fact I went into Pete's bedroom. I wanted to write him a note, but my heart was pounding. Mum and Pete and Sarah were not really settled down, and Mum in particular has a habit of suddenly walking around on a whim, and what's worse she moves completely silently; Ninja Mum would find it easy to get to Pete's doorway and ask me what I was doing. If I shut his door it looked like a sign of guilt, so there was no easy option.

I needed a piece of paper to write on, but there was nothing I could use in Pete's room at all. So I felt flustered and that my absence from the main room would be noted. In desperation I turned to the bookshelves and tore a page out of a book and wrote a note using my wrong hand and upside down for good measure; I left it by his bedside.

I then flushed the toilet the bathroom and walked back to the living room. Mum and Pete were squinting at Mum's phone and Dippy Sarah was the only one who noticed my movements, but it was not her house or her family, so she wasn't in a position to wonder what I was up to.

My thinking was that our best bet was still to the get the body back into the mountains where the 'correct' police would be in charge of the case, and preferably it was just Sarah who did this. I didn't want Pete involved a fraction more than he was already.

Pete looked up at me and said, 'Are you alright?'

'Yeah,' I replied.

After all that, I was worried that my face had gone pale from the adrenaline and that someone would notice it, but after sitting for a while with the three others, that emotion gave way to a quiet satisfaction that I would make a really good spy. Undercover Emily, international spy. Job description: espionage. Physical description: totty. I am pretty sure I could do it. I would have to wear thick foundation on my face for when I went pale from the adrenaline surges, and drink a lot so that my hand tremor from nerves could be passed off as the DTs; but apart from that, yeah, I could be a spy.

TWO

So. I took mum off to her place and I drove out to the lodge in the mountains. I still had a box of surgical gloves in the car, but apart from that there was nothing else of use. I considered stopping off at a shop to buy cleaning materials but I worried that I would be remembered by a shop assistant or filmed on the CCTV in the shop, and if I ended up under suspicion by the police then that would be like something extra and difficult to explain away, so I decided against it and took a chance that we could find cleaning materials at the house.

When I got to the lodge there was no car parked outside the front and I didn't notice one at the right hand side of the building, but it was dark and looking back Jacob's car must have been there. There were lights on in the lodge and that made it a little harder to see in the nearby shadows. Given that I didn't think there was a car present I couldn't understand how Antone had got there if he didn't have a car. I then worried that it wasn't Antone in the house at all, but by then I had already driven my car up and parked. In fairness, I did better than park: I turned the car round so it was facing forwards for a quick escape. I sat in the dark and gave myself a little talking to. I kept meaning to move. But I didn't move: I just did some more thinking. I kept trying to think through in my head what my actual crime was by this stage, but I was getting so confused and tired. I jumped a mile when there was a tap on my car window. It was Antone peering in at me.

I wound the window down.

'How did you get here?'

'My cousin gave me a lift.'

'Where is he now?' I asked.

'He's driven off back to Bastia to see if he can track Sarah. He's hoping to follow Sarah,' he said.

'How far have you got with the cleaning?' I asked.

'I was waiting for you,' he said.

'But you'd had an hour's head start on me,' I protested.

'I'm joking,' he said.

He wasn't joking; it was just that he had seen my face; I looked appalled. When we got inside the house, he had made a bit of a start. He did have some yellow kitchen gloves on, which I found really amusing, but apart from that, I found it all very irritating. Where was his urgency? Or did he feel there was no real worry and somehow all the police were in his pocket. To this day I can't explain it. I suppose Antone is a relaxed person and so that is all I have to understand.

So, one thing is for sure. I hate bloody cleaning. I mean, let's face it, normal cleaning is bad enough when there is no blood involved, but a crime scene? In fact, I'd say that cleaning a crime scene is the very worst kind of cleaning; even worse than cleaning an oven. In fairness, I've never cleaned an oven, but I have a very vivid imagination. At least with an oven there are special sprays and foams you can buy, or you can get a man in to do it, or buy a new oven, or just resolve to live on takeaways. There are no special sprays and foams for a crime scene. Or if there are, it is incriminating to even own them.

I think what is particularly bad about cleaning a murder scene is that you can't miss out any bits or give it a little bit of a clean and make a promise to revisit the problem at a later date: a promise that even when you are making the promise you know you are going to break. Like most of my promises, in fact. Like all of my promises, in fact.

I was surprised to discover that Antone had brought his own cleaning materials. It was like a large plastic box with a handle and it contained sprays and bleaches and wire wool and all sorts.

'It's best not to use the cleaning materials in the house,' he said. 'Also they don't always have what you need.'

How many murder scenes had he previously cleaned up? Best not to ask. The truth would be a liability.

A particularly difficult bit was under the bed. To give it a scrub I had to climb under there, but by climbing under there I was potentially leaving my own hairs and cells behind. Not just potentially; we later discovered I did indeed leave hair and the like down there. It was almost inevitable; I had gloves on but that was scant protection in real terms.

The second problem was that the shotgun had made a hole in the mattress. Shotgun cartridges are pretty destructive things. I had held the gun high over the bed and pointed it down vertically at the general direction of Jacob's face as he lay back on the bed. He didn't look surprised. Of course he didn't. He kind of disintegrated and a whole chunk of the bed, or in fact the mattress, hollowed out with it. I didn't have time to linger on the sight at the time, but now I could see not just the blood and the flesh left on the bedding, but also a shredded mess of blown away duvet cover and mattress stuffing. There was no chance of cleaning it all up. The only option would be a new mattress altogether. The cousins didn't source this until the next morning, but they were pretty efficient. For an immediate solution, I found a duvet from another room and a spare cover for it.

'Okay,' I said. 'In the short term if we put the cover on this duvet, and change the sheet below then that will look as if there is no hole in the bed.'

'If anyone peels back the duvet and sheet we are stuffed. They will see the bed has a hole in it.'

'Yes,' I agreed. 'If anyone peels back the sheet then we are stuffed. Or rather it looks like Sarah concealed evidence. It makes it look like she did a murder. Not a suicide. But we'll get a new mattress asap.'

Antone was not exactly then throwing himself into the duvet cover changing thing. He saw himself more as an advisory/gazing into space kind of guy.

'Is this a Corsican thing?' I asked.

'Is what a Corsican thing?' he replied.

'Letting the woman do all the work.'

'No it's a laziness thing,' he replied.

I suspect it is also a Corsican thing, but I don't want to slander all Corsicans; just one in particular.

'Where's the gun?' I asked.

'We've taken care of it,' he said.

I didn't ask any more; the less I knew, the less I could let slip if I was being interviewed. Oh dear, I hope I wasn't interviewed. I assumed that the cousin took the gun off in his car and threw it in a lake or off a cliff.

I changed the sheets of the bed.

'Do you think we should burn these sheets? Or take them home and wash them?' I asked.

Antone looked at me as though he had forgotten I was in the room.

'We can't put them in the washing machine here,' he said. 'They've got a big hole in them. I'll put them in a bin liner and we'll burn them. Have you ever stayed here?'

'Yes,' I replied. 'You know I stayed here. I stayed here with you a few weeks ago.'

'Yeah of course,' he said. 'That'll be something at least if they did find any of our prints, or some DNA. I have wiped everywhere obvious; door handles, cupboard fronts.'

The fact that he'd forgotten whether he'd stayed here with me made me wonder how many women Antone had taken here for a weekend away in the past. I dismissed the thought at once. It is the sort of thought that eats away at a relationship.

We finished as quickly as we could and when we left the building we locked the front door and replaced the key where it was kept outside and got in my car. It was then that I nearly had a heart attack.

I turned the keys in the ignition and turned the lights of my car on, and for a split second I was sure I could see a car in the driveway ahead of us. But in the time it took for my eyes to become acclimatised it seemed to reverse and disappear. But I definitely saw it. We now know that it was Pete and Sarah in Sarah's car with the body of Jacob in the back; they had been sitting in the dark watching us. But had they seen me walk from the front door to my car? If you know someone well enough you can recognise not just their shape but also the way they walk, and Pete would certainly recognise my car. I was so stuffed. There was no way in a thousand years I would be able to think up a crafty excuse for why I was at that lodge at that time, and I didn't want to fall on Pete's mercy. I was fed up with falling on Pete's mercy.

As we were driving away, I realised Antone was talking to me.

'Do you reckon we should get Jacob's car back and then we should just store it some place for a bit?' he asked. 'It makes it look he was there.'

'He *was* here,' I said.

'Yeah but we are trying to muddy the waters,' he said.

'I think the waters are muddied more than enough. I just want to get away from that place as far as I can,' I said. 'We might have been seen. I'm getting spooked.'

My brain was beginning to hurt.

‘Seen by who?’ asked Antone.

‘I don’t know. I swear there was a car sitting just ahead with its lights off. The moment I saw it, it reversed back.’

We got back to Bastia. We were nearly home when Antone said, ‘I think I’ve lost Jacob’s phone. I haven’t got Jacob’s phone. Where do you reckon it could be?’

‘I’m beyond caring,’ I replied.

THREE

We drove to my place and picked up a few items and then went on to where Antone was staying.

I think looking back, my emotion was that I didn't fancy being on my own in my own flat gazing at the ceiling. I am not good on my own at the best of times. I only keep a flat for form's sake. I mean what is the point of living on your own? What are you supposed to do? Grow some window boxes? Rearrange the window boxes so that only I can admire them? Put some pictures on the walls? Putting pictures on the walls would take half an hour. What are you supposed to do for the rest of the year? I am a people person. If I hung out with Antone, we could discuss our thoughts with each other and not leave a paper trail of texts or calls and the like. In the event we had sex.

I know that most people in my position would not have had sex. It had been a very stressful, very fatiguing day. But in my defence, I really like sex. I find it reassuring. If you have sex with someone that means there are no issues with them; you are at one with them, and it's all alright. And anyway, what was the alternative? Thinking endlessly about our predicament? I can get really lost in sex. It's like an adventure with lots of different twists and turns. Especially with Antone. It's never the same twice. I mean, okay if I'm planning it and thinking it through then I will know what's going to happen. But usually I just surrender to Antone; it is like falling, a blissful kind of endless falling.

I was lucky that Antone was up for it. People say men are all alike, but in my experience this isn't true at all. A lot of men wouldn't have wanted sex after the evening we had. They would have freaked out or got grumpy or obsessive, or started blaming me for stuff, or sat there drinking heavily.

I had one boyfriend who I recall just pacing up and down on the carpet in front of me, forwards and backwards, forwards and backwards. Sometimes he would walk in circles. I can't even recall what the issue was. He was very agitated. It was something like he'd lost his wallet, or he didn't like the colour of his new dental work and couldn't think what to do. It was nothing. It was nothing to worry about. Women don't want that. They want a man who has something solid about them. They want a man who can take a punch.

I would bite Antone. I would stand behind his naked back and tilt my head sideways and feel the muscles of his back nestle against the edge of my teeth and I would trace my teeth sideways across his flesh causing the slightest line of white scraped skin, and when my head was under his arm I would inhale his smell and sink my teeth into the muscle. His palms would be against the wall. He wouldn't flinch or make a sound. Then I would press my cheek against his back and close my eyes and breathe out through my lips. I loved it. And for those moments, it seems, I am happy to commit a crime with him.

In the event, that night Antone brought things to a conclusion quite quickly, so perhaps he wasn't really in the mood; he's just a nice guy who picked up on my cues and wanted to please. This makes him an even greater guy.

In fact, after the sex Antone looked profoundly disconsolate. I tried to catch his eye and flash him a smile, but my smile felt anxious and I realised I'd done the wrong thing. I've noticed in relationships I often double down using sex. Why do I do that? Then I heard myself answer my own question.

'I won't judge,' I began.

'Right,' he replied.

'I won't be judgy.' Then I knew I had betrayed that I cared about the answer to the upcoming question because I'd rearranged my own sentence before I'd barely said it. 'I won't be judgy,' I repeated, just to make matters worse. 'But have you had sex with Dippy Sarah?'

'Sarah? Er, no,' he replied.

'Er no, or no?' I asked. I had totally over played it. I should have simply asked 'Can I ask if you had sex with Sarah?' I should have kept it simple like that. The thing is he obviously likes English girls and there is a small dating pool in Bastia and Sarah is in and out of the fringe of our group. To use murder parlance, with Sarah he definitely had the means, the motive, and the opportunity. Most importantly, I have seen the way he looks at her and the way she looks at him. So I know what I know.

Antone kindly knelt and took my hands in his and looked me in the eye.

'No,' he said simply.

Then he kissed me.

Okay, so it turns out he's perfect.

Then I reflected on Sarah. In fairness there was probably no temptation there. For sex to be any good someone has to take charge, and that certainly would never be Sarah; she is just too wet. The worst that could happen is that a man would take advantage of her; she would get flung round the bedroom like a ragdoll. Because she is wet, she would never be sexy. You could dress her up in latex and give her a whip, and she would just end up looking like a garden gnome with a fishing rod. No, Antone would never go for her.

Antone's phone was the sort that knows when you are awake through his Fitbit or whatever, and when you do wake up it alerts you to messages that have come in the night. Somehow it sparked into life at about four in the morning. So I suppose that this meant Antone had woken up early; perhaps he had been worrying and couldn't sleep.

'I've got a message to meet my cousin,' he said.

Antone has a lot of cousins, so I didn't clarify which one he meant. In any case, some of them looked the same as each other and I hadn't really paid attention enough over the months to work out which was which or if any of them had, oh I don't know, individual names.

'Now?' I asked.

'Yes now.'

'It's four in the morning.'

By five we were in Antone's car driving off to see the cousin.

'Which cousin is it?' I asked.

He laughed. 'You know how you say my cousins are shady? Well this is the most shady of them all.' Categorising one of the cousins as the shadiest was no small accolade; there was a crowded field to choose from.

Antone had arranged a place to meet and chat up in the hills north of Bastia, and we sat there in my car waiting. It was dark, and events were getting a bit much for me at this stage; I felt nervous and tired.

Antone's cousin drove his car up next to our car. He bent one finger at Antone to go and talk with him. The rustic Corsicans I have met can sometimes come over as profoundly anti-women, and certainly I was not allowed to hear them talk for that meeting. But equally, the traditional Corsicans can be all about the family and that was as likely a reason as to why I was excluded: I wasn't in fact part of their family. Families trust each other and stick together on this island, and thousands of years of foreigners invading and exploiting and leaving again had done little to make the Corsicans change their opinions on the subject.

Antone's Shady Cousin was handsome, as Pete would say, or dishy as mum would say, in a swarthy hook-nosed tumble-haired, just-about-washes-enough, Italian kind of way. He had good hair, and I am a sucker for good hair. And he had proper presence. He is the sort of man where people murmur in his ear. He is the sort of man whose eyes never move around the room, and yet somehow he already knows who is in the room, where they are in the room, why they are there, and how best to kill them.

I tried to imagine what sex would be like with him. I think he would very much be in charge. I think he had a normal size penis, maybe slightly small, and I don't think it would be a case of me in front of him on my knees. I think it would be a case that he would take me roughly from behind, while I was on all fours or bending forward against a wall. I think he would also want sex up the derriere and wouldn't feel any guilt in going for it. Most men I have ever met have want sex that way, but they work up to trying to get it after several months of dating. But Antone's Shady Cousin would expect it on day one. So I won't be dating Antone's Shady Cousin. In fact, I can't believe I even considered dating Antone's Shady Cousin. Yes, someone should be in charge during sex, but as I've said before and said often, pick the right man in the first place.

He smiled at me from his car. I smiled back. I added a little wave to be a bit flirty. It looked like they had finished their conversation.

Antone got back in my car.

'Cristofanu says Petru picked Sarah and your brother up in his car last night,' he said.

'What?' I replied.

Cristofanu was the younger, handsome, cousin Antone had been talking to in the car whom I took to referring to as Antone's Shadiest Cousin. Petru was the older cousin or uncle who had given Antone a lift back to the lodge last night.

'Petru left me at the lodge to clean the place, then he drove towards Bastia to see if he could find Sarah and discover what they were doing. He was driving round in the mountains without any progress for ages and he was going to stop looking, when they were standing in the road.'

'Standing in the road?'

'Standing in the road. Evidently they looked terrible. They asked to get into his car. He pretended he only spoke Corsican. Then Petru accidently spoke English. He didn't know what to do and he panicked and stopped the car at the lodge. He said to them to leave the car. The other thing that made him panic was that Pete was telling him in Corsican that he wanted to be taken to the police. The last thing Petru wanted was to go to the police.'

'Pete was trying to speak Corsican? That's a worry.' I tried to weigh all this up. 'If he dropped them back at the lodge then it looks as though Petru knew who they were and what they were doing?' I said.

'Exactement.'

'Exactly,' I said. I hate it when I accidentally correct Antone's English. He is good at languages and it makes me sound patronising. Jesus wept, there are signs that I love him. I wouldn't care about such minor things with anyone else. Grrrr. Bad Emily. Curse my greedy eyes. It's just that he smells so good and Emily deserves treats.

'There is something else,' he said. 'The cousins have found the car with the body in it. Pete and Sarah must have had an accident. The car fell off the road.'

'They fell off the road?' I asked.

'They fell off a road.'

'How did they find the car?' I asked. I wanted to get things clear in my muddled mind.

'Petru figured that they were limping so badly that they couldn't have walked far. In fact, his actual words were that they looked as though they had been in a car crash and so he put two and two together and checked the roads nearby.'

'So we should rescue the car,' I said. 'If they rescue the car and they rescue the body, there is no crime. If there is no crime, then Pete is not in trouble. They can tell any story they like to the police; there isn't a body. The police will just believe they'd had some weird hallucination, like when people claim they are abducted by aliens and given an anal probe. People don't believe the story is true, but they do believe the person telling the story believes it is true.'

Antone wrinkled his nose.

I tried to sound firmer. 'Look I can just about stomach Sarah being done for Jacob's death, but I won't have my own brother being done for it.'

'French prosecutors don't think like that,' he said. 'They may still arrest them.'

'If we get the body then we can have a nice think about our options,' I said. 'If we leave the body, the wrong person could find it. The wrong police could get involved. Either way Antone, I don't want Pete involved. Let's just remove the crime altogether.'

Antone reflected on this and then got out the car and talked to Cristofanu through his open window. He looked at me a couple of times during their conversation and you could see by the way he raised his eyebrows amicably and tilted his head that he was considering my plan.

Antone returned.

'Apparently the car is down by a farm track and they can probably get it removed,' said Antone.

'What about Jacob's car?' I asked.

'What about it?' asked Antone.

'Can we get that as well? Let us just totally remove the whole crime, otherwise anything Pete and Sarah say will have a bit of traction.'

'It makes sense,' he said. 'It's not hard to steal a car.'

He went back to talk to his cousin.

'Oh and change the mattress!' I shouted. 'Don't forget a new mattress for that bed! And a duvet to replace the one we took from the spare room.'

They both nodded. It would have been quicker and easier if I had sat in the car with them all along.

FOUR

It's the little mistakes that are the annoying ones.

On the Saturday night I kept to my original plan to go out with some friends to Pinocchio's and unusually, Pete joined us. Before we knew it, he was mouthing off in front of my friends and, frankly, to half of Corsica about having Jacob's body in the car. What was he thinking? Surely he would shut up about a thing like that; he was acting like an idiot. But what annoyed me even more was that I reacted incorrectly. If it was all news to me then I should have rung him up the next day, or talked to him that Saturday night, and been like WTF? I mean, when your brother says he has been riding around with a body in a car, this is huge news. You would ring him up and ask supplementary questions and bug him all night. I did nothing of the kind. Instead I was in shock and probably tired from the weekend as a whole, and my instinct was that I wanted to talk it over with Antone. Even then, oddly enough, I forgot to do it. It wasn't until the Wednesday that Pete found me at work and showed me that he was on the front page of a newspaper, and I started discussing events with him. That was a whole four days later.

The only good news was that by Wednesday we had quietly thought up a strategy to deal with Sarah and Pete. Basically, I figured that Pete was only involved because he felt he owed a duty of care to Sarah. If we could get Sarah feeling better about everything, then Pete would slack off and get back to his daily diet of drinking wine and growing his stomach. For Sarah, we devised a two prong strategy. As well as removing all the evidence of the crime, we would introduce her to a modern day 'witch' and lay on a lot of Corsican folklore to sow ideas in her mind that she might have hallucinated the whole experience. It opened our options up a bit and also if she started babbling about witches and dreams, it would make her an unreliable witness.

The upside was that meeting a mazzere and interviewing her for the job of freaking out Sarah was a complete hoot.

'Being a mazzere is like a drug,' explained Bernard. 'You first dream about someone and then they die and it is a shock, but you soon get another dream and then you look forward to the dreams and the power of knowing who will die.'

'That's macabre,' I said.

'Sure,' he said gleefully. 'Macabre sells documentaries. I am a documentary maker. You see the amazing thing is that this bears no relation to any other European culture. These are not witches. There has never been a persecution of them; there were no witch trials in Corsican history. This is more about the idea that before people understood the medical basis of death, they would feel the spirits or the gods had earmarked the next person to die. On some instinctive level people knew who had terminal conditions: they had the wrong pallor or swollen ankles; perhaps the gods had marked the next to die with swollen ankles. They knew who was going to die but they didn't understand the science.'

'Bernard I love you,' I said.

'What?'

'I have literally no idea where that came from,' I said. 'Rest assured, I don't love you.'

He shrugged and laughed and ordered more drinks.

I like the men who don't fancy me. I am particularly drawn to them. My experience is of course the same as everyone's; that it is always easier to deal with people who aren't trying to make a pass at you at the time; on the other hand if you are good looking, people tend to notice you in the first place. I had long since discovered that Bernard didn't fancy me and that allowed us to just get on with being pals. Clearly he was gay. There couldn't possibly be any other explanation as to why he didn't fancy me. I am joking: he is not gay.

I realised I had zoned out of what Bernard had to say. I concentrated for the next thirty seconds and discovered to my happiness that he had everything in hand. We were going to interview some mazzeri.

So Bernard rustled up a couple of mazzeri to interview and we travelled to meet the first one in a town down the coast. She lived in a crummy apartment that smacked of social housing.

She inevitably wore black; black leggings that had lost their shape and a black top that seemed constantly surprised by her lumpy shape. She washed a lot less than I was hoping. Worse, it was only ten thirty in the morning but it seemed she had already fortified herself with her morning brandy. Bernard could see what I was thinking and raised a finger at me to keep my thoughts to myself.

We sat side by side on a threadbare sofa while our host poured something out of a pot. I will be charitable and call it tea; there was certainly a lot of foliage involved. Some leaves were brown, some of them were yellow; a lot of them looked rotten.

'Tell us about yourself Tempête,' said Bernard.

'Tempête?' I asked.

'My name is Tempête Brouillard,' she began. 'I was summoned by the spirit world over twenty years ago. I have seen many deaths. So many deaths. It is my calling.'

Storm Fog. Her name translated as Storm Fog.

As if she had read my mind, and who knows perhaps she had, she said 'Storm Fog is my given name.'

Okay, but given by whom? And how was I going to avoid drinking the tea? She pushed my cup closer to me. It smelt of pond. I was pretty sure I could see a tadpole lurking.

'One night I dreamt a dream deeper than any dream I had had before. Even the woodland, even the animals warned me in my dream that my hunt that night was going to be dangerous. My own life would be in peril,' she said. She was swaying at the time.

She closed her eyes, remembering. The more she swayed, the more we got whiffs of her body smell. She was damp in strange places.

'I travelled deep into the forest using only the tracks that the wolves have known for a thousand years.'

There are no wolves in Corsica. There are some nasty little weasels, some malevolent looking bats, and if a wild boar is charging at you though the undergrowth then get out of the way; but there are no wolves. Pete would never be taken in by this woman. I could feel his emotions in me as I watched her. Storm Fog was clearly not our girl.

However, there was no easy way to interrupt her; there was too much rhythmic moaning going on. And now she was chanting. Perhaps we could tiptoe out and when she finally realised we were gone she would put it all down to being a dream. Then no doubt we would be the next to die.

The monologue continued, now in a baritone.

'I ran deeper and deeper into the forest with thorns slashing my ankles and branches swiping my face and then my prey was ahead of me. I couldn't see it, I couldn't hear it, I could sense it. And other mazzeri were running in parallel, sweeping through the forest; the animals were scattering in fear, but they did not need their fear because we knew we had only one prey and only one objective, only one we needed to kill. At last we found him. He cowered and whimpered. He knew the game was up.'

By now Storm Fog had reached quite the state of frenzy. She started emitting a guttural moan, a pain of a wail deep from her gut. She was shuddering. Her eyes were flickering under her eyelids.

She screamed 'I was terrified!' Then reverted to baritone: 'My terror was even worse than the terror of the prey itself. All the mazzeri were towering over the exhausted prey and we all pointed our asphodel down into his heart. We had to kill, we had to kill, we had to kill! But though I knew I must kill, I felt such a grieving.'

Her entire body was shaking and throbbing. It was an uncontrolled jitter which sent waves through her body.

Something caught my eye. I nudged Bernard and whispered in his ear. 'I think she's wet herself.'

Her crotch was at our eye level. We both leant forward to examine.

'It was terrifying!' she boomed above us.

A neighbour in the apartment below banged the ceiling for her to keep the noise down.

'Then I knew who it was! I knew why I was so terrified. I knew why he was so terrified. For it was a he.'

There was a merciful break in the shouting and swaying.

'It was my own husband.'

She and her wet behind collapsed back into a chair. That was clearly a chair to avoid in future.

When she had got her breath back I asked, 'So how did your husband take it?'

'Take what?'

'The news that you had dreamt he was going to die,' I said.

'I don't know. We got divorced soon after.'

On the way back to the car we exchanged looks and raised eyebrows.

'Well she's genuine,' I said. 'She really believed all that stuff. I just really don't think that's what we are looking for in a mazzere.'

Our second interviewee was a well-dressed lady in her fifties. Bernard couldn't make this appointment; he had to be elsewhere that evening.

She was pleasant, smartly-dressed and tiny. She worked in a dry cleaners. We were in my own apartment after work.

'You want what exactly?' she asked.

'Well my brother and his friend are agnostic about these things and I thought it would be good for them to meet a mazzere.' I then explained a little about my predicament. A very little. Less is better than a lie. 'He is more likely to believe something if it comes from the right person,' I finished.

'So you want a flavour of the whole thing and you want me to put on a bit of a show,' she said.

'Well when you put it like that...' I said.

'No that's fine. I sometimes do corporate events.'

'How did you get into this if you don't mind me asking?'

'I used to live on the south west of the island and I had a normal life. I had a young family and I started getting these vivid dreams. They were nothing at first, just me running. I am a keen jogger so it was not strange to run in a dream. But one day I dreamt I was chasing someone I knew, and a later time I was hunting and the thing I was chasing was afraid of me. The dreams got progressive and then there was a death. I told the person about it, but almost as a joke. It was a lady in my village. She was very nice about it. She said the oddest thing. She said, "That's alright dear. You're not the first to tell me this." She died within the year. She was old, you know?'

'Did she tell you who else had predicted her death?'

'Yes, and we became friends,' she said. 'So anyway, let's get our diaries out. When did you want me?'

'Well, a couple of weeks' time?' I said.

'Oh dear,' she replied. 'I can't I'm afraid. I'm going to Ibiza.'

'What?'

'My daughter lives there. When she was twenty, she went for a holiday and she never came back.'

I looked crestfallen.

'What, you can't see me in a fluorescent bikini and Ugg boots?' she laughed.

'You are going clubbing with your daughter?' I asked.

'No,' she said. 'That was a pleasantry.' She changed tone. 'You look upset.'

'I need a mazzere,' I moaned. 'My brother would have loved you.'

She held my forearms with her hands. 'I can do this week if it helps?'

'Life saver! I'll see if I can get everyone together asap,' I said. Having confirmed her as our option I then got a bit greedy. 'Er...'

'Yes.'

'Out of interest, can you dress it up a bit? You know, make it a bit more witchy?'

'What do you mean?'

'Well,' I began. 'What clothes do you wear? Do you wear these clothes?'

'Oh no dear, I dress up in lots of flowing black and I'll choose a dramatic bit of countryside to add to the drama. Trust me, I know what I'm doing.'

'Great!' I said. 'Oh and can I ask one more question. What is an asphodel?'

'An asphodel? It is the Flower of the Dead. It has a long strong stem and then a flame like top, a bit like an artichoke shape. You can stab people with it. It is thought to have sacred powers. They are rather pretty. They grow in the hills and mountains.'

'Bring one of those,' I said.

'Is it a deal breaker?'

'No.'

'Then no,' she replied.

FIVE

It was a Monday lunchtime and I remembered with a jolt it was my turn to have lunch with Mum. I was late picking her up and so I knocked on her door and when there was no answer I let myself into her flat with my key.

I found her in a chair in her kitchen fast asleep.

She woke and looked disorientated.

When her face cleared and she realised who I was she said, 'You're late.'

She then looked pleased - of course she was pleased - she had the double joy of having something to moan about, and having a nice little nap while waiting for me.

I took her down to the old harbour for lunch in a nice bar restaurant that overlooks the town's smaller more picaresque boats. It's the sort of decent restaurant a dutiful daughter takes her ageing mother to. My ageing mother couldn't have cared less; she didn't care about the standard of the cuisine, she didn't care about the ambiance, and she couldn't have cared less that her daughter was kindly paying – although she would have cared if I *hadn't* paid.

But all that notwithstanding, she wouldn't eat anywhere else, because the restaurant affords a direct view across the harbour to where her paramour lives.

I ordered a nice lunch, eschewing a starter of blackbird pâté on offer, while Mum settled in to abuse the waitress.

'Well she's put on weight,' said Mum.

'She can hear you, you know,' I said. I smiled an apology to the waitress. 'I thought we were doing that thing where we select the better of our thoughts before speaking.'

'Are we still doing that?' she asked. We do keep each other amused.

My mother placed her bags on the chairs around us as a barrier to other people sitting near, and then set about ignoring both me and my light conversation. Instead she stared like a predatory bird across the water at Ludic's apartment. She was as obsessive as Gatsby staring across the bay at Daisy - only three times older and with a slight whiff of stale urine. I followed her gaze and could just about make out Ludic and his wife pottering around in their apartments. Watching them move from one room to another was oddly absorbing.

Then my mother, without explanation, stood up and left the restaurant. For an old woman, she could really scurry when she wanted to. I watched her as she took the road round the harbour, past the yachts and car park, and then disappeared into an alley beyond.

The food came and I tucked in. I was due back to work in half an hour and it was more than likely that I wouldn't see my mum again before I went back. I got as far as ordering a coffee when the door of the restaurant opened again, and my mother shuffled in and sat down.

'What have you been doing?' I asked.

She ignored me, and started texting on her phone instead. When she had finished, she settled into a happy daze, as old folk do - a daze that is at the satisfying midpoint between reminiscence and sleep. I wasn't having any of it. I grabbed her phone and found her messages. I read them out.

'Dear Ludic. I've just sneaked round to your place, I placed a rounded pebble on the window ledge outside your room. When you find it, pretend to look surprised.'

Good grief.

'Pete wouldn't treat me like this,' said Mum.

'No because he wouldn't take you out to lunch in the first place.'

I wouldn't have minded, but I had a lot on my plate that day.

To complete the circle of evidence that Sarah was just a fantasist, the cousins decided they would replace Sarah's lost car. They did it surprisingly quickly, but it did nonetheless involve stealing a car and filing off the chassis details. I thought the whole thing was unnecessary but it wasn't down to me.

The trouble was I had to wait until Sarah was in the office and then slip the keys of the stolen car into the bottom of her handbag. When she found her car returned, the keys had to fit.

It is easy enough putting a key in a bag, but I also wanted to check that she didn't have her original car key in there as well.

Sarah had popped out of the office but not given a reason, so I didn't know if it was for thirty seconds or half an hour and it is amazing how much time it takes to go through the contents of another woman's handbag.

I fished around among the make-up and notebooks and pens. I found a little plastic bag carefully folded up with some spare knickers in it. Who routinely carries a spare pair of knickers? But still no key.

I was just about to give up when two things happened at once. I heard the door open and I felt the shape of a car key in the lining of the bag itself. There must be an internal extra pocket.

I could hear Sarah talking. I got the impression she had half opened the door to come back in but was now chatting to a colleague. I found the zip that related to the pocket with the car key in it. I unzipped it. The key was definitely a car key but it had a key fob on it that was like a plastic unicorn. I would need to get the key off the key fob and replace it with the new key.

'What are you doing?' asked Sarah. She had caught me red handed.

'Sorry,' I replied. 'It was like my sinus was leaking and I needed a tissue in a hurry.'

'Your sinus is leaking?' queried Sarah.

'Don't ask; it's disgusting, it's kind of a thin liquid that's fluorescent yellowy-green,' I said. 'But please get me a tissue.'

Sarah, bless her heart, ran out of the office to get tissues from the staff toilets. So I had time to remove her key and re-zip the little pocket they were in. I ran back to my desk with both the new key and the old unicorn key and held my head back as though I were preventing a major medical emergency.

'There you go,' said an unseen Sarah, placing a tissue into my outstretched hand.

I would now have plenty of time getting the key sorted and back in her bag.

Job done: another mission accomplished for Emily the international spy.

During that time, Antone and I had to meet in out of the way places if we were to see each other at all, which in Corsica always involved a lot of time and travel. I got the feeling there was a lot of work going on in the background that involved the cousins and Antone having to be elsewhere and I hadn't had anything out of it yet; I no longer even had my boyfriend to play with. But it was no good moaning or dwelling; we all had to knuckle down and help.

One of the final pieces of the jigsaw where I was directly involved was that we needed to get rid of Sarah's original car. It had been dragged away from the side of a mountain easily enough and the chassis number and plates removed, but the next problem was disposing of it without leaving any evidence. For all sorts of reasons, this job had been kicked into the long grass. It was a long time later that we were formulating a plan.

We were in a house deep in the countryside. The sort of area synonymous with bandits and freedom fighters; but these days robbing from whom, the taxman? Freedom from what, the EU? It was one of the houses that belonged to Antone's extended family, where the forest and the mountains keep their secrets and you can't even hear yourself scream. Antone and Antone's Shadiest Cousin were deep in conversation at one table, and I sat on a chair a little further away with a cup of coffee and the internet.

There was also a daughter around who was perhaps in her late teens or early twenties; she was brushing the bare wooden floor. She wore a white embroidered dress that I loved for its country simplicity. I decided not to admire it in case I came over as patronising. In truth I was generally a bit out of my depth when amongst Antone's family, but I liked them. These were people who were at one with the world; easy with each other and easy with the tasks in hand. They had murders in their past and blood on their hands, yet nothing seemed to faze them. For all their crimes, I felt they had a purity at heart that I could never have. And I *always* want what I can't have.

'Can I ask your name?' I asked of the woman sweeping.

'Lisabetta.'

'You have a lovely smile Lisabetta.'

'Thank you. You are very pretty.'

I smiled for a bit. And tried to look pretty.

She had great teeth and perfect skin. I could hate her for that alone, but she was no threat, so I decided not to.

Lisabetta went off to the kitchen and returned with a big bowl, some wooden blocks and some old kitchen knives that had been sharpened so many times their cutting edges were undulated and delicate but deadly. They were the kind of knives you could run clean through a person's stomach and pin them to the wall behind.

'Would you like to cut some vegetables with me?' she asked. 'We need to chop them for a stew.'

'Lisabetta makes great food,' called Antone.

I put my phone away and I followed Lisabetta's cues. She knelt on the floor and made a work area for herself. There was some newspaper for the vegetable peelings to her left and a chopping board in front of her and a bowl to the right for us both to place the chopped vegetables.

'What do you like to cook?' she asked me.

'I don't cook,' I said.

'Then how do you eat?'

'Well it's not that I never cook,' I said. 'I don't know. I eat out I suppose, or go to my mother's house. Or my brother's house. Or eat cheese.'

'Your brother cooks?' she asked.

'Yes. He is a good cook,' I said.

'What does he do?'

'He works at the same insurance company as me,' I said.

'You both work,' she said. 'And your mother, does she work?'

'No. She is old.'

The onions were a bit fiddly to cut because they were tiny, but they didn't seem to make my eyes run which was good. Lisabetta saw me struggling and showed me her favoured trick that involved spearing the onion with the tip of a knife to trap it. She must have thought I was an idiot, or perhaps she thought that I was so gloriously urbane and sophisticated that I didn't know how to peel vegetables. It was kind of insulting and flattering at the same time, but she was so kind in her manner I could forgive her anything.

She decided to make conversation.

'So you work 9 to 5 every day,' she asked.

'Yes.'

'So how do you get your jobs done? The cleaning and the cooking?' she asked.

'I don't. Well, I do. I have to do them in the evening after work and on Saturdays and Sundays.'

'That's a long day,' she said.

'Yeah, but it's fun.'

'You like work?' she asked.

'Er, no,' I confessed. 'I've got a week off at the moment, so I can do what I like.'

'So you can get your jobs done?' she asked.

'No, I won't do my jobs,' I laughed.

We chopped for a bit.

'What do you do Lisabetta?' I asked.

'I do the cleaning and then I chop the food up for the family. I put it in the pot in the kitchen. I will show you!' she said. 'I will show you in a minute. The food then cooks all day and everyone can eat when they want but mostly we eat together in the evening. Often I bake or roast.'

'Great,' I said.

'I can get my jobs done in about two hours. I am usually finished by about 10 o'clock.'

'Then what do you do?' I asked.

'Sometimes I walk into the village, especially if I want something from the market. Sometimes I sit outside and read. I have a favourite walk down by the river. Then in the afternoons we all sit outside and we look at the view.'

'Who is we?'

'The family. Mum and Dad and brothers, cousins. I haven't got a sister. Have you got a sister?'

'No,' I said. 'I haven't got a sister.'

She brightened up, not that she was ever anything apart from positive, and she said, 'I can be your sister. If you marry Antone. We will be sisters.'

'Oh. I don't think there is anything like that going to happen. I am sorry.' I don't know why I apologised.

'I just thought,' she said. 'He has never brought a girlfriend here before. So I just thought. I am sorry if I have said the wrong thing.'

'You haven't said the wrong thing,' I said. I tried a bit of smiling and nodding to help the situation.

She gathered up the peelings.

'I need to get potatoes,' she said. 'Don't move.'

Soon we were peeling potatoes. It is not as though I haven't peeled potatoes before (honestly, I have done it before) but peeling potatoes with a stranger felt like an act of friendship.

'So why do you work?' she asked.

I shrugged. 'To earn money.'

Lisabetta nodded amicably.

'What do you do with your money?' she asked.

'I rent an apartment. I have a car...'

She nodded again.

'We have a car!' she said brightly.

'Sure.'

'You don't live with your brother?'

'No.'

'He has a car as well? Our family share a car. When we go to market or we go to the coast we can all fit in the car. Then we can talk. How do you talk if you have separate cars?'

'Well,' I replied. 'We can phone each other.'

'So you drive in your separate cars and you phone each other? I thought you worked together.'

'We do,' I replied. 'We work in the same building.'

'Well you could share a car. And you could share an apartment. Then it would be cheaper and you could talk.'

'Indeed.'

'I don't think I would like a job,' she said. 'My brothers have jobs, they help at the car garage but they also look after the chickens and the pigs, and they go hunting. Will you visit again with your boyfriend? He likes you, you know. And I like you. We could walk and we could sit and read and we could go to the market. You know, while the men do their thing.'

She had stopped.

'I've made you cry,' she said.

'No,' I replied. 'Okay a little. I don't know what's wrong with me.'

'I am so sorry,' she said. 'Did I say something wrong? I am such an idiot. I have said something wrong.'

I reached out and touched Lisabetta's wrist with the tips of my fingers.

'You have done nothing wrong,' I said. 'And you are not an idiot.'

'I don't know what to do,' she said. She was visibly distressed.

'I'll be fine. You are lovely Lisabetta. I guess I am having a bad time at the moment. You are very lovely. Maybe you're the first person to be nice to me.'

'I feel terrible,' she said. 'But please do come again on other days. And you are not going now?'

'You can show me your walk,' I said. 'I promise to stop crying.'

I swallowed and smiled.

I started peeling again.

'So you make a stew and it is for everyone?' I asked.

'Yes I am told I am a very good cook.'

Lisabetta got me some tissues and a fresh cup of coffee.

What with one thing and another, I hadn't been listening to Antone and his shadiest cousin and the whole reason I was at the house was to ascertain our next move.

'We don't know anyone we trust who can crush a car,' said Antone. 'There are already too many people involved in this.'

'Everyone will get paid,' said the shady cousin. 'They are good people. We can trust them.'

'Can you bury the car?' I asked.

There was more conferring.

'It seems to me,' said Antone. 'It seems to me that the problem is that we don't want more people to know what we are doing.'

My suggestion had been ignored.

'You could push the car off a cliff?' I said. 'Or the same cousin who helped us get the car off the mountainside, the cousin with the tow truck, could pull the car apart?'

They conferred again.

I reflected that on the various occasions I had met Antone's Shadiest Cousin, he had never been closer to me than about three metres. That was fine by me.

Lisabetta was cleaning up the chopping boards.

'Would you like to chop the meat? She asked earnestly. 'It's rabbit. Rabbit is...'

'Fiddly?' I offered in English. 'Delicat,' I offered in French.

'Fiddly,' she said. 'I like that word.'

'What about burning out the car?' I suggested.

'Burning out the car is the best,' said Lisabetta. Then to me she said, 'They pretend not to listen to us, but they do listen to us.'

We resolved as a group to burn out Dippy Sarah's car.

SIX

It is astonishing, but somehow Dippy Sarah's beaten up car was still drivable; it was like it had long since accepted its fate and resolved to keep going come what may. Or maybe it was a tribute to the ingenuity of the family's paramilitary car mechanic wing who no doubt had to bend bits of chassis and exhaust pipe to make it happen. The car had been towed in the first instance to a garage owned, inevitably, by a cousin or a nephew or an uncle. They had put a large sheet over it to hide it, and it became part of the furniture in no time.

When the car was first towed from the mountains they left the body in the back and pulled the car behind a tow truck. I am told it was the fastest of the options. The trouble was what then to do with the body. It had seemed to my eyes that the family had rallied round entirely effortlessly in the crisis but no doubt it just looked easy to an outsider; I am sure there were worries, discussions and upsets, but I was not aware of them. Jacob's body had been taken off to cold storage by one side of the family, and disposing of the car had somehow became our responsibility.

I got to the garage one night and the boys were busy checking out Sarah's original car.

'The engine turns!' announced Antone. 'The wheels work!'

'Always a plus when driving a car,' I replied. As usual I was ignored.

'There's a good spot in the hills where a lot of cars get taken and burnt. One of us will drive Sarah's car and one of us will drive another car to get away in.'

I have found that I get quite revved up at this stage of anything vaguely criminal. It feels like a hollow feeling in my stomach but also my feet tap rhythmically and my neck does a little jig. I have to be honest; I get a buzz from crime.

I volunteered to drive Sarah's car but I had no idea where we were going, so I closely followed the lights of Antone. We drove for about five miles on a major road and then left it unexpectedly to drive down a lane through the woods. It was barely wide enough for a car and it was bordered by boulders that were covered in green moss. After another careful mile we were at a natural hollow amongst the trees where the road sloped sharply down and away to one side.

Apparently the trick to burning out a car is to start with the engine and the inside of the car but not start with where the petrol tank is at the back; the petrol tank will most likely explode, but you want to first guarantee that the middle of the car was burnt of any DNA evidence, fingerprints, bits of body and the like. Once the petrol tank is on fire you can't go back and adjust the fire to make sure it reaches the passenger area, and if someone comes and puts the fire out then you want to feel the driver area has already been burnt out.

The other trick to burning out a car, I now know, is to not leave your handbag in the car.

Also, it would make sense to cover your face, because unexpectedly another car came down the lane and we had our faces bare.

I thought I could duck down to avoid being seen but there was nothing obvious to duck behind, so for whatever reason I reached for the hem of my dress and pulled it up over my face leaving my arse and knickers bare. It was nothing terrible and I suspect the locals driving around these woods didn't care what they saw going on and had seen worse, but the fact remains someone in a car got a nice look at my bottom caught in the headlights and that would have made them remember the incident. If it hadn't been for my bare arse, we would have just looked like some people standing outside a car. You learn a lot about a person when you commit crimes together and one thing I noticed about Antone was that he never tells me off or guides me. He sometimes ignores me though, which can often feel worse.

Antone seemed quite the expert in the matter of burning out cars and he got on with the nitty gritty of it. He opened the bonnet (which he called the hood because he seems to have learnt American English not English English) and poured petrol all over the engine. Then he closed the bonnet and poured petrol down over the front windscreen so that it poured into the vents. Then he opened the doors and threw some petrol on to the seats. He then had an aerosol can of something flammable and a match.

It was then that I remembered my handbag.

'Stop!' I shouted. 'No one move.'

I opened the car door again and held my breath and leant in and grabbed my bag from the foot well. It doesn't take much to get something smelling a bit of petrol, but my handbag full-on stank of it.

I went off to stand a distance away and Antone readied himself to set up his impromptu flame thrower.

'Stop!' I shouted again.

'What?'

'We should put the back seats up. The back seats are down where the body was kept. It will be a giveaway that this is Sarah's car if the seats are down.'

Antone considered this for a while.

'Okay,' he said.

He pulled his t shirt up over his nose and dived into the car and wrestled with the seats. It took a long time but he took the view that it was worth doing properly.

After he got out of the car he took all his clothes off. This involved a lot of fussing around getting his shoes off and back on again.

'What are you doing?' I asked.

'I have too much petrol on me. I could go up in flames,' he said.

I looked down at my own dress.

'Me too, coming to think of it,' I said. I wrestled with the concept for a while, then I wrestled with my dress for longer; trying to get it off without the petrol on it touching my hair was difficult.

So we threw our clothes into the car and Antone readied himself with the aerosol and the match. I held the matchbox and he lit the match on the side of it. The car needed no persuasion whatever to burst into flames.

'We will just check that the clothes and the seats all burnt,' he said. 'Then we just want to check we are not setting fire to the forest.'

'Then we go?'

'Then we run,' he laughed.

We drove home happy side by side. Antone with his body glistening, me in my knickers and bra.

Back at the house, Lisabetta was sitting outside on the veranda with an elderly man who was new to me. It was a bright night from a well-lit moon.

Lisabetta saw us arriving. She didn't ask why we were nearly naked. She stood up and went inside the house. About fifteen seconds later she came back out with a white cotton dress for me to wear. She hadn't brought anything for Antone. He just stood there wearing only his shoes and his underpants and made conversation. Lisabetta got back to reading her book by the porch light.

This family is the best.

Let the record show I looked hot in that dress.

Then there was a blaze of sirens from two police cars careering through the woods. They pulled up on the grass in front of the house. Two policemen jumped out from the second car and went round the back of the property; they had determinedly sombre faces that struck me were a contrivance but it was hard to tell. They had the look of people who hit other people and felt no remorse. Two more police got out of the first car and walked towards us. They had a 'we're fed up with your antics' look on their faces.

'Nobody leave the premises,' said the first one. The family looked nervous of him but were trying not to show it.

Antone threw a look at the older man on the veranda. It was a look that meant that something needed hiding or covering; something could be found if the police knew where to look. These police were a threat to us.

The little terrier of a police officer in front of us plainly hated the Lluberas family and had long since taken the view that he was going to get them for something and then everything, and he'd prefer sooner rather than later.

'Would you like to tell us where you have been for the last half hour?' he asked. His neck was twitching independent of his body. He was one of those men who did too much bodybuilding, so when he went to turn his head, his whole body moved with it.

'We have just been driving, officer,' replied Antone.

Antone looked subdued. In fairness to him, he was, like, standing there in his underpants; it was difficult to look authoritative.

The other policeman was eyeing me up in a very disconcerting way; it was like he knew he was angry with me, but hadn't yet worked out why.

So I smiled at him. I ran my tongue slowly across my upper lip. It made him look away at least.

'Where have you been driving?' asked the first officer.

'We took a cousin back home. She had been hanging out with us. I didn't want her out on her own. The woods can be treacherous,' said Antone.

'Don't make me laugh. You're standing there in your underpants. It's not exactly consistent with...' He trailed off. He started again. 'We have reason to believe you were burning out a car,' he said.

'No. We saw a car though,' said Antone. 'We passed by a burnt out car, didn't we?' He was looking at me.

'Who is she?' asked the policeman.

'*She* can be addressed directly,' I said. 'My name is Emily.'

'Have you got any ID?'

'I have. Shall I get it from my bag?'

The policeman didn't answer me; he addressed Lisabetta instead. 'I don't know what you're smirking about. You are on parole aren't you?'

Lisabetta nodded and shrank.

'Look officer,' I said. 'If you actually had something on us you would have come out with it by now.'

'Oh we have plenty on this family,' he said. 'The only issue is where to begin? Why hasn't he got any clothes on?' This last was to no one in particular.

It all continued like this for a while. I didn't like the way the police were reluctant to leave. They knew that if they ruffled everything enough they would find something.

The two police who had gone to the back of the house came through the front door; they must have let themselves in through the kitchen. One of them fixed eyes with the lead policeman and raised his eyebrows happily. Had he found something?

'I'm seeing you on Monday,' the policeman said to Antone. 'Perhaps we should discuss that.'

I never plucked up the courage to ask Antone what the policeman meant, but a few days later I did ask him why Lisabetta was on parole.

'A misunderstanding,' he replied.

I turned to one of the policemen who had emerged from the house; I picked the one who looked least aggressive. I went to speak, but one of the others said, 'Whose car is that?'

We turned to look at a car parked some way away under a tree. It was Jacob's car. We now realised that the policeman who had gone through the house was holding some car keys. He dangled them in a knowing fashion.

'Okay well we are going to round you all up,' he said.

'You're arresting us?' asked Antone.

I don't remember any more, because without warning my legs gave way. I collapsed.

Part Three

THE WORLD ACCORDING TO PETE

ONE

I spent an entire day jumping every time my phone rang, and panicking every time someone walked through the office door. It seemed inevitable to me that if Sarah had been arrested then so would I. But when the first day passed and then another I realised that I wasn't just being paranoid, I was being selfish; we hadn't done anything yet to help Sarah.

At length, we found Sarah a lawyer and he took a lengthy statement from me, but when I subsequently phoned for updates, I was rebuffed. And when I tried to ring the police about the case I was rebuffed. I had somehow become a pariah amongst the professional classes. So much so, it was hard to know what to do to help.

The structure of justice itself was interesting in that according to the French system there were two prosecutors involved, both part of the judiciary; the first one guides the police in their investigation, and then when the evidence has been amassed, it is turned over to a second prosecutor who takes it to court. Bastia only has a population of about 40,000 and so there are only a couple of prosecutors for this level of offence. As a result, I was to find when trying to help Sarah that I was forced to deal with the same few faces again and again. If any of them got annoyed by me, I was sunk in terms of communication.

One Saturday morning there was a knock on my door and Inspector Fortini was standing there.

'Are you arresting me?' I asked.

'No,' he answered. He then didn't say any more.

'So what can I do for you?' I asked.

'We'd like you to not leave the island,' he said.

'I wasn't intending to.'

'To that end, we would like you to voluntarily surrender your passport to us.'

'Am I a suspect for something?' I asked.

'We feel we may need to interview you with short notice,' he replied.

And that was that. I wasn't being interviewed, I wasn't being arrested, but they did feel the need to stop me travelling. It struck me as very odd. But then odd things do happen.

I took to visiting Sarah in prison.

Just visiting a prison makes you feel vulnerable. It's like walking through customs at the airport; no matter how innocent you are, you feel you have done something wrong, and the staff know exactly what that 'something' is, even if you don't.

It is not as though they design a prison to look inviting. If an architect is awarded the contract to design a prison, presumably their next thought is 'How can I make it look intimidating?' They are never going to win any awards at the World Architects Awards for designing it, so they might as well indulge their darker side instead.

You can see Bastia prison from the railway tracks as you go south along the coast. It has its own railway platform that is imaginatively called 'Prison' and the train won't stop there unless you ring the bell. Or rather you used to have to ring the bell. The trains recently got state of the art rolling stock, but they have used the same recorded announcement in the carriages from the old rolling stock, so the intercom announces that to stop at 'next stop prison' you have to ring the bell. But there is no bell on the modern trains; you have to ask the guard instead. First you have to find the guard, and then you need to ask the guard to stop at the prison. That way the guard can judge you; look you up and down, purse his lips as if to say 'Yeah I can see you might want the prison.'

It is best to visit the prison by car.

My visits to see Sarah tended to a format as follows:

Me: How's it going Sarah? Can I get you anything?

Sarah: Food. It's like, well, they only give me French food. I can't eat the food.

Me: French food, like snails in garlic or something?

Sarah: (giving my comment the disdain it deserved, given that she was the one in prison) No. It's like cous cous.

Me: That's not French.

Sarah: Well it's certainly not English.

Me: But you go out and about and eat different cuisines, surely?

Sarah: Yes.

Me: So you are used to different foods.

Sarah: Yes.

Me: Do you want, like fish and chips or something?

Sarah: (considers this) No. I don't like fish and chips.

Me: I'm not sure I can bring in food for you.

Sarah: Really?

Me: I'll ask. But more important, how is your legal preparation going?

Sarah: Oh that.

Me: Oh that? You could, like go to jail forever. What is your defence?

Sarah: I keep telling you. Jacob is alive. I will be okay.

Me: You do keep telling me that, but you offer no proof.

Sarah: I just know it.

Me: How?

Sarah: I just know it in my heart. There was something off about the whole thing.

Me: Off?

Sarah: Jacob wouldn't kill himself. And there was no one else there. And I didn't do it. So he's alive.

Me: If he's alive, it would be useful if he would show his face.

Sarah: Whatever. And the mazzere. That was life changing wasn't it? It's completely opened my eyes.

Me: Sarah, you need to focus on how to defend yourself against the charge of murder.

Sarah: That's what the lawyer lady keeps saying.

Me: Perhaps she has a point.

Sarah: What point?

With each visit I would raise the subject of Jacob.

Me: I want to pin down if you have any specific concrete reason to believe Jacob is not dead; something your defence could work on.

Sarah: Yes. The timing was wrong. I was in the kitchen. How long was I in the kitchen? Not long. When I first arrived we walked through the house and it was empty. Where did the gun come from? He would have had to come past me to get the gun. And where would he get the gun from? There was nowhere.

Me: I can see how that shows it wasn't suicide. But it could have been murder. After all, there was definitely a gun.

Sarah: Who did the murder? It wasn't me.

Me: Someone else must have been in the lodge.

Sarah: There was no one else in the lodge. Was someone lying under the bed with a gun for hours waiting for the off-chance that Jacob would bounce on the bed? Did Jacob open the window to his own killer? How did the killer get there? There was no car. There are three ways Jacob could have died. A person broke in and killed him. I killed him. Or he killed himself. I didn't kill him. The most likely is that he killed himself. Have you seen a picture of him? He didn't kill himself. And I feel it here (she pointed to her heart) he isn't dead. Does it feel right to you? It doesn't feel right. The flooring here is really cold.

Me: The flooring is really cold?

Sarah: The flooring is made of something really solid like concrete and it is really cold.

Me: Sarah, you're not making any sense.

Sarah: (considering this) Yes I am. Who opened the window in the bedroom?

Me: Jacob did.

Sarah: To let in a murderer?

Me: No he just opened it anyway. It had to be him.

Over the weeks I was treated to plenty of other grievances apart from the food and the material used for the floors.

There was the water fountain:

'I know they are supposed to be hygienic, but the jet is only a dribble and so people are sucking on the spout to get the water out, so I think it is spreading germs. I tried cleaning it, but I got told off.'

The library:

'Most of the books are in French.'

The view from her window:

'A wall. A grey wall at that. I saw a bird go by once. That's my excitement to last me a whole day. A bird going past my window.'

A guard:

'She has one fat thigh, where she holds all her keys on her right hip. The keys are so heavy it has made her right thigh bigger. She should swap sides with the keys; left one day and right the next. To even up her thighs.'

'It would be muscle, not fat,' I said. 'If it's the exercise of lugging a big bunch of keys.'

Sarah looked angry. 'How would you know?' Then she said, 'Look. I know what I've seen.'

'Have you told the guard your views on her thighs?'

'No. I will. I'll do that.'

'Don't.'

'If she could stop wearing tight trousers that would be a help,' she said.

'How would that help?'

'Then I wouldn't have to see the size of her thighs.'

One day she ruminated about Jacob as a person. She explained, 'You see, I think of what he looked like. I think of Jacob. His face. His kindness. His hair. The way he would stroke my face with his hand. There is no way he would kill himself. He was always full of life. Like a performer. I was late once for a meet-up. And I saw him on a stool by the bar and he had a cup of coffee and when he heard the door creak as it opened he turned and I can picture his face and he focussed on me and when he realised it was me, his face beamed. Now when you are in love like that you don't kill yourself. It's not as though I had dumped him. Would I dump him? I wouldn't dump him.'

Unlike Sarah, I was favouring the theory that someone else had been present at the lodge that night. Someone had hidden out, perhaps in the house, or maybe they had approached the house stealthily. They had shot Jacob and hopped out the window. This had to be the front runner explanation.

I explained this to Sarah but she replied, 'Just look at a picture of him. Look long and hard at his face. You tell me whether he looked like an unhappy person.' I think she was going a bit crazy. Even more crazy.

When I didn't respond, she tapped the table with her finger, rat-tat-tat. 'I am simply asking you. Look at a photo of him. Go into my flat and find my phone.'

'Your phone is in your flat?'

'I think so. I am not sure in truth. The police might have it. I was arrested so fast. I mean you don't expect to be arrested. I was arrested so fast that I haven't seen my phone since. Go and find my phone. I will give you the pin number. Look on my phone at photos of Jacob.'

I didn't do any of those things, not least because I didn't know how to get into her flat, but largely because I couldn't see the point.

I was quietly making inquiries about the case, though. I thought I might unearth something to help Sarah but also, indeed, me if the police started taking an interest.

'Sarah-Jayne!' I announced to my colleagues one morning; it was largely to Niculaiu, but Jean-Marie and the office manager Benedettu were also present. It was Benedettu who had introduced Sarah to Jacob but I hardly knew him to talk to so I hadn't followed that up. He seemed very friendly with Jean-Marie though.

'Sarah-Jayne!' I said louder, when everyone had ignored me.

'The girl from upstairs who was arrested?' asked Jean-Marie. He knew perfectly well about whom I was talking. Benedettu skulked off straight away.

'What do we know of the man who died?' I asked.

'Jacob Lluberas?' asked Niculaiu.

'Jacob Lluberas?' I confirmed. 'I have been doing what I can, but I have no official status in the case, so the police are not sharing evidence with me and, basically I am at a bit of dead end. Where did he live? Who knows him? Who can I talk to about him?'

Niculaiu was looking pretty animated for a corpse. 'Well we know he comes from one of the villages in the south. Fozzano, or near there. It is proper old school down there; independence from France, gun toting farmers, granite castles, prehistoric stone effigies; insult another family's dog and the feud will last a thousand years; you know the score,' he said. 'I've made a few notes.'

'You've made a few notes?' I asked.

'You think I sit here working every day?' he laughed. 'I've got to do something with my time. We can't just sleep.'

I walked around to Niculaiu's desk so that we could both see his screen. He had made a file. We both started whispering out of instinct.

'The Fozzano area is a long way from here. I wonder what Jacob was doing up here in Bastia.'

'Have you got a picture of Jacob?' I asked.

He tapped a little at the computer.

There were four photos of him. One was an official style photo, such as you would have in your passport, and a second was him socialising in a group. There were also two pictures of Jacob from Sarah's Facebook and in them he looked older and more wizened than the passport style photo. I found myself studying one of the four photos in particular. It was of a group of friends, all male and all looking pretty similar. They were handsome lads, who had a 'group' look; their dark hair was tousled but their beards were well groomed. They all looked physically fit, and were ruffled from the sea and the wind; their legs sandy from a day on the beach. Jacob was seemingly oblivious to a woman in a bikini who was just behind them; he was just smiling. It was such a kind smile that I could see why Sarah thought of him as a good man, and why he would never kill himself.

'In theory, there is a fifth photo,' said Niculaiu. 'It is a riot and he was tagged as being in the photo but I can't see which one he is.'

'What are they rioting about?' I asked. 'The burqa ban on the beach? A football riot? A riot against the French?'

'One of those,' shrugged Niculaiu. 'For us Corsicans, any excuse to riot is excuse enough. We pride ourselves on our rioting. We once rioted because they tried to ban rioting.'

I searched Niculaiu's eyes for signs that he was joking. It was hard to tell with Niculaiu.

'And Sarah mentioned that there was someone in the office who introduced her to Jacob. Do you know who that is?' I knew the answer to that, but I was interested in how much my colleagues were actually helping me.

Jean-Marie thought for a while. 'I will ask around,' he said at length.

'Oh and then there's the insurance,' said Niculaiu.

'He had insurance with us?'

'No, he didn't, but I cast my net a bit wider to databases of insurance companies where we have a working relationship and I got a hit quite quickly. He has a life assurance policy with... I forget the firm; Assurance de Province perhaps. I'll find it in a second. Do you want to see his policy?'

'Yes please,' I said. 'But, if Sarah didn't kill Jacob then who did? How can we find out more about Jacob? Did people have grievances against him? Who can we ask?'

'I don't know,' replied Niculaiu. 'The police?'

A little time later, I put in a call to Inspector Fortini.

I was surprised to be put straight through because he hadn't previously returned my calls.

'Good day Mr De'Ath,' he began.

'I thought I would call because I might have something of interest you.'

There was silence on the other end of the phone – of course there was – what else did I expect from the Taciturn One?

'Go on,' he said at last.

'Okay,' I said. 'I don't know if this is important but Jacob Lluberas was insured. I went through the database and he had some standard style life assurance with a company that is affiliated with us. It was about 40,000 Euros.'

Another long pause.

'Who is the beneficiary?' asked the inspector at last.

'No-one is named, so it would go to his estate and his family would get the money I guess,' I said. 'But 40,000 is hardly enough to murder for.'

'I have known people to murder for a cigarette,' said the inspector.

'Well Corsican's do take their smoking seriously,' I joked.

'But your colleague Sarah-Jayne Hoskins. She is not a beneficiary,' he said.

'No. And neither am I,' I said. 'This is a good thing. We had nothing to gain by his death.'

There was a silence again.

I felt I had already lost my fragile momentum with him.

'Is everything okay?' I asked.

'Yes of course,' he said. Perhaps he was writing things down. 'Can you send me the name of the insurance company he had the policy with?'

'Will do. Also I am going to check other databases,' I said. 'He may have more than one life insurance policy.

'How old was the policy, roughly?' he asked.

'About six years. I think it related to a loan.'

Another silence.

'Um,' I said.

I hated the silences. I gave up hoping he would fill them. I had only rung him about the insurance as a way to get him talking about the case. I might have known the ruse would fail.

'We both came in and told you about the events that Friday night,' I tried. 'It was both Sarah and I, and then the body went missing and the car returned. Um...'

'You are asking why we arrested your friend and not you?' he asked.

'No, not that,' I said. Yes that. Exactly that.

There was a pause on the line that the inspector refused to fill.

'Well okay, now you mention it. Why Sarah, not me?' I cracked.

'She said she was present when he died. Neither of you said that you yourself were there.'

'Yes, but you could do me for preventing a burial,' I said. What was wrong with me? Just move the subject on, don't give him bright ideas about how to arrest me.

'We've got evidence against your friend. Proper evidence. We haven't really got evidence against you.'

'Evidence?'

'Evidence has come up, yes.'

Why did he keep saying she was my friend? I barely knew her.

'Can you tell me what this evidence is?' I asked.

'No,' he replied. 'But we did go back to the lodge that was the crime scene and we had a proper forensic team look at it.'

'Yes, you said.'

Another silence.

'So I have been helpful telling you this,' he concluded.

Had he?

I wondered what they had found at the lodge with a second visit.

'And you will tell me if you find more life assurance?' he asked. 'That would be helpful to me in return.'

'I will inspector.'

The next silence was long enough for me to believe that the conversation might be over.

'Can I ask?' I ventured, down what sounded like a dead line. 'Can I asked if any people had a grievance against Jacob Lluberas? If there were any people with a grievance against him?'

The phone really did sound profoundly dead but I was determined not to check verbally if he was still there.

After an eternity Inspector Fortini said, 'We know of no grievance against Jacob Lluberas.'

That man needs lessons in being a human.

I let the phone remain silent for a full twenty seconds before I rang off.

That man should not be allowed to make phone calls.

A day later and I was having an excellent meal in the harbour. Of course I was. There is a great bar cum restaurant on the north side overlooking the boats which not only does cracking wine, but also has a strong range of eats. If you are not quite sure what you want then they do a long thin slate with a little example of everything. A little burger in a tiny bun, a little square of onion tart, little bowls of bread, of olives, a little china bowl of interesting wild mushrooms. It is... gorgeous. Happy days.

Now I would like to stress at this stage exactly how much I may or may not have drunk with my meal, and I would like to mention the quality of the evening light and stress at length how tired I was.

I was very, very, tired.

I was sitting in the bar restaurant and, as requested by Sarah, I was gazing yet again at the printed picture of Jacob I had taken to carrying around. I was trying to imagine what could possibly have happened that could explain the murder or suicide, and I was indeed a bit drunk. I had been drinking gin. The trouble is at times like this I actually think gin is my friend. Well okay, I know gin just pretends to be my friend. Then she turns on me in the night. Then two weeks later she sidles up to me like nothing happened that other time wanting to be my friend again. But sometimes friends are like that. In my anthropomorphic world of alcohol, incidentally, gin speaks with an eastern European accent, Pinot Grigio is a perky Italian lothario which is not as good looking as he thinks, Sauvignon Blanc is a suave French James Bond-style figure, and they all live at Jacob's Creek.

Okay, so to recap, there is evidence I do spend too much time drinking on my own and get lost in my own reverie, and I had been drinking that particular night. Whatever the explanation, I was aware of the lights from the other bars and restaurants lighting up the harbour and reflecting in the water and I was contemplating the stagger home and wondering what temperature it was outside, when I saw him.

Jacob walked past the window.

TWO

Now, I am not 100% trusting of my brain's facial recognition software. I have on occasion addressed the wrong twin socially, or failed to take into account how a lad might have changed when getting older. As a result of the latter I once mistook a lad for his own father and asked him how his girlfriend was, when he was married at the time, and then caused a divorce a little down the line because the son had then reported the story back to his mum who confronted the father. In mitigation, the lad had grown a beard that was obscuring his face - and this might be relevant - I was fully refreshed at the time.

So yes, I have made my share of mistakes when identifying people over the years. But sometimes you just know when you have seen a person.

I had seen Jacob and he was alive.

I ran into the street and looked left to where he had walked and I saw no one. It was more than possible that in the time it took me to react and get out of my seat, he had walked round the corner towards the main harbour area, so I ran - yes ran – after him, albeit with my stomach bouncing and lurching out of sync with my varicosed legs.

When I got round the corner, I still couldn't see him. There are a couple of bars on that stretch of the road overlooking the sea, so he could have gone into one of those. Or there are some alleyways which take you back to the old town square, but if he was going that way then surely he would have cut into the system of alleys in the first place before walking past where I was sitting? So I felt he had either gone into one of the bars round there or possibly pressed ahead to the new harbour and was going much faster than I thought. The other train of thought is that he somehow saw me and had darted back on himself into the alleys to hide, but I didn't see any evidence that he had looked my way at all, and would he really be wary of me? Why would he even know who I was?

I wandered back to my restaurant table and gave all this a nice think. If Jacob was indeed alive and Sarah's car had indeed been returned then at least Sarah is off the hook for a murder, but only if we could find Jacob and show him off to the police. And how exactly is that conversation going to go? 'I hear you thought I was dead. Well surprise!' Corsica is not a huge island and the 'murder' had been reported extensively. It would have been the talk of every bar and workplace in the land. And none of this explains who the dead body was in the back of the car that I got up close and personal with.

The longer I sat at the restaurant table, and the more I refreshed myself with gin, the less sure I was that I had seen Jacob. I reasoned with myself that I couldn't have seen him. It was hardly broad daylight out there. And yet, I felt in my heart that I knew what I saw.

I resolved that my next move would be to visit Jacob's family and find out what they knew. Perhaps they could even put me in touch with him. Imagine that; I have never talked to the dead before.

I resolved to go and visit Jacob's mother.

It was an experience.

Before going, I read Jacob's life assurance documents that he had with our affiliate company a few times – I was hoping some titbit would jump out at me that I hadn't noticed before. There was a handwritten application form that had the usual questions about health, and being a young person there was nothing to report apart from mild asthma as a child and an appendix that was removed in 2005. I found myself looking at his handwriting and his signature, but there was little I could glean except that the handwriting was untidy but better than many that I come across on insurance forms. Other details included that I discovered he came from Sartina, not Fozzano, and I wondered if I had been deliberately misled by my colleagues about that, but if so, why?

Sartina is a fine example of an old Corsican town.

The town itself is proudly grey: it rises up from the maquis that surrounds it with towers of vertiginous granite fused to the mountain as if they are one and the same. In the internal alleyways there are antiquated Paris-style street lamps and some tourist cafes that ease the portentous nature of the buildings that loom over you, but it is easy to imagine the years when vendettas between families lasted centuries and meant that if you walked the streets after dark, you walked with a knife and a purpose scurrying to get to the next safe doorway.

At first I couldn't find anyone in the town to even talk to. I walked along the cobbles and had the feeling that unseen people were watching me from the windows above. I had an address for Jacob's mother but I didn't know where I was going. I figured I would ask in a bar or restaurant to get my bearings.

At last I found a man setting up a few café tables.

'We're closed,' he said in English.

Did he know I was English, or is it the best bet with tourists?

'Sorry, I said. 'I wonder if you can help me. I am looking for this address.'

He was a round man with an affable face. He got his reading glasses from his top pocket and studied the piece of paper I was holding. I was expecting him to be unhelpful, but instead he said, 'I will take you.'

He left his restaurant without locking it, and walked in a busy manner across the street and off toward a grim block of a house that seemed to be half building, half monolith. The shape of the house followed the shape of the natural granite and was built upwards and sideways in the manner of a threat. Instead of proper windows, there were perches high up to allow the residents to pour boiling liquids over invading armies or – I half suspected – insurance claims adjusters.

The man seemed to be leading me towards a solid wall but as we approached, the wall revealed a kink and then a low beam which we both had to duck to get under.

'These were originally secret walkways, so that if the town was under siege you could escape in the night and get supplies or attack invaders,' explained the restaurateur. 'Now we use them to escape the tourists.' He chuckled at his own joke.

We were now seemingly within the mountain itself, in a cold stone tunnel that was unlit apart from a semi-circle of light in the far distance. The ground was a series of steps that were each two paces in length and which themselves sloped down; these were largely hewn from the rock, but some of it was cobbled. There was an occasional rusted metal rail to hold on to, but between the lack of light and the unevenness of the steps it was all wilfully dangerous.

At the darkest part, midway between entrance and exit, my guide stopped walking.

'And now I will rob you,' he said.

'What?'

'Will you relax,' he said. 'Where is your English sense of humour?'

This 'English sense of humour' concept gets used against the English far too often.

He pointed to an unlit side tunnel and we walked up a spiral of steps and back into the light.

He knocked on the first door we came to.

'There you go,' he said.

I thanked him, and he was turning to leave when the door opened and a well-dressed woman in her sixties appeared.

'This is a man from an insurance company,' he said.

How on earth could he have known that?

'Well!' she said, looking me up and down. 'Come in!'

Mrs Lluberas ushered me in through the house and we were soon sitting in a well-appointed kitchen with a stunning view over the valley. She had the air of a woman who had never asked a question in her life; instead she just offered a series of assertions. This was mitigated, however, by a ready willingness to smile.

'You will have tea.' she announced. She had a box of Lipton Yellow label tea bags in her hand and two mugs in the other. 'English tea is the best,' she explained.

'Thank you, yes,' I replied.

She had one of those taps that gives you boiling water instantly. I can never decide whether they are a gadget that will seem very dated in a few years' time - like Laser Discs and pagers - or whether I want one. Probably both.

'Well this is mysterious,' she said. 'There is little I can do to help a man from an insurance company.'

'It is a very odd and delicate matter,' I began. 'We had a report of the death of your son Jacob and he has an insurance policy with us.'

'Okay,' she said.

'But we have no death certificate,' I said. In truth I didn't know how to approach the subject; I was just fishing for information.

Mrs Lluberas laughed uproariously. She had a rich round laugh that enveloped the air.

'And could you tell me if Jacob had any enemies? If anyone had any grievances against him?'

'No one has any grievances against my son,' she said.

'No one at all?'

'I will save you some bother, Mr De'Ath,' she said.

'I didn't tell you my name,' I said.

'I can read newspapers,' she said. 'I have the internet, like everyone else.' Her hand swept around the kitchen to point out invisible newspapers and the Wi-Fi in the air.

'My son is not dead,' she said. 'If he died we would have contacted you about his insurance. He is not dead.'

'Okay,' I said.

'And no one has made a claim on his policy, have they? They have not made a claim upon his policy because he is not dead. You need to tell me why you are really here.'

'A woman has been arrested for his murder,' I protested.

'Oh that!'

She studied my face for a while and said, 'I tell you what, I will phone him. It will put your mind at ease!'

I tried smiling a wide smile to match hers.

'My colleague in prison accused of his murder,' I said. 'So if I could speak to your son. In fact, if I could meet him, it would solve a lot of problems.'

Mrs Lluberas got her mobile phone from a china bowl on the kitchen counter and played with the screen.

She then hunted around for her reading specs, and with them perched low on her nose, she played with the phone some more. She held the phone to her ear for a long time, then looked at the screen. It was a little dramatic for my taste, but what do I know? I've never had to pretend to ring my son who is dead; I don't know what precise Gallic gestures it would involve.

'I'll try again,' she said.

She tried again.

She shrugged again.

'I can't get through. So there it is,' she said.

'Where is he?' I asked.

Sometimes when the French are thinking, they make a sound that is a kind of 'Bahhn' noise; it is mostly Bah with only a hint of n at the end.

'Bahhn,' she said. 'He's working.'

'Can I have his number?' I asked.

She thought about this.

'If he wanted you to have his number, it would be on his policy application,' she said. 'If you are who you say you are, then you would have his number.'

She was sharper than before. She was implying the conversation was at an end.

I persevered. 'Where is he exactly now?' I asked.

'He is working away,' she said. 'I am not my son's keeper.'

Somehow, I had fallen out with her. I had only been there a few minutes and I thought my questions were reasonable enough. 'Could you please tell him that he needs to contact the authorities in Bastia, because there is a woman in prison charged with his murder,' I said.

'I will be sure to do that,' she said.

She walked me to the door.

I hadn't had my cup of tea.

As I stood in the street, I imagined her pouring my cup of tea away. I imagined her turning her head to look out the window at the view. I imagined her pursing her lips and making another phone call. But who would that be to?

I walked along the cobbled streets and the echoes of my steps seemed to fade to become silent. I found myself dwelling on this; it struck me as odd. I think perhaps that on the first part of my walk the alleys were tighter and more resonant and then, particularly after I was out of the tunnel, the alleys were wider. But then I noticed another oddity. The sun was strong now and I had a sharp shadow. But my shadow didn't seem to quite keep up with me. It was like it was on a time delay. I would move, and my shadow on the cobbles was a little delayed at moving. I stopped and I decided to do an experiment. I opened my briefcase and found a clean piece of paper. I scrunched it up into a ball. I threw the ball forwards through the air at shoulder height.

The ball of paper went forward through the air.

And its shadow was slow to catch up.

It was on a half second delay.

Okay. The sun, the stress, the everything, was getting to me. I had seen corpses walk, and mothers try to ring their dead sons. I went to pick up the litter I had created, then walked on to source some restorative lunch and some coffee. Perhaps the whole thing was just low blood sugar. I concluded as a result that a restful afternoon was in order, and a restorative nap at home.

THREE

I have friends in mediocre places and when dealing with insurance issues that involve the police I usually deal with a particular inspector called Luc Cadin.

I decided to give him a call.

'Peter! How is it going?' He sounded pleased to hear from me, so I obviously wasn't social poison with every last person on the island.

'I am wondering about a case and I wondered if you could help me?' I tried.

'Your colleague Sarah-Jayne Hoskins?' he asked. 'You know I must not talk on that subject. Also it is not my case.' Yes, but this is gossipy island where everyone knows everything?

'I never said it was about Sarah-Jayne,' I tried. Of course it was about Sarah.

There was an awkward pause.

'In any case,' he said. 'Let's meet up for a drink. Just two friends. I'll meet with you at the place we often drink together? Eighteen hundred hours?'

'Perfect,' I replied.

Brilliant. That conversation was great in every sense.

Luc knew my phone could easily be tapped – standard procedure in France during an investigation - and so he wanted it to sound clear to anyone who might be listening that he wasn't going to help me at all. But on the other hand, Luc and I were not in fact friends – we were at best acquaintances - we had had a total of one drink together out of hours. So when he said 'the place we often drink together' he was laying down the concept that it was in fact natural for us to meet up for a drink , and that meant not just that he thought people might be listening to our call, but also that he was willing to help me. What wasn't clear, was why.

At six o'clock, I was at an outside table at a large café overlooking a main road. It's near to my house and a good place to meet because there was the constant noise of traffic and it would be difficult to overhear what was said.

Luc was punctual. What a fine young man.

We ordered a simple beer each and got down to the point.

A man walked towards the café and sat down at the next table. He had evidently been walking a little behind Luc and could easily have been following him. He was wearing an old fashioned mac and looked like a detective of some sort. I was very alert to new ways to feed my paranoias, so it all probably meant nothing, but I felt as though he was listening to us.

'You want to discuss Sarah-Jayne Hoskins, your colleague?' asked Luc in the lowest voice he could get away with that sounded nonchalant.

'Yes.'

He waited.

'There is no body,' I said. 'The car has re-appeared. The family of the dead person say he isn't dead. Why has she been arrested?'

He nodded.

Luc was a jovial man who liked to list.

'A, we have found some camera footage of Sarah-Jayne Hoskins's car and the images show what is probably a corpse in the back. B, the bed in the hunting lodge. When we lifted the mattress, the frame of the bed was broken. There was gunshot in the wood of the bed and some flesh material. Human flesh. C, the DNA match. The DNA on the phone we found at the lodge is the same thing as the DNA we have from his house and the DNA from the wood of the bed under the mattress. We think someone had changed the mattress completely. It was a new mattress and it was without DNA. Have you ever heard of a mattress with no DNA? Not the DNA of a bed bug even? So that's four things.'

'So to be clear,' I said. 'You have got DNA of Jacob Lluberas from his house? And it matches the phone we found and the DNA you found from some flesh in the bed?'

'Correct,' said the smiling inspector.

'Well that blows a few theories of mine.'

I had a think about the mattress. When we were at the lodge with Inspector Fortini we had pulled the mattress up a little way, but we hadn't really inspected the frame of the bed underneath. To look at the bed frame where the head would have been shot, we would have had to remove the entire mattress. It was much further up than we looked.

'Oh and there is another thing,' said Inspector Cadin.

'So five things,' I said.

'Five things,' he nodded. 'E, there was an incident called in to us that night. Someone heard a noise and telephoned the police.'

'Ah, yes.'

'They heard a gun at the lodge. A policeman went to the lodge and looked but there was nothing there. The lodge was locked and there were no lights. He knocked on the door.'

'He didn't go in the house?'

'No, it was locked,' he replied. 'There was a car there. He felt the front of the car to see if it was warm. It was cold.'

'Whose car was it?'

'It was the car of the missing man. Jacob.'

'Was he a policeman from Bastia?' I asked.

'No. Local police,' he replied.

We both did a bit of drinking and thinking.

'Jacob lived with his mother?' I asked at last.

'Yes,' he said. 'From time to time. Not always. But that was the address he gave when one has asked.'

'I visited her,' I said.

'Yes we know. Could you not visit her, please?'

'Is there a reason I cannot go and see her?'

'You are a possible suspect,' he said. He laughed loudly. 'So no, you must not see her. You yourself are not far from being arrested!'

'So to repeat,' I said. 'There is DNA from the murder scene bed and it is the same as Jacob's DNA from his mother's house. So we are sure he is dead.'

'Yes. But also we have the informers. We have information that he is dead.'

'Do we know of any grievances that anyone had against him?' I asked. 'Do we know who else might want to kill him?'

The inspector shrugged. 'If there were the grievances, there are no people who will tell us. They will be secrets. This is a family that do not talk to the police. But in the mountains there are lots of vendettas.'

For whatever reason, the inspector and I looked the same direction at the same time to the man at the table next to us.

'Do you know him?' I asked.

'I don't believe so,' he replied. But the inspector did something with his eyes implying we should not speak for a while; it was like a friendly glare from his eyes to mine, but I could have misinterpreted it. He spoke generally for a while. When a particularly noisy lorry lumbered up the hill Inspector Cadin spoke again. He had another list.

'Let me list the elements that are most important that you might want to consider. A is for Corsica: it has the mountains in the middle. Things that pass on one side are difficult to see on the other side. B is for family: I imagine it is the same thing in your country; there are some families who are no good and simply we don't trust them. C is for DNA. I think the DNA will prove the key.'

I wasn't quite sure what he was getting at, but he was clearly trying to steer me to something. I reflected idly that when people make lists it changes information through the way it is presented. It could make something appear important just by making it onto the list in the first place, and something else seem less important by not being on the list.

'One thing I must say,' he continued. 'Is that the mother of Jacob; she reported that he was missing.'

'What?' I asked. 'When?'

'On the first day. She reported that her son had not come back home. She filed a report.'

'And?'

'And she later retracted it. She said he returned home,' he said.

'When?'

'I do not know,' he said.

Again, the inspector pointed with his eyes to the man at the next table. He was going to speak but then he shrugged.

When the traffic was noisier again I said, 'If the mother says she has seen her son then there cannot be a murder. Certainly the defence would call her as a witness. It would help Sarah's case.'

'But we know he is dead from the DNA,' said Luc. 'Anyway, you should not worry. Inspector Fortini is in charge and he has taken the point of view that your story fits the facts, but Miss Hoskins story does not fit the facts. So you should be okay.'

I had refrained from asking about my own situation, but I was glad Luc had sought to reassure me. Another question did occur to me however. 'Do you mind me asking why you are being to helpful? I know we have worked together on some insurance investigations, but to be frank, I don't feel you owe me one.'

'Well that is simple,' beamed the inspector. 'I do not trust the families involved. Things are never what they seem, and now that your sister has been arrested, I am worried for her. For you. Your family.'

'My sister? Emily? Has been arrested?'

Inspector Cadin looked alarmed that I didn't know.

'What has she been arrested for?' I asked.

'Something to do with stealing cars,' he replied.

'Stealing cars? Seriously? Where?'

'Ajaccio, I think. I'm not sure.'

'Why would she steal cars? What else do you know?'

Because this was all news to me, Luc suddenly felt he had said too much; he clammed up.

He waved his hands as if he was now talking generally instead. 'Well anyway, my thinking is,' he said. 'Now that the police are taking an interest in the stealing of the cars, well... fin de souci.'

The noise of a lorry had made it difficult to hear Luc well, so in fact I had assumed he said 'Fin de souci' – end of worry – but he might have said something else.

Either way, my mind was too busy racing about Emily for me to listen properly.

FOUR

I spent a furious evening ringing around trying to find out about Emily. The police station at Ajaccio were unwilling, or unable to tell me anything, so I tried a few other police stations on spec. I drew a blank everywhere I rang.

In the morning I tried a different tactic. I rang the local police station in Bastia and reported Emily as a missing person. I knew she had a week off work, and I hadn't seen her for about ten days in total; she wasn't answering her phone, so I had just about enough to justify registering her as a missing person. I hoped it would give me a bit more clout when I rang the police in Ajaccio. It didn't.

I tried ringing Luc Cadin to see if he had any more information about Emily that might help but I couldn't get through to him. I left a few messages, but he didn't reply.

I had a vague idea Emily was dating someone, but I hadn't knowingly met him. It's not as though she would bring a new man home for tea to show the family. If Emily was dating then I would tend to find out by chance when socialising. It's not that Emily and I weren't close, it's just that we didn't give each other a constant blow by blow of our lives.

And Emily being arrested could not have come at a worse time from my point of view.

It was now the day before Sarah's trial; and the authorities had finally granted me access to the prosecution's evidence dossier.

Sarah had given me written permission to see the evidence weeks ago, but I had been met with delay after delay. When they did finally grant me access the day before the trial, they set various conditions. I had to sit in an airless room in the police station while a police woman, who looked about sixteen and who sat on a chair in the corner playing with her mobile phone. The file itself was on a computer and I was given my own username and one off access code. When I tapped in the code the screen came up with exactly one icon on it. I clicked on it and found a mass of information but no apparent way of searching it; they were not trying to make it easy for me.

The nearest I had to a way of searching was to bring up an individual Word document and place a name in the search box. But I would have to do this endless times in endless documents.

My first instinct had been to put my own name into each search box, but even when I did find something I would discover the paragraphs were heavily redacted – mostly to remove the names of witnesses. I smelt a rat about the whole thing, but what could I do? I figured they just wanted to be able to say that they had 'granted full access even to a friend' and that was that.

I wasn't allowed a phone or a camera but I did have a notepad with me. I was surprised at the enormous amount of evidence there was – the investigation and the story was far wider and deeper than anything I had myself perceived. There was certainly far too much to read in one go. I reflected that if you had this much evidence you could fashion all sorts of different narratives from it and a painstaking search of the entire file might be needed to refute the story so formed. For my sins, I spent a lot of my allotted time reading the evidence that directly mention me; it didn't take long to find stuff.

I soon discovered that unbeknownst to me, the police had gone to the trouble of interviewing large numbers of people to ask them about me, including my neighbours; and although these were people to whom I had barely said hello in two years, they all seemed to have opinions about me. One claimed that they knew 'for a fact' that Sarah and I were in a relationship. Another claimed I was gay. Where were they getting all this nonsense from? One source, who didn't sound like a neighbour at all – it seemed more like a colleague – said I must have clearly been infatuated with Sarah and that is why I went along with things; their proof seemed to hinge on the idea that I come over as lecherous when dealing with young women. One quote was, 'Of course he helped her; he always has an eye for the ladies.' I was flabbergasted – the only reason I helped Sarah was that she was a colleague. As I read these strange accounts, I was struck by the story of the famous popstar who sat down and tried to correct his own biography on Wikipedia, only to find that within minutes his fans kept changing it back to their version of events – it simply wasn't possible to assert the truth against the tidal wave of other people's opinions. There were two kinds of truth it seemed; what actually happened, and what the world as a whole agrees has happened. But what if I was in fact attracted to Sarah and hadn't realised it? My version of the truth - no matter how first hand – might be less accurate than the view of people who observed me. It was a thought for another time.

I moved onto Sarah's stuff; guilty that I had spent so much time on my own.

There was a grainy photo from some CCTV of Sarah driving her car and you could clearly see something that might just about be a body in the back, but it wasn't clear enough to be a killer piece of evidence in its own right. There was another photo of me and her in the car at a different time, but I was relieved to note that this photo didn't show the back of the car at all.

The forensic search of the lodge was interesting. They had endless photos of the bed where Jacob had died – photos from six different angles taken again and again as each layer was removed – the duvet, the sheets the mattress and so on. The final photos were the most interesting. They showed the wooden frame of the bed with the mattress removed and a frayed gap in the woodwork about two feet in from the pillow end, where the boards were splintered. There were close ups of pieces of shot from a gun and red stains that were thicker than blood. The final photo was of the floor itself - evidently they had removed the bed altogether – and you could see gunshot embedded in the floor and dark shreds, like woollen fibres, that I couldn't identify. Also under the bed, according to the report, they found some hair samples from two separate people. I wondered whose they could be. The report said that the forensic team could find 'no match from the current database.'

In the kitchen they had taken photos of the handles of brooms and mops and the triggers and necks of kitchen sprays. It was noted that Sarah's fingerprints and DNA were found on these, but only sparcely. Elsewhere in the report the question posed, 'If Ms Hoskins had just arrived at a holiday let, why would she clean?' Er, because she is Sarah. She could have arrived to find the place more sterile than an operating theatre, and Sarah still would have had the impulse to clean.

I made a note to tell Sarah's defence team that they needed a witness to the fact she was an obsessive cleaner. But what good would it do? It would somehow look feeble in court compared to the mental image that the jury would have of her doing the murder and then cleaning up afterwards.

There was then a lengthy section on whether or not Sarah would have been able to get a body into a car or whether she would have had help – just as we ourselves had wondered throughout. At this point a photo of me appeared in the file and my own strength and ability to move a body was discussed. There were photos of 'a similar Renault Clio' with the back open and two expert witness statements about the mechanics of moving a dead body. Who the hell was an expert witness in moving bodies? Do they just get to call themselves expert witnesses and we all just accept it as a fact? Or are they reformed serial killers who have finally given up a life of crime and 'want to put something back' by offering impromptu advice on how to dispose to dead bodies?

One section was more heavily redacted than the others. It was a short report from what was tantalising called 'local sources'. These unnamed people testified that they 'knew for a fact' Jacob was dead, but would not say how they knew. I didn't know what to make of that. I am naturally suspicious of all secret testimony – if you were accused anonymously how would you defend yourself? How can we judge the honesty of the informant if we don't know who they are? – but it did make me aware that the police had moles in various communities throughout the island. It struck me that this section was unlikely to be useful in court because it was hearsay, but I did find it intriguing. Another very odd thing about this section was that according to two different 'sources' I had claimed to people that I was married to Sarah.

Married to Sarah?

It made no sense whatever. I would never say anything like that, for the simple reason that I am not married to Sarah. It was such an odd thing that I dismissed this oddity on the spot, and therefore I didn't bother to go to anyone to try and put this story right. Why would I? What I wasn't to know was that by not putting it right, it came back to bite me badly a year or so later.

There were various witness statements where the police were following a line of thought about the mazzere. Evidently Sarah had been quite garrulous to a number of people that she had had visions about Jacob dying and at least two written quotes that Sarah had said she needed to tell Jacob that she had dreamt about his death, to warn him he was going to die – even though he was already dead. One of these statements was from Bernard – the very man who took us to see the mazzere in the first place. I found this a bit rich, but I tried to put myself in Bernard's shoes: if he was interviewed by the police then he was right to factually relay anything Sarah said. This whole section of Sarah's file was somehow 'stand alone' in nature and not referred to in any other documentation. Nor were there any comments about it. They were just kept as statements with no inferences drawn from them.

Sadly, the net result of all my reading that day was that I just ended up feeling inadequate and overwhelmed. When the day of the trial came, I sat in that courtroom in my best suit – okay, my only suit - feeling I had let Sarah down. My theory at the time was that someone else had murdered Jacob and covered it up, but I hadn't made even the slightest inroad into finding out who might have a grievance against him. My sole consolation was that I had stressed to Inspector Cadin, Sarah and the defence team that Jacob's mother had claimed categorically that Jacob was alive. They did seem to know about this, but no one else seemed to be stressing this but me. In my imagination I felt the mother might be used as a surprise witness later in the trial – a sort of 'big twist' ending – but I could find no one with an appetite for this.

Usually I love a good court case. I love the to and fro of the evidence; I love the way that juries can be swayed by instincts rather than facts; I love the pomp and ceremony; I love the way that at the end, just one word from the foreman of the jury and the defendant goes from being presumed innocent of all crimes to being a murderer; I love the way that on appeal, you can go from being a murderer to not having done the crime at all - a world where the truth is what is decided by whoever's in charge that day.

In all my excitement I realised I had got to the courtroom far too early, and when I realised I would be almost alone sitting on the benches, I scuttled off to get coffee and go to the toilet.

I had a new system in place to quell my prostate paranoia. I had taken to timing my peeing as I did it. If the pee took twenty seconds or more then I could reassure myself that it wasn't my imagination, I really did need that pee and I definitively didn't have an inflamed prostate or cancer. If I wasn't convinced in my heart that I had twenty seconds of urine in my bladder then I would force myself – force myself, I say – to not visit the toilet at all. The system had been up and running for a few weeks, and it was going very well. My personal best was 54 seconds of urination. I was a medical marvel.

I popped to the toilet safe in the knowledge that there would be no issues as I hadn't had a pee for hours.

I couldn't have been more wrong.

I stood at the urinal expectantly, and after a long time the best I managed was to coerce a tiny dribble out.

Since I have had prostate trouble, I have found I listen out to the sound other men make when they pee. In the time I was standing there, a younger man walked past me and into a stall. He had barely got his flies undone before I heard what sounded like he'd got a full bucket of water and simply upturned it down the toilet. Then within a second he was out again. Well that's just taking the piss. Show off. And he didn't wash his hands.

I jogged up and down in a rhythmic motion but another person had now joined me at the urinals and he was giving me a terrible look. I continued jiggling unabashed while looking his way apologetically; I was expecting some brotherly understanding. Not a bit of it. He looked completely rattled, and hastily did up his flies and scurried off. When I returned to the court room, it was almost full. It felt odd that we had gone from empty to full so quickly. I hadn't been gone many minutes, or so it seemed, but the French can be very punctual even on a rural island.

I am no expert in the French legal practice but I got the feeling this was a sort of pre-trial to see if there was enough evidence to continue; it wasn't clear – at least not clear to me. The judges wore black capes and had two white bands that fell down from their neck. They did not wear the wigs we are used to in the UK.

The public benches were full of locals and the media, but I barely recognised anyone. Emily's friend Bernard was present but too far away for me to get his attention. I looked for a sign that any of Jacob's family were there. I felt confident that I would easily spot Jacob's mother but as far as I could see she hadn't arrived. I had also done a little homework to identify his various cousins and uncles. I couldn't see any of them.

Sarah appeared in the wooden dock. It was a high security area with thick Perspex glass. I had not been to this courtroom before and so I wondered if this was just the design of the court in that they might occasionally have to deal with terrorists or the mafia or the like, or whether they had specifically elected to have this Perspex cage for Sarah. Whatever the reason for the thick glass, it had the effect of making Sarah look even smaller than usual.

We all stood when asked. We all sat when asked. We all stopped talking when asked. We all checked our mobile phones were off when asked.

'We are here today to consider the case of the state versus Sarah-Jayne Hoskins of... ,' began the judge.

After various protocols and announcements, the judge gave way to the prosecutor. He was a very old man. To my eye he looked above retirement age and then some, but just possibly he had the face of someone who had aged badly from too much time outdoors. He fumbled alarmingly with his glasses – so much so that it felt like a miracle that they didn't drop to the floor – and when they were finally perched on his nose, his sheaf of notes became a flutter instead. I thought it very odd that a man this doddery should be allowed such an important job.

But then he gathered his poise, his body fell still, and a gravitas descended upon him and the room.

I inhaled deeply.

Here we go.

This is it.

'The state has withdrawn its charges,' he said.

'All charges?' asked the judge.

The elderly prosecutor consulted his notes as if he himself had made a mistake.

'The state has withdrawn all charges,' he said.

Sarah's head turned slowly up and left as though the fixings in her neck had gone. She asked an unheard question, then her shoulders slumped and she disappeared from view. Presumably she fainted. Hopefully there had been a chair behind her that she had simply fallen in to, but it wasn't clear.

Then the only sound I could hear in the courtroom was the hum from the air conditioning. The only movement was a couple of reporters tapping information into their phones – phones they had clearly not turned off when previously requested. Then, as if a dial was being turned, the noise of people talking to each other went from silence, to scattered whispers, to a hubbub, and soon it was so loud that an official had to call order so that the judge could dismiss us at all.

My next thought was that the presiding judge should have been angry that the prosecution didn't announce it was withdrawing its case before we all gathered - it represented, to my mind, a mass waste of time for scores of professional people - but there seemed to be no acrimony about it. Perhaps it was the formula a court had to follow; if the prosecution was dropped it had to be done in public, above board and on the record. Who knows? Either way, in the time I was thinking this, I had forgotten to look at Sarah. When I did look again that whole area of the court was clear of people and so presumably she was gone.

I tried to push through the crowd that was now jostling for the doors, but it was like trying to get out of a stadium at the end of a football match; you could only go at the speed which the crowd allowed.

I saw Luc in the distance.

'Luc!'

He didn't hear me.

I pushed hard though the crowd and managed tap him on the shoulder.

'Luc, can I ask?' I started. 'My sister Emily. Are you sure it was Ajaccio where she was arrested?'

'Quite sure.'

'It's just I can't get any news of her.'

'She's safe and well,' he said.

'Yes but,' I began. 'Should I go there?'

'They won't let you see her,' he said. How did he know that?

'Why not?'

'Look it's all going to be fine. It's all going to be fine now. It isn't my case, so I can't ask questions.'

Luc was the only person who was being helpful to me at the time, so I didn't want to press him too hard; I might lose my only source of information. I let him disappear into the crowd.

My thoughts turned to Little Sarah. I tried to think through the layout of the courts to try and guess where she may emerge. Were there some backroom formalities she had to go through, or would she just be told she could leave? Were her belongings ready for her already, or would she have to apply for them to be returned? As far as I knew she had no relatives or close friends, so did she then just walk home on her own to her empty flat? Did they give her a lift? Then what would she do? Watch TV? No one to celebrate with, no shoulder to cry on with relief.

I walked around the periphery of the building a bit to see if there was a side door or similar. I came to the conclusion I must have gone the wrong way and when I doubled back it seemed too late; there was nothing and no one to see. I figured instead I would wait an hour and visit her at home.

I was walking back to my own place to change when my phone rang.

'You were trying to reach me?' It was Emily.

'Yeah, where the hell have you been?'

'I'm on holiday,' she said. But her tone of voice was off; it was flat.

'Luc Cadin said you'd been arrested.'

'Why would he say that?' Probably because you had been arrested.

'Stealing cars or something,' I said.

'Oh that. Oh that was a misunderstanding.' I have known her literally all my life; she was lying.

'I managed to report you missing to the police,' I said.

'Why would you do that?'

'Because you were missing.'

'Well you can unreport me,' she said. 'I'm fine.'

'Where are you exactly?' I asked.

'I'll be back in a few days,' she said. She rang off.

I rang her straight back. She didn't take my call. I tried her a few minutes later; her phone went straight to messages.

My house was up the hill from the court. Hell, my house is up the hill from absolutely everything; what was I thinking renting it? I needed to rethink the house situation - perhaps a nice little place close to the bars in town - somewhere with a lift that worked, and not one of those crazy French lifts with a concertina of sharp metal specifically designed to chop your fingers off.

When I was finally home I had a nice sit down from my exertions then I got changed and drove to Sarah's place. I parked in the spot where Jacob's car was parked on the famous Friday night and that felt a bit eerie, but the sun was shining and that always dispels my darker thoughts. Like all good Brits, I am easily distracted by sunshine.

I pressed the buzzer for Sarah's apartment. There was no answer. I pressed again for a bit longer. I realised that it was only my conjecture that Sarah had gone straight home. I tried to think how long I had been at home changing and then how long the journey was for me; it was not impossible that Sarah was still at the courthouse. The French are very bureaucratic - this a country where you have to apply for a licence just to play golf – so who knows how many forms you had to fill in when you were released from prison. I had only just had that thought when Sarah's voice came on the intercom.

'Hello?' she asked.

'Hi Sarah, it's me, Pete!'

'Er, yeah okay. What do you want?'

'I wanted to check how you were.'

'Now?' She seemed to be giving me a hard time. She was, after all, the person who knocked on my door with a dead boyfriend in the back of her car; what right did she have to funny about me visiting?

'Okay, well come up,' she said at last.

I walked up the stairs and knocked on her door. Sarah opened almost straight away but only about half a foot.

'Hiya,' she said.

'Hi! How are you doing? Amazing about the case! How are you? How are you feeling?' I asked.

But she clearly wasn't letting me into her apartment.

'Fine. Fine, yeah great,' she said.

She was wearing a bath towel. She was clearly naked, but not wet. Perhaps she was just about to get in a bath or shower; it might be a nice idea after a court case and all that time in prison.

I paused, not quite sure what to say next. Surely this was a huge event in her life, and it should be marked in some way.

She then drew a little determined breath inwards through her mouth and twitched her head up a bit.

'I'm a bit busy?' she said.

'You're busy?'

She twitched her head a second time and opened the door another half a foot.

'This is Jacob,' she said. 'Meet Jacob.'

I could half see a man beyond her, a few yards into the room.

'So can we talk later? Like at the office?' she asked.

'Sure,' I said. 'No problem.'

She didn't then say anything, so eventually I added, 'I just wanted to check you were okay.'

'Cool,' she said. She shut the door.

FIVE

A few days later we arranged to meet as a group. We chose Pinocchio's out of habit. The group was to be Emily, Sarah-Jayne, Jacob and myself. The three of them had a lot of explaining to do.

Sarah and I were there first.

Sarah was showing no signs whatever that she had been in prison per se, but she did have a completely new look. Her hair was cut in a pixie cut and it looked glossy and stylish. She was wearing something figure hugging in a rich purple colour. It had an oval window at the front for her cleavage.

When she stood up to go to the toilet I took the chance to eye up how her arse looked in the dress. I did this by pretending to look at my phone, and then I nonchalantly looked up in what I hoped was a distracted manner as if contemplating some recently gleaned information. I can report that her rear looked well-turned, rounded - almost a bubble-butt - and that the dress fabric shimmied over it as she walked. There was no way she was wearing knickers; it would have left a line in the fabric.

I wondered if she had taken advice on her look. She was a world apart from the woman I had spent the evening with while 'dead' Jacob was in the car, and she was a world apart from the forlorn and picky figure she cut in the prison. Perhaps jail in fact made a huge difference to her; she seemed to now be a woman. I wondered how long this new 'womanly' Sarah would last. Sarah always seemed to be different according to the different fates that befell her.

When Sarah got back from the toilet she sat across the table from me. She sat upright with one leg folded over the other.

'So to clarify,' I started. 'The prosecution dropped the case because Jacob turned up and explained to everyone he was alive.'

'Yes.'

'When did you find out this?' I asked.

'Moments before the trial. He came to the court and talked to the judge.'

'He talked directly to the judge?'

'Yes,' she replied.

'And the judge made him prove he was indeed Jacob?'

'I guess,' she said. 'But can I ask you something?'

'Sure.'

'How do I look?'

'You are asking me how you look?' I asked.

'Yeah. How do I look?'

'You look great Sarah.'

'Really? You sure?'

'Really!' I said. I was going to mention how her bum looked in her dress, but thought better of it.

'It's just I'm so nervous. I have got stomach ache with nerves.'

I said, 'This isn't the first time you have seen Jacob since the court case, Sarah?' I couldn't bring myself to say the word prison.

'No,' she said.

She thought for a while and evidently felt she owed me some explanation.

'I saw him the once,' she said. 'Then he was away for two days.'

'Have you spoken on the phone?'

'I am so nervous,' she repeated. Her eyes were widening and moving a little to the left and right like when you are wondering if you are going to be sick. She then reached out and placed her hand on the back of my hand.

'You're going to be fine,' I said. 'Have you spoken to him recently? Often?'

'Yes. But he was in Italy or somewhere, I think on business. He couldn't speak long.'

'What does he do? On business?' I asked.

'Import, export. Wine. That kind of thing,' she said. 'I think.'

'Did he offer an explanation of events?'

'He didn't really have time. I feel like this is all a dream.'

She looked down at her own body. Her eyes were big and wondering.

'I do know what you mean. I had some almost hallucinations a few weeks back, when I was in a village on the other side of the island. '

We were both silent for a while.

'Do you ever feel you are being drugged?' I asked. I don't know where that came from.

'No.' she replied simply. 'Maybe it's the island. Maybe it's all the pollen. The air. It was a dream, but it was him. I have felt so strange since I left prison. I felt so strange at prison. I went back to work and everything was the same, everyone treated me the same, but it wasn't the same. It was like I was taller or drifting or, I don't know. It is really odd. I could do with being taller.'

'And it is definitely Jacob?' I asked.

'Yes, of course,' she laughed.

'What did Jacob actually say about what happened?' I asked.

'He said he, er...' Sarah rose from her seat. From the colour of her face, I thought she was going off to be sick but in fact she was looking beyond me to the doorway.

Jacob was walking into the restaurant.

Jacob was a handsome man with a well-groomed beard, tousled hair and a lot of presence. He had a crisp light blue shirt and a toned body. He had an energetic, friendly bounce to his walk. He made straight for Sarah. Upon seeing Sarah, he opened his mouth and eyes wide and threw his arms open, and advanced forward. He was theatrically thrilled to see her.

Sarah came round the table towards him and they hugged, and he lifted her up in a sweep and swung her round.

'Sarah!' he said. 'You look fantastic!'

For my part, I put my hands to my face – one palm on each cheek - and sat observing them.

What story would he offer?

He was dead. He really was dead. I know this because I saw him with my own eyes and Sarah saw it with her own eyes and there was DNA evidence to boot. But here he was: larger than life and twice as charming.

He clasped Sarah's arse in a palm and squeezed. She was comfortable with this; in fact, she was thrilled with this.

Prior to the meet-up my big question was going to be whether this was in fact Jacob, but judging by Sarah's joy and her previous assertion, it clearly was the right person; and he certainly matched the photos I'd seen. I wondered at what stage was she going to sit down and ask him a few basic questions though, like, er, are you immortal? Can you come back from the dead? If that wasn't you who died, then whose dead body was it in the car?

They pulled apart and Sarah just looked at him and looked at him and looked at him. Her face was a picture of love stripped bare - no side, no guile, no British cynicism, no reservations: just love. She threw herself a second time at him. Her tiny arms were wrapped around his neck. He was smiling like the Cheshire Cat. He was laughing.

'You really are pleased to see me,' he said.

'Oh you have no idea,' she said. 'I thought you were dead. I thought you were dead. I thought you were dead. Then when I saw you and then you went again, I thought I would never see you again. This is going to take a lot of getting over. I mean, I know I have seen you, but then I thought you might go away again. I thought maybe you just came back for the trial and you didn't really want to see me. This is going to take a few weeks for me to process.'

It's going to take her a few weeks to process? It's going to take me a whole *lifetime* to process.

'Yes, sorry about that. I was working away. I was in Italy,' he said. I felt this might have been said for my benefit. 'I had no idea there was all this fuss. My mother called me. It took a while to get back.'

'You could have called Sarah!' I said. He didn't seem to hear me. 'You could have rung the authorities.' I said, realising that perhaps you can't ring someone who is in prison.

It turned out he had heard me; his head turned as best it could, given the grappling he was getting from Sarah.

He said, 'I thought it was just an odd confusion that my mother had got wrong. I thought it was the imagination of an old woman.'

'Your mother seems quite clever to me,' I said.

'Who are you, by the way?' he asked.

'This is my friend Peter,' said Sarah. She was bouncing up and down now. I felt like putting a hand on her head to stop the bobbing, but instead I put out my hand to shake Jacob's.

'I am a colleague of Sarah's,' I said. 'We just about met before. Just after the trial.'

He nodded and smiled, 'You work at the same insurance company?' he said. He leant forward to examine my face. 'You must be Emily's brother.'

He looked at me longer.

'I can see you look like Emily. I can see it,' he said.

He was bonkers charming - he was hit the ball out of the park charming - this would make it harder to pin him down and be cross; perhaps that was the point. If we swallow his story about his mum ringing him up, why did he not ring Sarah the moment he heard the rumour? In fact, why was he not in touch with Sarah all along? I hadn't actually checked Sarah's phone to see if she had missed calls but, presumably, she had checked. After all, we are talking about a couple of months.

'Did he try to ring you?' I asked Sarah.

Jacob had open, friendly, slightly theatrical body language and posture. He turned smiling to Sarah, waiting happily for the reply from her to my question.

Sarah looked from him to me and back again and then back once more to me all the while bouncing happily.

'What?' she said.

'When you got out of prison and you checked your phone, were there missed phone calls from Jacob?' I asked.

'Yeah tonnes of them,' she said. 'I mean, first I had to recharge my phone, but then lots of texts all came through at once and lots of notifications of missed calls.'

'Can I see your phone?' I asked.

'Sure,' she said but she didn't then proffer the phone.

'I want to see a list of your missed calls.' I sounded very hard-arsed, especially compared to her enthusiasm.

'Sure,' she said.

She scrolled through her phone and showed me the screen I wanted to see. I guess she was happy to indulge me because I had been her ally in prison, and because she was in such a good mood now she had Jacob back.

'Can I get Jacob a drink?' she asked me.

'Of course!' I said.

'Sorry,' I said to Jacob. 'I am being a party pooper.'

Sarah was fair skipping about; she got her handbag and went off to collar a waiter.

She called back, 'Jacob! What do you want to drink? Have you eaten?'

'Thrill me!' he announced. He turned to me. 'I love your sister. I totally love your sister. She is so much fun. She often talks about you. It's great to meet you.'

Emily had never once mentioned to me that she knew Jacob. Given the circumstances; if she had met Jacob on even one occasion, surely she would have mentioned it to me.

It was all a problem. It was one of those situations where you have to keep reminding yourself of the truth because everyone else in the room was acting differently. Sarah had been in prison because this person was thought to be dead, I myself had had a torrid time and been in the newspapers; but given the enthusiasm of the happy couple, if I kept pressing for an explanation I felt like some horrible old misanthrope. Instead of getting to bottom of events, evidently we were going to - judging by the Kir Royales coming in our direction - drink cocktails to celebrate life.

I returned my attention to Sarah's phone. I scrolled down through Sarah's missed calls but I couldn't see any mention of any phone call from Jacob.

'Look, I'm sorry Sarah but I can't see any missed calls from Jacob,' I said.

Sarah looked at her phone for a while. She scrolled down and she scrolled up. She became stock still and did a lot of thinking. She scrolled a bit more.

She started to speak slowly, as if she was not quite sure.

She said, 'Jacob has changed his number. He lost his phone. When he rang, I didn't recognise his number either. He's got a new number.'

This made sense because Jacob's phone was found just outside the hut where he was shot.

Sarah turned to Jacob and put out her hand to touch him without looking at him, the way you do when you are relating to someone who trusts you with their body; a lover.

'Jacob?' she asked still looking at the screen. 'What's your mobile number?'

Jacob was less bouncy than before but still very happy; he scrolled through his own phone to read out his number.

Sarah said, 'Yep. There it is. Look at the date. There you go.' She said this to me without resentment, then got back to the all-important job of rubbing her face against Jacob's.

I looked long and hard at those texts on that phone. The fact remained that there was a long time where there was no evidence that Jacob had contacted Sarah. When you are getting on well in the early stage of a relationship, you don't suddenly have a long period of radio silence. I checked her WhatsApp. Nothing there, as far as I could see. One possibility was that when a phone is off for a long time through lack of juice, not all texts come through when you turn it back on – they get timed out in some way. Another possibility was that Jacob was a bit of a player and had blown hot and cold about Sarah; but that wasn't the evidence of my own eyes.

Another possibility was that he was dead at the time.

I decided to change tack.

'Okay, sorry, but bear with me,' I said. I was now addressing Jacob. 'Tell me something only you could know.'

'What? He asked.

I was trying out the thought, 'What if Jacob had a twin?'

'So... tell me about the first time you and Sarah were alone,' I asked. 'Where did you meet?'

'The Black Sheep,' he replied.

'What did Sarah drink?'

He pointed to the Kir Royale. 'Kir Royale,' he said.

'I love Kir Royale,' enthused Sarah. She looked thoughtful, albeit in a happy way. 'No. I didn't have Kir Royale.' She looked at Jacob as if teasing him. 'What did I drink on our first date? Or rather what was my first drink?'

'Yeah Jacob, what was her first drink?' I jeered.

He thought about it.

'You had Kir,' he said eventually.

He turned to me with the enthusiasm of someone with an anecdote to tell; there was no whiff that he felt only one difficult question away from being found out as a liar.

'Sarah loves Kir Royale which as we know is made with Champagne, but she didn't realise that if you just say Kir to a barman you will get a white wine from Burgundy with Crème de Cassis. There will be no bubbles.'

Okay so he was probably not a twin. Or if he was a twin, he was one of those psychic twins that only existed in fiction. I reflected that in truth, the most I could possibly hold against him was that he seemed to be expecting questions that queried whether he was Jacob or not.

Emily appeared.

I had seen her earlier at the office and she was now wearing different clothes. This was highly unusual for her; she had evidently slipped home to change into something less comfortable. She was wearing what, to the casual observer, would pass for work clothes but were demonstrably more glamorous than she normally wore either at work or at play. She had some cream coloured trousers made from a rich thick material; they were baggy at the thighs and tapered down to her ankles, but tight round the waist with a leather belt to accentuate an hourglass look. She wore a white close-fitting blouse which left her cleavage pouting. The hourglass effect was further enhanced by her having her hands in her pockets and she was playing with the fabric by moving her hands inwards and outwards. It was the smartest I had seen her for a long while. She was in a very sunny mood.

'I didn't know you knew Jacob,' I said to her.

'I don't,' she said.

She tilted her head to one side for a professional appraisal.

'A good looking boy,' she said. She turned to me. 'As you can see I am not in jail myself.'

'Well that's a relief,' I replied. 'Were you ever?'

'This is no way to greet your sister,' she replied. She looked at Jacob. 'I might have met him,' she said belatedly. 'Why, what does he say?'

'He says you talk about me a lot,' I said.

Emily reflected on this. 'Is he Jean-Marie's cousin? Nephew or something?'

'So you do know him? And you know Jean-Marie from my office?' I asked.

'Pete, this is a small town. I can believe we've hung out. You've seen us. We hang out in groups. Has he always had a beard?'

I had visions that Jacob had indeed been in attendance on one of the many occasions when Emily had held court in a restaurant or bar. His would be just one of many faces, whereas everyone present would have remembered Emily swinging her leg on a chair and launching into a story with a glass held to her cheek.

I sourced some more Kir Royale. I needed some thinking juice.

'Emily help me out here,' I said. 'We need to pin Jacob down on the issue of him going to the lodge in the mountains with Sarah. She went with him to the lodge for a dirty weekend. They were getting something out of the car and Jacob was bouncing on the bed or whatever. Sarah heard a bang and he was dead. We need to ask Jacob where he was at the time. We need his account of events.'

'Sure,' she said.

'His phone was found at the hunting lodge for heaven's sake!' I said.

'I know.'

Emily sniffed a bit and called out, 'Oi! Lovebirds! I want to talk to you.'

The happy couple sat down contentedly, side by side.

'Before today,' said Emily. 'When is the last time you saw Sarah?'

'About four nights ago?' he said, looking at Sarah for confirmation.

'You've had sex?' she asked; a bit direct for my taste, but evidently important in Emily's view.

They shrugged a yes.

'Okay, and before that,' persevered Emily. 'When was the last time you two saw each other?'

'We were here in town. In Bastia,' he said.

Sarah was silent.

'Sarah?' asked Emily. 'Before four nights ago, when was the last time you saw Jacob?'

Sarah looked slightly agonised but spoke firmly. 'Well I certainly saw him in town here in Bastia. We spent the night in Bastia.'

'But what about the weekend at the lodge in the mountains?' asked Emily.

'I went out to the lodge on my own and my recollection is that Jacob was there. Then there was the whole terrible thing.'

'Where were you at the time Jacob?' asked Sarah. 'Your car was at the lodge.'

'My car would have been in Bastia. It was parked outside Sarah's apartment.'

'And where were you yourself Jacob?'

'I was in Sartina,' he said. I knew from his tone of voice he was lying. What am I saying? We knew he was lying because he was at the lodge and he was shot dead and his mobile phone was there, and I myself had driven from the lodge to Bastia in his car. Okay, so my version of the truth had a hallucinogenic quality that was markedly missing from Jacob's version of the truth, but that didn't change the facts.

Emily decided to go for a similar angle that I had used earlier.

'Why did you not phone or text Sarah for all the time you were away?' asked Emily.

'I did,' he protested.

'The texts and missed calls were a number of weeks later,' I said. 'I have just been looking at Sarah's phone. Why the big gap?'

'I lost my phone,' shrugged Jacob. I didn't like the shrug. 'I took a while to get a new phone. I thought my original phone would re-surface. I then got another phone, but I was working away. I let down Sarah. I can see that. I didn't know she was in trouble. Sometimes when I fall in love I panic a bit and I find myself backing off. It is silly. I am so sorry.' He said the last bit to Sarah who was now melting.

'You're in love with me?' she cooed.

Oh good grief. And no no no no! This is a generation married to their mobile phones. They get twitchy if they haven't checked a screen in the last two minutes, let alone not even owning one for a couple of months; in fact, that generation are so obsessed by their phones, the only possible reason they wouldn't own one for several months would be because they were dead. Ha!

Okay. First principles. I am not prepared to believe in witchcraft, voodoo or local superstition so I am going to have as my first immutable fact the idea that there was indeed a dead body. We know that Jacob was standing in front of me, so the dead body was not Jacob. So that is my second immutable fact. But my third immutable fact was that I had been told to my face by the police that the dead body was indeed Jacob. They know this from the DNA on the bed frame.

'Okay! Team!' I shouted - the alcohol was kicking in handsomely - 'So who was the dead body?'

'What?' asked one or two of them.

'So if we can accept that Jacob is alive.' I pointed to Jacob. 'Who was the dead body?'

'There is no dead body,' said Emily.

What? Emily, of all people, hadn't backed me up. My own sister. Half-sister more like.

She saw the look on my face and said, 'But the thing is Pete, there is no body.'

'No!' I said, head already in both hands. 'There was a dead body. There was definitely a dead body. Sarah back me up.'

Sarah?

Sarah didn't back me up. She just looked at me and twitched slightly. I was the nasty man who was spoiling her lovely evening with the man she loved.

'Sarah?' I asked again.

Sarah had her man back and wasn't going to question whatever the gods had done to make it happen.

I looked at all three of them. The group sentiment had completely run away from me.

What the hell, let's just drink. I ordered some wine from a passing waiter and let the matter rest. I couldn't think what else I could do.

We settled down to socialising as a group. Jacob was good company, and the re-energised Sarah and Emily were in great spirits. Something that was profoundly odd, however, was that it became increasingly clear that Emily was flirting with Jacob.

The exact interchange was as follows...

Jacob was telling a funny story about how he used to go to dances with his sister, to nightclubs or similar. As teenagers do, they used to practice their dance routines in their mum's front room, trying not to smash any fragile objects.

'My sister and I learnt a dance that was on the TV. It was the US comedy 'Friends' – we loved Friends, and there is an episode where the brother and sister Ross and Monica do a dance they have practiced in their bedrooms when they were children. It is a bit comical? It is an episode about New Year's Eve. So we do this dance.'

'Show us the dance,' said Emily.

'Yes show us the dance,' said Sarah.

'No, no, no, it takes two people,' he said.

He showed us the dance, acting out both sections in their entirety in the space between the tables in the restaurant. It was funny. It involved a variety of 'white people can't dance' moves such as flapping chicken wings, stirring an imaginary cauldron, robotics, and for a grand finale the girl takes a run up and lands in her brother's arms.

'But no!' said Jacob. 'My sister ran at me and somehow I dropped her and there was a bump. On her head. Her head hit the side of a table and we had to take her to hospital.'

By this stage Jacob in the excitement was speaking in French, and he had used the words 'baisser' and 'cogne'. These words mean to drop and to bump. Both these words are pronounced in a very similar fashion to two very well-known rude words that you would never say in polite conversation.

Emily, without missing a beat, said in French, 'Well you can baise my con any time you like.' She said it with a body gesture that sort of opened herself up to him; her thumbs hooked her pockets outwards as if opening her hips and in the same manoeuvre she pushed her crotch forward towards him.

This was clearly a sexual thing to say and do, and I couldn't see that it quite caught the mood. She barely knew Jacob and we weren't that drunk. It piqued my interest because Emily rarely flirts. I mean, yes, she flirts her whole life through, but she is not specific in her flirting. She attracts men in general, and then choses the one she wants from the ones who offer themselves. She doesn't ever specifically target a man; and yet she was doing it that day.

Apart from her suggestive remarks, Emily continued with a series of what I can only describe as micro-flirts all evening. She occasionally traced her finger across her lips while listening oh-so-attentively to Jacob; from time to time she would flick her hair to behind her ears or look at him through an imaginary fringe; the tip of her tongue might rest on the edge of her upper teeth; she would do all of this while facing Jacob squarely and in a relaxed manner and giving him her undivided attention. She didn't overplay any one tactic, and it all had plausible deniability, but Little Sarah didn't stand a chance. Jacob was soon hanging off Emily's every word and simpering.

At one stage Emily stood up – I don't know why - and Jacob instinctively stood up as well; it was the tiniest of observations but Sarah and I both registered it. Jacob checked himself, then turned and smiled at Sarah, but Sarah's face had changed colour; she was mortified.

As previously stated, my sister could give lessons in flirting. She has an industrial strength flirting technique that she unleashes like a water cannon; breaking men's ribs on impact, and the hearts that they encase. Emily, Emily, Emily, what were you doing? This is plainly why Emily has so few female friends; she can't stand not being first pick with the men and so she flirts with their boyfriends.

I surveyed the three of them over the rim of my wine glass, and despaired at the antics of all of them.

SIX

It was my turn – again - to take mum out for lunch.

Incidentally; never let old folk go on about their pensions and lack of money. A lot of them are loaded. Mum eats out twice a day, most days. If you can eat out twice a day, then you are doing alright. This is partly the French way of doing things - a surprising number of apartments don't have a fully equipped kitchen - partly my mum's laziness.

So we were out for lunch at a simple little eatery near to where I live and my mum put great stress on wanting to pay.

'I insist Peter,' she said. 'When the bill comes, I want to make a contribution. You are always paying. If I can't treat my own son to lunch once in a while, then what is the world coming to?'

And when the bill came, she was good to her word. Her arthritic blue fingers stretched out and pulled the little tray towards her that held 'l'addition' and she scrutinised the piece of paper for an interminable minute.

'That's correct!' she pronounced.

She then unzipped her purse and placed one solitary coin on the tray with the bill. It was a 1 Euro coin. Satisfied, she pushed the bill back towards me.

Satisfied?

Of course she was satisfied. She had taken the moral high ground of saying she was treating me to lunch and then only had to part with a 1 Euro coin. She probably expected change.

I placed forty Euros of my own on top and awaited a reaction from my mum. But reaction came there none. I looked into the middle distance and breathed in and out ten times slowly. I have learnt to do this a lot.

And in the middle distance, on the pavement on the other side of the road, I was astonished to see Jacob with my sister Emily. They were walking along chatting in a very amicable way - more often than not talking over each other. Hells bells my family are irritating. What on earth were those two doing together?

'I need a favour,' said my mum.

If she asked me to thank her for lunch, I was going to have a go at her. The experts say that with old folk you are supposed to agree and smile at everything they say but if these so-called experts ever meet my mother they would be in for an abrupt rethink, followed by years of self-flagellation.

'What is this favour?' I asked.

'I need you to drive me to Ludic's,' she said.

'What? You want me to drive you to your elderly lover's apartment block? Your gentleman caller? Your little friend?' The French have an excellent euphemism for lover. 'She's got a little friend.' It has a gorgeous gossipy ring to it.

'Don't call him my little friend,' she said.

'Okay,' I replied. 'Your elderly friend.'

'He was round my house the other day and he didn't have long because he just said to his wife that he was just popping out.'

'Okay...' I said.

'So we were in the front room and we were having a little...'

'Minty clinch?'

'Don't be disgusting. We were standing!'

'That's how you have a minty clinch. If you are lying down, it's a love wrestle.'

'But the trouble is we lost our hearing aids,' she said. 'They just went shooting off across the room.'

'Okay.'

'All four. All lost. Well you know what my place is like.'

My mum's place is very untidy with piles of items littering the floor: books, trinkets, mugs, magazines - everything really. There are vague forest paths through the undergrowth; one from her armchair chair to the toilet, one to the kettle, and so on, but basically it is a mess. So I can well believe that if two elderly people lost their hearing aids in a tryst emergency, then those hearing aids would not be found again for many a year.

'So Ludic had to go home to his wife, but he no longer had any hearing aids. He was most unsettled,' she said.

'When was this?' I asked.

'This morning.'

'You were having a minty clinch in the morning with your little friend?'

'Stop saying little friend and stop saying minty clinch.' Despite her protests, she was laughing. I like making her laugh; in a few years, when her memory goes, it will be all we've got.

I now realised Emily and Jacob were no longer in my line of vision. What the hell were they up to? There is an underground car park near where we were sitting; they might be parked there. It is also possible they were visiting me, but they would have phoned first surely?

'So how can I help you?' I asked my mum.

'I found one hearing aid.'

'Okay.'

'I tried it in and it isn't mine,' she explained.

'You tried the hearing aid in your ear? What if it had someone else's earwax on it? That's disgusting.'

'It didn't have any earwax on it,' she said.

'How do you know? Your eyesight is terrible.'

'My eyesight is perfect. The trick is that I never wore it out by reading.'

That's another irritant right there. Her house is full of books but, as my mum often says, she never reads. I think what happens is that old people just foist their books on other old people because they hate waste.

'So I want you to help me get the hearing aid back to Ludic's house,' she said.

'How?'

'By driving me there.'

'You're kidding,' I said.

The good news was that we could walk to my house and fetch the car and I could see if Emily and Jacob were there. The bad news was that this was all so irritating.

We walked to my house.

No sign of Emily and Jacob.

My mum and I got in my car and we drove to Ludic's place. The street that gives access to his apartment block is quite narrow and difficult to navigate.

'Stop!' she said. 'Now let me out. If you turn here, then your car won't be seen, and we can make a quick getaway.'

'Getaway?'

'I'm going to sneak in his back door, and I am going to hide the hearing aid somewhere in his house.'

'Okay...'

With that, she dashed out of my car.

Dutiful son that I am, I turned the car around, doing a thirty-three point turn in the narrow road. It felt like my mum was gone forever, but no one is that lucky.

I kept looking in my rear-view mirror to see if I could see her, but somehow I didn't and I jumped when the passenger door suddenly opened and she got in.

'Drive!' she said.

I drove. It was like we were in a heist movie.

She ferreted around in her handbag and produced her mobile phone.

'Hold the car still,' she said. 'I am having trouble texting.'

'Who are you texting?'

'They were both in the house. Ludic was there. I saw him, and I saw his wife.' She was very excited.

'How did you get in? I asked. I thought they had an apartment?'

'There is a balcony round the side. You can hop over the railing.'

'Good grief. That is very agile for someone who had a hip replacement.'

'I've never had a hip replacement,' she announced. She has had a hip replacement.

'I hid the hearing aid behind the armchair in the front room. I was almost caught. She half walked in the room and then walked out again.'

'What are you texting?' I asked.

'"I found your hearing aid. I have placed it behind the big chair in the front room. When you find it, pretend to look surprised,"' she said.

We drove along in silence for a minute. My mum was texting away on her phone.

'Mum?'

'Yes?'

'I have run out of words to describe you,' I said.

'Well that's a good thing surely?' she said.

Why did everyone assume I wanted to be the driver in their heists and misdemeanours? On a whim I decided to check my face in the rear-view mirror to see if the word 'Mug' was written there.

Intermittently around that time, I was trying to get through to the police to find out quietly what their official view was on the disappearance and re-appearance of Jacob. None of my calls were returned and I didn't feel it warranted me marching down to the police station just to satisfy my curiosity. One afternoon, however, my passport arrived back at the office by courier and I took it as a sign the case was now completely settled, and the police might be happy to talk to me again. I picked up the phone and managed to get straight through to Luc Cadin.

We chewed on a few neutral topics for a minute and then I said, 'Can I ask what the official conclusions were in the case of Sarah-Jayne Hoskins?'

'Well,' he said after a little thought. 'We had the conclusion that she was a little bit of a fantasist. She reported that Jacob Lluberas was dead, but then she started to say to everyone that she was going to talk to him.'

'And I'm a fantasist too?' I asked. 'Did you interview Jacob?'

Again, another long pause.

'Look, I am not sure we should be talking,' he said. He went silent and then seemed to change his mind. He said, 'Jacob Lluberas said he had for certain stayed at the lodge a few weeks earlier, and he said there was an accident with the bed. A bedroom accident.' Was this a euphemism or was it Luc's take on English? 'He went under the bed to repair the wood of the bed and he cut himself. In the lodge in the mountains, I mean.'

'But there were shotgun pellets found in the floor under the bed,' I protested.

'Certainly, yes, but he is alive!'

Also, Jacob's car was seen there by a policeman, and there was a photo of Sarah driving a car with what looked like a body in the back

'Okay,' I reasoned. 'But I was in a car with the dead body. Am I a fantasist too?'

'No but sir there is the bizarre history of how you were walking and your shadow was slower to budge than you, and there was the story that you thought Sarah was your wife.' He was getting in his stride now and was set to go on, but I butted in.

'This has nothing to do with anything; the strange thing that happened to me with the shadows in Sartina, was that even in the prosecution evidence? Either way, it was just weird and I put it down to low blood sugar levels. And I have never said I was married to Sarah.'

'For sure, but if a person does not know you, the person will judge you by...'

'Also, another thing I have been dwelling on...'

'Yes?' asked Luc.

'Some time ago, you and I sat and had a drink and you used the words "Fin de souci" and I was wondering if I misheard you. There was lots of traffic, and I thought you said "End of worry" because it was a logical thing to say, but in fact I reckon you said the French word sosie, not souci...'

The line went dead.

I thought Luc had terminated the conversation his end, but I then realised it was because a hand had extended over my desk to disconnect me. The hand belonged to Sarah. She was standing in front of my desk looking very angry. Just as intriguing, one of her arms was in a surgical sling. I tried not to look alarmed at the fact I was caught on the phone talking about her, but I was furiously wondering how much she had heard.

'What's happened to your arm?' I asked.

'I fell over,' she replied.

Jean-Marie had been observing us and asked her some supplementary questions before I had the chance and she replied, 'I like my apartment to be just so. So when I vacuum clean the mats I like to make scrape marks on the mats with the nozzle.'

'You make lines on the carpet?' asked Jean-Marie.

'Exactly,' she said. 'And then I like to leave them. So I don't like to tread on the carpet for a couple of days. I jump over it.'

'How often do you vacuum your carpet?'

'Most days,' she said.

'So you never really walk on your rugs,' I said. I noticed I was the one who was a bit rude to Sarah; this was not for the first time. Sarah didn't seem to notice though.

‘So how did you break your arm?’ asked Jean-Marie.

‘I broke my collar bone jumping over the mat,’ she said. ‘It’s a big mat and I tripped over.’

‘You poor thing,’ I said, trying to be the nicer one in the room. ‘How long will you have to wear the sling?’

‘It’s not clear,’ she said. ‘It might be a precaution.’

‘Poor you,’ said Jean-Marie. ‘Is it inconvenient? Can you drive?’

‘I walk to work. The worst thing is trying to change my bra. It takes two people to change my bra. But I haven’t got a boyfriend. So I have to come to work and get a friend to change my bra for me. And that brings me to my problem.’

Sarah paused and looked at me accusingly.

‘Your sister has stolen my boyfriend.’

I knew it.

A little time later, Sarah and I sat at a café table across the street and ate pastries.

‘Can you have a word with her?’ she asked. She was very cross.

‘It really isn’t up to me who my sister dates.’

‘But it’s not fair!’ said Sarah. ‘Emily could have anyone. Why does she have to pinch my boyfriend? It’s so unfair.’

I would like to pretend I was torn on this issue and somehow see it from Emily’s point of view, but I had to agree with Sarah. She looked so forlorn. She kept sighing and gazing at the table.

Then she started crying. I hoped initially it was going to be a short lived cry that would require no reaction from me, but usually if that is the case the woman starts dabbing at her eyes, or sits up, opens her eyes wide and places a horizontal finger under each lower eyelid. I think this is something to do with preserving make-up integrity, but no man has ever asked. A similar mystery is when a man is in the hairdressers and there is a woman sitting silently in the corner with bits of tin foil in her hair; no man knows what that is, nor has ever asked. In any event, it became clear that Sarah’s tears were not going to stop.

I leant forward over the table, as much as my stomach allowed, and did that restrained half hug which the British have perfected where our fronts didn't touch but the palm of my hand tapped her shoulder. This just made her cry more.

'I'll have a word with my sister,' I said.

This concession took her from a state of crying to a state of sniffing. It was an improvement of sorts.

She did a big breath in and out of her (snotty) nose and said, 'Do you want the rest of your cake?'

You've crossed the line, Sarah.

'You can have it, if you like,' I said.

'When I was first told, I didn't believe it,' she said.

'Told what?'

'That Emily was sleeping with Jacob.'

'Ah.'

'I called the woman who told me a bitch. I mean, I really shouted at her. I think I spat at her. I have to work with her, you know?'

'It wasn't very helpful, a colleague telling you something like that,' I said. 'Even it is true.'

'It *is* true,' she said.

'Indeed.'

Apart from the one phone call to Luc, I had more or less stopped delving into the situation of Jacob and his death, or non-death. If I had been armed with more information, then I would be better prepared for any subsequent event. But at the time it wasn't clear there was going to be a subsequent event. There was no dead body; in fact, the dead body was alive and well and dating my sister, so the police had lost interest. They had originally made much noise about getting to the bottom of things, but evidently it just took one word from the official prosecutor, and they saw things through the lens that Sarah and I were fantasists and moved on. The newspaper article mentioning me had proved to be a one-off. Everyone, it seemed, was either shrugging, forgetting, or treating the incident like a weird dream – worse; they were treating it like a premonition that tied in with some half-baked local folklore.

There were a number of lines of inquiry I could have pursued. For example, Sarah's car looked like Sarah's car, but I knew it wasn't Sarah's car, because Sarah's car was smashed up on a mountainside. I could have checked the engine number. There is a number inside the bonnet of a car or within the door frame, and it should also appear on the documentation. It would be easy enough to check. I could also have run a check for cars that had been reported stolen at that time and whether any of them were the same colour and model as Sarah's car. I had done none of this.

Also, I could have asked around about Jacob more. He seemed jolly and he seemed like he wouldn't kill himself, but life isn't that simple.

I fancy myself as an armchair psychologist, so let us call this the Owen Wilson Paradox. Owen Wilson is a relaxed looking actor who is hugely successful, rich, has enjoyed a lengthy career and has even been nominated for Oscars. He looks comfortable in his own skin and is the sort of man who will never grow tired of asking 'So, where's the party?'

And then he tried to kill himself.

And then he was treated for depression at more than one medical centre.

And yet, despite this knowledge, we still haven't changed our perception of him. I, personally, would love to be Owen Wilson, I would kill to be Owen Wilson, he's the one of the coolest guys on the planet. Perhaps Jacob was an Owen Wilson figure. Perhaps he wanted to fake his own death and start a new life, possibly with some life assurance in his top pocket. One aspect that I felt wasn't fully explained was the shotgun pellets and DNA under the bed in the lodge. Was Jacob there or not? I decided there was one line of inquiry I definitely wanted to pursue, and it wouldn't be too hard.

SEVEN

I had Emily and Jacob littering my life on a luxurious Sunday afternoon.

I decided to make use of it for my own devices.

I moved the patio furniture and sat them close to the wall of my house, in a patch that catches the evening sun. We were within feet of the bougainvillea.

'I don't like the look of your pointing,' said Jacob. 'I think the plant is harming it.'

'What on earth are you talking about?' I asked.

He reached out and picked at the wall to show that some of the cement on the wall was flaking to dust.

In common with a lot of buildings in Bastia the house had originally had a painted plaster layer over a brick construction. Over the centuries, the plaster had largely crumbled away to reveal dark bricks that were quite flat with mortar between.

'I don't think plants truly harm walls,' I said.

'That's his wall of metaphor,' chimed in Emily.

'What?' asked Jacob.

I sighed. 'Emily is alluding to a conversation we had sitting here. I said facts are like bricks and inevitably we don't know everything about every subject, so the mortar is like supposition or faith or theory in that it fills in the voids around the bricks. The bigger the bricks, the less the mortar, and the house is stronger as a result. The bigger your knowledge and the less there is conjecture, the better.'

'My, what urbane conversations you guys have,' said Jacob.

'And I said people of faith have their bricks too,' said Emily.

'And I said so they have to mould their facts, like mortar, around their beliefs. But that's not how facts work.'

'And I said no one cares,' said Emily. 'They just care about the outcome. Does the wall stand the test of time, or not? Does it get the job done or not?'

'You don't look interested,' I said to Jacob. 'Which I totally understand.'

'No, I just think you two obviously spend a lot of time together,' he said.

'What do you mean?' asked Emily.

'You two are so similar, it's bizarre,' said Jacob. 'And freaky. I have to have sex with that one.' He pointed a thumb at Emily who cooed. Cooed! 'Now I'm going to have Pete popping into my brain at the same time.'

'Why?' asked Emily.

'Because you're so similar!' he said.

'No we're not!' protested both Emily and myself.

In unison. In the same tone of voice.

'Ah we're just two young and crazy kids,' said Emily.

'Well you got that half right,' said Jacob.

I have to say I really liked Jacob. In other circumstances he would be a great match for Emily.

'I am going to take some selfies,' I announced.

'Please don't,' said Emily. Then, suspiciously she said, 'You never take selfies.'

Undaunted, I took a couple of pictures of the happy couple. Purely for my records.

'Have you seen the Oriu?' said Jacob. He had been doing some thinking.

'The what?' I asked.

'The houses where there is a natural rock formation that is perhaps the shape of a wave and by adding a few extra bricks it just about turns into a house.'

'Yes, we saw some recently,' I said.

'Oriu are a curiosity to look at and the world is a better place that they exist,' said Jacob. 'But they would be ugly and impractical to live in. No one wants to live in an Oriu.'

I looked blank.

'I was furthering your analogy about bricks being the truth,' he explained. 'People say they want the truth, but it is unwieldy and impractical. Look, what's the point of the truth?'

'It helps us get our jobs done and helps us make decisions,' I replied.

'So we should evaluate the truth purely on whether it helps us and nothing more,' he said.

'Literally no one takes that view,' I said.

Emily had an expression that I read as 'I knew you would both get on.'

'And anyway the heart always rules the head,' continued Jacob. 'Emotions trump facts. Look. Look at Emily; she is beautiful. I can't explain why I love her. It is not a fact thing.'

'You love me?' asked Emily.

Hold on a fracking second, didn't Jacob use that same line on Sarah and get away with it? What has got into Emily? She heard him use the same line with Sarah; I was there are the time. In Pinocchio's.

I went in the house to fetch a tray of drinks - and try not to throw up my stomach contents from all the cloying sweetness outside. I also got a pair of scissors. When I went back outside, the happy couple were kissing. The tongue action was wilfully visible.

'You haven't worn your dress for ages,' I said to Emily, flicking her head with a finger. Hard. Making sure it hurt.

'What dress?' replied Emily.

'The dress you wore non-stop for two years.'

'I got some petrol on it,' she replied.

For some reason this made Jacob laugh; it was evidently an in-joke. Perhaps by petrol they meant sperm.

'You two seem all loved up,' I said.

'We're just organising going away for the weekend,' said Emily.

'Is that wise?' I asked. I wasn't joking. Somehow it had just slipped off my tongue.

They were playing footsie now, and Emily's finger was tracing the top of Jacob's thigh.

'We are walking along the coast on the west of the island,' she said. 'We've got ourselves a speed boat and we've booked a hotel in Ajaccio and everything.'

They were ridiculously loved up. I was not going to able to put in a good word for Sarah as promised.

Jacob and Emily both drunk from their glasses.

'I asked for white wine?' said Emily.

'Indeed,' I replied. I deliberately chose red wine so it wouldn't create condensation on the outside of the glass.

I stood and started snipping at a few leaves of the bougainvillea.

'What are you doing?' asked Emily.

'Trimming the bougainvillea,' I said.

'No you're not,' she replied. 'Not with that little pair of scissors.'

'I can't find my shears,' I said.

'They're in the bathroom,' she said.

'No they are not. Why would they be in the bathroom?'

'I don't know. But that is where I saw them.'

I snipped at the branches ineffectually with my scissors.

'Oh you're doing my head in,' said Emily standing up. 'I am going to get the shears.'

'From where?'

'From in the bathroom,' she said.

'They are not in the bathroom,' I replied.

They were in the bathroom. I knew perfectly well they were in the bathroom, because I had placed them there.

Emily went inside the house.

'Did you just cut some of my hair?' asked Jacob.

'No,' I replied.

I had just cut some of his hair.

Emily returned with the shears.

'Ha!' she said, handing them over.

'Pete just cut some of my hair off,' protested Jacob. He didn't sound too riled; he certainly wasn't going to hit me or anything.

'Pete is this true?' asked Emily. 'Have you cut Jacob's hair?'

'No,' I replied.

'Turn out your pockets,' she said.

I wasn't going to turn out my pockets.

'Turn out your pockets!'

'Shan't.'

At that moment I had an amazing stroke of luck. An unseen bird flew overhead and shat in my drink.

'Good grief,' I said. 'What kind of day is this?'

'And what aim!' marvelled Emily. 'Now there's a metaphor. Forget your stupid wall.'

The glass of wine the bird had shat in was the last of my bottle of Villa Maestracci 2015; among the finest wines made in Corsica. I wanted to weep. I leant over the glass to see if the bird dropping had fallen straight to the bottom without dissolving into the wine on the way. It was hard to tell.

'Don't even think of drinking it,' said Emily.

'Come on let's take you into town for a drink,' said Jacob. 'I know of a bar that sells wine that would make your bottle of Villa Maetracci sick with jealously.'

What a fine young man.

'I'll just clear the table,' I said.

And turn out the contents of my pockets and place them in a clean plastic freezer bag.

I picked Jacob's wine glass up only touching it at the stem and placed it along with the other two on the tray. I took it inside and placed it carefully on a high shelf in the kitchen where nothing could disturb the fingerprints on it.

'What are you doing?' asked Emily from behind me.

'Tidying up,' I replied.

'No seriously. What are you doing?'

Part Four

THE WORLD ACCORDING TO EMILY

ONE

The points along the path of this tangled tale where I felt the game was up are too numerous to mention, but certainly when the police rolled up outside the Lluberas house I feared the worst. They were going to arrest me along with the family, but somehow, for whatever reason, I fainted.

When I woke up in the hospital, I was handcuffed to the bed.

I wanted to say something, but it wouldn't come out. I had some words in my brain, but they slipped back into a fog.

'Don't tell my brother,' I said out loud.

There was no one there to hear me.

Then there was a policeman there and a nurse.

'Have I been arrested?' I asked.

'We are waiting to charge you, until you are well enough,' he replied. 'In the meantime, we are detaining you pending charges, on order of the judge.'

'What have I done?'

'You were involved with the theft of a car belonging to Jacob Lluberas from Bastia.'

I passed out again.

Jacob Lluberas? They couldn't get us for burning out Sarah's car, so they went for that charge instead. Perhaps. I had a terrible thirst. I tried calling out, but no one heard me. I called out in French, I called out in English. I called out in Corsican.

'Emily?'

'Emily!'

'Emily?'

It was Lisabetta, but also there was a man.

'I've just had the weirdest dream,' I said.

'Emily look into this light,' said the man.

There was a light.

A man turned away. He was writing something.

'Lisabetta?' I called.

'Yes,' she replied.

'People mustn't know I am here. Pete mustn't know I am here.'

'Everything is okay. Everything is good,' she said.

She held my hand.

'I love you,' I said.

'I love you,' said Lisabetta.

'Do you know your name?' asked the man.

Lisabetta squeezed my hand.

'I am Emily Fisher.'

'When is your date of birth?'

'1st of June 1982.'

'Who is the President?'

'Of France? President Macron.'

I am Emily Fisher. My date of birth is 1st of June 1982. And this is the first time in my life I have told someone I love them.

'What have I been arrested for?'

'We are sorting it out,' said Lisabetta. 'It is just the police trying to poke the fire.'

'What's poking the fire?'

'They can't make the charges stick.'

'But why are they interested in Jacob Lluberas's car? It makes no sense.'

'They have had half the family in a prison cell for questioning. They are saying that if Jacob says he is happy with his car being stolen. If he says he just lent the car, then they will drop charges.'

'But Jacob is dead,' I protested.

'Yes. But his mother says he is alive. They are flushing us out. Getting us to make a move. Or just doing us for anything they can, 'cos they have it in for us.'

I swear that even if you were fully well, and even if you weren't pumped full of drugs, you would still feel ill just lying in a hospital bed for a day.

I needed a pee. Lisabetta had gone. Because my arm was handcuffed to the bedframe it was difficult to manoeuvre. I had to ask for a nurse, and she brought me a thing that looked like a wheelchair but in fact was a toilet. It had a papier-maché trilby in the middle that was upturned to catch my urine. It was the highlight of the morning. Or afternoon.

I was sitting on the side of my bed and trying to take control. I wanted to look like discharge material. It was a hard look to pull off, given the surgical gown and the handcuffs.

For the first time, I noticed I had a plastic cannula stuck in my vein on the back of my hand. How had I not noticed that?

A lady with a clipboard appeared. She removed the clock from the wall ahead of me. That clock had been my companion – watching the second hand go round. She placed it face down on the bed. Why would someone do that?

'I would like to do a test with you,' she said. She was middle aged and had an annoying blue cardigan with distended pockets where she'd put too many things in them over the years.

I had to do a test that involved drawing a clock face on a piece of paper. Then I had to identify a number of cartoon animals. I had to count backwards from a hundred in units of seven. Then I had to remember a list of random words and repeat them on the spot. Then, much later as a trick she asked me if I could recall them again. I had to remember sentences and then some numbers. I quite enjoyed it. Anything to do in a hospital is a blessing.

The lady got a pen and marked the test.

'How did I do?' I only asked by way of conversation.

'Not very well,' she replied.

'You're kidding,' I said.

So I pulled the sheet from her hands and scrutinised it. I had dropped marks all over the place. I had failed to remember the sentences. I had failed to remember the numbers. I couldn't count back from a hundred in sevens (well who can?) I had even dropped points when naming pictures of animals. Like I can't name an animal. According to this woman, I had pointed to a picture of a rhino and announced grandly that it was a wild boar. It looked a bit like a wild boar, and we were in Corsica, which is so lousy with them it might as well be the national animal. But the fact remains the picture was clearly of a rhino. I was astonished.

I looked at that piece of paper for an eternity. How had this happened? Because I felt better in myself, I had assumed I was well.

'How did I do in the test?' I asked the woman. But she had gone.

I felt bile rising up. I tried to choke it down. I breathed calmly and waited. It should subside soon.

And I remembered that bile like it was yesterday.

I would have a pint of water next to my bed every night and I would drink it so that if I was sick it would dilute the bile. It was etching my teeth and sometimes when I vomited it, it would come through my nose. Those were crazy times. I knew I had a problem; of course I knew I had a problem. And I was young, that was my excuse of late; I could be emotionally down and wiped out for days and I started looking for ways to climb out of the downer days. I was popping pills and taking stuff I didn't even know, and then there was the alcohol, of course there was the alcohol. And the hospitals. Then we were at a concert. It was one of those venues that was just a bit too big, so the band was in the far distance, but it was a band I loved, like the Killers or something, or maybe it was a club and maybe it was dance music. We were hemmed in with people seated and I needed to go to the toilet and the music was great but I remember tensing my thighs and the boyfriend I was with was looking at me strangely. He said, 'Do you want to pee?' and I was shouting 'Yeah, yeah, I want to pee. I need to pee. I might have left it too late.' And I thought it was odd because he wanted to come with me. I shuffled along the little walkway in front of all the people sitting and I think it was a football stadium now I look back, or maybe it didn't happen at all; maybe it was a compound memory. There was a disabled woman at the end of the row in a wheelchair and I trod on her foot and I remember thinking in that way that only makes sense with drink or drugs, I remember thinking, 'Oh it's alright I stood on her foot she can't feel a thing, she's disabled.' And I remember her carer or her friend gave me a terrible look, and I said, 'Oh how English! You are upset with me, but you don't say anything you just stare at me; you just give me a look. What would I have to do to get you to shout at me? Spit in her face?' And then someone remonstrated with me and so I did spit in their face, and I remember twirling around in a concrete corridor and there was shouting and I couldn't make things out. 'I'm alright, I'm alright,' I said. And I realised I was on the ground. There was a face over me and then I said, 'I'm alright.' It was a woman with a round face and badly dyed purple hair. I went to stand up and there was a crack as my face hit the concrete floor, teeth first. And there was blood in my mouth. And the boyfriend's face, then Pete's face. Then nothing. Then nothing. And then there was Pete. There was Pete in the hospital.

One day he made an album of photos.

I opened my eyes and Pete was sitting in the sensible chair that every hospital places besides the bed (perhaps that is why I am thinking of this now) and he was doing a crossword and he noticed I was awake.

'I have made you an album,' he said.

'An album?' I asked.

'You are having trouble remembering things and the hospital asked me to bring in photographs to jog your memory.'

'You have got an album of photos to jog my memory? What am I a hundred?' I asked. 'Isn't that what you do for old folk?'

I looked at the album. It was the sort we all had before smart phones; a thick folder made of plastic that pretended to mimic an old fashioned leather bound book, and inside there are lots of plastic sleeves to put your photographs.

I pulled my face into an expression of interest or gratitude or some such. But Pete looked at me strangely so I pulled my face into another expression that I hoped was more appropriate.

Pete opened the album and said, 'I want you to tell me who everyone is in the photographs. Tell me if you recognise anyone.'

The thing is I must have really been out with the fairies on previous days and I must have simply forgotten my antics or forgotten my amnesia because when Pete showed me his album I certainly knew who most of the people were in the photos.

There was a picture of Mum of course, and there was an old picture of Dad. But after that Pete had floundered. What he had done was to go online to Facebook or MySpace or whatever was the social media at the time and he had printed off pictures of me he'd found there. But here is the thing. Although I did have a Facebook page and I am indeed an Instatwitter and the rest, I hardly ever post photos and neither do my closer friends. I mean, for example, the kind of antics I got up to with Antone are the last things you would want to post on the internet, so the photos that Pete had found online were quite peripheral to my life. Yes, I was in a nightclub with people and someone had tagged me, but they were tiny fragments, random snapshots, of my life and not the main story at all. These were pictures of bit players, colleagues, acquaintances; they weren't the lovers and the main men.

So I looked at this album and I recognised the images from my life but it wasn't my life at all. It was like if you looked through the keyhole at a famous art collection in a famous art museum but all you could actually see through the keyhole was the fire extinguisher on the wall opposite and a bit of curtain. But Pete wasn't to know that. As far as Pete could tell the fire extinguisher and the bit of curtain was my life, because these were the images he found where I was tagged on the internet. Pete knows me better than any other human in the world, and yet he doesn't really know me at all. It doesn't take much to make you depressed in a hospital bed, and that thought made me depressed for a week.

'Can you recognise these people?' persisted Pete. I had obviously gone quiet.

'That is Sam and Laura from the office, at my first job. We are in a club in Norwich,' I explained.

Pete looked pleased.

'And that's another Laura,' I said. 'And that's Chloe and that is Richard. I think I had sex with him once.'

'Very good.'

'Twice to be fair,' I said. 'Once was a sort of accident and then it turned out he was rather fond of me, so I had sex a second time because I felt sorry for him. It just made matters worse.'

I kissed Pete on the brow. What I loved, what I really loved, was the effort Pete had gone to in order to make the album in the first place. 'I shall keep this forever,' I said. And I did keep it for a while, though I've lost it now.

And the point was that Pete stuck with me; he was always there. There was Pete in the rehab place. There was Pete in reception when I was released. There was Pete with the paperwork. There was Pete finding me a drugs support counsellor. There was Pete finding me another counsellor when I fell out with the first one because he made a pass at me, and okay, I did flirt with him first, but I reported him to his professional body when he flirted with me and there was a whole to-do, and I only flirted 'cos I was bored. Pete had to extricate me from that one. And Pete never said a word. And he never said a word when I got into trouble with the police and I ended up with a record and they had my DNA and my fingerprints and all that irritation. And he must have spent money, he must have spent thousands, and he must have covered for me at work. He just never said a word. He didn't even hug me. If he had hugged me I would have cried and cried.

He would try and make conversation and he would talk about the past, and sometimes he would hold my hand as I lay in a ward and we said nothing forever.

I owe Pete one.

Actually, I don't owe Pete one. I owe him everything.

Sometimes I can see it in my face. I look in the mirror and I wonder if other people can see that I used to do drugs. I have made my peace with alcohol, but I never did drugs again. Can people see that in my face? A certain asymmetry? Are the eyes a little deep set? Is my skin not quite right? How could they see it? I can see it. But is it my secret or does everyone know? I've made a new life in Corsica but do they all somehow know, and talk about me behind my back and never mention it to me? Poor Emily they say, well what with her past what do you expect? This is my belief as to who I am. I can live clean for thirty years, but this will still be who I am.

TWO

The next morning when I woke, there was action going on by my wrist. The policeman was unlocking the handcuff.

'To what do I owe the honour?' I asked.

'Jacob Lluberas has dropped charges,' he said.

'He never pressed charges in the first place,' I said. 'He was dead.'

I found Lisabetta's dress – the one I borrowed after we burnt out the car – it was in a locker by the bed. I planned to put it on but fell asleep with my mouth open, saliva dripping from the corner of my mouth. I am one sexy bitch.

Where was Lisabetta? Where was Antone? I had done nothing for these people. But they had been so kind. They were all I had.

'I want to leave,' I said to a doctor.

'Do you trust me?' he asked.

'I trust you.' I said.

'Do you believe that I want the best for you?' he asked.

'I believe you want the best for me,' I replied.

'Please trust me when I say I need you to stay in the hospital.'

Lisabetta was sitting beside my bed. She was knitting.

'How come the police have dropped the charges?'

'We've brought Jacob back to life,' she said. 'He went to talk to a judge in Bastia. Jacob said he was fine with his car being in the wrong place. He said he hadn't been murdered by Sarah.'

'Jacob Lluberas?' I asked.

I passed out. I going to have to accept I was very ill.

Jacob Lluberas. I found I even dreamt about him. Jacob Lluberas; it began with love as all good stories should.

He was a lad from the South West of the Island. He came from the kind of village that wears its heritage with pride, that have lived and breathed resilience to all comers despite centuries of poverty and hardship. These are people who look after their own and nurse a grudge for centuries. These are kind, good people; but they never forget.

Jacob had been dating a girl called Sofia from the next village.

Sofia got pregnant.

Sofia was from a traditional-minded family and, worse, a family that had some ancient grievances against Jacob's family. There was no single big issue between the families that I could get to the bottom of, but according to who was telling the tale, there were sagas of murders in the 17th century, a few more in the 18th century, and then in the 19th century an out of control killing spree that involved the kidnap and death of dozens of the family. It was so bad it resulted in the army being called to restore order. But many of the finest rural Corsican families would claim a similar history to this; and if they couldn't, they'd probably make one up.

The fact remained, however, that there was enough history between the two families for a lot of people to raise an eyebrow about Jacob and Sofia to be dating at all, let alone about her getting pregnant. When the news got out, gnarled uncles thumped kitchen tables, ruminating widows pursed their denture-less lips. 'No good has ever come of that family,' both families muttered about the other. A delegation of hot headed brothers and cousins drove off to confront Jacob and discover his intentions toward Sofia.

They found him in a bar with Antone, myself and a few others from Antone's family. We were having a drink and a chat, like normal people do on a Saturday night.

I swear some people think they are in a wild west movie.

Sofia's brothers and sundry irate male relatives came storming through the door with shotguns at shoulder height, sweeping them around the room.

'Lluberas!' called one of the brothers with a gun.

The entire bar looked round; their surnames, after all, were mostly Lluberas.

Jacob was not someone I knew very well. I had perhaps met him twice. He was handsome and good natured, but like the island itself he had a core of solid rock; and if you come up against rock, it is you who will get hurt.

Jacob knew that of all the Lluberas men present, he was the one they wanted, so he turned to square up to Sofia's brothers.

'What are your intentions to Sofia?' asked a brother. He was the smallest and busiest looking.

Jacob moved forwards towards the shotgun. He then folded his legs down slightly so that he was lower and the end of the shotgun barrel level with his nose. This was both an act of bravery, and an insult intended to show how short the brother was.

If the intended outcome was to make matters worse, then job done. In a blink, the Lluberas contingent had knives in their hands. Do they all carry knives all the time? The owner of the bar evaporated, and I was eyeing up the path to the toilets. Could I plausibly pretend to the police that I was in the toilets all along? Was there a window in there I could climb out of? My handbag was on the back of a chair in the middle of the room, while I myself was somehow standing by the bar. I often think we women are held back by our use of handbags; my bag had my ID in it and my money; I couldn't leave it behind. Plus, it was a Birkin bag. Some misguided former admirer had kindly shelled out thousands of pounds for it. So either way, I wasn't going to leave the bag. I mean who takes a Birkin bag to a murder? Me evidently.

The room, I remember, was made of stone. It was a lovely bar, but it was solid in every way. I was pretty sure that if a gun went off then a few glasses would get broken and the odd glass shelf would shatter, but the building itself was so solid it would pretty much go unharmed; the bar had seen bigger fights than this one. But the fact remained, there was a gun and it was pointed at Jacob's head, and Jacob was determined not to calm the situation down.

Jacob pulled a face at Sofia's brother that was both brazen and somehow sad. He sort of swaggered left and right in a manner that was meant to provoke him, but to my eye there was a sadness about it. It was very odd and very hard to put into words.

Sofia's brother responded with a low growl.

Jacob went, 'Go on then pull the trigger.' At least one other person present agreed with me later that his tone of voice was somehow one of surrender.

Antone meanwhile was to the left of Sofia's brother. He had spotted a hefty looking stool. His hand crept towards it.

Jacob's hand, meanwhile, reached forward slowly but resolutely and pressed the man's trigger finger. He appeared to be trying to push the trigger himself.

Antone hadn't seen what Jacob was doing. He picked up the stool with two hands and swung it hard at the head of Sofia's brother. The stool was made of wood; it hit the ear and temple of Sofia's brother and because he wasn't expecting it, he hadn't braced himself. His head snapped sideways on his neck.

The trouble is, in the same manoeuvre, the shotgun went off.

Sofia's brother, whose name I can't recall, was on the flagstone floor on his back. There was blood on the floor, and I got the impression that he would have sustained two injuries: the hit from the wooden stool and the hit as the back of his head hit the stone floor. He was twitching. The twitch was in his neck and down his right arm. It was very alarming. I felt weak and sick.

In fairness to the men present, there wasn't then a sudden escalation in violence. There were still some shotguns in evidence, and there were still plenty of knives in the hands of the Lluberas contingent; but suddenly everyone had gone into containment mode. Some people were dissolving into the night, while others were bending over the body of Sofia's brother.

There was no one bending over the body of Jacob. There was no point. His face had been blown clean off by the shotgun cartridge; he was definitely dead.

I felt hands move under my armpits and I was half lifted up and carried forward. It was Antone. He guided me out of the door and into the parking area.

'Wait in the car,' he said.

I just sat in the dark in the car. I could have been there forever, or for only a few moments.

I had no clear idea about a plan. I was a witness to murder, but it didn't occur to me to ring the police. I suppose I felt I was waiting on what was decided by everyone else; I felt it was not my country, so it was not my place to make decisions. I felt that traditional Corsican families would always welcome a chance to address their own problems without recourse to outsiders and I was an outsider.

The car door opened and Antone sat beside me.

'Let's get out of here,' he said.

We stuck together from that day.

I don't know who came up with it first.

Jacob's body had been spirited away to a meat storage butcher's place owned by the family. I never saw it, I just always imagined him hanging up amongst the beef and pork carcases but with a white cloth over him and some frost around his ankles; but in truth I don't know and I don't want to know in case the police started asking me questions.

I do know that a little time later we were sitting at a table and Jacob's wallet and ID and keys were right next to me and I said, 'He looks a lot like you.' And I held up his photo next to Antone and said, 'You just need to shave a bit differently and cut your hair a little different.'

'People often say we are brothers,' he said. 'We have been mistaken for each other.'

'Are you known on the other side of the island? Bastia, Calvi?' I asked. 'What if we establish you for a few weeks on my side of the island. Date a girl. Establish you as Jacob. Then stage your suicide.'

'We would be best to just dump the body,' he said. 'Dump it in the mountains. One day it will be found but the animals will have got it first.'

So, at that stage we dropped the idea.

But a few days went by and because I was dating Antone I ended up once more with a group of the Lluberas boys. They were buzzing and conspiratorial in a friend's house. None of us were sober.

Antone seemed to be well respected by the family. When he spoke, they listened. My contributions, such as they were, were largely ignored.

'The thing is,' Antone explained to the group. 'The older members of the family have all got involved. They have grievances that drive me crazy. The old folk; they never remember to take their medication, but they do remember some grievance from four hundred years ago. So they want a sum of money for Sofia to bring up a baby, and our family have somehow agreed to this and the young brothers...'

'But they killed Jacob!' someone reasoned. 'They shot him in cold blood. He did nothing to provoke them.'

'Didn't he?' I asked.

I was ignored. Instead, they debated the difficulty of raising money to compensate Sofia's family. They then discussed the opposite course of action; upping the stakes and turning it all into a feud.

'I have an idea,' I offered.

No one looked my way.

'I have an idea,' I offered again louder. Was I invisible? Could these men not hear the frequency and wavelength of a woman's voice?

I stood up tall.

'Excuse me!' I called. I tapped the side of a glass. I kept tapping until everyone was silent. They still didn't actually look my way, which was disconcerting.

'Go on,' laughed Antone. 'They are listening in their way.'

'I work in the insurance industry,' I began. 'I know how insurance works. I have an idea for a plan.' I described in detail a couple of different ways the family could take out insurance policies on Jacob and stage his death anew. They all listened in silence. I laid it on thick about my industry knowledge and my experience, probably because I was annoyed at being ignored. When I finished, there was no tangible evidence I had even spoken, so I was just left standing in silence, then sat down again unacknowledged.

The Lluberas men started talking to each other again. Occasionally one or two of them would look furtively my way.

Finally, Antone spoke loudly so that the whole group had his attention.

'I am up for it,' he said.

'What?' asked one.

'Posing as Jacob on the Bastia side of the island and taking out insurance on his life,' he replied. 'Emily, tell them what you told me about the girl you mentioned in your office. The girl called Sarah.'

'Sure,' I said. 'And out of interest, how easy is it to get an Italian identity card?'

'It can be done,' said Antone.

'Do you fancy a trip to Italy?' I asked.

'Where?'

'Livorno.'

'Tell them about the girl called Sarah at your office,' he said again.

And so it all began.

THREE

'I need to get out of here,' I said. 'Out of the hospital. I think they have my handbag. And my phone. Maybe my shoes.'

Lisabetta conferred with her father. Lisabetta pared off to leave the room. I wanted to make conversation with the father, but I didn't know what to say. I smiled a lot.

A while later Lisabetta returned with a woman who looked like a head nurse. Lisabetta was holding my handbag and shoes with an air of triumph; an unseen event had clearly happened.

'You wanted to see me?' asked the head nurse.

'Yes,' I said. 'Is there any legal reason why I cannot leave this hospital?'

'No,' she replied, but I could see her guard was up and there was a lot of thinking going on behind her supposedly helpful eyes.

'In that case could you please remove the cannula from the back of my hand?'

'I cannot do that,' she said.

'Why not?'

'It is the job of a haematologist,' she replied.

'Or a nurse surely?' I asked. 'Never mind. I will do it. How hard could it be? I just take off the tape and pull.' I felt sick even saying the words, so I added, 'Why exactly can't a nurse do it?'

'I am going to get a doctor,' she said. It was my belief she meant she was going to get a doctor to remonstrate with me, not a doctor to pull out my cannula. In either event she disappeared.

I was feeling bloody minded so I put out my right hand and with the fingernails of my left hand I started peeling back the surgical tape. I now had full access to the plastic cannula with its well of lifeless blood.

Lisabetta and her father were wide-eyed in silence.

I felt faint, but pushed through.

I gripped the tube between finger and thumb and shut my eyes.

I pulled.

I just about got the needle onto the bedside table before my stomach did a dry heave.

The doctor appeared with the head nurse we had seen before. The latter was looking indignant and empowered by having summoned a colleague. She fanned her two palms out like she was going to catch a cricket ball. I have no idea what she meant by it.

'I am leaving,' I said firmly.

'Okay, but first you must sign some paperwork,' she said.

'Then get the paperwork,' I said.

'It will take twenty minutes to organise it.'

I looked at the clock that was back on the wall.

'I will give you twenty-five minutes. When the big hand gets to the top of the clock I am going. And I can draw a clock by the way.'

They never did return with the paperwork, but when the big hand got to twelve, Lisabetta and I walked through the corridors and out of the hospital.

Her father had brought the car round the front.

'They will report us to the authorities,' said Lisabetta. She sounded concerned. I was letting her down, I was adding to her problems; but she was supporting me regardless.

The energy I had shown getting out of the hospital was soon spent. I collapsed in the back of the car. I felt I had a fever. I was hallucinating and remembering the oddest combinations of things from my past. The day I sat by a swimming pool reading High Fidelity. Walking through Brooklyn in my twenties and being wolf whistled. I felt sick. But I wasn't sick. But I knew that feeling. The illness, the letting people down. These were feelings I had had before.

'Stop the car!'

We were in the countryside now. In some foothills.

'Open the window. Stop the car,' I said.

Somehow I leant forward and just about got my mouth out of the window and threw up down the side of the car. At least it wasn't on the inside. The vomit wasn't in the car. I would soon be home.

Home was with the Lluberas family.

I was in a bed in the house in the woods. The Lluberas family house. I fell prey to a number of moods that dragged me forwards and backwards and always helpless, like a body being washed up on the shore. At first I was relieved to be out of the hospital, then within a day I felt depressed that I was stuck in someone else's house. Then I simply submitted to the whole experience.

Lisabetta would sit by me and talk or sew.

She would prattle on in a constant stream about nothing in particular, but I loved it.

She was prone to making me thick soups with beef and carrots and potatoes. She called it 'English food' but English from which century? I tried to eat what I could, to please her. It was likely I simply had a nasty virus. The most common things are the most common. In truth, if it had been a virus, the hospital would have mentioned a high temperature so I felt in my heart it was a combination of stress, being weirded out by events, and my deep-seated belief that I wrecked my body in the past and sustained some damage so deep that it cannot be found and cannot be undone.

The nights were the worst. When your reality involves dragging corpses from under beds and dressing the dead to look like the living, it can be difficult to differentiate between dreams and reality.

Sometimes I would hear voices from beyond my wooden walls.

'If we feed his head to the pigs,' one said.

I would crane to hear better, but just hear the sounds of the forest or the ticking of a clock.

'If we place him so that his head is in the pen with pigs and the body is beyond their reach, they will gnaw at the head,' said a man in a whisper that somehow caught the wind.

'Do they want to eat a human head?' asked another.

One day it was Antone's voice. He talked and reasoned and pleaded but I couldn't understand a word.

Someone replied, 'Tow the body out to sea. Far out to sea. The flesh will rot and bloat, the pathologists will be confused, the fish will eat the body. One day it will wash up on the shore.'

'Couldn't he fall headfirst into some farm machinery? Far more respectful,' said another.

They all laughed at that one.

Antone was standing over me and I relaxed into the sheets happy to see him.

'What have you been doing?' I asked. I knew what I'd been doing. I didn't have much news.

'Working out how to dispose of Jacob's body a second time,' he said.

'Didn't you say that before?' I asked. 'Have I been dreaming this?'

'I visit you every day,' he said.

Then Antone was there again, but his clothes were different.

He was relaxed and loving.

'I have brought you clothes from your apartment,' he said.

This felt good. It felt like recovery was in sight.

'What news with you?' I asked.

'Ah the usual,' he said. 'We have been trying to pick out the shotgun pellets from Jacob's face.'

'The usual Friday night in the Lluberas household.'

'Exactly,' he laughed.

'And why are you picking out the pellets from his face?'

'Well we feel that if he dies again, it won't be from a shotgun wound this time. We don't want the pathologist finding pellets.'

'That body can't be in a very good shape now,' I said.

'No. We are going to have to factor that in,' he said. 'We might tow it out to sea and let the fish do their work.'

I was very conscious of how I must look. My face was clammy from illness and the last time I'd seen a mirror all I could see were dark rings under my eyes and matted hair. I didn't want Antone to see me this way. I squeezed his hand and he squeezed it back. I couldn't think what to talk about. I tried to remember what we usually talked about. I couldn't recall a single conversation we'd ever had. Everyone knows that when it's hospital visiting it's near impossible to make conversation.

I gave Antone's hand a big definitive squeeze.

'I'm sorry, I don't feel well,' I said.

'No worries,' he said. 'I'll see you soon.'

When I was feeling better, I would be able to go on a flirting offensive and put matters right.

Then one afternoon I found I was sitting on the side of the bed.

'Why don't you change into some clothes and sit on the veranda?' said Lisabetta. 'It will make you feel good.'

I went walking in the woods with her, and rather than illness it felt more like a holiday from my life. She took me on trails through the trees and along by the brooks, then she took me on a trip in the car to show me menhirs and stone burial chambers. She told me folklore about how they got there and what they were taught in school about them. It was mystic and beautiful and apart from getting some itchy eyes from hay fever, I began to feel much better.

'Can I tell you a secret?' Lisabetta said one day.

We were harvesting wild figs. Lisabetta had provided us with a linen sack each. She wore hers on her front, I wore mine on my side. We only needed about twelve, so I think the linen sacks were mostly decorative.

'I have told no one this secret,' she said. 'So you must promise not to tell anyone.'

'I promise.' I made a little saluting action with my hand.

Lisabetta pulled her lips into a smile. She looked like a six-year-old confessing to kissing a boy.

'I have a boyfriend,' she said. As predicted.

'A boyfriend?' I replied. 'Why is that a secret? Does he belong to the wrong family?'

'Silly!' she said. 'My family won't mind who I date!'

'Sorry,' I said.

'Why are you sorry?'

'I am just afraid that I am always close to saying the wrong thing,' I explained.

'You can never say the wrong thing,' she said poking me in the side. 'We are friends!'

'Okay, so why is it a secret?'

'People can make a big deal of things. If my family knew I even kissed someone they would go and visit the family and ask their intentions.'

'I got off lightly then,' I said. 'No one has quizzed me about my intentions with Antone.'

'Oh, we all know what your intentions are with Antone,' she said.

'What?'

'Sex!'

It was her turn to wonder if she had said the wrong thing.

'So to be clear, I don't have to marry Antone just because I kissed him,' I asked.

'Oh no. It's easier for you,' she said. 'Do you want to marry him?'

'I don't suppose so,' I said.

'Me and my boyfriend have sex!' she said.

'Er... good for you?' I ventured.

'I just wanted you to know that,' she said.

It was my turn to dig her in the ribs.

'It's a secret,' she said.

'I know,' I replied.

I found a really plump fig to pick.

'Do you enjoy the sex?' I asked.

'Yes,' she replied. 'It is just that traditionally for a girl to be marriageable she should be a virgin. In fact, she should be untouched at all by any man. And of course these things don't matter these days but my grandmother is lovely and I have a great-grandmother and they are lovely and they like to think I am pure and my family like to think the best of me, like you said about your brother and we mustn't tell him what has been happening.'

We picked some more figs and Lisabetta turned her conversation more generally.

'We used to have a traditional way of marrying where the bride and the groom meet in the house of the bride's parents and they kiss in front of witnesses. And then we all eat fritters made of chestnut flour and then the couple have to go to bed.'

'Straightaway?' I asked.

Lisabetta giggled. 'Straightaway, with everyone downstairs.'

'You'd have to be quiet,' I said.

'And then if they have a baby they then go to a church or the town hall and get married in the normal way.'

'Wow! Remind me to turn down chestnut fritters, if Antone's dad offers me one.'

'And that is why a bride wears a veil,' she explained.

'You have lost me,' I said.

'If a woman wears a veil then she has not been kissed by a man. So in the marriage ceremony when she lifts the veils and allows the man to kiss her, the lifting of the veil proves it is the first time she has been kissed. And then they are betrothed.'

'Well I never,' I said.

'Why did you think a bride wears a veil?' asked Lisabetta.

'I had no idea. To hide her face if she's ugly?'

Lisabetta laughed loudly. It was gratifyingly easy to make her laugh.

'But as you know,' said Lisabetta. 'It is still a big thing in some families if a woman gets pregnant and there is no promise from the man.'

We'd gathered enough figs so I eyed up a sunny patch on a riverbank to sit on instead.

'Do you want to see where we do it?' she asked.

'Do what?'

'Have sex,' she replied.

'Does it involve a walk?'

As we walked she shared some of the local gossip.

'We have a thing coming up in a few weeks where the lady is pregnant and she doesn't want to marry the man who made her pregnant, but also he hasn't offered to marry.'

'So?'

'So the brothers of the pregnant woman have booked a church and they are taking the bride to the church and they will be armed.'

'Armed?' I asked.

'You know. Knives, guns.'

'The usual for a wedding.' I said.

Lisabetta laughed loudly. Evidently I am hilarious. I should so do stand-up.

'They won't use the guns, silly! It is part of the ceremony. In your country if it is a military wedding do you not have a guard of honour? Perhaps the men have kilts and swords?'

'You have an intriguing view of our country, but maybe? And all the men in London wear bowler hats and have umbrellas under their arms and all French men in Paris wear berets and have a string of onions.'

'Exactly!' Another hearty laugh from Lisabetta. It's like I kill in rural Corsica. Sadly, this is not a metaphor. She continued, 'The kilts and swords relate to some tradition from the past. Anyway in this case for the honour of everyone, the groom must stand on the church steps and offer to marry the woman.'

'But you said she doesn't want to marry him.'

'Well he has been charming her! He has taken her on dates, even though she is not keen. The family told her to go. He does want to marry her and so we shall see whether she says yes on the day.'

'We?'

'We are all going! We're all really looking forward to it. It is a long way from here but we are going. So she then, in front of the whole village square, can either lift her veil and agree to marry him, or she can leave her veil down and then she has her honour back. Because she was asked to be married in front of the community but she turned him down, so she has her pride and honour. Then we will all cheer.'

'Then everyone has a party?' I asked.

'Pretty much.'

We had been walking upstream and uphill. We reached a sun trap; a flat rock at the top of a waterfall with a grassy glade nearby.

'This is where you have sex?' I asked.

'Maybe?'

This was where she has sex.

To be fair, the days were good. But I had to find ways of staying busy or I would dwell on events, and it's hard to stay busy in someone else's house.

I would get visual flashbacks of pulling Jacob's body around; we had to get the same clothes on Jacob's body that Antone, posing as Jacob, would be wearing when he went up to the lodge for the dirty weekend with Sarah. Lisabetta and I got the task. Evidently this was 'women's work' in the Lluberas family. We decided on a loose t shirt with a second shirt on top that buttoned up the front, and for his bottom half we had some loose fitting trousers; it is difficult enough to dress a dead body without trying to get them into skinny jeans.

Don't get me started on how disgusting it all was. The body was clammy. It was like it was sweating. Presumably, the tension in the glands goes when you die and all the tiny glands in the skin release their sweat. Or perhaps the body was rotting. It was totally gross.

Lisabetta took this all in her stride and seemed to know what to do; surely she hadn't done this before? I got a roll of paper towel from the kitchen and patted it against the skin of the legs and feet and thighs. I felt nauseous just walking back with it to kitchen bin, although in fairness I felt nauseous a lot during my stay at their house; but dressing a clammy dead body was not going to help. I didn't tell anyone those tissues were in the bin, not even Lisabetta; it would only freak people out, and then I'd have to fish them out again or something.

I got the legs more or less dry and we somehow shimmied some trousers on him, but when we went to lift the top half of his body to get the shirt on, the body made a wheeeeeh noise through the mouth. It gave me a heart attack. It must have been air in the lungs. No wonder I was having nightmares. Lisabetta laughed at me and then apologised. I kissed her on the cheek.

Sometimes I would dwell on how we could get caught out. I tried to think like a detective to work out what they could find. The mobile phone had Antone's DNA as well as the DNA of Jacob. Would that come back to bite us? What about the note I left by Pete's bed? That was a rash moment of panic that ultimately didn't help and had left a loose end. I kept dwelling on how lucky we had been so far. Would our luck balance out and we would now get a run of bad luck?

We had been lucky in the hunting lodge. We had successfully got Jacob's body under the bed well ahead of Sarah's arrival, and we left some sheet from the bed trailing down to obscure its presence. Sarah toddled off to get food and drink out of the car, while

Antone bounced up and down on the bed. When Antone felt the coast was clear he opened the window and I hopped in.

We went to drag the body from under the bed, but inexplicably it got snagged on something unseen. We pulled and pulled one leg each but I can only believe there was a nail sticking up from the floor because as we pulled harder and harder we felt that something had snagged and I got the impression it was pulling at the back of Jacob's flesh. There was then a ripping sound and the body gave and we both fell backwards. That was not a worry so much as the sense we had lost a lot of valuable time. It was then that I spotted a problem.

'Where's your shirt?' I asked Antone.

'I took it off. I got hot,' he replied. He was just wearing a t shirt.

'Yes, but Jacob is wearing a shirt. We can't have the same two shirts in the house. We just want the one shirt and that should be on Jacob.'

There was no time for recriminations. Antone looked out of the bedroom door and down the corridor. He nipped out and left me struggling with the body. I managed to get it clear of the bed and then propped up against the edge of the bed frame. It felt unlikely that Sarah would be gone for more than a few moments. In fact I now realised this was the part of the plan we didn't think through; Antone should have made Sarah go off for some errand in the nearby village. He could say he only drank a certain kind of beer, or a certain type of milk and she needed to get some in. These thoughts were unhelpful, but I couldn't stop my mind racing. We still hadn't got the body on the bed, staged the shooting and run off to our place of safety, and in my mind I kept picturing how long each of these tasks would take.

Jacob re-appeared wearing his shirt.

'I can hear Sarah back in the kitchen,' I whispered.

We both froze. I was panicking big time.

'Just keep going,' I said. 'If we're lucky she will go back out again to the car.'

'Wedge the door,' he said.

'What?'

'Wedge the door with something, and if Sarah does manage to get in we'll jump from behind her and put a blanket over her head.'

In the event there was no need to mug Sarah. We got the body on the bed, shot at his face and jumped out the window; there were only seconds to spare, but we managed it.

I woke one afternoon in bed to hear a lot of people talking somewhere unseen. I walked through to the main room and found the whole family having a meeting.

Antone looked up at me and smiled. 'We have something to tell you,' he said. 'We have worked out a plan and it involves you dating me, as Jacob.'

Part Five

THE WORLD ACCORDING TO PETE

ONE

And then it was Emily's turn to be on the front of newspapers. I heard about it from Jean-Marie at the office and soon found the article online.

MAN DIES IN CLIFF TRAGEDY

Friends watched on in horror as a man plunged to his death after attempting to take a selfie photograph at a popular tourist hiking route by the sea near Piana.

The international student Jacob Lluberas, 34, was "mucking around" with his girlfriend when he fell 40 metres onto rocks at the famous Calanques cliff region on the west coast. He was then swept out to sea.

"We were new to this part, we didn't know it well, he was taking pictures and lost his footing," the man's English girlfriend, Emily De'Ath, 38, said.

The friends, from Bastia, were on a coastal trip, having boated around the island to see the famous red rocks and cliffs.

The couple were walking with another group along the same path who they had met along the way on the Sunday morning, when he veered off the designated path to take photographs.

At around 11.30am the group saw him fall over the edge, hitting a number of rocks along the way. He landed and hit a rock at the bottom of the cliff.

A witness called 112 and said the man looked like he was unconscious after the fall.

Moments later a wave swept through the basin and took the man's body out into the ocean.

'I had to stop a man from jumping in after him and going over the edge,' Miss De'Ath told our reporter.

Sources at the local police say that a body has not yet been found and a search is continuing by air and sea. More to follow.

There was a photograph of the cliff and there was a photograph of Emily. She looked tired and her hair was like straw, but otherwise she was okay. Despite the fact that they got Emily's name and age wrong, I took the story at face value, along - no doubt - with all the other stories in the papers that day.

I had not heard from Emily for a few days. That is not too unusual - we do not have a routine for when we chat or phone each other. The moment I saw the story I tried her mobile, but I couldn't get through.

I walked upstairs to her office. Okay, that's a lie: I took the lift up one floor. I was told that she had the week off; she's had quite a few weeks off over the summer.

Sarah appeared from nowhere.

'He's dead!'

'Yes.'

'Jacob is dead!' said Sarah.

'Apparently so. Perhaps for good this time.' I felt guilty saying that. Almost.

'This is just awful,' said Sarah. 'It's just... I haven't been able to work. I haven't been able to do anything. It is just awful.' She started crying.

A colleague behind her back mouthed 'She's been crying a lot.'

'It was just like I predicted,' said Sarah.

'What?'

'I foresaw his death and I didn't... I didn't...'

'You didn't what?'

'I should have made him more careful. I should have got him to take precautions. We could have prevented his death.'

'He was taking photos on the edge of a cliff. These things happen.'

'He should have been more careful!' wailed Sarah.

'You're making her worse,' mouthed the colleague.

I shrugged a helpless shrug.

'We don't know for sure what happened. Anything could have happened.'

'I suppose,' sniffed Sarah. 'Have you heard from Emily?'

'No.'

Sarah's crying got worse.

'The thing is I love him,' said Sarah. In fact, what Sarah actually said was 'The thing is I luhuhuhuhuhve him,' and it was said with her shoulders heaving up and down.

There was nothing for it; I had to forget my roots, my forebears, and centuries of my culture. I pulled Sarah in for a lengthy smothering very non-British hug.

'We are meant to be,' she continued in a lower voice. 'We are meant to behehehehehehehee.'

Even though the man had clearly run off with Emily, and he was 100% dead at the time: they were meant to be.

'You see I know. I just know this,' she blubbed. 'He loved me. I know he loved me.'

I wonder what would have to occur for Sarah to concede it wasn't meant to behehehehe. Jacob getting a zombie virus? A nuclear holocaust? No matter what facts present themselves to Sarah, in her mind Sarah and Jacob were meant to be.

'Still, look on the bright side,' I said after a while.

'What?'

'Given his form, he might not be dead at all,' I said.

And then there was a horrible pause in which I wished, I really wished, I hadn't made that joke.

Sarah's wail got louder. Her sobbing was now uncontrollable.

At length I was frogmarched from her office by a disdainful colleague.

On the way back to my desk, Daniel called out my name. He could obviously tell by my footsteps it was me. Damn. I was going to have to change my walk. I trudged to his office, hoping he wasn't planning to breathe when talking to me. Gasp gasp breath, gasp gasp breath. All I could ever hear was the breathing.

He closed his door.

I braced myself for a world of irritation.

'Um. We need to talk,' he said.

'Okay,' I said sitting down. Nothing good ever began with the phrase 'We need to talk.'

'Um, tell me what you know about this Jacob Lluberas. Tell me what your theories are.'

So far, I had to concede, there had been no weird breathing - no gasp gasp breath, gasp gasp breath – but I had only been in his office five seconds.

'I have been digging around and contacting our colleagues at other insurance companies. There is an old phrase "Follow the money" and I have been wondering about whether he has taken out other life assurance policies recently,' I said.

'And?' he asked. He was continuing to have the temerity to breathe perfectly normally.

'I have found a number of policies and the dates they were taken out is very telling.'

'Go on. You are the man!' Daniel was trying to be pally - it came over as a bit 'fake mates' but at least he was trying - and in truth he could easily have given me a hard time about both Emily and I being in the papers and all over the internet, seemingly up to our necks in trouble.

'There is the original old policy we all knew about from years ago, but there was also a huge life assurance policy taken out over at Ajaccio. It is close on a million Euros. It was with a completely different company so it didn't show up on my original search.'

'Um, who is the beneficiary?'

'He was. Jacob wasn't married, so it would go to his family.'

'When was it taken out?'

'A month or two before the incident in the lodge in the mountains,' I said.

'Er... um. Okay,' said Daniel. 'Presumably you can provide the details.'

'Indeed. And there is a third policy for a quarter of a million with a company out at Livorno in Italy.'

'And who is the beneficiary of that?'

'An Italian company I've never heard of. The details are a bit hazy.'

'What kind of Italian company?'

'They registered an interest in Jacob as a key worker or a key supplier. Contrary to what the newspaper said, Jacob was not a student, he was involved in import and export.'

'Um, when was this policy taken out?'

'A similar time to the other big policy.'

'And what do you think the story is? Um, the underlying truth?' asked Daniel.

I paused for effect. I felt I deserved a dramatic undertow to my revelation.

'I think they are deliberately getting me and Sarah and my sister involved as witnesses to the death of someone heavily insured.'

'Okay.'

'I think that if you die soon after a big policy is taken out we are likely to investigate at least to a degree. But if we ourselves are the witnesses to the death, then we will be likely to accept it and process the claims on the policies. If we say it is a fraud then it drags us into the investigation and reasonable people don't like being interviewed by the police, so we are likely to rubber stamp the claim and move on.'

'Okay, so they have insured someone they knew they were going to kill?'

'Yes,' I said. 'And I think the plan went wrong somehow and they had to hurriedly disappear all the evidence.'

'A family wouldn't murder their own son.'

'Maybe there was a big feud? Maybe the family had a loss of honour and he had to die. You know what the Corsicans are like about their feuds and the pride of the family. It's like the Montagues and the Capulets, or the Borgias, or some other mythical family from literature, I am not sure which.'

'So you said chase the money. You want to find out who claims the money,' said Daniel.

'Whoever ends up with the money is in on the murder,' I said.

'But what about the death at the cliff edge? Are you claiming that your sister Emily pushed Jacob off the cliff?'

'No,' I said. 'Firstly I haven't had a chance to speak to Emily yet so I don't know the details. I would never want to believe what I read in the papers; they didn't even get Emily's age right. My guess is that Emily temporarily lost sight of Jacob. The article in the newspaper can be interpreted in more than one way but the most likely interpretation was that the so called group of friends passing by were the ones who saw him fall, not Emily. They could have pushed him perhaps, but my theory is quite different.'

'So, er, um, what is your theory?' asked Daniel.

'It wasn't Jacob at all.'

'Okay.'

'I think Jacob was murdered at the lodge in the mountains. I think the crime went wrong. Perhaps they were hoping to report it to a certain detective who was friends with them. I think they had to backtrack on the plan and disappear the murder and then they got someone to pose as Jacob to show he was alive. This person dated my sister and then he "died" again. This time it was investigated by a "correct" detective. I want to see a body. There is no body at the moment. And if there is a body I want a DNA test.'

'So, er, the second death was a staged death that didn't happen?' asked Daniel.

'Yes. They will want the death certificate in order to get the pay off, so we need to keep an eye on that.'

'They have got Emily to vouch for it being an accident. I see what you are thinking.'

Daniel clapped happily; in the manner of a seal who'd been thrown a fish.

'So to conclude, we are interested in whether they find a body, and we want a DNA test, and we want to see who claims the money.'

'You are looking well,' I reflected.

'Thank you!' he said. 'It turned out I had mild asthma. There is a lot of pollen on this island and it was giving me a bit of a wheeze.'

'Really? I lied,' I hadn't noticed.'

'Yes, it was a kind of gasp gasp breath kind of noise?'

'Really?' I replied.

'Yes Pete. I heard you from the other office bitching about it more than once and you mentioned it to my face.'

'Oh yes,' I replied.

'So, I thought I would ask a doctor, I now have an inhaler and it has worked wonders. I have a lot more fresh air going in and out of my lungs.'

'Well I am glad that worked out well for you,' I said. It was suddenly very hot in the room.

I went to go.

'There is a slight problem with your theory about the murder,' he said.

'Which is?'

'Sarah identified the new Jacob as the being the real Jacob. The Jacob she knew all along. Presumably the court was convinced as well, when they dropped the court case.'

Daniel was enjoying himself. He had entirely blown away my theory with one question.

'But you are right,' he said. 'Something is very off about this whole case. Oh and the Borgias weren't a fictional family; they existed.'

Pedant.

Still, I was right about Daniel's breathing difficulty; it turns out he had had asthma. I am often right about these things. So, ha Emily!

I rang the pathologist in Bastia. We often liaise on insurance matters and had a straightforward working relationship. I wanted to impress upon him that if a body turned up his DNA should be checked against all DNA samples that have appeared in the case so far. I also checked that they would analyse any stomach contents to see what time of day Jacob died. He promised to keep me informed.

Almost straight after, my phone rang. It was Emily.

'You've been trying to ring me?'

'Yes Emily, you are all over the papers and the internet. Are you okay?'

'I am fine. It was awful though. I mean. One minute he was there. Then I couldn't see him. I had walked on a bit, but I didn't think it was too far. But when you take photos it is amazing how the person you are walking with gets quite some way ahead, so it turned out I was a lot further ahead. I could see a group of people back at the cliff edge...'

'How many?' I asked.

'Four,' she said. 'But. Well anyway, they were quite some way back and so I didn't think about it. There were a few twists and turns to the path and so I didn't really realise he was gone for a long time. I tried ringing him but there was no answer.'

'The phone was dead? Or he didn't answer?'

'I don't know. I can check on my phone maybe.' She was sounding very composed but we were a few days on and she must have told the story a few times.

'Where are you now?'

'In Ajaccio,' she replied.

'Are you coming back to Bastia?'

'I was going to but they have just found a body, so the police have asked me to hang around and identify it.'

'Wow, there's a body?' I asked. Things were happening fast.

'It might not be Jacob,' she said.

Oh, it'll be Jacob.

'So you walked back and there was the crowd of four people and what did they say?'

'They were all looking over the cliff edge. They said they had seen Jacob fall. He was taking a photograph or a selfie and he stepped back and fell.'

'Did the passers-by know Jacob?'

'What do you mean?' she asked.

'Were they tourists? Were they locals?'

'They were locals as far as I know,' she said.

'Did they know Jacob?'

'What are you getting at?'

'I am just trying to get things straight in my head. They might have recognised him, in which case they could identify the body and you could come home.' This isn't what I meant at all.

'Jacob comes from this side of the island. You know what Corsica is like; everyone knows everyone in your own part of Corsica.'

Of course they knew him; they were in on whatever the scam was.

'So anyway, poor you,' I said. 'How traumatic for you.'

'We hadn't dated long, but it is really unsettling,' she said.

'How do you feel?'

'Flustered.'

'Where did they find the body?' I asked.

'Floating at sea. It was further along the coast.'

The conversation somehow petered out but Emily stayed on the line. I think she was upset.

'But you yourself didn't see him fall off the cliff?' I asked.

'No,' she replied. 'And why couldn't the journalist get my age or name right? Actually I don't feel well. I'll ring again later.'

With that, she rang off.

TWO

It transpires that being patient on the island of Corsica is not always a good strategy; events overtake you.

'What do you mean they paid out on the policy?' I asked.

Niculaiu shrugged. 'I've been keeping an eye on things and the smallest of the policies has been paid out.'

I was stunned. It had only been a few weeks since Jacob's official death and I assumed it would take months for any claims to be submitted and settled. Above all, I assumed someone would have told me.

Niculaiu turned his monitor around to show me.

I scrolled down the page to find out who had okayed the payment. It was no one I knew.

'Right,' I said. 'Well I feel an idiot. I phoned the other two insurance companies and impressed upon them that they shouldn't pay out unless there was proof that the corpse was the correct body, but then it's our own company that is the one that pays out.'

'Well it turns out there is proof that the dead body is the correct body,' said Niculaiu. 'There is a DNA test result,'

'What?'

He clicked on a PDF file and we both read for a while.

'Apparently the body was in such a terrible state from being out at sea so long that there was a limit to what the pathologist could be sure of.'

Jean-Marie wandered into the office.

'Did you know they had paid out in the Lluberas case?' I asked.

'I wondered,' he replied. He looked over our shoulders at Niculaiu's screen.

'I mean how is that possible with no one telling me?' I asked.

'Insurance policies get paid out all the time,' shrugged Jean-Marie.

'Yes but I wanted to see who got the money,' I protested. 'And I wanted to see the DNA test.'

'The DNA test showed that the body which fell into the sea was Jacob Lluberas. There is nothing more to know,' said Jean-Marie.

'Well you could probably still ask where the money was sent,' shrugged Niculaiu.

'I feel like I'm the only one who cares,' I protested. 'And not for the first time.'

'You probably are,' said Jean-Marie. 'Man dies. Life assurance is paid out. It happens. I know it hurts. I know it is against everything we stand for in this office. But I think the public have got it into their silly heads that insurance companies are supposed to pay out on such occasions without making a fuss.'

How dispiriting.

I sat at my own computer and brought up the details of the insurance pay out. I found the name of the clerk who okayed the payment and rang him up. He was a chap in England called Miles Hoskins.

'Hi,' I started. 'I've just sent you an email about an insurance claim that we flagged up that it shouldn't be paid without checking with us first. The case of Jacob Lluberas.'

'Yes I've just seen that. I was a bit confused,' he replied.

'Confused how?' I asked.

'Well I rang your office the moment that claim came in. I rang straight away. You said you were fine.'

'I said I was fine?'

'Well it might not have been you,' he replied. 'I talked to someone called Jean-Marie something.'

Seriously?

I looked up from my desk. Jean-Marie has disappeared.

I rang the Livorno insurance office and the lady on the end of the phone was very understanding and helpful.

'All I am asking,' I pleaded. 'Is that if you pay out, you will let me sit in and ask a few questions. Before paying out, get the beneficiary to come in with their documentation.'

'I promise,' she said.

My next concern was the office in Ajaccio where Jacob's largest life assurance policy had been taken out. I had been dealing with a man on the phone who was middle-ranking. I felt that given the size of the policy, and therefore the size of the potential fraud, I wouldn't leave anything to chance. I made an appointment to see the head of department. I even got Daniel to ring her to make her take me seriously. I was very gratified when she then took the time to ring me.

'You are the famous Peter De'Ath?' she began.

'Famous?'

'You are the claims adjuster for some of the biggest insurance contracts in Europe. I have been following your work for a long time. I am a big fan,' she said.

What a fine woman this Madame Fournier in the Ajaccio office was.

A few days later and I was sitting in front of her desk. It transpired she was a pleasant French woman of a similar age to me. I soon got the impression that she was from mainland France rather than from the island and I was intrigued to discover how much that made me warm to her. I was obviously getting very sensitised to the ways of the native Corsicans.

There are a number of tell-tale differences between the French and the Corsicans which you pick up on as they talk. For example, when a Corsican talks about France they say 'the mainland', whereas a French person would simply say 'France' or 'home', and unlike the French, and very like my own mother, the Corsicans routinely talk about 'their village'. This will be a village inland that has magical properties. Not only is it the most beautiful village in the world, but the grass grows richer, the streams flow fresher, it has the best view, the best school, the best people, it has never had crime, and every day is sunny. It is extraordinary, therefore, that the person saying all this ever left the village in the first place. Why give up such a nirvana? In truth, this little slice of heaven on Earth is quite the bugger to get to, has no paid employment to offer, and the last village shop closed down a decade ago.

So in this instance when I asked Madame Fournier where she was from, and she simply replied 'Lille, back in France,' it was a truly excellent start.

'So as we know, I have a concern about the insurance claim on a life assurance policy you issued,' I began.

'Go on,' she said. 'How do you say in English? I am all ears.' She moved her hands up and down to indicate her whole body. 'In fact, I am covered in ears.' The unintended result of her pointing out her body was to alert me to the fact she had a cracking figure and a particularly fine pair of legs.

'The same person had a policy with an affiliated insurance company, but somehow we paid out on this policy before I had a chance to stop it. And we all know it is easier to not give out money in the first place than to get the money back after it has gone.'

'This is exactly what I tell colleagues,' she said. 'They don't listen. What difference would it make to anyone to delay paying out for a few weeks? We are the region with the highest murder rate in France, we should always be cautious.'

'Precisely!' An ally, at last. I wondered if she was single.

I explained the saga so far and outlined my theories. As Madame Fournier heard each new detail she would nod and smile; she plainly loved this kind of stuff, and it confirmed all her prejudices about the locals. She then brought the details up on her computer and did some reading for a minute.

'Some of these people are from villages where I don't trust the families,' she reflected. 'You shouldn't take anything at face value. If you ask me, they had a death, perhaps a shooting accident or a murder they were trying to cover up, and they figured they would take out insurance and then stage a second death for the body and claim on the insurance.'

'Thank you!' I said. 'Why does no one else think like this?'

'Because they are all in it together!' she said. 'They stick together on this island. The stories I could tell.'

'By any chance, do you know if someone came into these offices personally to sort out these policies? And if so, is there CCTV in your lobby?'

'We certainly have CCTV,' she replied. 'You are hoping we have a picture of the person who took out the insurance policy?'

'Yes,' I replied.

'It's worth a shot. I'll look into it,' she said. She made a note on her pad. 'Tell me, who was the detective on the case?'

'Inspector Fortini,' I replied.

'Really? He's one of the ones I trust.' She thought for a while. 'Who else?'

'No one else.'

'No other policeman took an interest at all in the case?' she asked.

'Not that I know of,' I replied. 'Inspector Luc Cadin, I suppose, but he is a friend.'

'Luc Cadin?' she said. 'I trust him less.'

'Really? I like him.'

'Oh I *like* him!' I said. 'Heaven knows there are all charming. Who was the judge investigating?'

'I don't know his name,' I said.

'Find out. It may be important.'

'Are we going to prosecute a judge? We can't prosecute a judge,' I said.

'No, but I want to always know who is doing what on this island. Nothing is ever quite how it seems. Did they try and fob you off at some stage with some mystic mumbo-jumbo?'

'Yes I had to go out and meet a witch in the woods. They wanted me to believe I might have hallucinated the dead body.'

'Typical! That's just the sort of thing they'd try. Do you want to have dinner together tonight? Perhaps a drink? I mean, we will discuss all this now, but the things I could tell you over a drink in private...'

What a wonderful woman.

Marry me.

I particularly loved the way she went seamlessly from talking about business to talking about food.

'Did they ply you with that myrtle berry liquor that they brew up themselves and gives you hallucinations?' she asked. 'One glass of that and you end up speaking fluent Corsican, two glasses and you're speaking fluent Corsican to their dead relatives who are standing in the corner silently judging you.'

'Three glasses?' I asked, to show I appreciated her humour.

'Three glasses and you *are* the dead relative standing in the corner silently judging you, and they have taken out insurance on you and faked your second death. But you knew that one Mr De'Ath.'

'Call me Pete.' Please call me Pete. 'In fairness, they have never given me the myrtle liquor. Although, now that you've told me about this wonderful stuff I feel a little insulted that they *didn't* ply me with it.'

'Perhaps they wanted you alive.'

She leant forward, all the better to whisper.

'What do you want me to do?' she asked. 'As you say, I can certainly get them to come in to claim the money in person. We will tell them we need some witnessed signatures and a bit of paperwork sorted out. You could be here when they come? I can't necessarily refuse the pay out if their death certificate is in order, but whoever is claiming the money will be involved in the fraud, so we want to be clear who they are.'

'That's what I say! That would be fantastic,' I said.

'I think you are a genius,' she said unexpectedly. 'You have kept at this against the odds and...' She trailed away.

Validation - whenever it comes and from whomever it comes - is always such sweet nectar.

Marry me Madame Fournier.

Bear my children.

I might need to find out her first name before this was possible.

'My name's Armelle by the way,' she said. She was clearly a mind-reader: always useful in a relationship... useful until she learnt to read my darker thoughts, at which point the relationship would be over.

'I think the murder was earlier than the incident at the lodge,' she continued. 'Sarah was never dating Jacob. She was dating a faux Jacob.' My new best friend, soul mate and future lover Armelle Fournier appeared to have it all sorted out in her mind.

'I think that Inspector Cadin was trying to tip me off,' I said. 'The police clearly had a bit of intel from a source. He said to me – no, I thought he said to me – the sentence, "Fin de souci." But in fact he said "Sosie."'

'Which is the French word for Doppelgänger,' she said. 'Luc said that?'

'Yes.'

'The thing is,' she said. 'The date the big insurance policies were taken out tell us when the death really occurred. Any death after the big insurance policy is a fake death.'

Exactly! What a truly wonderful woman.

Marry me.

Bear my children.

Take a sperm sample as a down payment.

'Have you any questions?' she asked.

'Yes. Two questions.'

Then I paused.

'And the questions are?'

'Were you serious about dinner tonight and where can we get this myrtle liquor wine of which you speak? It sounds wonderful.'

'I know just the place.'

THREE

Despite Armelle's slight reservations about Luc Cadin, he was still my preferred port of call at the police because he was more likely to actually tell me something. I rang him and he very generously agreed to see me for half an hour.

'Good morning Mr De'Ath,' said the inspector. 'And what have you got for me today?'

'Insurance fraud. Failure to bury a body. Perhaps a cover up of a murder,' I replied.

'Fantastic!' he said. He rubbed his hands in a comedy style.

'Let's say there is a murder up in one of the mountain villages and everyone wants to hush it up.'

'Okay,' he replied. 'Does this corpse have the name called Jacob Lluberas by chance?'

I outlined my theories to the inspector and concluded, 'I need to talk to the people who took out these policies.' I then paused dramatically. 'But,' I began. 'I have got a photo taken from the lobby on the day one of them visited the life insurance brokers in Ajaccio and filled in the forms.'

I offered the inspector a grainy picture that Armelle had supplied; it was of a man pressing a button to call a lift. It was taken by a security camera. Just after he had pressed the button he looked up to see on the display what floor the lift was currently on. It captured his face quite well.

'This is definitely the man that Sarah knows as Jacob. I have met him and I can confirm it is him.'

'And have you got the pictures of the original Jacob?' he asked.

'Well that is just what is so interesting,' I said. 'There are some photos on the internet tagged as Jacob Lluberas which look substantially different and there are some tagged as Jacob Lluberas that look like the man I met and who dated Sarah and then Emily.'

'I suppose any person can tag a photograph,' said the inspector thoughtfully.

'I wondered if it was possible to get his driving licence or passport, to see those pictures?'

‘Possible,’ ruminated the Inspector.

‘I was thrown at first because my colleague Niculaiu showed me photos on the internet of Jacob and they were definitely the same as the man I met,’ I said.

‘So your conspiracy theory now is involving your colleague Niculaiu?’

‘He and another colleague introduced Sarah to the fake Jacob.’

‘So, yes, your conspiracy theory involves your colleagues,’ he smiled. ‘It seems to me you have a lot of people in your conspiracy theory, most of whom have no advantage by their involvement.’

‘Yeah okay, so that bit may be chance. But yes, my conspiracy theory involves a lot of people,’ I laughed.

‘I suppose as a stranger to the island, it looks as if we Corsicans all work together.’

‘Niculaiu comes from the same village as Jacob.’

‘And me also!’ said the inspector.

‘Really?’

‘No, not really,’ he said. ‘But not far. But your theories also need a policeman to visit the crime scene who will not ask the wrong questions.’

‘Yes,’ I said.

The inspector laughed. ‘So now the police are also involved in your conspiracy? Can I suggest you do not go around the island with accusations that the police are in collusion with the crimes?’

‘Fair enough,’ I said. I had probably been a bit out of line.

‘So we now have a third death,’ said the inspector. ‘The death where he fell off a cliff when he was walking with your sister.’

‘Yes, they faked a death.’

‘But we have his corpse still in the morgue,’ said the inspector. ‘We know from the DNA test on the corpse that is indeed Jacob Lluberas. We have DNA from his mobile phone and also from his mother’s house.’

‘Yes,’ I said. ‘But I’m interested in the person in between? The fake Jacob? When he arrived, alive, at court to exonerate Sarah, did you take his DNA then?’

He considered this, then tapped with his computer for what seemed like an age. It looked as though plenty of thinking was going on behind his eyes,

He finally replied, 'It is not my place to tell you.' He sat back in his chair to signify he was talking generally rather than giving away secrets. 'He was not a suspect. He had committed no crime. It would have been a subject for the prosecutor or the judge. We know they were happy so that is that.'

I leant forward with a small plastic sachet with some hair in it.

'What, I ask myself, is that?' said the inspector.

'I have a sample of fake Jacob's hair. At home, I also have a wine glass with his fingerprints on it.'

'I doubt we will analyse the hair,' he said firmly and quickly.

'What?'

'Because the case is closed!' he said. 'I will keep the hair and I will take the wine glass you mentioned and we will label it and keep it. But the case is closed. We need more to open the case. It was decided the fall off the cliff was an accident, so there is no investigation. You have to understand that we conducted a major investigation and it collapsed. We got egg on our face. There is no appetite at all for re-opening the case.'

I must have looked disconsolate, because after a while he added. 'Peter, why is this so important to you?'

'This is an insurance fraud to the tune of one and a quarter million Euros!' I replied. 'This is major crime. Also, the way the previous case collapsed, it left Sarah and I looking like fantasists. Like we imagined the whole thing. It's humiliating.'

'Okay fine,' he agreed. 'It is not like I haven't had similar thoughts myself. The trouble is...' The inspector took some time to drink a coffee I hadn't previously noticed. 'One,' he said finally. 'If there is insurance fraud, we need more evidence that there was a faux Jacob. Two, we need to see who benefits from the insurance and if there was fraud in the creation of the policies. Three, and most importantly, this is a case for Inspector Fortini and the presiding judge to re-open, not me. But I promise I will talk to him and tell him what you have said.'

'Exactly. Thank you,' I said. 'You are being more than fair.' I thought for a while we were going to go a whole conversation without Luc numbering his sentences. Panic over.

'For my part,' I said. 'I have made an appointment to be present when the insurance companies talk to the people claiming on the policies. I expect to see the man who impersonated Jacob but now looking different to walk through the door, or if not him, at least the mastermind behind the crime.'

Luc Cadin nodded.

We stood and shook hands.

'When are you going to these insurance offices?' he asked.

'I am going to Ajaccio on Wednesday,' I said. 'The family claim it was the only day they could do.'

'And the meeting in Livorno?'

'That is on the Thursday straight after, but it has changed to Nice.'

'Why?'

'The company taking out the life assurance took it out in Livorno, but the life assurance company has bigger offices in Nice. Apparently when the beneficiaries heard this, they jumped at the chance of going to Nice to settle matters.'

Luc Cadin wrote this down.

'I have a theory,' I said.

'That goes?'

'If the company who took out the policy really is in Livorno then why move the meeting to Nice? I think the beneficiary lives in Corsica.'

'Why do you think that?'

'Corsica to Italy is a slow boat trip, but Corsica to Nice is a fast flight by plane,' I said. 'Nice is much easier to get to if you are based in Corsica.'

As I left Luc's office I was amazed to see Jean-Marie from the office sitting just outside. He could easily have heard everything we had been talking about.

'What are you doing here?' I asked.

'I am waiting for a chat with Luc,' he said.

'About work?' I asked.

He shrugged a reply.

'Also, it turns out that our colleague in the UK, Miles Hoskins, phoned our office before paying out on the Lluberas insurance and he got you on the phone.'

'I don't recall that,' he said.

'He is very clear. He said you okayed the claim.'

'I have no recollection of that at all,' he said.

Unbelievable.

I walked back down the police corridor with its polished click-clack floor trying to contain my fury. It should have been a satisfying day, but I was repeatedly confronted with evidence that a lot of people were somehow working against me. I had always found Jean-Marie a bit annoying but this was the limit.

On the upside, my meeting with Luc had gone quite well. I felt that if I could just get a bit more evidence, they would probably re-open the case, and I felt that over a number of conversations – with people – I had got to the bottom of the most likely scenarios for what had occurred. I had been groping in the dark but it was now getting clearer to me.

Jacob died.

They insured him.

They staged a second death for him.

It went wrong, so they removed all the evidence it had happened.

They staged a third death.

To make this all possible they needed a fake Jacob, and he dated people who didn't know what the original Jacob looked like and were the very people who could okay an insurance pay out. I felt that some of the police might have been in on the scam, but others, like Luc, were probably not involved but had a fair idea of what had happened. When it looked like Sarah might be wrongfully convicted, they tried to flush out the LLuberas clan by trumping up an accusation they had stolen Jacob's car; this re-activated the fake Jacob and somehow Emily got caught up in the wash. But they didn't really have a case that the fall off the cliff was a fraud - the body they ended up with was indeed Jacob, after all – so the police then let everything rest rather than get more egg on their face, particularly now that no one innocent was going to prison. But I don't think they were against re-opening the case if there was decent evidence to go on.

I felt it was just a matter of meeting face to face the beneficiaries of the insurance policies; they were the perpetrators of the crime.

Apart from my astonishing levels of irritation that Jean-Marie was somehow involved, my sense of satisfaction was beginning to grow that I was finally getting to the bottom of things.

FOUR

On the Wednesday morning I had my papers ready in my briefcase, I had an overnight bag, and I had got myself to the train station at the crack of 11 o'clock in order to start the four hour journey to Ajaccio for the appointment at 4pm. I could have driven but I needed to then take a plane from Ajaccio to Nice, and from Nice I could fly straight back to Bastia, so leaving my car at Ajaccio wouldn't make any sense. There are no coffee facilities on the train so I went to a nearby kiosk to get a coffee to take with me.

There is no road to cross between the coffee kiosk and the train ticket office; it is pavement. As I walked across it we all turned our heads – the coffee drinkers at the cafe, the tourists pulling their trundle luggage, the workers having a sit in the sun - to a noise behind me.

A car was over-revving and its engine was making such a racket that it was impossible to ignore.

I had stopped in my tracks and turned my head towards the noise but somehow turned my head the wrong way, so the offending vehicle was already next to me without me seeing it. As my head swivelled back to the left so I could see the car, I was hit hard on the back of the legs by something unseen. I had no physical option but to fall forward.

I was expecting to hit the pavement with my face but something was already in the way – a hand perhaps. I was also aware of someone's foot on my ankle. Whoever was attacking me, they knew what they were doing. I was now being carried.

I still hadn't seen my assailants; the only person I saw at that moment was a man across the street who was a worker in heavy overalls sitting on a barrier. We somehow locked eyes as I fell.

I remember seeing the pavement swim a bit in front of my eyes, and then the buffers at the end of the station which were basically a large block of painted wood and which suddenly struck me as odd. Then I was being tipped bodily and there was a scrapping feeling on my shin and, clunk, I was in the boot of a car and the back was slammed down.

There was an overly loud noise of the car revving off again and I was in complete darkness, huffing and puffing and totally confused.

FIVE

If someone has deliberately thrown you into the back of a car you know straight away that there is no point to making a big noise about it. No one is going to hear you as the car is driving along, and the people in the car already know you are there and are obviously not planning to let you out no matter what kind of drama you make.

So my first instinct was to stay quiet.

But what the hell are you supposed do when you are kidnapped? Literally, what do you do?

My next instinct, oddly, was to wonder what had happened to my briefcase. Had it been pulled from my hand? Had I dropped it?

I realised my earlier logic had been a bit faulty – to be fair to me, I was new to this 'being kidnapped' lark - if I was going to make a noise, then it made sense to do it when we were still in town. Presumably we were going to get stuck at traffic lights and junctions at first, but less so as the journey progressed. If we left town we would be travelling more freely and there would be fewer people about. I had an image that we could get stuck at a junction and people would be crossing the road in front and behind the car. If I made enough noise some passer-by may take an interest.

But then what would they do? Shrug and move on?

It was worth a try.

We stopped; presumably at a junction.

'M'aidez, m'aidez!' I shouted. Help me! Help me! In English this is, of course, 'Mayday! Mayday!'

The car engine stopped. We had either parked, or the car engine has that setting where it temporarily turns off if stopped for too long at lights. The car engine started again. It was the latter. I think that meant it was a German make of car; a BMW or a Mercedes, but I couldn't be sure.

We drove for another thirty seconds and stopped again.

'M'aidez! M'aidez!'

We started again. This time the car drove for about a minute before stopping once more.

'M'aidez! M'aidez!'

No answer. The car didn't move.

'M'aidez! M'aidez!' I shouted.

Then I heard someone click the catch on the boot and it moved open a fraction. Then it was pulled up about 30cm.

Whack!

I was hit with something very hard on my shin bone. It was perhaps a metal spanner.

It really hurt.

My shin bone. Of all places.

It really, really hurt.

The door to the boot was closed as fast as it had opened. I reasoned that if I made another noise they would stop the car and hit me again.

I decided to do some thinking instead.

What did I know about the men who attacked me? They had the element of surprise in their favour, but the fact remains I am quite large, so they must have been quite big people themselves to wrestle me and carry me so easily; they had got me into a car without much huffing and puffing.

I think I saw that they wore dark clothes. Perhaps even leather jackets. Had I seen the leather jackets or perhaps smelled them? Perhaps I had imagined them altogether.

Okay, so why was I being kidnapped and where was I being taken?

It was possible that it was a coincidence. Random kidnapping is not unknown in Corsica; but like any western country, it is rare. I reasoned that the chances were that it was not a coincidence; it was me they wanted. They wanted to stop me getting to my meeting with the insurance companies.

I had my phone. I got it out. I had reception. All five bars! Now we are talking. But to whom?

I decided to ring my sister.

I pressed her name on the screen and my phone appeared to try to phone her, but I couldn't get a tone to say it was ringing her. I looked at the screen.

'Connecting.'

I placed it against my ear again.

Still no sound.

The car went over a bump that somehow jarred my neck.

There was still no sound and then just when I was giving up hope there was a repeated tone that implied I had been disconnected.

Okay. Let's not panic yet. Mind you, what difference would it make if I did panic? There would be no one to see my shame. What if I needed a pee though? I wouldn't want to wet myself. As usual, the moment I thought about needing a pee, it was all I wanted in the world. When did I last have a pee? I was instantly and hopelessly obsessed. I last peed some time at home, but when? Think Pete, think.

I made myself snap out of it. How could I possibly be obsessing about my bladder when I had been kidnapped? Perhaps it is a stress thing. Coming to think of it, stress often makes me want to pee. I might need to factor this into my prostate protocols; perhaps work even less hard?

I played with my phone again.

I rang Sarah.

She picked up quickly.

'Hi Sarah?'

'Hi Pete, how are you?'

'I'm fine thank you.' I clearly wasn't fine, but it's a conversational nicety. 'I have been kidnapped.'

'What?'

'I have been kidnapped,' I said. 'I am in the boot of a car being driven somewhere.'

'Wow,' she replied. 'Where are you? Who's kidnapped you?'

'I don't know. I was bustled into the back of a car at Bastia station. I have been driving about five minutes.'

'Oh. Right. What shall we do?'

'Ring the police,' I said. 'Actually, I don't know what we can do. Perhaps they can trace my calls with geo sat or whatever it's called.'

'How come they've let you have a phone?' she asked.

'Good question. They were in a hurry to get me into the boot of the car, I guess. They didn't check my pockets.'

'What's your battery life like?'

'Another good question.' I looked at my display. 'Pretty good.'

'You should hide your phone. And you should put it on silent. Stick it in your sock.'

'Why?' What?'

'Well if the police track it, track the phone, you don't want the kidnappers having found it and thrown it away.'

'You are thinking far clearer than me,' I said.

'I was kidnapped once,' she said.

'What?'

'Yeah. I was working in a drugs halfway house and one day we lost the key to the cabinet where they kept all the drugs and...'

'Actually Sarah, you can tell me later.'

'Oh okay.' She sounded disappointed.

'It does sound like a good story though,' I said.

'Okay,' she said, half placated.

'Ring the police,' I said.

'Sure. And you put your phone in your sock.'

Good old Sarah. Today she was Good Old Sarah.

I had a bright idea. I went on the internet. I Googled 'stuck in a boot of a car' then before I even checked the results of the search I changed it to the more American 'stuck in the trunk of a car'.

I wasn't the least bit surprised to discover there was an entire website dedicated to the subject and it was very helpful. Firstly, it said that every car sold in America after 2002 has an internal release leaver.

Excellent news.

Except I think I had worked out that this car was German. And we weren't in America.

I had a hunt around in the dark for this no doubt mythical lever.

I wriggled myself over to face the other way. The movement put pressure on my bladder. I really did need a pee. I undid the top of my trousers.

I used my phone as a light to look for the boot release lever. It was hard to move my head more than a little, but I couldn't see anything.

I consulted the website again for more guidance. Apparently the handle will have a glow in the dark sign on it. Crap. Or sometimes it hasn't. Well that detail was just irritating. My thoughts returned to my bladder. Must... have ... other... thoughts...

My phone vibrated.

It was Sarah.

'I've rung the police,' she said.

'Who did you talk to?'

'The police.'

'Yes, but who exactly at the police.'

'Um, I don't know. He did say. I didn't write it down.'

'So you rang the police generally?' I asked. 'You didn't ring Inspector Fortini or Inspector Cadin?'

'Why would I ring them? We went to them and they arrested me!'

'No, yes, I mean, they aren't going to arrest you again,' I said.

'That's what you said last time.'

'You were driving around with a dead body in the back of your car!' I shouted.

'No one speaks to me like that,' she said.

'What?'

'You were shouting!'

'I am sorry I shouted,' I said.

'Well it's very upsetting,' she said.

'I am sorry.'

'Okay,' she said. She paused and changed her tone from irritating to condescending. 'I can understand that you might be under a lot of stress at the moment and so you might not have thought through what you said.'

For heaven's sake Sarah.

Still, a least she answered her phone, unlike my so-called sister Emily.

Her phone was cut off. My reception had gone.

I had to wait about ten minutes and when reception was back I got back to the internet and the very useful website I had found.

Did I want to accept their cookies?

Yes.

What cookies would they be? Was I now marked digitally as a person who often gets stuck in the boot of a car? Would I be offered more information in the future to help me extricate myself from other emergencies? Locked in a meat cold storage unit, perhaps. Trapped under ice in a frozen lake. Just how accident prone did they think I was?

Focus Pete, focus.

The website had diagrams and photographs to help with my escape. Some showed an actual man, who looked Hispanic, curled up in the boot reaching for various levers and so on. Perhaps this sort of going-on is very common in some countries. I had a mental image that at any given time there were dozens of cars being driven around the roads of Latin America with kidnapped people in the boots Googling the same website.

The website said, 'If there is a trunk release cable available, pull on it.'

I suppose that related to the cable that runs from the driver's seat area that the driver can pull to release the boot remotely. This was a good tip; such a cable must surely exist.

I felt around in the frame of the car and couldn't find a cable. I tried pulling at the upholstery and was partially successful but could find any cables.

I scrolled down to read more text but then I lost the image again.

'Press play on advert to unlock rest of text,' said the screen.

I now had to watch an advert and wait for the 'Skip Ad' sign to appear. It was an advert for adult incontinence pants. How do these adverts get chosen for me by the internet? Are they based on my previous search preferences? The other day I was sent an advert for 'Senior Singles Dating.' What age do they think I am and how do they know I'm single, or indeed that continence was an issue with me? Actually, I might have answered my own questions there; I really needed a pee. My entire lower abdomen was now one big ache.

The text of the website was back again.

'Disconnect the wires from the tail lights and smash out the tail lights. This may allow you to wave at other cars. At the very least, the car may be stopped by the police for having faulty lights.'

I wasn't sure the police in the mountains of Corsica would stop a vehicle for a wonky brake light, but it seemed like a plan.

I pulled at the carpeting of the corner near my head and it hurt my nails a lot. This seemed to be quite a well-constructed car with no sign of skimping in its manufacture. Curse the Germans and their forward-through-technology pursuit of excellence.

My phone lit up and vibrated. It was an unknown number.

'Hello, Monsieur De'Ath?' said the voice. 'Peter?'

'Speaking!'

'It is Luc Cadin.'

'Luc! What a relief to hear your voice.'

'Your colleague has phoned to say you are stuck in your car?'

'I have been kidnapped,' I explained.

'Kidnapped?'

'I am in the boot, the trunk of a car.'

'Okay.'

'I have been kidnapped by the people who want to stop me investigating the insurance claims. They want to stop me from going to Ajaccio and Nice. At least I think so.'

The phone then cut out. It was not clear how much the inspector had heard.

If there was no reception, then there was no chance of being tracked by my phone.

I think.

I wasn't sure.

Luc Cadin rang again.

'The conversation before stopped,' he said. 'Where are you or what are you certain you know?'

'I am in the back of a black saloon car, possibly German, I was abducted at Bastia train station. We have been driving about twenty minutes. Once we left Bastia we haven't had to stop much at junctions. We have perhaps turned at two junctions, left then right, but the road has been intermittently winding. We are going uphill.'

'We have talked with the phone companies to see if they can find you,' he replied. Can you remember the details about the kidnappers?'

'Not really.'

'Men or women?'

The phone went dead again.

I felt sick in my mouth. It was like the taste of Feta cheese. Had I had Feta that day? It was unlikely. I was getting a bit addled.

The dull pain across my bladder area was getting more insistent. I really did need a pee. I also needed to repress such thoughts.

What to do?

My keys.

I had my keys in my pocket.

I would see if I could get the sharpest of the keys and burrow through to the lights by my head and break through them that way.

I placed the keys in my palm and had the sharpest of them coming through past my knuckles like a blade. By scraping with them, I managed to pull back some upholstery and was able to work on what I felt was the light panel.

My thoughts returned to my bladder. If it got any worse, I would just need to pee in the car and lie in my own urine. At first it would swim around the floor a bit, but soon it would soak into my clothes. Class. I had had three cups of tea that morning. What was I thinking? That's a lot of fluid. Try and think of something else.

I hacked at the light panel with renewed vigour but I was somehow making a lot of noise. The car stopped and the boot opened again.

A spanner hit my thigh. Ow! A big ow by the way.

The man said, 'Stop wrecking the car!'

He hit me on the shin for good measure.

'Just stop being so irritating!' he said.

Why would I stop being irritating? It's all I've got.

Then his hand came through and took my keys. The boot shut again, and the car moved off.

A lesser person would have been dispirited.

It turns out I am a lesser person.

I lay in the back of that stifling car for what felt like a hundred miles - but given the nature of Corsica was probably only two - and felt very sorry for myself indeed.

Who had betrayed me? Who had I told I was going to Ajaccio? Everyone. I had mouthed off my masterplan to literally anyone who would listen. It would have been quicker and no less effective to have hired a plane to write in the sky 'Pete is going to Ajaccio on Wednesday.'

I realised I was putting off attacking the light fitting now I no longer had my keys. I figured I would need to get my jacket off and wrap it round my hand, and punch at it with my fist.

First to get off the jacket.

Given my bulk, the idea I could just slip my jacket off in a confined space was pretty comical. As a manoeuvre it was going to take me ten minutes or more; still, at least I would be cooler with fewer layers on.

I eventually got my jacket wrapped round my fist and punched the glass hard. At my third attempt I broke through the first layer then a little later I was making an impression on the outer layer; I had to consider it a success of sorts. I kept expecting the car to stop and for my attackers to hit me again with a spanner, but perhaps I was making less noise now.

Sarah sent me a text. 'I am off on a yacht for a day with friends. Hope it works out for you.'

What?

Sarah has friends? With yachts? And what about me? Still, it was nice to know that if you are banged up in jail, our employers let you still use your holiday entitlement.

I summoned up all my strength and belted my hand through the hole I had made.

Success! I got most of my forearm through the hole.

The aim was to wave my arm around to attract attention, but in the event my arm was badly wedged – the best I could manage was to flick my palm and fingers, and even then I soon got tired.

On a whim I tried pulling my hand back.

It was stuck.

It was really, really stuck.

What if they reversed the car against a wall and I got my hand crushed?

And what about my bladder. This journey had gone on such a long time, I was probably going to have to pee myself, and that's that.

The car stopped.

I could hear noises as a car door opened and then there was some talking. Then I heard what was probably a garage door being lifted up and out.

There was a pause where I couldn't discern anything and then the car started to reverse backwards. We were backing into a garage. It was like they had heard my previous thought. All I could think about was that if they backed against a wall it would then crush my arm.

I wriggled my arm furiously forwards and backwards.

It was properly wedged.

The car continued to reverse.

Now I could feel the wall with my fingers and still the car went backwards.

I curled my palm inwards and I twisted my body so that I could bend my hand as much as I could.

It was only a matter of seconds before my hand would be crushed.

The car stopped moving. Then I heard the engine being turned off. Again a car door opened and then clunked shut again. Were they going to let me out of the boot, and if so, I wondered if they had a way of freeing my hand. I strained to hear in the silence.

Then I heard the garage door being pulled down and shut - they were leaving me in the back of the car. How long were they going to leave me here? And why?

I waited in the dark wondering if they would return.

Then I waited some more.

They had to be kidding. It is not as though they had forgotten I was in the back of the car. What on earth were they doing?

Okay. Think.

I would certainly have to prioritise getting my arm free. I had got the arm through in the first place, so it must be possible to retrieve it. On the other hand, my arm was now crooked on the outside to avoid the wall behind me; it was going to be harder to extricate.

I figured I might need to be brave – not my strong suit – and try and widen the hole in the glass and plastic. The reason this was brave was that I could end up severing a vein in my arm as I wriggled it against the serrated glass. My head was already full of images of blood running up my sleeves and down my arm. Or worse, would it cut an artery and the blood would pump and spray all over the garage? There would be long lines of red streaking and spotting the grimy walls and ceilings and meanwhile, silent and unseen, my face and body will be turning grey within. And then I would die.

Somehow during my death reverie my arm came free. It was easier that I thought; apparently it just involved turning my body a bit and not panicking. I almost felt short-changed.

Right. Now to get out of the boot and garage before my abductors got back.

It took me far too long to remember that I had in fact made a little progress during the journey. I had managed to get some of the fabric carpet-like lining away from the metal of the internal chassis. Perhaps if I kept pulling I would be able to peel it back enough to find the boot opening cable that had been suggested on the internet.

This was fine in theory but the material was very stiff and also my own bulk was in the way of me peeling it back. On the other hand, I had no other choice but to persevere, so persevere I did.

I found the cable that led to the back latch and it was like the brake cable on a push bike; it had a firm outer sleeve with, presumably, a metal cable within. Pulling on it, in itself, might not make a difference because it was, presumably, the difference of the inner sleeve compared to the outer sleeve that made the latch trip. Either way, I gripped the wire with my hand and pulled hard.

Nothing happened.

I yanked again really hard. I was bitter. I was angry. These people had kidnapped me, they had hit my shin with a spanner, they had previously caused me to look like a fantasist in the eyes of the police and my colleagues... suddenly the boot sprang open.

There was a small door at the back of the garage. It had a gnarled Bakelite style knob that was cracked. I turned it and I was out and blinking in the sunshine straightaway.

I had no idea where my kidnappers had gone, or why. Surely they weren't going to just leave me in the boot of a car without any water or food, and no way to pee. That's a point; what happened to the pee I thought I needed? As I lumbered away from the garage I checked my abdominal signs and symptoms. Nothing. I didn't apparently need a pee at all. The whole thing had clearly all just been in my imagination. How irritating. How extraordinarily irritating. It had all been in my mind all along. What a ridiculous time to have an epiphany like that.

Oh well, no time for a prostate protocol re-evaluation now; time to get as much distance between me and my kidnappers as possible.

SIX

I was in a back street; it was narrow – little more than the width of a car. It had a sand and stone surface rather than tarmac. Ahead of me I could see a proper road. I ran down to it and a vista fanned out before me where I was clearly in a hilltop town of quite large rectangular houses with terracotta roofs. I couldn't hear anyone behind me. I could see no other person in the streets, so if I did come across my kidnappers there was no way for me to blend into a crowd.

I reached a T junction and facing me was a stunning view across a valley that was bouncing around in front of my unfit eyes – I was already completely out of breath. The good news was that I could see we were not too far from the sea – perhaps five or six miles. Getting to Ajaccio seemed unlikely now, but perhaps I could get to the coast and then to Nice. I wasn't going to let the buggers win.

My passport. I didn't have my passport. It was in my briefcase and I had lost my briefcase. The briefcase was possibly in the car, or lost on the pavement near Bastia station when I was bundled into the boot.

I dithered. Should I continue my escape, or go back for my passport? Neither. I should ring the police. It was what I should have done months ago when Sarah appeared with a dead body in her car and it's what I should do now. But of course I wasn't going to do the right thing. I was angry. I was so angry. I was so very angry with whoever had kidnapped me that I wanted to get to that insurance office and confront them and get the dirt on them and bring them down. It didn't matter how long it was going to take me; I was going to bring the Lluberas family down.

Then I saw them in the distance, and they saw me.

The two kidnappers were walking in a street parallel to mine but quite slowly. We locked eyes and I ran forwards. One of them ran towards me, and the other ran forwards in the street they were in so that he could cut me off.

I knew I wasn't fit enough to outrun them, and I had been curled up in a car which wasn't going to help my joints. So I felt my best bet was to find somewhere to hide. In an alley perhaps, or in the forest that seemed to surround the town, or perhaps a crowd. The road layout largely dictated my route, however; I had little choice but to run forwards and away from them, and this took me on a path upwards towards what I presumed was the middle of town. And when I got there, presumably, the second man would cut me off.

I was aware of my phone clattering out of my sock and onto the road. I decided I couldn't go back for it.

As I ran, I could see a white church tower bobbing intermittently above the rooftops and between alleyways, and I could hear a bell donging which I felt was from the same church and I felt it was calling me somehow, and then all I could hear was my laboured breathing.

I daren't look round to see if the man behind me was catching me up. I felt the game was up, but that I should keep fighting on regardless.

And then I was in a town square in front of a church. There was a large crowd - a huge crowd - and the crowd was silent and all facing the same way. It was eerie.

Something strange was happening.

I followed their collective eyes to see that at the top of the steps by the entrance to the church there was a bride and groom. The bride was in a traditional white dress with a veil over her face. She was obviously pregnant. The bridegroom was to her left, dressed in a dark blue suit and a crisp white shirt.

I slowed my pace - from lumbering to exhausted – and tried to slip into the edge of the crowd. Everyone at the back was hovering on their tiptoes to get a view of the happy couple.

Except they weren't a happy couple. They seemed unhappy. Worse than unhappy; they seemed afraid. The bride and groom were plainly tense and there was a brittle anxiety amongst the group that was with them on the steps. Next to the bride was a man who was probably her father, but apart from that, there was an array of swarthy looking Corsican men – the inevitable brothers and cousins that populate extended rural families in this part of the world.

They looked armed.

Each of the men had one arm missing – that is to say one hand was partially out of sight. As I got my eye in, I saw that some of them seemed to be holding the handle of a barely concealed gun. Then I saw that one of them blatantly had a knife in plain sight; it was a thin sharp stabbing kind of knife with a worn wooden handle that was black with use. What kind of a wedding was this?

I moved forward through the crowd trying not to dislodge too many people as I went.

'Sorry. Sorry. Excuse me,' I went. When you are fat you have to say sorry a lot, just to get from A to B. I didn't know where my kidnappers were, but I felt they would be monitoring the crowd for any disturbance that might give a clue to my position.

I felt that this crowd was a little different from the people I usually met in the Corsican coastal towns. These were the more traditional Corsican families – the ones with a pride for their island that burned in their hearts. Families like this were fewer in number than even twenty years ago and more diverse that they used to be, but this was the emotional heart of Corsica assembled in a square; brave proud people. Something big was up, and it involved this groom and his pregnant bride.

The groom dropped to one knee in front of the bride and muttered something.

'Louder!' shouted a man from the crowd. 'Louder damn you!'

There was a pause and then one man a little behind and to the left of the groom drew a gun. It was a three quarters length gun; I don't know anything about firearms, but it was halfway in length between a pistol and a shotgun. It was an antique; it had a matt grey muzzle and on the top of the handle it had two shiny metal thumb catches that presumably you had to click back before you could fire it. I was reassured by the way it looked largely ornamental. Less reassuring however, was the man holding the weapon. He was the sort of man who lived to be angry, and his whole body seemed to be jittering and barely controlled.

It turned out to be the least of our problems.

There was another man on the side of the bride who, on seeing the first gun, had pulled out one of his own. Unlike the first man, his gun was a state of the art firearm; something James Bond might use. This gun was pointed at the man with the older firearm and the man holding it looked like a far cooler character - a man who would be perfectly sanguine shooting a fellow human being dead.

All eyes were on the two men until they themselves looked to the bridegroom.

The bridegroom, not unreasonably, took the guns as his cue to speak louder.

'I, Arturo Giabiconi, would like to ask the hand in marriage of Cristina Mariani,' he announced.

The crowd made no noise, nor did they move. A man next to me clipped his phone onto a selfie stick, all the better to take a photo. His wife or girlfriend tugged at his sleeve to stop him.

There was a sense in the square that the problem - whatever the problem was - lay unresolved.

The groom tried again, even louder.

'Will you, Cristina Mariani, do me the honour of marrying me?'

This seemed to settle the men with the guns a little.

I felt a tug at my clothing from behind. One of my kidnappers had caught up with me. I half turned to see a hand tugging at my sleeve.

I pushed forward trying to divide the crowd in front of me. My plan was to get to the right of the steps and perhaps run into the alleys behind the church.

I was making some decent headway and had got to the periphery of the crowd when I saw the other abductor standing squarely in my way. I was trapped.

The bulk of the crowd was still preoccupied with the bride; would she say yes to the proposal? It was almost as if she was supposed to say no, in which case why have a wedding at all?

I had no option. I climbed the steps to the church. I figured that the kidnappers wouldn't follow me up there, not least because they would be easier to identify to the police afterwards. The trouble was that I was now the centre of attention. The entire town turned their heads towards me. The bridegroom looked startled. He was already on edge, and looked like he thought I was tearing up the steps to attack him. He started backwards and fell back on his heels to get away from me. This, in turn, made all of the men at the top of the steps – every single one of them – reach for their weapons. Some of them pointed them at the groom as a warning for him not to move – so he froze in a position that was half in recoil from me - but most of the guns had their barrels aimed at me.

It was an eclectic mix of firearms – hunting rifles, shot guns, modern handguns, archaic duelling weapons, there was even a 'handbag' gun the like of which only America could have invented. The result was terrifying and dream like in equal proportions.

In my dazed logic I veered away from the groom. It seemed to me the groom felt under threat and so his allies, if he had any, might want to protect him from me. Probably by shooting me.

In my haste to avoid threatening the groom any further, I stepped back and bumped into the bride; the bride who was half my size and carrying an unborn child and therefore in need of protection from a middle aged portly man who was clearly acting erratically. The pregnant bride who had at least half a dozen family members in attendance who were there to protect her with random weaponry from over the millennia, some of which were ignited by flints.

I had no idea what to do.

I did know I had to move forwards not backwards. I was afraid of the men behind me, I was out of puff, but above all - and I am very proud to say this - I was still angry at the position I had been put in by the kidnappers.

It was an anger that fizzled out the moment the end of a gun – the solid metal aggressive and terrifying end of the barrel of a gun - got pushed into my cheek.

It was deep in my cheek. It was pushing my whole head sideways and towards the stone slabs of the church doorway. My eyes tried to see who was holding the gun, but I was pinned down hard.

Oddly, it all just made me irritated.

I had done nothing wrong, I repeat, I had done nothing wrong. But I was being kidnapped, chased, attacked… all because I was trying to get to the bottom of a million Euro insurance fraud.

It was this feeling of irritation, rather than fear, that made me do what I then did.

Instead of cowering or submitting, I put my hand firmly out and grabbed the barrel of the gun that was in my cheek.

I held the gun near my face and adjusted my body upwards. I used a full fisted grip and clenched that barrel tight.

I turned to face the holder of the gun.

'Really?' I asked.

'Really??' I asked again.

There was a tinnitus in my ears.

'Reallllllllllly?' I asked again. 'You are going to shoot me?'

The man holding the gun looked more than a little uncertain.

I stood tall.

The gun was now in my mid rift.

'You want to kill me?' I shouted. 'You don't even know me!' It was a cross between bravado and resignation to my fate.

The man looked startled, and this gave me some misguided confidence.

I shouted loud enough for the whole square to hear. 'You don't know why I am here. You don't know who I am. You don't know what I am running from. You have no... i... dea... ! And yet...' – at this stage I was now pointing my fingers near his face – 'And yet! You are willing to risk a life in prison and the chance that you are killing a fellow human being. And for what? What? Answer me. This is a question!'

He just looked at me.

'For what?' I shouted louder.

There was a long pause.

'Chi?' he said.

Seriously? He was a Corsican who only spoke Corsican? It seemed unlikely.

Then I heard the click of a weapon.

Then the click of another weapon.

I now had several guns in my face.

With the benefit of hindsight, my impassioned speech might have made matters worse.

I was dimly aware of the bride's facial expression through her veil. She seemed to be looking at me with concern, like when you are ill and you don't realise it yourself and someone stares at you because you're such an unearthly colour. I thought to myself that if they did shoot me they were probably comfortable that the entire village would back them and not me. Half the crowd would deny being there, and the other half would claim they were indeed in the town that day but at the exact moment in question had nipped off to the toilet.

Something about me had definitely snapped however. Even though it would only take one hot head to end my life for good, I swung around and drew myself as high as I could, and in the moment it took them to work out what I was doing, I surged forward towards the church doors. I was in the church before I knew it.

The church was dark and eerie silent; centuries of incense steeped the air. I wondered if having sanctuary in a church was an actual concept or just something from the movies, and then quickly concluded that the sort of person who thought nothing of kidnapping me would also think nothing of chasing me round a church. I was alone for now, however. I huffed and puffed my way to the altar end of the church to see if there was another door - a way out of the situation. It wasn't the biggest of buildings and so I soon found a side door at the back that presumably led to the vestry.

It was locked.

The handle wouldn't even turn.

I considered ramming the door, but with what? And also I knew I couldn't do it. This a church. It was a sacred place. Yes, it was a building like any other building made from bricks and mortar but psychologically, spiritually, you had to treat it differently.

I milled about for a few seconds with no ideas in my head. I was going to have to face the fact that the only way out of the church was the way I had come in.

I wondered if everyone outside was just standing there looking at the door in silence knowing I had to re-emerge, or had they all shrugged and got on with whatever weird ceremony they had planned; the ultimate shotgun wedding.

I figured that if I was going to re-emerge I needed a weapon of my own. I looked around. There were a number of candlesticks of various sizes. None of them seemed quite right; some were too small and some were too unwieldy.

Let's face it; I was stuffed.

There was a crucifix in my line of vision. It was exactly the right size for my purposes. It felt like a sign. It felt like the Almighty Himself was telling me what to do. This cross was my shield and my talisman; my protector and weapon. This was going to happen, and this was going to work.

I wanted to pull at it to see how well it was secured but felt in awe of even touching it. It was an ornate painted wooden cross with Jesus nailed on its front stoically suffering his fate and forgiving us for what we do. He had a crown of thorns and red blood was painted, dripping from his head and palms. There was a layer of dust on it where no one had disturbed it for centuries. Then somehow my brain just flipped and against all my previous instincts, I yanked at it. It was the single most awful thing I have done in my life – and I have used a corpse as a ladder. The crucifix came away instantly; the plaster of the wall crumbled where its fixings came free, releasing a cloud of dust that swirled in the shafts of light that fell from the windows above.

I walked as steadily as my nerve allowed back towards the main entrance of the church, and pulled the heavy wooden door towards me. I breathed deeply in, as if to jump off a cliff, then pressed myself out into the blinding light.

The bride was talking loudly, as if she had been repeating herself to be heard more clearly, 'I, Cristina Mariani, accept that you, Arturo Giabiconi, have proposed, have asked for my hand in marriage. I hereby tell you that I will not marry you.' It turns out they hadn't missed me at all.

The crowd responded to the bride with whoops and cries of hooray.

The groom bowed his head, and the bride pulled her head high in pride.

Seemingly satisfied with the actions of the bride and groom, the attention of the town fell back on me.

I was standing before them holding the crucifix by its base. I held it in both hands like a powerful sword. I felt I had not quite achieved the effect I had in mind, so I started to swing the crucifix around my head.

It turns out I'm not fit enough for that kind of thing; I stopped after two swings.

The guns, which had been briefly put away, all sprang back out into the sunshine. Twenty or thirty muzzles were aimed at my head, my legs, and all points between. I had no strategy. So I was as surprised as anyone when I found myself reaching out for the pregnant bride.

With my right hand I held the bride's forearm, and with my left hand I held the cross as if it was a weapon; I moved it slowly in an arc, pointing out the various gun wielding Corsicans.

I will never know who shot me.

There was a bang that was from close by, but I wasn't sure where.

Something happened to my foot. It was whipped away sideways. My left knee went down and away from my body.

I steadied myself on a nearby bride as I fell.

SEVEN

It was my foot, or my shoe that was hit. Who shoots a shoe? I had no inclination to find out the damage; I just tested my foot to see if there was any chance I could pick myself up and run, and it seemed that I could. I had not seen where my kidnappers were all this time, but I wasn't going to waste time scanning the crowd for them. The only option I could see was to somehow get away from the church and down a pathway to the right, and hope that my pursuers would get somehow stuck in the crowd.

I set off at pace. At least it was downhill - every road and path from that church led down a hill, not up. I have no idea what I did with the crucifix - I must have dropped it - I hope I didn't break it. As I ran I listened out for footsteps running behind me, but I couldn't hear anything. I was soon quite a distance away.

I favoured shaded streets; partly because it was so hot, and partly because I was a little less obvious in the relative shadows. It was one of those towns where you wonder how people buy stuff. Where were the shops? Was it just a group of silent houses, and everyone had to get into a car to get anything done?

I still couldn't hear footsteps behind me. That had to be good news. The other good news was that I was definitely able to run on my shot foot. Perhaps the bullet had simply hit the leather. I had previously also hurt my foot when Sarah and I were chasing around the mountains with the dead body in the car. Fate had it in for my feet.

Fate had it in for my feet.

Fate had it in for my feet.

I was repeating this in my head like a mantra as I puffed along.

I was now in some parched countryside; it was mostly smallish trees and bracken. There were no clear paths, but it was reasonably easy to make progress. I came across a road. Should I walk along the road because it was easier? - I would make more progress that way - but what if the kidnappers had gone back for their car? They would be cruising the roads looking for me.

I should have disabled their car; slashed the tyres or something. I should have looked for my passport. There were so many things that I could have done better in hindsight. I suppose most of us feel like that in life.

I had no idea what I was doing or where I was going. Because I was in the countryside without a phone the police would never find me - that's assuming they were looking for me at all – so it was up to me to get to safety. I was still determined to get to Nice though; it was a matter of pride that my assailants didn't succeed.

I trudged on.

And most importantly, what was I going to do about lunch?

I saw a glint of sunlight on metal.

It was about twenty metres away and down a steep bit of mountainside, but metal it was. I moved my head left and right to try and understand what I was seeing.

It wasn't the barrel of a gun. There was just a chance it was a railway track.

It was as good a plan as any. I could walk along a railway track. It was better than a river. A railway track always leads somewhere useful. Like a station. Or buffers.

I warily picked my way down the hill. What I thought was the train tracks soon disappeared from my view but at least it had given me some hope. The trees and undergrowth were dry and scratchy and the rocks were vertiginous. I had to hold on to trees and branches carefully for when, inevitably, I would slip.

I slipped.

My feet slid so suddenly from under me that the first true sensation I experienced was my ample arse hitting a rock. The dusty earth then formed a chute and my legs shot forward and I shot down the hill on my back. It was bumpy and relentless. There were snags of rock that tore my clothes. I tried to put my hands out to catch roots and branches as I sped past them, but it soon became clear that I was risking shredding my palms. I put my hands above my head and surrendered to the fall.

And then there was the edge of the mountain. I jetted off horizontally into the air above some sort of chasm at the mountain edge.

So this is how I was going to die: a lengthy fall, and my skull cracked open on the parched rocks of Corsica, cerebrospinal fluid pouring from my head, pooling on the ground and soaking into the cracks of the hardened earth to be lapped up by the jackals who would then move on to eat my flesh - flesh that I have lovingly marinated in red wine for twenty-five years knowing that this day would come; lucky, lucky jackals. If there are any jackals in Corsica, which I doubt.

I ended up, arse first, on the railway track. It turns out I hadn't died.

Obviously, as a rule, you should never walk on railway tracks. To do so would be a simple transaction with fate; a train will come, and then you will die. But Corsica – as so very often - is the exception to this otherwise inviolate rule. In fact, Corsica is possibly the only place on planet Earth where it is safer to walk on the tracks than beside them.

Firstly, the Corsican train system is single track, so you only have to look one way. Secondly, like the roads, there is frequently a solitary goat or a cow in the middle of the track standing there – just standing there – not moving, not eating; just standing – and usually just round a sharp blind bend. It is never a herd; it is always just one. It is not as though there is anything to eat there, so it makes no sense. But as a result, the trains in Corsica crawl along at a bucolic pace with the driver keeping a keen eye out for animals; despite these best efforts, however, animals still get hit. It could be argued therefore that it would be safer for me to walk to one side of the tracks, but the edge of the tracks in Corsica do not have a fence: there is simply a variable width of gravel and then a precipitous drop to a certain death on the rocks below.

I trudged along as purposefully as I could manage. There was the skull of a dead goat perched on a stick at the side of the tracks. The hollow eyes and sharp horns looked like something to do with black magic. I decided to not take it as an omen. Another twenty metres further on, and there was another skull on a stick stuck by the edge of the tracks. It looked like a human skull. It couldn't possibly be a human skull. I tried to decide to not take it as an omen. To be on the safe side, I didn't make eye contact with it.

I was now at the opening of a tunnel. The tunnel was long and curved to follow the shape of the mountain; so long and curved that I couldn't see the end. It was pitch black, but pleasingly cool – in fact it was easily the most pleasant part of my enforced journey that day. The cooler temperature was refreshing and there was even a slight breeze.

I trudged along doing my calculations. I reckoned I was maybe a couple of hours walk from the coast. That was do-able, even for me.

The breeze in the tunnel picked up a little which was great. I reflected what a great little micro-climate the tunnel afforded. The breeze picked up some more.

Because there was a train coming.

I could not see the train because of the curve of the tunnel, and therefore it could not see me. I could hear it though. There was a chance the driver would see me and stop in time.

And there was a much greater chance he wouldn't.

Perhaps if I lay down on the track?

If I lay down dead centre, presumably there was height between the ground and the train. But what if there was something metal that poked down from the bottom of the train that I didn't understand? What if someone flushed the toilet of the train as it went over me?

Okay. I would move to the side of the tunnel and hold my stomach in. Surely there was enough space for me? They wouldn't make the tunnel for the train exactly the width of a train, would they? They would surely leave a bit of space round the sides for it to rock a bit on its axles, plus an extra bit of width for a portly Englishman's stomach.

I tried it. There just wasn't room enough to tuck myself in.

Perhaps if I stood in the middle of the track and waved? The train was still behind the bend and so there was no chance the driver could see me with much notice. And what is the stopping distance of a train from when the driver first applied the brake? Even with a slow train it couldn't possibly be less than ten metres because of its total weight; twenty or thirty metres seemed a more reasonable guess.

Of the various terrible options available, I decided the most viable was to lie in the middle of railway. I figured that the height of the rails off the ground plus the radius of a train wheel must surely be enough height for me and my ample frame.

If I held my stomach in.

In a parallel reality where my stomach was smaller.

Okay so this was probably the fast-track executive route to meeting my maker; but here goes nothing. I gingerly went to sit midway between the two tracks.

The train was upon me.

It had a light that blinded me, and then I saw what was probably a cattle guard on its front – whatever it was, there was no more that ten inches between the front of the train and the ground. I would never survive being hit by that.

EIGHT

I have never moved so fast in my life.

I rolled and spun with my legs still lying on the gravel, and with my torso, arms, stomach and head all corkscrewing over the rail to the right and onto the edge of the sleepers. My left shoulder was the first part of my anatomy to make it to safety. A rush of air heralded the impending impact and somehow with a twist of my back and a flail of my legs I was over the rail.

It took me a few seconds to make sense of my position. I couldn't work out why I couldn't move my right leg. I wasn't in pain – which was great of course - but something was nonetheless wrong. I was being buffeted by the train – thump, thump, thump – it was jarring my body – but somehow I was powerless to move.

I got both hands onto my thigh and pulled my leg.

Nothing. No movement.

Perhaps the edge of my trousers were caught on the track. It was a working hypothesis. The wheels weren't continuous – there were surely gaps between the wheels – so I decided to pull rhythmically on my trousers rather than on my leg.

The leg of my trouser ripped. It was about the same moment that the last wheels of the train passed on. If I had just waited another four seconds I wouldn't have ruined a perfectly good pair of suit trousers... was just one of many delusional thoughts I had up there on the railway tracks: I had fallen down chutes of dusty earth and rock and wrecked them long since.

The next problem was that the trains in Corsica are very few and far between; because of the single track – if a train was going in one direction there couldn't possibly be one coming the other way. If I didn't catch this particular train, then there might not be one until the following day.

I sprang to my feet as best I could. The train was not moving very fast, but it was faster than I could run for more than a few yards. Running after the train was not an option.

Happily, it turns out I'm heroic. With a hitherto unsuspected athleticism, I somehow spun and twisted and leapt, all in one movement, up and onto the back of the train.

There isn't much to grip onto on the back of a modern train - I now know - it is all smooth contours and flowing glass and metal beauty. By contrast, early steam trains were lovingly made objects resplendent in their irregularity; there would be plenty to hold onto if one of those passed by, and it would be going slowly enough for me to choose my best options for a foothold; not so with modern designs; society seems to have gone from the functional to the aesthetic without any thought for the little man - or the not so little man - who needs to escape kidnappers and get to Nice in time to confront and slay – yes, slay - his tormentors and prove that he had been right all along and not a fantasist; yes, my anger had persisted at turbo-charged levels all afternoon and was not going to abate now. I was so riled by how I had been treated that whoever was the ringleader in all of this, I really wanted to see them with my own eyes at the insurance office. And kill them. With my bare hands. My thumbs would press into their eyeballs and push so deep, I'd be picking out bits of retina from my thumbnails for a week.

I somehow got my feet into a groove around the bumper and my fingers got a vague hold around the casing of the train's headlights. Provided the journey was smooth and not too long, I was in with a chance of staying on.

The train continued on a pleasant stroll along the mountain edge, occasionally slowing at bends, and on any other day I would have enjoyed the view. The trains in Corsica have repeatedly been voted in the top five most scenic train journeys in Europe and there was me getting a ride for free. Get me!

We passed a station without stopping. Well, when I say station, it was a solitary wooden platform with a slightly overgrown path through the rocks leading down to it. The station didn't even have a proper name. Like the other stations on the Corsican train network that were simply called 'Prison' and 'Swimming Pool' this one was called by some numbers and letters: PK 79 + 800. Presumably this is the map reference for how to find it, which is fine, but why stop there? Why not call London Kings Cross station by its map reference or by its postcode: N1C 4AS? It would be so much more, er, practical? Baffling? Either way, the train didn't stop at the practically named PK 79 + 800 and so I didn't have a chance to put my plan into operation.

My plan was that when the train did next stop, I would jump off the back of it and run to the side and tap desperately on the windows. I had visions that the train would nonetheless set off without me, much as when a bus driver deliberately ignores a late passenger running as he moved away from the bus stop; but at least I had a plan. The trouble was that the train was only going to stop at a station where the passengers wanted it to stop; the train may not stop at all until we got to the coast. And it was very unlikely I could hold onto the back of it that long.

The view was at least beautiful. Pools of cloud were nestling between nearby peaks and lapping at the cooler valleys; the green parallel lines of a vineyard flicked by. A child in a field waved at me. I smile back as best I could and mouthed the word 'Help.' I wondered what he would tell his parents, and whether they would believe him.

The train was slowing. It was possible I would be able to outrun it. It slowed some more. And then it stopped.

We were at a station.

I extricated myself from the back of the train and dropped to the tracks. I discovered my joints had seized up in transit, but I decided to break the habit of a lifetime and not dwell on my minor ailments; I hopped, limped and hobbled to the edge of the platform. Mercifully, the decking was slanted down at my end. I got to the side of the train in time for the door to open. A young couple with dirty hair and even dirtier rucksacks got off, and I - nonchalantly as you like - got on.

So there I was on the train to Calvi, and the whole carriage of people were looking at me. They didn't even look away if I stared back. I matted down my hair a bit, and was addressed by a guard.

'Have you got a ticket, sir?' he asked.

'No, I need to buy a ticket to Calvi.'

Miracle upon miracle, I still had my wallet. I handed over some cash and the guard tapped away at his machine. I was now the owner of a train ticket and the guard moved on.

I pulled a face at the other passengers as if to say, 'What you staring at?' – apart from my torn trousers, muddy clothes, and the shoe with a bullet hole in its side.

Most of the carriage looked like tourists. Perhaps they thought I was some 'colourful local'. Perhaps they were right.

In the central section of the carriage, near the automatic doors, there was a lady with a dog. The dog was lying down; it looked stressed by the heat of the day. The owner - a sensible looking woman in her thirties - was crouched beside it, evidently concerned. There was a bowl of water for the dog which I thought was nice. The woman caught my eye and smiled at me. She was stroking the dog's stomach.

'Could you help me a second?' she asked.

'Sure,' I replied. She, for one, was not put off by my appearance. Ha! Rest of carriage.

'My dog has got stomach trouble. Can you comfort the dog and stroke him while I find the guard? He's called Napoleon.' Of course he was.

As I sat with Napoleon and comforted him, I reflected that with my tattered clothes, unwashed face and supine dog, I had now completed my new look; that of a homeless person.

Our next stop was at a proper functioning train station with uniformed staff, hanging baskets and all sorts of decorative frippery. There was a very fetching platform guard in figure hugging trousers and a well pressed jacket. Evidently she had just re-applied her lipstick, and when the train stopped our guard got off to kiss her on each cheek; he then handed over various parcels.

Napoleon and his owner got off and walked to a tree about ten metres away. The passengers watched with half-hearted interest as the lady asked the dog to go to the toilet by the tree. The dog had other ideas. He had been stuck on a boring train for hours – which are probably 'dog years' to a dog – and this was a chance to indulge in every dog's favourite hobby: sniffing stuff. His tail was wagging. He was burying his nose in clumps of grass where other dogs had peed before him. Then, glory of glories, he found a stick. The stick was far too big for him, so it took several attempts for him to get it balanced and wedged in his mouth. All the while, the woman was imploring the dog to go to the toilet and intermittently made apologetic shrugs at the guard who was looking on from the doorway of the train. We were clearly going to be waiting a while. The passengers seemed unfazed by the hold up; this was island life; the rolling stock of the train may be state of the art - shiny, efficient, and air-conditioned - but that counted for nothing; this was a rugged part of the world where everyone had to go with the flow in order to make life function. The whole episode pleased me greatly - it was the highlight of my day - which says something, because I had also been to a wedding.

Eventually the woman gave up and led the dog back to the train.

The train set off again along the side of the mountain. It had been moving no more than two minutes - I stress, no more than two minutes - when a jet of diarrhoea, the strength and colour of battery acid, shot horizontally out of the dog's arse and across the width of the carriage. It hit the doors. The stream was impressive both in terms of its force and duration; it must have continued for a good five or ten seconds. Then there was a pause of three seconds, and then the stench hit us like a nuclear blast.

It was going to be a long trip to Calvi, now we no longer had air to breathe.

Once at Calvi, my next task was to get to Nice without a passport.

First I would need a some clothes. Also I was hungry. Also I needed a pee. Also I needed a drink. Okay, upon reflection, Nice was going to have to wait a while.

On the way from the station to the centre of town there was a very welcome tourist shop that sold everything from rubber rings to cartons of milk. The range of clothing was appropriate for a happy go lucky holiday maker who wanted a t shirt and a pair of beach shorts. It would have to do.

I emerged with a Hawaiian shirt, a t shirt, a pair of pink shorts and some blue canvas shoes. The t shirt was aimed at tourists and had the Corsican logo on its front: the silhouette of a black face with a white bandana. I had lost the will to be decent and decorous, so I stood on the pavement and took off what was left of my suit trousers and shirt, and put on my new clothes instead.

As I walked into town I dropped my old clothes in a bin.

'Alright Pete?' asked a passer-by. 'How's it going?'

It was a restaurant owner I often chat to. And habitually give lots of money to.

'Could be worse!' I replied. How? How could it be worse?

Now for food and drink: it felt like a steak and chips with a nice cold lager kind of day. In truth, what day isn't?

I found a seat at a restaurant in the little square in front of the church and although they didn't have steak and chips, they did some very nice potatoes that were half fried and half roasted with thyme, and suckling pig. And yes, there is no predicament in the world, that would put me off savouring my food. The suckling pig was delicious. What greater joy is there than knowing a baby animal has been torn from its mother's teat at dawn and freshly spit roasted, all for my transient oral amusement? I'm kidding of course. Sort of. To accompany the feast, I had some excellent ice cold lager. I didn't take much persuading from the waitress to have a second lager and probably a third – only when drinking can I lose count after two - and then before I knew it, it was evening and I was ready to go down to the harbour to talk to a man about a boat.

'Pete, you're drunk,' he said.

'I'm not drunk.'

'You are slurring your words,' replied Francois, my boat guy.

'I just need to hire a boat for twenty-four hours,' I said. 'I have had an exceedingly trying day, and I could do with no further obstacles.'

'Where are you planning to go?' he asked. I have never known him to be obstructive before so I must have been giving off very bad vibes – perhaps accentuated by an ill-fitting Hawaiian shirt and whisky breath - I may have had some whisky after the beers. The net effect was to make Francois stand ever more firmly between me and the hooks with the keys on for the boats.

'I am planning to go down to Bastia,' I said.

'You've had too much to drink Pete,' he reasoned.

I could see two sets of keys for Bayliner power boats; they were side by side on the last two hooks on the right. I tried to not stare at them. I turned my head away from them and looked at them from the corners of my eyes. It was plain to even me that I was drunk.

I turned towards the window as if to make more general conversation. I was now trying to see where the two Bayliners were docked. Would I be able to get to one of them, start the motor, and cast off before Francois could stop me? It seemed very unlikely, particularly given our relative physical prowess.

'Ah, you're right,' I said. 'You're right. How's business?'

'Okay,' he replied. 'Would you like to sit down? I'll make you a cup of coffee.'

He removed some files and papers from a wooden chair and moved it towards me. I obviously looked in such a state that he didn't even suggest I walk the few feet necessary to cross the office.

I sat in the chair. It creaked ungratefully under my weight.

Francois unhooked the plastic reservoir from his coffee machine and walked off to another room to fill it.

I sprang up and took the two sets of keys to the power boats and made for the way out.

The key to the outside door was dangling in the lock so I also took that for good measure and locked Francois inside the building. I saw him emerge almost straight away and his eyes locked with mine through the glass; they widened with alarm.

'Pete!' he called.

I lumbered down the jetty looking for one of the two Bayliners. They are usually easy to spot; they are racy looking and mostly white in colour with a long wide blue or black strip down the side. I could hear shouting from the office. Francois was now banging the window with his palm. He then dashed out of sight. There was clearly another way out of the office, but it was a longer way round the building.

If I was very lucky, I had fifteen seconds.

I found a Bayliner. I clambered on board and set about undoing the mooring rope. It had canvas over the central section to keep it dry; it was going to take some undoing. I reasoned if I could just get it folded back enough to get to the ignition, I could do the rest at sea.

'Hey! Hey!' shouted Francois.

He was round the corner of the building and running towards the jetty.

I unhooked a couple of fastenings and just about got behind the wheel. The boat had been moored awkwardly - the buoys from my boat had somehow interlocked with the next boat - which is a very rare occurrence - as a result I needed to push my own boat hard aside before setting off. I clambered up onto the side decking and placed one foot hard against the next boat to try and get a bit of space. I thought I'd rocked the boats apart, but it was far from certain. I scampered back to the ignition and fumbled with one key and then the other.

'Pete stop! Please stop! What are you thinking? Are you mad?' He was sounding closer.

I turned the key in the ignition.

The boat did not start.

Think Pete, think.

Perhaps I needed to open a fuel valve or something.

'Pete, stop, now! Please!' He sounded very close, but I wasn't going to waste time looking.

I was pretty sure I had to pump some fuel, but I couldn't remember how.

Was there a rubber squeezy valve I had to pump with my palm to get fuel to the engine? Surely Bayliners are a bit too posh for that kind of thing.

I could hear Francois's feet clanking on the boards of the jetty behind.

I had half an idea that the way to start the motor was to push the throttle forwards and backwards a few times; perhaps it pumped fuel into the motor.

I swung the throttle forwards and backwards. I turned the key in the ignition. It half spluttered. I was on the right track. I pumped the throttle again forwards and backwards five times.

I could see the boat next to me dip down low where Francois had stepped onto it.

'Pete!'

I felt my own boat dip where Francois placed his first foot on it. I turned the ignition key again and the engine caught straight away.

I surged the boat forward.

Francois swore loudly in French. I turns out I'm a whore.

'At least bring the second set of keys back!' he shouted. But I daren't even do that.

I was off into the night.

NINE

I am not an expert sailor.

I have sailed around a little here and there, but in real terms I don't really know what I'm doing; I have always stuck to rivers or hugged the coast.

Firstly, how the hell was I going to find Nice? It is about 120 miles from Calvi. And it's dark. And there are no signposts.

Secondly, the particular boat I had stolen was basically a fun power boat for recreational use. It was sturdy, but it was certainly not intended for international travel. It could go perhaps forty miles per hour which is fun and amazingly fast for a boat, but it absolutely burns through fuel while doing so. As a result, the range might only be a hundred miles or a lot less. Okay, in truth I didn't know what the range was but I was pretty sure it wasn't going to be enough to get me to mainland France, even if I travelled at a more moderate, fuel efficient, speed.

I headed forward into the dark of the night, aiming the boat roughly north. I didn't have a phone; all I had was the rudimentary geography in my head and my common sense - heaven help me.

I felt I would fix on the North Star and keep aiming the boat for it.

So, first I had to work out which was the North Star.

I couldn't see anything because it was cloudy.

Then I saw the compass set at the front of the dashboard – hopefully that would help. But was Nice due north? Surely it was bit more to the left? And were there currents that might push me off course without me knowing? I could keep my boat facing north as long as I liked, but still be pushed sideways by currents and never even realise it.

I then had a vision that I would simply run out of fuel and drift in the sea for days.

I checked my fuel.

The tank was half full.

It was not enough.

Perhaps I should sail back and see if the other boat had more fuel in it – after all I did have the key for it - but I imagined police standing on the quayside listening to Francois and making notes. They would be talking into crackling radios and shaking their heads about the antics of the English. It would be better to keep going north.

I decided on a strategy to save fuel. I would get the boat to do about 30mph and maintain it for about twenty seconds, then cut the power for thirty seconds and let the boat drift forward under its own momentum. Then I would start the motor again, get the boat back up to 30mph, and then cut the motor again. That way, the engine was only on about half the time; that would surely be more efficient? Or was it the other way around, and if I went at full speed I would skim across the top of the water and so the boat would suffer less resistance? I had no idea. I did know that in my heart a full tank of fuel would not get me to France, let alone half a tank. What had I been thinking even setting out? No matter what strategy I tried, I was doomed.

Clearly this was how I was going to die. Adrift in the middle of the sea, ready to be eaten by jackals - somehow they would still find me. They would arrive in boats, with more fuel in than mine; because they'd thought ahead, and I hadn't.

And even if I got to Nice, what about immigration and customs? If I was stopped, I didn't have my passport. It was factually correct that I was travelling from one part of France to another, and so a passport shouldn't be needed, but immigration wouldn't know that. I was clearly not a French person and I could have travelled from anywhere.

Deep breaths. I was not to worry: the customs and immigration problem was only a theoretical question. Because before that, I was going to die.

I kept up my routine of starting the engine, counting to twenty and cutting the engine, keeping about twenty degrees to the west of North – I kind of figured that was right for Nice. Sometimes in life all you can do is choose a strategy and stick to it, even if you know in your heart the strategy won't work.

Then it started to rain. Heavily. I only had two layers on. The rain was in my eyes and all over my face; matting my hair and clumping it into thick strands on my forehead. The rain was freezing. My hands were painful with the cold.

My vision was so poor that a container ship would rear up in the dark without me seeing it and chop my little boat in two. I literally wouldn't know what hit me.

I was getting obsessed by the fuel gauge. It was already markedly down. Was it like in a car where the last bit of the dial actually had more fuel than you thought? I doubt I would be so lucky, and in either case I was too far from anywhere for it to make much of a difference.

I spent another hour or perhaps two in the dark, freezing with cold, wet to the bone, and counting to twenty then thirty. Sometimes I counted in English and sometimes I counted in French. It was something to do.

Inevitably, and finally, the fuel ran out and the engine spluttered and I drifted in silence on the sea.

I couldn't see anything at all in the wet and gloom.

Perhaps the boat had a flare I could set off.

I hunted around a bit in the lockers. Nothing. I clambered over the screen and onto the front of the boat. I clung on as best I could and opened up the storage hatches at the front. Shouldn't it be some sort of law that you had to always sail with a flare? If it was, then I couldn't find it.

I figured my best bet was to find the most sheltered part of the boat and curl up and rest. Sooner or later I would be found. Dead. And eaten by the cunning sea jackals who were gloating about their surplus fuel.

I tried curling up on the floor under the wheel. This had the theoretical advantage that the screen offered a bit of protection against the wind and rain. The trouble was that as the boat tilted and rocked, a puddle of water would wash along the flooring and soak me, or to be precise, soak me even more.

I then tried the floor near the secondary fuel tanks; it was a bit drier for some reason. I curled up in a ball so that I had fewest limbs exposed to the elements. The height of the tanks at least afforded some shelter.

Secondary fuel tanks?

I stood up and kicked them to find out if they made a hollow noise where they were empty.

They were full.

I am officially an idiot.

An idiot who panics too easily. First my bladder when I was in the boot of the car, and now this. Good old Francois, supplying his boats with spare fuel. I must remember not to screw him over too often in the future.

I soon rigged up the necessary fuel line and got myself going again. I swear the rain even got a little less wet. I didn't even bother with the twenty seconds on, thirty seconds off thing; the gods were now smiling at me and I was going to Nice.

I would sit in the flower market in the old town and have some well-earned breakfast. I would treat myself to socca – a local delicacy of crepes made from chickpea flower. I would admire the orange and pink Italianate architecture. I would watch the flower sellers at work and the antique dealers setting up their stalls for the day. No customs officer would see me arrive, so I would have no need for a passport.

In short, I now felt my luck was finally in.

TEN

I sat on a low wall opposite the insurance offices in Nice. I was ten minutes early.

I would savour the moment.

I had battled my way by train and boat, and escaped kidnappers to be where I needed to be. I deserved my moment of victory.

I would interview the person who was claiming the money on Jacob's life assurance. It would probably be Fake Jacob, but it might be a close associate. Either way I would be able to get to the identity of the people behind the fraud. They were possibly responsible for the murder of the real Jacob, and therefore the police would get involved. This time they would be on the right track, and the evidence would click into place.

Nice is one of the most pleasant cities in the world. It is stylish, but down to earth. It is friendly, but classy. As I sat there, its Mediterranean weather bathed my soul with calm and happiness.

I could have gone into the office and introduced myself to my colleague at this stage - I was just about neat enough to not be turfed out, despite my Hawaiian appearance. We could sit together in her office and discuss a strategy; what questions to ask and what evidence I needed. But somehow having come all this way, my instincts were against it.

What was stopping me?

The truth was – and I hated to admit it because I am not spiritual - I had a horrible presentment. Something was nagging me. On some deep level my heart had put together the pieces of information I had encountered over the weeks; the omens, the facts, the sideways glances and whispers that you notice but can't interpret. And I knew – I just knew – I couldn't go into that office. Was it low blood sugar that was making me feel so odd? I had had the hearty breakfast of socca I had promised myself, I had had coffee. In fact, I had been in such a good mood I had even drank an orange juice, and to hell with its likely effect on my bladder!

Then I knew. I just knew why I didn't want to proceed. I knew perhaps ten seconds before the evidence of my own eyes confirmed everything.

I spotted the well-dressed woman in a business suit and dark brown hair from a long way off. She moved purposefully in high heels along the kerb and past two policewomen on horseback. A couple of young men at a café table stared at her unapologetically. The woman smiled back and then raised an eyebrow at one of the policewomen who raised an eyebrow in return; men, eh?

The woman was within about five yards of me when I called out to her.

'Emily!'

She faltered, her face just about changed colour, then she gathered herself.

'Hi Pete,' she replied.

She gave me the widest and toothiest of grins - Reese Witherspoon would have been proud - and pushed on the doors of the building to disappear from view.

Emily.

How had I not realised this all along?

ELEVEN

A day later and I was safely back in Bastia.

I had returned the boat and keys and had grovelled an apology to Francois. He sniffed around the boat to look for damage but when he found none and I paid him handsomely, he was pretty good about the whole thing. I might have to avoid him for a while, though. And perhaps leave him something obscure in my will.

The following Monday, and I was back at work.

My immediate impression upon entering the office was that the atmosphere was completely off. It was like the time I was plastered all over the local newspaper, only this had more of a finality about it.

'Has someone died?' I asked.

Niculaiu was the first to reply. 'Inspector Fortini wants to talk to you. Soon as possible. He phoned us last Thursday, last Friday, and today first thing. Has he not phoned you?'

'I lost my phone,' I replied. 'I lost it last Wednesday in the mountains. Do you know what? I don't miss it.'

'You're going to need to ring Inspector Fortini,' said Niculaiu.

'Has someone got his number?' I asked.

Jean-Marie still hadn't said a word. He knew what he'd done. Or didn't do. It was hard to tell.

Niculaiu handed me a piece of paper with Raphael Fortini's number on it.

Thoroughly spooked by the atmosphere at the office, I organised a meeting with the inspector and was soon sitting in front of his desk.

He motioned with his hands as if he was somehow parting his desk like the Red Sea. It was an odd gesture.

'Great news!' he said. His deadpan face did not match his words.

'Okay,' I ventured.

'I am re-opening the case into the death of Jacob Lluberas!' he said.

Oh crap.

'Oh great!' I said.

'It is what you asked for,' he said. Had he read something in my face? I was going to need to try and keep it blank.

'It is indeed what I asked for.' Before I realised that solving the case would mean Emily would have to go to jail for insurance fraud, covering up a death, car theft, and a variety of other serious crimes.

Inspector Fortini sat in silence, as is his way, then unexpectedly smiled. 'You survived your kidnapping then?'

'Kidnapping?' I asked. I wasn't even sure I was going to admit to that. Why hadn't I thought everything through before coming to see him?

'So as I understand it,' he continued. 'A key factor in your thinking is, as the Americans say, to follow the money. Whoever claims on the life assurance policies is probably involved in the death of Jacob Lluberas.'

I nodded slowly in what I hoped was a thoughtful but inscrutable manner.

The inspector paused. Perhaps he was used to other people filling the silences he created. Well, not today mister; he could wait all he liked.

Eventually he spoke again; to lay out his thinking.

'There was hair found under the bed in the lodge,' he said. 'We previously analysed its DNA.'

I nodded phlegmatically. I added a top note of mildly pensive.

He paused again.

'You kindly provided a sample of the fake Jacob's hair and his fingerprints,' he added.

So they were now accepting the concept of a fake Jacob. Oh hell.

'We have had them analysed. The DNA and the fingerprints.'

What?

This is a disaster. I thought they were not going to analyse the hair unless they had grounds to re-open the case. And I had previously been told it was inadmissible evidence. And as for the hair under the bed, I was pretty sure Emily's DNA is on a British police database from her drug years – was it her hair they had found at the lodge that time?

I was more determined than ever that none of my panic would spread across my face. I conjured in my head the look of an 18th century widow on a clifftop looking out to sea for her lost love. I would be wearing a black woollen shawl stiffened with my dried tears. I didn't feel it worked. Perhaps Marlon Brando looking enigmatic playing poker with the Mafia. That should do it. I am clearly insane.

'You look a bit strange. Are you okay?' he asked.

'Yes?' I replied.

'Even if we can't arrest them for the insurance fraud or murder, we can arrest them for your kidnapping,' he said.

'My kidnapping?' I asked.

'You said the two were related.'

'I said the two were related?' In my panic, I had even slipped into Australian inflection. Think Pete, think.

The inspector looked at his notes.

'There is a recording of the conversation you had with Inspector Cadin when you said you were kidnapped in the back of a car. In this recording you said the kidnappers were trying to prevent you from going to the meetings at the insurance companies. You were very clear on that point.'

I had indeed been very clear. They record conversations?

'It was only conjecture,' I tried. 'I have to stress I can't prove anything.'

'What's your sister's name?' he asked unexpectedly. So she was in the frame.

'Emily.'

'Her second name? Emily De'Ath?' he asked. 'Is she married? Does she have other names?'

My inscrutable look was now – I can only imagine - replaced by one of shock.

'The DNA from the hair under the bed and the hair you provided from the fake Jacob. We have been checking it on international databases throughout Europe.'

Mary mother of Joseph. Or something. He was coming at me from all angles.

The inspector appeared to be thinking hard about what to say next. The suspense was awful. How much was showing on my face? How do other people keep their faces so blank? Botox? I had been too quick to dismiss Botox; there were clearly many advantages. What felt like an eternity later, I managed to speak.

'My sister isn't married, no. Emily is Emily.' It was lame, but the best I could do. It wouldn't be difficult for him to find out Emily's surname – he just had to ask Luc - and now it looked as though I was obfuscating. Which I was. Most importantly, why was he mentioning her at all?

'You requested the pathologist consider what was in the stomach of the body they fished out of the sea,' he said.

He knew everything. On every subject.

'I did,' I said.

'The body was very decomposed. The stomach contents also. But it was most likely that his last meal before death was an evening meal. There was a lot of meat in his stomach. He fell off the cliff in the morning, but the sort of food he had in his stomach implies he died in an evening soon after eating. He had also been drinking alcohol.'

'Really?' I said. I didn't feel that was a smoking gun, but it still pointed to the two fake deaths – the lodge and particularly the cliff - both being at the wrong time of day.

He said, 'A defence will say, yes Jacob and Antone are friends, they are related; one of them once used the other one's phone and that explains the DNA.'

'Who's Antone?' I asked.

'You sister's boyfriend,' he replied.

'My sister was dating Jacob Lluberas,' I tried. 'It was Jacob who fell off the cliff.'

'And before that she was dating Antone Lluberas,' he said firmly. 'Surely this was the point of what you were explaining to Luc?'

So that was it. This was the first time I had a name for the fake Jacob. I had never met Antone - or rather I had never met Antone playing Antone - I had met him as Jacob. Presumably he was still alive somewhere - on the other side of the mountains maybe; sitting in a room with the blinds down, counting huge piles of cash from the insurance pay out.

'So,' continued the inspector. 'If the Lluberas family, either Antone or the mother claim the insurance, then that is normal, but if Antone was proved to be passing himself off as Jacob that may be a crime. Sarah-Jayne Hoskins would be a witness to that. But, better, if the hair DNA under the bed matches the woman who claimed the money in the insurance office in Nice we may have a case. After all, why would a business owner from Livorno, Italy, be in the hunting lodge that night?'

Fortini had put it all together. Emily was so stuffed.

'You have details of who claimed the money in the Ajaccio and Nice insurance offices?' I squeaked.

'Thanks to you, Mr De'Ath!' he boomed. 'In Ajaccio it was Jacob's mother who claimed the money, but the woman in the Nice office is of real interest.'

He smiled a huge smile of satisfaction. The man was being wilfully happy.

'When Inspector Cadin explained your theories to me, I thought Mr De'Ath is right,' he continued. 'So I phoned the offices in Ajaccio and Nice. When you focussed us on the stomach contents. The hair samples. Mr De'Ath you are a genius!'

I nodded meekly. I was looking as inscrutable as a startled rabbit.

'It's just,' I said.

'It's just?'

'It's just I don't think you really have enough good proof,' I protested weakly.

Of course they had enough good proof.

'A piece of hair,' I continued. 'Two Lluberas cousins who look like each other. Of course they look like each other, they are cousins and they are Corsican. The stomach contents; Jacob could have had sausage and bacon for breakfast the morning he fell off the cliff. He was staying in a hotel with an English woman; it is what the English eat at breakfast in a hotel.' I warbled on as best I could. I couldn't think of too much. The inspector was leafing through some notes as I spoke. I wasn't sure he even heard me.

I didn't know what to do. Worse, my brain was now slumping. It was just about possible they didn't have enough proof to tie Emily to the insurance office in Nice. She had worn a wig or dyed her hair for the visit – that was something – and she had dressed differently; that was a slight help perhaps. And it was hardly that she would have left a DNA sample behind her.

My brain, in defeat, just went with doing what it knew best.

I rambled.

I just started talking, and then I didn't stop. I talked and talked at the inspector in verbose and never-ending circles. I flung in non-sequiturs of logic. I flung in needless and convoluted conversational tangents. I gesticulated. I tapped the inspector's desk. I inexplicably broached the subject of Corsican cuisine. I threw in stories about my prostate and my bladder. I talked about my childhood. I even – for no reason clear to even me - started talking about my bowels. I must have talked for over twenty minutes. The least I thought I could achieve for Emily was to muddy the waters. But I feared we had got the stage where they had so much evidence that pointed to the truth, and the police were so close to solving the case that no diversionary tactic was going to work. The truth was we were only one step away from Emily being arrested, and if the police had Emily in their sights then my talking nonsense for twenty minutes would just look like me covering for her.

The truth was we were stuffed, and I knew it with every fibre of my being.

Part Six

THE WORLD ACCORDING TO EMILY

ONE

Happy days! I was a quarter of a million up. So I can finally get the new frock I've had my eye on. A new frock, a new pair of shoes, a new pair of knickers, and I can walk into town, seat myself on a bar stool, order a fancy cocktail, and be somebody.

'Waiter!' I will call. 'A margarita for me and one for all of my friends!'

My spangly new dress will light up the room like a glitterball.

Also, I can pay off my credit card debts.

But first to face Pete. I had been avoiding his phone calls, but according to all sources he was very angry. Very angry indeed.

I decided to visit him in his natural habit; a restaurant. He didn't take much tracking down. I stood outside and looked through the front window to check that his bottle of red wine was now at least half in his stomach and I took the plunge through the door. The door made far too much noise, but everyone looked up except my brother. In fact, he didn't see me until I had slumped down in the seat beside him. His eyes turned to the right to take me in, but his head remained set forward. I wasn't in a position to read his expression so we both looked forwards for a while taking in the events of the old market square beyond.

As time moved on, I took his silence as despondency. I had expected anger or sarcasm, but this smelled dank and musty. It wasn't good.

'How is your case coming along where you are trying to show there was a fake Jacob? A Facob, if you like?' I ventured.

Pete scraped his fork around in his food.

'Far too well,' he replied. 'The police are very close to arresting you. They routinely mention you Jacob and Antone in the same sentence. It's not good.'

'Oh what do you think of Antone, by the way?' I asked. 'I want to date him for a bit so you might have to rub along with him? I really like him. Do you like him? Tell me you like him.'

'Emily, the police have a hair sample of yours from under the bed where you shot Jacob. If memory serves, the police in England have your DNA on file. They are circulating the data as far as England.'

'And?' I asked. 'I have stayed at that lodge. I stayed a few weeks before that evening, and with Antone. The weekend was dirty. Very dirty.'

Pete didn't laugh. Instead he said, 'And the police think it is you who visited the insurance offices in Nice.'

Pete really was looking very depressed about all this.

'It's going to be fine,' I said. 'It's all sorted. What wine are you drinking?'

'How can it all be sorted? The police know the whole story,' he said.

'No Pete. The police understand the whole scenario that you have been piecing together. Good work by the way! Good sleuthing!'

Come on Pete, laugh. I will you to laugh. Pete was in a deathly mood.

'So exactly which of them were involved?' he asked.

'What do you mean?'

'Well you all made me feel like a paranoid madman conspiracy theorist. To explain events, a lot of people would have had to be involved,' he said. 'Some of the police, the guys at the office, Jacob's mother, whoever had a tow truck to remove the car with the body in it, the witnesses on the cliff, maybe even a pathologist or two.'

'You'd rather be a conspiracy theorist than spiritual,' I said.

'Huh?'

'One explanation for all the events was that you foresaw a death in a hallucination.'

'Oh come on,' he said. 'I was never going to go for that.'

'Sarah did.'

'And that was not your finest hour Emily. You got Sarah so confused with the mazzere nonsense that she was barely going to defend herself in court.'

'She knew in her heart Jacob was alive,' I pointed out. 'And she was right. The mazzere allowed her to believe that she could see things other people couldn't. She was far closer to the truth than you ever were. Anyway, the mazzere idea was a good one. The idea was to try and get Sarah to burble a lot of witchy nonsense to the police. It would discredit her.'

'Emily!' cried Pete. 'The police are taking statements from the insurance agents in Ajaccio and Nice!'

'Let them. I didn't use my real name. I had set up a whole identity over in Livorno. I did my hair a bit different. I'll grow a moustache. By the way, you wouldn't believe how good the Lluberas family are at sorting out IDs. If you ever need to go on the run, or fake your death...'

Pete was not going to soften. 'The Nice office could easily identify you as you, visually. It's a huge problem.'

'I am telling you I have it sorted,' I repeated.

'And did you leave that note on my bedside table?' he asked. 'It scared the bejesus out of me.'

'Yeah that might have been me,' I replied. 'Come on Pete, I'm a quarter of a million up. Let me have my moment. You can never see the good in a situation. It's all "Oh you broke the law this" and "Oh you got people to people to kidnap me that" Little Mr Glass Half Empty.'

I perused the menu and tried to look contrite.

'Is dinner on you?' I asked. It was funny in my head.

'After all you put me through? The meal is definitely on you,' he replied.

'If you don't pay, I'll have you kidnapped, I'll have you bundled into the back of a car. I'll have you cracked on the shin bone with a spanner. You know I would.'

'Shut up Emily.'

'Too soon for that joke?' I asked. 'Aw come on Pete. We love "too soon" jokes.'

'That really hurt by the way,' he said. 'I don't know what shin splints are, but I am sure I now have them.'

'You'll be fine,' I said.

I drew some solace from the fact he was at least, to a degree, interacting with me.

'One huge problem is the hair I stole from Antone when he was sitting in my garden pretending to be Jacob,' said Pete.

'I knew you stole his hair!' I said. 'I don't go around stealing hair from your girlfriends.' Not least because Pete doesn't have any girlfriends; perhaps not the best time to bring that up, though. 'And you gave the hair to the police?'

'Yes, and they did a DNA test and it matched a sample found on Jacob's phone,' said Pete.

'Because it was Antone,' I explained.

'Yes!' said Pete. 'So we have DNA proof that Antone was masquerading as Jacob.'

'No we don't,' I explained. 'I will simply say you got yourself confused. I was sitting having a drink with you and Antone, and somehow you got it into your head that he was Jacob.'

'Emily! I have just heard they are going to interview Sarah and see if she will identify Jacob.'

I admit that threw me a little, and Pete seized on my prevarication.

'There, that is a problem isn't it?' he said. 'Sarah will identify Antone, and the insurance woman in Nice will identify you.'

'Sarah is a problem,' I said. 'But I'll fix it. I'll do something about Sarah.'

'You'll do something about Sarah? What, in the Mafia sense?'

'No, in the Lluberas sense,' I said mimicking his voice. 'Oh come on Pete, let's not fall out.'

'Let's not fall out?' he said. 'You had me kidnapped!'

'Hmmm.'

'I notice that speech impediment of yours hasn't improved,' said Pete.

'What speech impediment?'

'The one you've had since childhood where you have trouble saying "sorry"?'

'Oh, uh ha, ha ha, ha ha!' I said.

He'd almost forgotten himself. He can never resist a bit of sarcasm; but he then remembered he was determined to be cross, and went back to looking resentful.

'Sorry,' I said.

'Sorry what?' he asked.

'Sorry I had you kidnapped.'

'And?'

'And I promise I won't do it again,' I said.

He sighed.

'I'm just going to have to pretend it never happened. That my sister would never do anything like this,' he said. 'Otherwise I won't be able to tolerate you.'

Well, that was brutal.

I wanted to say something perky, but felt defeated.

It was Pete who finally spoke.

'You looked ill by the way. When you were outside that insurance office in Nice.'

'Yeah. I've had a virus or something. But now I feel 250,000 times better!'

'Droll. Just order your food, pesky sister who had me kidnapped and has a lot of making up to do.'

He smirked and squeezed my hand.

Thank all the gods for Pete's good nature.

I beckoned the waitress over and ordered a bottle of Pete's favourite wine and a second glass. I figured it couldn't hurt the situation.

'Jacob's mother was in on it,' I said. I offered it like a peace offering. 'And Jean-Marie at your office was in on it.'

'I knew it!' he said.

'No, you didn't.'

I got a drinking straw and blew bubbles in my red wine while looking at Pete through my fringe. He smiled.

'And you are going to sort out Sarah? Make sure she doesn't identify this Antone as Jacob?'

'Don't give it another thought,' I said.

There will be other adventures, and I won't always be the one in the wrong.

Hell, I hope not at least.

Part Seven

THE WORLD ACCORDING TO PETE

ONE

I was enjoying a pleasant Friday night at home pottering around getting jobs done and deciding what to watch later, when there was a knock on the door. I put some trousers on - a precaution I have recently learnt - and answered it.

It was Sarah.

She was dressed like a vamp. She was wearing thigh high black boots that were shiny, a black plastic mini skirt, and a low cut white blouse tied in a Britney Spears knot. Of the various items of apparel, the worst offence was the plastic skirt. A stranger looking at Sarah that day would have been incredibly charitable for the words 'crack whore' not to pop into their brain.

In the De'Ath family tradition, I tried to select the better of my thoughts before speaking. In this instance, there weren't any. I settled for a bright 'Well look at you!'

'Hi Pete. Can I come in?' she asked.

'Sure!'

When, oh when, will I learn not to open the front door?

She walked towards the sitting room and sat down.

'Do you have gin and tonic or prosecco?' she asked. 'I'm feeling nervous.'

I got us some drinks.

'I want to talk,' she said.

'Okay?'

She looked very earnest.

'You and me we get on, yes?' she asked.

She drained her prosecco alarmingly quickly and held her glass out for more. She did it without irony. I was unnerved.

'The thing is,' she said. 'I feel we connect.'

Oh no.

I was very aware of her cleavage. It dominated the room. Was it a push up bra, or had I simply not noticed her ample chest before? As she spoke, I tried to look everywhere except her breasts. I looked at the ceiling; I looked at the floor; I looked at my glass. It was like when you are at the gym and a man in the locker room insists on talking to you even though he is stark naked. You try and look everywhere except his penis and yet the penis is all you are aware of. I am speaking figuratively of course; I have never been to a gym.

'I don't think I connect that often with people,' she began. 'And I know we are a very different age, you and me.'

'Yes,' I said. We could certainly agree on the age thing. I was afraid of where this was going.

'Can I ask you a question?' asked Sarah.

'Of course you can Sarah.'

She pulled herself up. She thrust her chest forward and her bottom back. She elongated her left leg and tilted her foot forward.

'Do you think I'm attractive?' she asked.

I tried not to panic. I gave myself a talking to instead. If this beautiful young woman wants to make a play for me then I should be flattered, not alarmed. It had taken a lot of courage for her to dress up like a hooker and knock on my door – and at least two hours studying Pretty Woman. Plenty of older men date younger women. I should rise to the challenge.

'You are very attractive. You are very sexy,' I said.

'Thank you,' she said. 'And you are a good looking man.'

'Thank you.' I topped up her prosecco and realised gloomily that the only other bottle of fizz I had was very expensive and for a special occasion; I didn't want to open it for Sarah.

'So why are we both single?' she asked. 'It doesn't make any sense. We don't have to be single. What am I doing? I just sit at home on my own every evening waiting for life to happen. Am I expecting a man to just walk through the door? I have to make things happen. I have to choose to exploit options from the life I have got!'

Fair dos. I don't mind being exploited.

She was holding my hand now, and looking earnestly into my eyes.

Had I made the bed and tidied the bedroom? Were there old underpants on my pillow and a half eaten takeaway curry on the floor? Was the toilet clean? Had I even flushed it?

'So I have got a proposition,' she said.

'Okay,' I replied, noting a shrill tone to my voice I usually reserve for the police.

'I think you and I should go out.'

'Right!' I said. It was very shrill indeed.

I felt I was letting Sarah do all the hard work. I should reciprocate a little. She had been incredibly brave approaching me.

I half closed my eyes and tilted my head. I leant in for a kiss.

'Now,' she said.

'Now?'

'We should go into town and get out and about. This is a friendly town. If we sit in a bar we can talk to people and we both might be able to find someone. If we don't go out, we won't find someone. I mean look at you. You need to go out. I need to go out.'

'Ooooooooh!' I said.

'Why? What did you think I meant?'

You really do not want to know what I thought you meant.

I topped up her glass with the last of the bottle.

'So you and I should go out on the pull?' I asked.

'Yeah and we can catch up!'

Catch up? Catch up on the times we drove around with a dead body and had to deal with the police? In fairness, I didn't have any better plans for my evening.

I stood up brightly.

'Okay,' I said. 'This is a good idea, and you are quite right. Let's do this. You and I can be out on the pull as friends.'

And she was right; I need to get out more. And in her funny-crazy-Sarah way she was good company.

'Let's do this,' I repeated.

We walked in the evening sunshine down to the harbour. I love that I live in a country where I can say the word sunshine so many times on any given day. Sunshine, sunshine, sunshine.

We chatted as we walked.

She said, 'Also I suppose I wanted to touch base with you on a similar topic. Your sister.'

'Emily?'

'Yes Emily. I have decided not to be resentful about Emily taking Jacob from me, but I think I want you to understand that I won't be playing fair in return either. If she can play the vamp. I can play the vamp. It is just that I consider you a friend and so I wanted to check that you and I are good about this.'

I really didn't think Sarah had much of a chance out-manoeuvring Emily on the man front. Or out-man-ouevring I should say. Hell, I'm funny. I kept all my thoughts to myself.

I then opted to say, 'Do you want a little advice?'

'I definitely want a little advice,' she replied.

'Your outfit.'

'Yes?'

'It is just slightly too...'

'Yes?'

'Okay,' I said. 'What if you button up the blouse a bit higher and unknot it at your waist. Just lead with your legs. Let your legs do the talking.'

She seemed to not hear me. She certainly didn't adjust her clothing. Then she stopped in her tracks.

'Well now I've lost my confidence,' she muttered. 'It's all your fault.' Of course it was.

We went to take the ornate steps down to the harbour, but then Sarah seemed to change her mind about where we were going.

'We'll go to Pinocchio's first,' she said. 'They sometimes have dancing. Do you dance Pete?'

No.

'Yes,' I said.

We went to Pinocchio's.

There was a party of sorts going on. Loud music, loud chatter, dim nights. They had assembled a very long table for about thirty people.

I instinctively looked for Emily, but couldn't see her.

'This is like a weird dream I had recently,' said Sarah who took hold of my arm for reassurance. 'Look, there is the policeman. Look, there is everyone.'

I wasn't sure at first what she meant, but then I got my eye in.

I could see Inspector Fortini and Inspector Cadin sitting chatting. Luc Cadin appeared to have a girlfriend or wife. She had short dark curly hair and was doing most of the talking. Then next to them I could see Jean-Marie from my office and a little further beyond was Niculaiu. There was even the office errand boy Benedettu. The more I looked, the more people I recognised. None of the table had seen us yet, and I wasn't sure what to do.

I steered Sarah towards the bar area to buy some thinking time. The barman wasn't ready for us yet, so we instinctively leant against the bar and gazed at the group.

'There's the pathologist from the local hospital,' I said.

'Oh and there is Bernard, the man who took us to see the mazzere,' said Sarah. 'We could talk to him. Do you think he's single?'

'You are casting your net very wide.' I observed. 'That is admirable.'

'I am going to make things happen,' she said. 'I am fed up with myself. I have promised myself to take some chances.'

'Exactly right. After all, what's the worst that could happen?'

'I end up with a dead boyfriend in the back of the car and go to prison,' said Sarah.

'Exactly!' I leant forward to talk in her ear. 'Who are the men at the end of the table?'

Sarah squinted at the group.

'They are cousins of Jacob,' she said. 'Or nephews.'

On an impulse I walked across the room to them. I affected a bit of a swagger.

'Did either of you likely lads kidnap me the other day?' I asked.

'What?' asked the nearest one.

I just knew in my heart they were my kidnappers, but I couldn't prove it.

'If so, can I have my passport back?'

'What are you talking about?' he replied. 'Who are you?'

I couldn't think of an answer to that, so before I knew it I starting skulking back towards Sarah.

I was stopped in my tracks by an elderly voice.

'Peter!'

I peered into a dark corner.

'Mum?' I asked.

My mum was sitting near the others in an alcove waving at me. Evidently everyone in Bastia was invited to this party except me and Sarah. My own elderly mother had a better social life than me.

Mum was talking to an elderly man next to her; I had to presume he was the famous object of her desire. I focussed on him. He was very dapper. I felt I'd seen him before but couldn't quite place him.

I went over and he looked inquiringly at me.

'I am Peter, her son,' I said.

'I am Ludic,' he replied.

He greeted me with good old fashioned manners, but he didn't then maintain conversation.

I tried to imagine him receiving the lascivious texts. I tried to imagine him getting so jiggy with my mother that they lost all four of their hearing aids in one centripetal clinch. My mouth felt nauseous.

My mum spoke. 'I know you think I am a batty old woman,' she said.

'No of course not,' I said. As in yes of course, and then some.

'But we weren't going to let you get arrested,' she said.

'Okay,' I replied.

'And we weren't going to let Sarah go to prison. We wouldn't do that.'

'No, of course you wouldn't,' I replied, mentally patting her.

'And we certainly aren't going to let Emily be prosecuted,' she said.

'What do you mean?' I asked.

'Well don't you recognise Ludic?' she asked. She pointed to Ludic who was now talking to someone else. 'He is the chief prosecutor in the district. If he says there isn't enough evidence, there isn't enough evidence.'

So that was where I had seen him before. Ludic – my mother's elderly boyfriend – was the prosecutor at Sarah's trial who had unexpectedly dropped all charges. He was probably the one who had accepted Antone's word that he was Jacob Lluberas.

I got myself back to the bar and the relative safety of Sarah's company. Of all the emotions that I could have felt at that moment, and all the thoughts I could have thought, my next thought was an odd one; that I myself had never felt so strongly about a person that I had left a pebble on the windowsill outside their bedroom. Good for Mum. I suppose.

'Shall we get a bottle of champagne?' asked Sarah.

'As a good a plan as any,' I replied. 'I'll pay.'

There was a voice behind me.

'Well if it isn't the odd couple!' said Emily. 'What are you two doing out? Is Porn-R-Us.com down or something?'

'Thanks for that insult Emily, but we are allowed out, you know,' I replied. 'Also Porn-R-Us is not a real website – I might happen to know. Also, you are insulting Sarah.'

'Also we're not a couple,' said Sarah. She sounded bristly but then quickly rearranged herself - she remembered that this evening she was trying on the mantle of man-eater and all round sophisticate.

Sarah did a little shimmy manoeuvre that was supposed to somehow confront or square up to Emily. She had plainly prepared the move earlier in a mirror. It involved rolling her shoulders a bit and moving forward towards her intended victim; in this case, Emily. Emily didn't notice it at all. Sarah tried it again and then visibly shrank and turned away. 'Oh this just isn't fair,' she said.

Emily, for her part, looked in a fantastic mood. She had a brand new off the shoulder dress and was very nearly wearing it.

'So basically you have assembled your crew for a celebratory meal?' I asked Emily.

'My crew?' she asked.

'Who helped you with your crime,' I said.

'What crime?' she asked. She was more confident than when we had met in the restaurant a few days before.

I pointed to the whole table.

'Think about it,' she said. 'Let's take the example of the pathologist, and not even that pathologist you are pointing at; he did his job correctly. Then there is Bernard the journalist: all Bernard did was take us to see a mazzere, which you thoroughly enjoyed incidentally, so no crime there. All Jean-Marie did was get Sarah to bump into Jacob and keep us informed of your antics; no crime in that. The police, no matter what you threw at them, did their job correctly. Every time there were new events they methodically looked into all the details. When you yourself asked them to look at the DNA and fingerprint evidence, they very kindly went above and beyond their duty to help you out. Hell, they even arrested Sarah: because that is what the evidence demanded, and they let you see the case file. The prosecuting judge, he did his job correctly.'

'Did he though?' I asked. 'He could have checked Antone's credentials more carefully when he claimed to be Jacob.'

'A judge doesn't take a DNA test of a person every time they say what their name is.'

'And you knew,' I continued. 'You knew deep down, as a backstop, if it all went wrong he should be able to prevent a prosecution, but what if the evidence kept turning up against you?'

'The evidence only kept turning up against me, because you kept turning it up. Frankly, it would have been a lot better if I had just kept you kidnapped dear brother,' she said.

'You have been riding your luck Emily face it,' I said.

'The insurance companies,' continued Emily who was on a roll. 'Only paid out when they saw a valid death certificate from a source they trusted. Not one of these people I mention, not one, has committed a crime. So in conclusion why don't you chill out and join us?'

'Because I wasn't invited?'

'Pete, this is a small town where the professional classes have to rub along with each other. It's called networking. You, on the other hand are always setting yourself against us. That's why you don't get invited to things.'

'Cheers for that. And who is paying for all this food and drink?' I asked.

'I am,' she said.

Emily will always be broke, if this is how she acts when she gets a bit of money.

'Look,' said Emily. 'I'll tell you one thing. The police you see there, Inspector Cadin and Inspector Fortini, are straight. They were not involved even one inch. You should take them seriously Peter.' She prodded me sharply in the chest to emphasise her point. 'And as a result, you should learn not to talk to them so much.'

'Okay, fine,' I replied. 'But can you do me one single favour?'

'Maybe?'

'Can you do something about Stripper Barbie here?'

We both looked at Sarah.

'Can you hook her up with a suitable man? You must have a cast off you can spare?' I asked.

Emily eyed up Sarah's clothes as if seeing them for the first time. She winced visibly. 'I told you,' she sighed. 'I've got it all in hand.'

Luc Cadin, Raphael Fortini and the judge, Ludic, were in my line of vision; they were chatting and then occasionally looking my way. Eventually Luc stood up from his chair and walked over to me. He tucked his shirt into his trousers as if preparing himself for something.

Sarah saw him approach and peeled off me. 'Remember what I just said,' she whispered.

'Hello Inspector,' I said.

'Hello to you. So you are safe and well?' He looked in a very good mood.

'I escaped unscathed,' I replied.

'I had heard it,' he said. 'You will need to visit us and give us another statement about what you know of your kidnapping,'

'I will? I thought I had done that?'

'We found a car that matches the description of the car where you were in the back,' he said. 'You'll perhaps be able to identify it.'

The inspector changed tone and placed his hand on my arm. He wanted what he said next to be taken seriously. 'And then there is the matter of the alleged insurance frauds.'

'Okay?'

'We feel... we all feel, that the case depends on you Mr De'Ath,' he said.

'In what way?' I asked.

'Well,' he replied. 'We have a situation where all three insurance companies say they are happy with the death of Jacob Lluberas. They are so happy that they paid out over one million Euros. That includes your own company!'

'Yes,' I said.

'And the forensic team and the pathologist are happy that the corpse they have is truly Jacob Lluberas and that he probably died from falling from the cliff and the drowning in the sea.'

'Yes,' I said.

'The idea that he died before, in the lodge; there is some little proof for this,' he said. 'But it largely rests on your testimony.'

'Yes, I suppose it does,' I replied.

'But you talked to my colleague Inspector Fortini and he says you seemed to be not so sure. He said you talked for thirty minutes, forty minutes on the subject. He was beginning to believe your ideas about the faux Jacob, and was considering opening the case anew, but when you talked; you yourself now seemed to doubt it.'

'Inspector Fortini said that?' I asked. So my lengthy diatribe in his office had had some effect. Gò me and my interminable verbosity!

'You, Mr De'Ath, are the chief claims adjuster in Europe for your company,' he said.

'Put like that, I sound important,' I said.

'You are important,' he insisted. 'Your opinion is very important. Your status is very high. So I am going to ask you a question: are you content that Jacob Lluberas died by falling off the cliff north of Ajaccio, just like the other insurers are content? If you say you are happy then the case is closed. If you say you are unhappy, we will keep investigating. For a long time, you said you were unhappy. You worked very hard on this case, when no other person was interested. Now it seems you think the death is in order. So I don't understand what you think.'

The inspector's grip on my arm was strengthening.

He came to the crunch.

'And it is not just Raphael Fortini,' he began. He looked the way of Ludic and my mother. 'The prosecutor has said to us that if the chief claims adjustor in Europe is happy with these pay outs and that there is no insurance fraud, then the police will have no reason to re-open the case. So to repeat, are you saying there is no firm evidence of insurance fraud?'

'Yes,' I replied.

'Yes what?' asked the inspector.

'I am happy that Jacob Lluberas fell from the cliff north of Ajaccio, and was found dead at sea.'

The inspector held my arm for far longer than was necessary. He had been looking deep into my eyes.

A smile of satisfaction spread across his lips.

'Oh well, it was a nice theory,' he shrugged. 'The faux murder. It was a nice theory.'

He slapped me on the shoulder.

'By the way, your passport was given in to us. Evidently you let it drop near the station in Bastia.'

As he walked away, I felt someone squeeze my hand. It was the kind of squeeze you give when you want to thank someone.

I turned round to discover it was Emily.

'You see the truth, is what we all agree is the truth,' she said.

'Don't push your luck, Emily.'

TWO

We were in a car driving across the island.

Emily was driving, I was beside her, and Sarah was in the back seat looking like a sulky teen.

'I don't get what we're doing,' protested Sarah.

'Trust me,' said Emily.

'I am not going to trust her!' said Sarah. She had taken to communicating with Emily through me. 'And why are you here Pete?' she asked.

'Because I didn't think you and Emily could be left alone together,' I replied.

'Well you got that right,' she said.

Emily was driving us to the Lluberas house in the countryside. Apparently Emily had been ill there and convalesced a few weeks or months before. It was largely news to me. As we drove, Emily was keen to get things off her chest, I think with a view of drawing a line under events. The more she talked, the more she wanted to talk. She talked about her time with Antone and about stealing cars and burning them and falsifying Italian letterheads to create a company that traded with faux Jacob. She talked about the practicalities of moving dead bodies, storing dead bodies, dressing dead bodies; in one bizarre moment she even explained how she had sex with Antone after committing a crime.

'Seriously! Emily! You are my sister. I do not want to know about your sex life,' I said.

'I want to lay out the facts,' she said. 'It just feels good.'

I put out my hand and held the hand of my sister as she drove.

'The facts are you stole my boyfriend,' mumbled Sarah from the back.

'We've all done things to be sorry about,' said Emily.

'Mostly you,' I said.

'You stole a motor boat,' said Emily.

'Well you faked a murder,' I replied.

'Well you held up a bride on her wedding day.'

'Well you defrauded an insurance company.'

'Well you lied to the police about what happened in the Nice insurance office.'

'Well you stole a car.'

'Well you prevented a lawful burial.'

'Well you faked a death on a cliff edge.'

Sarah eventually cracked. 'Okay! I get it! You are both terrible people.' I then heard her mumble something like, 'I can't believe I hang out with you guys.'

Emily smiled. She was in a good mood and I was happy for that; I spend a lot of time worrying about her.

'And while we're talking,' said Emily. 'Are you going to go to the doctors about your prostate?'

'I've already made an appointment,' I lied.

Emily addressed her rear-view mirror. 'Pete is so obsessed by his bladder and prostate that when he was kidnapped, he considered peeing himself and lying in his own urine while in the boot of the car.'

'That's nice,' said Sarah.

As we drove along I reflected that of everyone involved in the whole tangled tale, the only person who I am sure had done absolutely nothing wrong, not even once, was Sarah; for all her randomness and unpredictability she was consistent in herself, and what's more whenever she had said anything she had resolutely stuck to the truth as she saw it.

Saintly Sarah.

Good for her.

'Oh by way,' I said. 'I've got one final question Emily. When you had me kidnapped, what were they planning to do with me, and why did they take me to that particular town? Were they going to torture me?'

'No, they just wanted to slow you up. That's why they didn't pursue you once you were in the square and there were witnesses.'

'But why that town?' I asked.

'Ah,' replied Emily. 'Everyone, and I mean everyone, wanted to go and see that wedding where the bridegroom had to ask the bride to marry him on the church steps, and everyone was carrying a gun. Apparently, it was very retro; they had seen nothing like it for decades. The cousins said they would only agree to help me if I promised they didn't miss the wedding.'

I reflected on this. 'This island is one crazy place,' I said.

'This island is the most fun you can have in the entire world,' said Emily. 'Serious, serious fun can be had here.'

'Oh that's alright then,' muttered Sarah. 'So long as you all have fun.'

We ignored the teenager in back.

We were clearly getting closer to our destination because the roads were getting smaller and more tortuous.

'Here we are,' said Emily.

We had slowed to a crawl. Sunshine pit-pattered the windscreen as we passed under the trees. The lane turned left to reveal a pretty house in a clearing that was sheltered by the woodland on three sides, but open to the view at its front. It had a wooden veranda with worn stone steps leading up. At the top of the steps was a willowy young woman with a warm honest face. She looked a bit like Julie Andrews. Julie Andrews, I reflected; nobody's favourite actress, in a lot of our favourite films. She appeared to be expecting us, or had heard our car.

'I am Lisabetta,' she announced extending her hand to me. 'And you must be Sarah-Jayne. I have heard so much about you. I will make tea!'

She conferred for a few seconds with Emily. They appeared to be friends.

'Yes tea is great,' I could hear Emily say. 'English breakfast tea.'

'Liptons!' announced Lisabetta with pride.

Lisabetta disappeared into the house and we settled on chairs to take in the view of the valley beyond.

There was a woodpecker tapping at a tree and a gentle breeze through the leaves. I am a town person at heart but if this is country living, give it to me. For the occasional weekend. Once in a blue moon. Provided there is alcohol to sweeten the deal.

Lisabetta re-appeared in the doorway.

'Sarah-Jayne,' she announced. 'Antone would like to see you.'

Sarah-Jayne did not move.

'You know him as Jacob,' I explained.

Sarah looked bewildered and wary. I couldn't blame her for that. She went inside the dark of the house and was gone for an eternity.

Lisabetta brought out tea and some scones made from chestnut flour.

'These have bacon and apple in, and these are plain,' she explained. 'I didn't know what you would like so I made both.'

'Pete eats everything,' laughed Emily. 'In fact, there's only one thing he likes more than food, and that is talking about food.'

She prodded me in my stomach to demonstrate matters to Lisabetta. Presumably the matter being that she is an irritating younger sister.

'These are delicious,' I said.

Lisabetta beamed a gratified smile.

She looked me straight in the eye and said, 'The last time I saw you. You were standing on the steps of a church threatening people while a bride and bridegroom ducked. And everyone was trying to shoot you.'

'It's what I'd like to be remembered for,' I said. 'You were there, then?'

'I wouldn't have missed that. What a great day it was. You were fantastic!'

'Well, I'm pleased to have added to the spectacle and to everyone's general entertainment,' I said.

'Oh you did, you did,' said Lisabetta earnestly.

I realised this gave me the opportunity to ask a question about something that had been bugging me.

'Tell me Lisabetta,' I began. 'You know how at one stage I was holding a wooden cross with Jesus on it?'

'Oh yes,' nodded Lisabetta. 'I loved that bit.'

'Well, what did I actually do with the cross? I don't remember putting it anywhere, but when I was running I didn't have it in my hand anymore.'

'You dropped it on the bride's foot.'

'I dropped the crucifix on the bride's foot?' I asked.

'I think she had some broken toes,' she said. 'She had to go to a hospital clinic. Her foot was in a cast. It still is.'

Lisabetta took my hands in hers. She looked into my eyes.

'Thank you,' she said.

'My pleasure,' I replied.

'We are going to talk about that forever.'

I could see why Emily liked her.

'I wanted to show you things,' said Emily unexpectedly.

'What kind of things?' I asked.

She waved a hand in a semi-circle as if scattering seeds. 'Everything,' she said.

'Great,' I replied, none the wiser.

'And you should have invited me to this wedding thing,' she said to Lisabetta. 'It sounded great!'

'You were busy defrauding an insurance company at the time,' I countered.

'But did I? Did I really?'

'Yes!' I replied.

'Okay, well either way,' she said. 'I want to be able to tell you stuff all the time.'

That was so not going to happen. She'll confide in me when she next gets into trouble, and not a moment before.

Sarah appeared in the doorway wrapped around Antone. She was happy too. I have rarely seen a woman more thrilled.

'Did they make you eat fitters made of chestnut flour?' asked Emily. She appeared to be addressing Sarah and I didn't understand the joke; the Corsicans, however, all laughed heartily. It turns out my sister is a hit with rural Corsicans. Let's face it, she's a hit with everyone.

Emily turned to me. 'In case you're wondering,' she began.

'Oh I am!' I replied.

'It turns out Antone has a thing for Sarah.'

'I can see!'

'Apparently they've got stuff in common, and nonsense like that,' she said. 'And when they chat it's "effortless". But all is not lost. I got Lisabetta in the divorce. Didn't I Lisabetta?'

Lisabetta beamed.

The happy couple settled down and we enjoyed a drink together in the sunshine.

'May I ask a question?' I was addressing Antone. 'When you played Jacob, did you play him differently to Antone, or were you just your normal charming self?'

I thought he was going to say something like he was more vivacious as Jacob, but in fact he said, 'I played Jacob on the balls of my feet and I play myself on the heels on my feet.'

'Well we all know which one was more flirty,' said Emily. It was the one time her voice betrayed a little bitterness. There will be other men, Emily. Many other men.

'But what about you?' Lisabetta was addressing me for some reason.

'I am fine thank you,' I replied.

'Emily says you sit at home and watch TV and drink too much.'

'It is true. I do have a perfect life,' I replied.

Lisabetta looked confused at my answer and turned to Emily for reassurance who, in turn, raised both eyebrows to judge me. I didn't care. I was in a good mood. In fact, everyone was in a good mood. I was feeling at one with the world, Emily was feeling rich... and Sarah was feeling Antone.

'You need a woman Peter!' announced Lisabetta. I have to say she was a total delight.

'Well thank you for your concern everyone,' I said. 'But I may have found a woman.' That shut them up. 'She is called Armelle and she works for an insurance company in Ajaccio.'

'You'll have something in common!' beamed Lisabetta. 'Insurance.'

'Indeed. I rang her last night and we are going out on a date. She is fun, she is good looking and we could both talk forever.'

'Excellent,' said Emily. She looked genuinely pleased for me.

'She does have a funny way she breathes though,' I said. 'There's a sort of sigh through her nose when she finishes a sentence. It is very distracting.'

'You are joking,' said Emily.

'I am joking,' I said.

I wasn't joking.

The nasal thing was pretty irritating.

A NOTE FROM THE AUTHOR

Thank you for reading De'Ath in Corsica. I hope you enjoyed it. When I wrote the book I was hoping to create a fun light thriller with plenty of action, a few laughs, and some memorable characters, but I also wanted to celebrate the island of Corsica itself; its food, beauty, folklore and history.

I have a small favour to ask. If you enjoyed the book, please do consider writing a review on Amazon and Goodreads, or just a star rating would be great. Although De'Ath in Corsica and De'Ath in Sicily have been well received and have sold well, there have been some glitches where some reviews and star ratings have got lost in the system. As a result, I would be pitifully grateful for any help you could offer.

Thank you

Paul Humber

EXTRACT FROM DE'ATH IN VENICE by Paul Humber. Available now.

THE WORLD ACCORDING TO EMILY

Ever woken up handcuffed to a corpse? No, of course not; it's vanishingly rare.

I had woken early because my bladder was full.

I was lying on my front, and my right hand wouldn't move. I wasn't concerned at first; why would I be?

I tugged on my arm. I tugged again.

I raised my head to see why my hand was caught.

There was a naked man next to me. Yeah okay fine, that happens. Then I saw the handcuff.

My right wrist was handcuffed to the man's left wrist.

And they weren't the pink fluffy pretend handcuffs you sometimes see in lingerie stores. They were real metal handcuffs. Police style. Designed to immobilise a suspect. They were probably still intended for sex and sold by some dodgy store that specialised in such things, but they were more solid than you would expect; I wasn't going to be able to get out of them without a key. Oh joy.

And I needed a pee.

A lot.

My bladder was really full. Painfully full.

As a basic courtesy, I didn't initially attempt to wake him up; there was a chance the key to open the cuffs was within reach. But my scope for looking around me was pretty limited by my position, and my scope for retrieving an object from elsewhere in the room without waking him was pretty much zero.

I couldn't see a key.

I scanned my brain for what I could remember from during the night.

Nothing from after about eleven. Absolutely nothing. Seriously? Nothing? It was both reassuring and alarming at the same time.

I prodded him.

'Hey!' I tried.

He didn't stir.

I leant up on my right elbow as best I could, and I pinched his nose. It's something I do with men who snore. Just pinch their nose and count to ten. The snoring will improve; roughly when you get to ten, and largely because you have just woken them up. Sometimes you have to close their mouth as well. It's also a sex move I sometimes do. Just sharing.

It didn't have any effect.

How about twenty seconds? It was worth a try.

Twenty seconds later, and any reasonable person would conclude he might be dead. Under any circumstances, this is a really horrible heart-stopping conclusion; the sort of conclusion that hits your whole metabolism, but it was worse in this instance because I had drunk far too much the night before and had a profound sense I had been poisoned.

I elbowed him in the ribs. I elbowed him some more. I shoved him.

His head lolled.

Was he cold? I felt his chest with my palm. He wasn't unduly cold, he wasn't fresh from the morgue cold, but it was quite warm in the room generally and presumably you can't drop below the temperature in the room, so it was hard to tell; and obviously I'm a total novice at this waking up chained to a corpse lark.

What else could I do? I felt under his nose. There was no sign of any breath.

I pinched his nose again with a view to counting to thirty, but now that it was clear he was dead, it seemed an immoral thing to do; disrespectful at least.

When I did reach the count of thirty however, it was beyond all doubt.

I was handcuffed to a naked dead man.

Made in the USA
Columbia, SC
22 October 2020